Under a
Greek Moon

Carol Kirkwood is one of our most loved TV personalities.
Millions of viewers and listeners know her for her
weather reports on *BBC Breakfast*, Radio 2's breakfast
show, Wimbledon fortnight and waltzing into our hearts
on *Strictly Come Dancing*. Carol was inspired to write her
first novel by her passion for travel and her love of
Hollywood glamour. Off-screen, Carol can often be
found ensconced in a book, singing, dancing and
taking long walks in the countryside.

To find out more about Carol Kirkwood:

f @OfficialCarolKirkwood
🐦 @CarolKirkwood

Carol Kirkwood

Under a Greek Moon

HarperCollins*Publishers*

HarperCollins*Publishers* Ltd
1 London Bridge Street,
London SE1 9GF
www.harpercollins.co.uk

HarperCollins*Publishers*
1st Floor, Watermarque Building, Ringsend Road
Dublin 4, Ireland

First published by HarperCollins*Publishers* 2021
1

A catalogue record for this book is
available from the British Library

ISBN: 978-0-008-39342-7

This novel is entirely a work of fiction.
The names, characters and incidents portrayed in it are
the work of the author's imagination. Any resemblance to
actual persons, living or dead, events or localities is
entirely coincidental.

Typeset in Meridien by Palimpsest Book Production Limited,
Falkirk, Stirlingshire

Printed and bound in the UK using 100% Renewable Electricity
by CPI Group (UK) Ltd

MIX
Paper from
responsible sources
FSC C007454

This book is produced from independently certified FSC™ paper
to ensure responsible forest management.

For more information visit: www.harpercollins.co.uk/green

For Donald and Steve,
for always listening and being there.

Prologue

The young woman looked out across the sea from her room, high up above what passed for a main thoroughfare on the small island of Ithos. From her vantage point, she could see the bustle of the harbour but was spared the heat of the midday sun and the throng of holidaymakers who swarmed the narrow streets, here on trips from the larger islands of Crete and Rhodes.

The room was sparse, furnished in the traditional Greek way: terracotta tiles on the floor, a simple bed, a pine dresser, crisp white sheets, shutters on the window. A light breeze lifted the thin voile curtain, which swirled around her like a veil before hanging limp once more.

She drank in the sight below – fishermen hailing each other across the boats which lined the jetty, each man moving with a rhythm handed down from the generations before them. Mooring their boats, hauling the nets, passing their precious cargo of sardines and mackerel from ship to shore. Watching them, it seemed to her that nothing had changed here for centuries.

She turned away, tugging the rucksack zipper closed

which was already carefully packed with everything she needed, and turned to survey the room one last time.

Catching sight of the postcard lying next to the bag, she picked it up and reread the words that were so familiar she could recite them by heart:

Always have hope. We have our dreams. Don't wait for me . . .

She turned the postcard between her fingertips, looking again at the image on the reverse, the shot of Ithos, a Greek island idyll with its white beaches and sapphire sea, cobbled streets lined with traditional buildings, and behind them the craggy hills of the interior, always changing, always the same.

With a sigh she propped the postcard up on the dresser, no longer wishing to keep it. She didn't need it now; the words were indelibly etched in her mind – she would never, *could* never forget them. Then she heard the clatter of foot-steps on the stone staircase leading up to the room. A knock at the door. She took one last look at the postcard and turned to answer the door.

PART ONE

Chapter 1

Los Angeles, September 2000

Shauna Jackson adjusted her dark glasses, even though there was no need for them with the early morning light barely penetrating the windows of Los Angeles International Airport. She checked her watch, impatient to reclaim her luggage and board the limousine that would take her home. *Home*, she thought; what a mass of contradictions that threw up. She'd just stepped off a plane from Ireland, a place that hadn't been home for years, but as the old adage said, you can take the girl out of Enniscrea . . .

There were times, and today was one of them, when she felt like an imposter in LA. As if Shauna Jackson, award-winning actress, widow of Dan Jackson, the directors' director, was a fraud and at any moment she'd be stripped of her Golden Globes and Emmys and sent back to Enniscrea with her tail between her legs – an outcome which would undoubtedly please her mother.

She shivered, wondering if the drizzle and mist of the west coast of Ireland had got into her bones, or maybe there was still a little shard of ice left in her heart that even the rising heat of California couldn't melt. If only her father were here to sprinkle some of his magical optimism over her. She could imagine him telling her, *C'mon, Shauna, buck up – there's joy and happiness underneath every paving stone if you'd only take a look.* Instead she was alone, and though she had wealth and all the trappings of fame, it couldn't shield her from the humiliation and anguish.

Oh Dan, why did you do it?

Shauna peered through her Chanel sunglasses, surveying the baggage claim area to see if anyone had recognized her. There had been a time when she would have smiled and been happy to sign autographs, but today she'd employed all the little tricks Hollywood's finest used to go undetected: she'd made sure she was the last one off the plane, she'd kept her luggage to the minimum and her flame-red hair was concealed under a fedora. Her green eyes were hidden behind dark glasses, and she'd travelled under her maiden name, Shauna O'Brien, in case anyone tipped the paparazzi off after seeing the flight manifest. She'd had enough of photographers to last a lifetime. In the aftermath of her husband's shockingly sudden death they'd hounded her, driven into a feeding frenzy by the news that he'd been unfaithful and had fathered a son by another woman. As if the loss weren't bad enough, she'd had to cope with Dan's mistress selling her story, airing all the dirty secrets. Her life had turned into a never-ending nightmare.

And in Ireland things had gone from bad to worse . . .

When she recalled stepping off the plane at Shannon Airport, it felt as though time had stood still. No paparazzi lying in wait, no one giving her a second glance. The taxi driver who delivered Shauna to her parents' trim white cottage chattered away oblivious to the fact he had a celebrity on board. It was as if she'd reverted to being Shauna O'Brien, as if she'd never left Enniscrea.

The blast of disapproval as she hauled her cases over the threshold was just like old times too. She'd known that the last thing her mother would want was her arriving unannounced, but it was the only way Shauna was going to catch her off-guard, get some answers.

'Staying a while, are you?'

'If it's a problem, I can always go to a hotel, Mammy.'

'I didn't say it's a problem,' she sniffed. 'I just wasn't expecting you to visit.'

'Your letter had me worried. I booked the first flight I could.'

'Well, your da will be pleased to see you.' Her tone implied that she didn't much care either way.

'What's wrong with him, Mammy?' She lowered her voice in case Da was somewhere within earshot, though if he had been, he'd surely have come to the door to greet her. 'Reading between the lines, I got the impression it's serious. I've been worried sick, not knowing what's going on. Why must you always be so mysterious?' Shauna knew why: it was a form of control, a way of keeping a tight rein on the flow of information between her daughter and her husband.

'I reckoned you had enough on your plate, what with that scandal all over the news.' Her mother's lips pursed, prune-like wrinkles radiating out from her mouth. 'I'm shocked that woman dared show her face, and at the wake, of all things. I can't help thinking it's a blessing the two you of never had children. The shame of it all . . . What must the priest have thought when he saw the papers? I hope you apologized to him. And to think your husband . . . I've barely been able to look Father Sean in the eye. This wouldn't have happened if you'd stayed in Enniscrea.'

Shauna knew to argue was pointless. 'Where's Da?'

'He's having a lie-down. He'll be awake shortly. I'll put the kettle on while you go get yourself sorted?'

Shauna knew there'd be no answers from her mother until she was good and ready, so she bumped her suitcases up the narrow staircase to her old attic bedroom with its view of the sea in the distance. It wasn't quite the panoramic view of Pacific sunrises and sunsets you got in California, but still the views in Enniscrea could take your breath away, with showers and sunshine combining to throw rainbows across the sky, two or three at a time. She'd never tired of gazing at them as child, shouting for her da to come see. She could picture him now, jiggling her on his knee and telling her stories of the *leipreacháns*, the mischievous little people who hid their pots of gold at the end of the rainbow where no one would ever find them.

'Sure, you don't need rainbows or crocks of gold to be happy,' he'd tell her.

Her eyes blurring with tears, Shauna turned away from the window. In the taxi on the way here she'd steeled herself for whatever news it was her mother was keeping back, but now that she was here, surrounded by childhood memories, her resolve seemed to have left her. Rather than go downstairs, she stood looking around her at the little bedroom under the eaves. It seemed to have been left pretty much as it was when she was a child. Her old clothes were gone from the wardrobe and drawers, but the shelves were still crammed with her favourite novels and school exercise books. She opened a cupboard, and her eyes lit up when she saw her precious collection of *Photoplay* back issues. While other teenagers had pored over *Jackie* and *Seventeen* with their pages full of pin-ups like David Cassidy and David Soul, Shauna had invested her meagre pocket money in old editions of the cinema fan's bible, preferring to lose herself in Hollywood gossip of days gone by. She reached out and teased a magazine from the pile, pausing to drink in the cover, unconsciously returning Grace Kelly's all-American smile as it beamed out at her from a 1956 edition. She turned the yellowing, well-thumbed pages, and read again Grace's 'Untold Story'. It was as she remembered: no revelations, merely a well-trodden recap of Grace's life up to the year of the issue, accompanied by a photo from *High Society* featuring Grace and Bing Crosby.

The Hollywood legend turned fairy-tale princess had been a lifelong obsession for Shauna. As a teenager, she'd hated her red hair and dreamed of being blonde and beautiful like Grace. It had taken years for Shauna to embrace her looks, despite Dan calling her his 'pre-Raphaelite dryad' and urging her to stop lightening her hair in an effort to be more like her idol. Ironically, it was after she reverted to her natural colour and pale complexion, realising that it set her apart from the perma-tans and facelifts of LA, that Dan betrayed her with another woman.

Shauna winced. She'd resolved not to keep torturing herself with memories of Dan. Instead, she steered her thoughts back to her idol, and the night they'd met. The memory was fixed in her mind, the graceful handshake, the charming smile. There was so much else she could never forget about that night, too. *A promise. A caress. A dream that could never be real. 'You're like no one else, Shauna . . .'*

If only Grace had lived and they'd had the chance to get to know each other. What advice would she have given to Shauna in her current situation? *Smile and act like you don't care, darling.*

Good advice, but impossible to follow. Especially with her

mother waiting downstairs to break the news she had come all this way to hear. Now that she was here, the prospect filled her with such dread that she wanted to run or hide, as if so long as the truth about her da's condition remained unspoken, it wouldn't be real and she could go on clinging to the memories of him as he used to be.

Shauna composed herself, readying herself to go back downstairs again, then reapplied her make-up, before closing the door on her old belongings and her youthful dreams.

The day they buried her father, the weather was a typical mixture of sunshine and rain – the classic Irish combination. Father Sean's eulogy was good-humoured and intimate, as befitted a long-standing member of his flock. The church was packed with old friends and colleagues, local acquaintances and the usual random people who no one ever seemed to recognize but who turned up at every funeral in the parish, usually for the free tea and sandwiches afterwards.

Shauna's mother clung to her, weeping as her husband was lowered into his grave, her brittle exterior gone for once. As she tried to find words to comfort her, Shauna felt like a child forced into the role of an adult, lost and uncertain, desperate for her strong and uncompromising mother to take the lead instead of looking to her.

At the graveside, Shauna had read from her father's favourite poem, 'He wishes for the Cloths of Heaven' by W. B. Yeats. Her voice faltered when she came to the line, 'tread softly because you tread on my dreams', her mind conjuring his musical voice reading it to her as a child. She drew on all her acting ability to get through it and prayed she was doing him justice. As a rainbow burst across the sky, she told herself it was a message from him that she was.

*　*　*

Shauna's thoughts returned to the present with a jolt as the limousine left the freeway and turned into North Knoll Drive. Her penthouse apartment wasn't in the showiest part of Beverly Hills, but she had bought it with her first pay cheque from her first Hollywood movie, *Only the Brave*. Her role as the wife of a paraplegic Vietnam vet had won her an Golden Globe nomination for Best Supporting Actress and launched her career. Perhaps because of that, the apartment had sentimental value and she had insisted on keeping it on even after she and Dan moved into their sprawling beachfront mansion in Malibu. Though she'd justified it to Dan by pointing out it was more convenient for the studios, the truth was she liked having what Virginia Woolf would have called 'a room of one's own', a sanctuary she could retreat to.

As she stepped out of the limo and into the lobby entrance, she immediately felt calmer, more composed. Yes, this was home now, and it was so good to be back.

Chapter 2

'Shauna, you're home!'

After eighteen hours of jet-lagged sleep, Shauna had come out onto her balcony to escape the persistent flashing light of her answering machine. She'd barely had time to take in the view of the West Hollywood hills when a red open-top Cadillac pulled up outside with Roxy Lennon, her oldest and best friend, waving excitedly from the passenger seat. Within minutes, Roxy had sprinted up the stairs and was at the door.

Five foot eleven inches in her Jimmy Choo heels, Roxy towered over Shauna, who was barefoot and casual in Levis and a New York Yankees baseball jersey. While Shauna kept her make-up minimal, her friend as usual had opted for a more vampish look, her black spiky hair a masterpiece of through-a-hedge-backwards chic, thick black eyeliner to set off her brown eyes, her lips a gash of scarlet currently beaming with pleasure. Resplendent in red tartan trousers with a battered biker jacket, she cut a dramatic figure.

'Shaunie!' Sweeping her friend into her arms, Roxy hugged her long and hard, then stood back to subject her to a close inspection. When she spoke, her once broad Liverpool accent was softened with a transatlantic twang. 'That bad, eh?'

Shauna's shoulders sagged. 'Thank God you're here. I feel like I've been going mad.'

'Oh, that's crap, you're the sanest person I know.'

'Not any more. Who's that in the Cadillac?'

Roxy winked playfully, took her by the hand and led her out onto the balcony. Below them, looking up from the driver's seat was a handsome, olive-skinned young man who looked to be half Roxy's age.

'That's Marco, isn't he gorgeous!'

Marco responded with a friendly wave and Roxy blew him a kiss. 'He was one of my models at Milan Fashion Week – doesn't speak much English but can read a road map, if you know what I mean.' She waggled her eyebrows suggestively.

'What happened to that young designer you were championing – the one you said adored you, and that you couldn't live without?'

Roxy frowned. 'Jason Turner? Got too big for his boots, wanted me to set him up with a new label. I might have been happy to oblige if I hadn't caught him screwing one of the interns. I told him to move out, fuck off and set himself up with his own money.'

'Shit, I'm sorry.' Shauna could see that, beneath the bravado, Roxy's feelings had been bruised.

Roxy waved her sympathy away. 'Plenty more where he came from, and no chance of Marco doing the same thing – he's got to go back to university in a couple of weeks, so we're on a timer and making the most of it.' Roxy grinned mischievously. 'Anyway, enough about me. It's time to talk. I need a drink?'

'Dry martini?'

'You know me so well.'

'That's what I call a proper welcome,' Roxy said as they settled themselves into the Spanish colonial style chairs that looked out over the view. Plonking her stilettoes on the low table, she took a sip of the viscous clear liquid, fished out the olive and popped it in her mouth. 'Divine. OK, spill.'

'Is Marco all right out there in the car? Shouldn't we invite him to join us?'

'Don't change the subject. Marco's fine – he's listening to the soundtrack for the next Ralph Lauren show on the car stereo. He's got the gig in Paris.' She took another sip of her drink while observing Shauna closely. 'So how are you? How did it go in Ireland?'

Shauna stared into her whiskey mac, swilling the drink without taking a drop. 'Da's gone. The funeral was last week.'

'Oh, honey, no.' Roxy was immediately out of her chair and kneeling beside her, hugging her fiercely. 'Shauna, why didn't you call me? You know I would have dropped everything and come.'

Finally with a friend she could unburden herself to, Shauna couldn't find the words. Roxy held her, soothing her while she sobbed.

'You poor thing. I can't believe what a shitty year this has been for you. As if you hadn't been through enough already with Dan.'

'I'm just sorry Da had to hear about all that before he died. He loved Dan, it must have broken his heart.'

'He loved you more, you were his princess. He'd have sent Dan packing if he'd been well enough.'

Shauna winced.

'Sorry, honey.'

'It's OK, maybe you're right. I just wish Ma could have let up. She spent the whole time reminding me of how much I'd let them down.'

'Jesus, come on! Two Emmys, a shedload of award-winning TV series and movies, more money than she could ever dream of – some of which you used to buy the house she's living in and the car she's driving – and still your mother can't bring herself to acknowledge that you're a success story? Sometimes I think she'd rather you'd stuck to accountancy at university, then gone home and got yourself a boring little job in Galway.'

Shauna managed a laugh, but immediately teared up again. 'Do you ever wish you could turn back the clock, go back to when we were students with it all before us?'

'Living in student halls in Manchester?' Roxy raised her eyebrows ironically. 'God, that seems a lifetime ago now, doesn't it? But deep down, we're still the same, aren't we?'

Shauna stared out over the rooftops of LA to Santa Monica in the distance, lost in thought. Then she shook her head sadly. 'The last couple of months have changed me, Roxy. I don't think I'll ever be the same again.' Then the effort of trying to hold it together became too much and she shut her eyes tightly, willing the tears to stop, but unable to hold them back.

Roxy squeezed her hand tightly. 'Hey, you're going to get through this, do you hear me? We've got through worse.'

Shauna was shaking her head again. 'I promised myself I'd never be hurt like this again, not after—'

'Hey, we got through that and we'll get through this. You're not some naive nineteen-year-old whose world is going to fall apart because you've been screwed over. OK, Dan behaved like a prick, but there's no question that he loved you. Forget about that nasty bitch who got her greedy little fingers into him – she meant nothing to Dan. You know the drill: you grieve, you learn, and then you move on – it's what we've always done.'

'Have we? Can I really move on from this, any more than either of us could move on from that summer in Greece? No matter what we do, that's going to be with us forever.'

Roxy nodded but didn't concede. 'I'm not saying you should forget what happened – that's not in your nature. The trick is not to let it eat you whole.'

Shauna took a deep breath and then threw the whiskey back in one shot.

'Easy, girl.'

'Don't try and stop me, I needed that.' Shauna took a deep breath. 'Look, Roxy, I know you're right, I have to move on. But I don't know how. I mean, what's next for me?'

'Baby steps, that's how we'll do this. Right now, you need to focus on getting through the next few weeks, facing down the press and the gossip columns. Remember that old saying: Today's news, tomorrow's chip paper. You ride it out, hold your head high.' She paused. 'And then maybe we set about slaying a demon or two.'

'I've got quite a few of those now.'

'Me too. So, we take them one at a time, pick them off.'

Shauna nodded, but her green eyes were filled with uncertainty. 'You and me against the world?'

'You betcha. Same as always – only this time, we're better dressed.'

Shauna couldn't help but smile, buoyed up by Roxy's boundless strength and confidence.

'We've got to get you working again, too – can't have some back-stabbing cow stealing the juicy roles, not when all the best directors would give their right arm to have you starring in their movies. And then . . .' Roxy held

Shauna's eyes with her own, 'maybe it's time for you to go back . . .'

'Back where?' Shauna asked the question, but her heart already knew the answer.

Chapter 3

With the delicious warmth of the Mediterranean sun heating her shoulders, which were already covered in tiny freckles, Shauna smiled, thinking of home. Summer here was a lot more reliable than on the west coast of Ireland. Her da would be pleased that she was enjoying herself, though she was less sure about her mother. She'd made it abundantly clear that she thought her daughter should be spending the holidays studying rather than 'gallivanting'. Shauna wondered if her mother knew what it was to have fun, so keen was she to make sure nobody else ever had any. She shrugged off the thought, determined not to let anything spoil this moment. Here she was, finally, in the place that she'd dreamed of coming to ever since she was a little girl, enchanted by the poise and beauty of Grace Kelly after watching *High Society* on their battered old television.

Shauna looked out across the rock of Monaco, picking out the famous landmarks: the Musée Océanographique, the prince's palace, the Palais de Justice and the cathedral.

Monaco was every bit as beautiful as she'd imagined, and she was abuzz with the thrilling prospect that around the next corner she might catch a glimpse of Princess Grace herself. From here she could see the white stone turrets of the palace, the terracotta tiles of the roofs. Was the princess somewhere within the cool stone walls? The family were in residence at the moment, as Shauna had found out when she'd made her pilgrimage to the palace two days ago. She'd even managed to drag Roxy along, suggesting that they might cross paths with the young playboy, Prince Albert.

With a happy sigh, Shauna leaned on the railings. She had the whole summer ahead of her. It felt like a miracle, waking up to sunshine each morning and not to having to worry about carrying a cardigan or a raincoat everywhere. Wearing flip-flops day in, day out was bliss.

Up here in the botanical gardens, the spectacular view was well worth the heart-thumping fear she'd endured, sneaking her way in with a coachload of tourists. How many Hail Marys would she have to say in penance for ducking the entrance fee? Surely God wouldn't begrudge her this sun-kissed panorama?

The atmosphere was intoxicating. Everywhere she looked there was wealth and luxury. Shauna had never seen anything like it and was dazzled by the beautiful people who frequented the cafés and restaurants in the harbour, with their fabulous designer clothes and tastefully expensive jewellery. She envied the glamorous wives accompanied by attentive husbands dressed in white slacks and navy-blue espadrilles, their Armani blazers slung over the backs of their chairs. Everyone seemed to be dining on *fruit de mer* and sipping red glasses of iced Campari. She longed to be one of them.

The unfortunate reality was, they were only ten days into

the trip and already their stash of francs was dwindling fast. Monaco was beyond expensive. Now she understood why it was called the playground of the rich; this place wasn't intended for mere mortals like her on a backpacking budget. She and Roxy had done what they could to save money, hitching to Dover and across to Paris, but they'd still had to pay for the ferry crossing, as well as food, accommodation and bus fare to Monaco. For all her grand plans and Liverpudlian cockiness, Roxy had turned out to be pretty clueless; she'd even managed to leave their tent in a service station en route. But thanks to her cajoling and guile, they'd made it to Monaco, laughing and revelling in their freedom all the way. They were currently sharing a single attic bedroom in a dilapidated hostel just off the Rue Bel Respiro, but they couldn't afford to stay there for much longer. Their bubble was about to burst if they didn't find a way to earn some money.

Shauna sighed, remembering this morning's conversation with Roxy . . .

'Oh, my head hurts.' Roxy Lennon ducked her head back under the sheets, even though it was almost noon. Her black hair was standing up in spikes, and her bloodshot eyes still bore the traces of last night's eyeliner.

'Serves you right for gallivanting until the wee small hours and then keeping me awake going on about how wonderful Thierry is.'

'Thierry, Thierry. Thierry. Oh, Shauna, he is *so* gorgeous. Like a Greek God – Zeus, or is it Apollo? Like one of these fellas you see in the clouds of a Renaissance painting. And his kisses . . . Mind blowing.'

'Well, do you suppose he could use some of his godly powers to help us find work?'

21

'Work?' Roxy's tousled head reappeared and she wrinkled her nose in distaste. 'Why do you have spoil things?'

Shauna grinned. ''Fraid so. Anyway, don't you think he's a bit too old for you? He must be in his forties at least.'

'Darling,' Roxy rolled her eyes dramatically, 'you have no idea, the benefits of dating a man with experience.' She fluttered her eyelashes.

Shauna laughed and threw a towel at her friend's head. 'I'm going to ask at that restaurant on the corner. They had a card in the window. And I'll enquire at the hotels near the station.'

Roxy swung her golden-brown legs out from under the crisp white sheets and was about to spring from the bed when the hangover struck again. 'Oh, God, I think I'm dying! Bring me a croissant or a French stick . . . and one of those nuclear coffees they all drink around here,' she moaned, flopping back onto the bed and flinging her arm across her eyes.

'A baguette to share is as much as we can afford!' Shauna said as she slipped her feet into flip-flops and grabbed her canvas bag.

It was impossible to get cross with Roxy. It was a beautiful morning and they were in Monaco for goodness' sake; they could always sleep on the beach if they had to. She and Roxy had met the previous October, next-door neighbours in one of the university's halls of residence. The first time she had seen Roxy, she seemed the embodiment of cool, wearing the shortest denim shorts over stripy tights, a tatty T-shirt slashed across the chest revealing a busty black bra underneath, with thick black eyeliner and blood-red lipstick. Shauna felt like a timid country mouse by comparison, with her safe plain woolly jumper and her Debenhams jeans.

'The name's Roxy.' She'd gone on to explain that she was

22

studying Textiles and Fashion. 'I'm going to be a famous designer one day,' she said matter-of-factly. 'All the great designers are great tailors, so I'm making sure I get the skills I need. What about you?'

Shauna hesitated before answering, 'I'm going to be an accountant.'

Roxy had looked from the overflowing suitcase she was unpacking. For a moment she didn't speak, staring in wide-eyed astonishment at her new room-mate before bursting into laughter.

'What are you laughing at?'

'I can't think of anyone less like an accountant than you.'

'What do you mean?' Shauna laughed, too.

'You look like a Rubens painting with that red hair and those green eyes – you should be a model or a movie star or something, not a bloody accountant.'

It wasn't long before Shauna had started to believe that her friend was right; poring over numbers all day was leaving her feeling like something was missing. Luckily, she had acted as an impromptu model for many of Roxy's creations and her wardrobe was now less Marks and Spencer and more Vivienne Westwood. Now that she was here in Monaco, she could feel her true self opening up. A sense of anticipation, of being on the cusp of something exciting.

She gazed out at the view of the distant boats moored in Port Hercules and shook her head. Maybe it was just that holiday feeling and the sense of freedom at being away from dreary old Manchester that was making her tingle.

If they didn't find some work soon, they would be back home before their trip had even begun, and she wasn't feeling quite so confident as she had first thing this morning. She'd visited the cheaper hotels down by the station and the railway line but found that few of the hotel staff spoke

English, or if they did they weren't letting on. They seemed unimpressed with her limited French, shaking their heads at her and waving her away as soon as they realized she was looking for work rather than a room. Her usual sunny positivism had been dampened but not defeated, and she'd come up to the gardens to regroup and plan her strategy.

Picking up her bag, she followed the path down the hill, exiting the gardens and walking down towards Port Hercules. She was fascinated by the boats, most of them bigger than the house she'd grown up in. Lined up along the pontoons, they offered an intriguing window into the lives of the wealthy. Woman with svelte, perfect figures in tiny bikinis – which she guessed must cost a fortune despite the scarcity of fabric – padded from deck to deck, parading their privilege with conspicuous awareness, carrying crystal flutes of champagne that glinted like diamonds in the sunshine. Groups of people in gauzy wraps and designer T-shirts gathered on the rear decks to eat, served by staff in crisp white and navy uniforms. It was another world and one that seemed impossibly sophisticated and exciting to Shauna. These boats belonged in films and magazines.

She skirted the lively marketplace, her stomach grumbling at the sight of the colourful stalls piled high with the rich red of ripe tomatoes, the glossy greens of salad leaves and the creamy yellow of so many different cheeses. She'd noticed the day before that the traders would toss less than perfect fruit into piles of rubbish at the back of their stalls, so she sauntered as casually as she could into the gap behind the stalls and made her way to one of the broken wooden fruit boxes. Casting a furtive glance to make sure no one was watching, she snatched up a couple of badly bruised oranges and some apples that were rather squished on one side. The traders might not be able to sell them, but she could certainly eat the good halves. At home nothing was ever thrown away. Squirrelling her booty away into a plastic bag inside her canvas bag, she moved along a few stalls and was about to pick up a rather battered head of lettuce when a voice drawled, '*Tu as faim?*'

Shauna looked up, startled, and shrugged with a smile, remembering her schoolgirl French. '*Un peu.*'

An attractive, dark-haired woman regarded Shauna with amused eyes.

'I'm not doing anything wrong.' She jutted out her chin, determined she wasn't going to be shamed out of her lunch. 'They're throwing it away.'

The woman appraised her and then addressed her in English, 'You do not look like a beggar.'

'I'm not . . . just a little short of funds, that's all . . . I'm looking for a job.'

'In the gutters?'

Shauna shrugged and gave the woman a wry grin.

'What sort of work?'

'Anything,' Shauna said. 'I'm a hard worker. I'm studying at university, I've worked in a bar, as a chambermaid and I can . . .' What could she do? 'I can clean, peel potatoes and I can type . . . a little.'

'Ever worked on a yacht?'

Shauna, eyes widening, shook her head. 'No, but I'm a quick learner.'

'What is your name?'

'Shauna O'Brien. I'm from Ireland. County Galway.'

The woman smiled and patted her overflowing basket. 'I'm Chantelle, I work on the *St Helena*, I'm the chef on board. One of the crew jumped ship this morning, leaving us short-handed.' She paused, scrutinising Shauna from head to toe. 'I like your face, it's one I can trust.' She smiled.

'If you come back with me, I can get you an interview with the boss.'

'You can?' Shauna couldn't believe her luck.

'That's all I can do, though; he will have to decide.' She indicated the basket and the two bags at her feet. 'I could do with a hand just with the shopping. *Viens*, we must go.'

Shauna immediately picked the two bags up. 'Yes, ma'am.' Maybe the good lord was keeping an eye on her after all. No doubt she had her mother to thank for that.

Chapter 4

Chantelle skipped nimbly back on board, putting down her basket and reaching for the bags Shauna carried. With her heart in her mouth, she handed them over, too dumbstruck to say a word. This wasn't a yacht; it was a floating palace. Virtually a cruise liner.

'*Allons*,' called Chantelle, nodding towards the gangplank as she skipped up a tiny flight of steps. 'It's quite safe.'

Nodding, Shauna stepped forward, still not quite believing that she was boarding a yacht in Port Hercules in Monaco. She couldn't wait to tell Roxy.

'Wait here a moment.'

'OK.' Her nerves suddenly kicked in as she looked around. On either side of the boat was a set of steps leading to the upper decks. In front of her was a shady seating area with wide white leather seats piped around the edges in smart navy blue, arranged around a low glass table. It was easy to imagine glamorous people assembling here in the early evening, dressed in their finery, sipping at pre-dinner cocktails before disembarking to visit one of the many expensive restaurants on the quayside.

Beyond was a light, airy salon, so huge that she blinked at the sight of it. Sunlight streamed in through the vast windows on either side, illuminating what looked like half a dozen plush sofas interspersed with glossy wooden tables adorned with perfectly placed lamps with heavy bases. How many people could sleep on this boat, she wondered. Who could afford to own a place like this? There were plenty of grand yachts in the harbour, but this was possibly the biggest and most impressive.

Shauna was suddenly seized by nerves. She had no experience of this kind of lifestyle or the people who led it. She was considering bolting for the gangplank and the safety of the quayside before Chantelle returned with the boss, when she heard voices approaching and light steps on the stairway curving away to the right. She straightened, lifting her chin, hoping to make a good impression.

A slim girl appeared, her deep golden tan emphasizing her platinum-blonde hair. She was wearing the tiniest of bikinis that left nothing to the imagination, above the longest, brownest legs Shauna had ever seen. She moved with the natural confidence of someone who had the world at her feet and knew it. Her head was turned, laughing back up at a man who paused on the steps, Shauna could make out a pair of strong, tanned muscular legs, though his torso was just out of sight.

'Come on, Demetrios. They'll take forever. Let's just go now.'

'Normandie. Always so impatient,' chided a voice as smooth and rich as molasses. Something in its low-toned timbre brought goosebumps to Shauna's arms, or maybe it was just standing in the shade after the sunshine.

The girl skipped down the stairs and darted past Shauna

without a second glance, her fancy sandals clicking on the wooden planked flooring.

A broad chest revealed by an unbuttoned white linen shirt, loosely tucked into shorts, came into view. Shauna felt her mouth go dry. She'd never been this close to a half-naked man before, and certainly not one as sculpted as this.

Before she could move, he spotted her.

'Well, what have we here?' he asked, his hazel eyes dancing with amusement.

'Er . . . I'm waiting to see . . . to see the . . . the . . .' Sweet Mary, why couldn't she remember the title of the person she was supposed to see.

'Oh, you are a shy one?' he teased, an unexpected dimple appearing in the heavily stubbled cheek that outlined a strong jaw. There was no attempt at subtlety as his gaze travelled down her body. At the sight of the sinfully sugges-tive smile curving his broad mouth, Shauna felt a blush staining her cheek. There was something so blatantly sexual about the man, it made her feel immature and foolish.

'Ah, sir. Sorry about this.' A young man in uniform, slightly out of breath, appeared beside her. 'We're inter-viewing replacements for the girl that left this morning.'

'Well, this one is an improvement already.' The man's mouth quirked at one side, his eyes roving over her face. 'She is here and on time, unlike her predecessor.'

Before Shauna had a chance to process this she was being ushered below deck to a large windowless galley kitchen where Chantelle was busy preparing a salad.

'Take a seat,' said Chantelle, opening an enormous fridge that was packed to the gunnels with food.

The man slipped into the seat opposite. 'Hello, Shauna, welcome aboard the *St Helena*. I'm Jeremy Prior, the purser.

Chantelle tells me you're looking for work. What can you do?'

Shauna repeated what she'd told Chantelle earlier.

'We're looking for someone who can work in the galley, make up beds, clean bathrooms, serve food – a bit of everything, in other words. It's got to be someone who isn't afraid of hard work, who is polite and efficient, and will look after the guests on board. You'll also need to adapt quickly to handle young Demetrios.' He laughed. 'I saw your face upstairs. He's got an eye for the girls, and he's not afraid to show it, but he wouldn't go any further.' He looked at Shauna directly. 'We've got rules about that sort of thing.'

Shauna nodded, all the while wondering what happened to girls who broke 'the rules'.

'Think you're interested? It's hard work, but the Theodosis family are good employers.'

'They're positive angels, compared to some,' said Chantelle, bringing over a plate of sandwiches and putting it on the table. She pushed the plate towards Shauna. 'Here, you look like you could use one.'

'Thank you.' Shauna shot her a grateful smile. The sliced baguette filled with chicken and salad was a lot more appealing than the squashed fruit in her bag.

'Got any questions?' asked Jeremy.

Chantelle rolled her eyes. 'The pay, Jeremy.'

'Ah, yes.' He named a figure that seemed depressingly low. It would just about cover her rent, but she wouldn't be able to eat as well.

'And is food included?' She nodded towards the plate of sandwiches.

'Oh, yes, full board and lodgings. Although you might want to see the cabin before you decide, if you've not been on board a yacht before.'

'Board and lodgings?' Shauna frowned and then immediately felt silly for not realizing that the job would entail living on board the boat. 'I thought . . .' She laughed at herself. 'I thought you were just looking for a maid or something while you were in port. Someone who'd come each day.'

Both Jeremy and Chantelle laughed. 'No, you sell your soul when you join the crew,' said Chantelle. 'It's not for everyone. But I think you'll fit in.'

'How long would you want me for? I have to go back to university in mid-September.'

'No problem. We'll be heading across to Corsica in a few days' time, then cutting across to Italy and the Amalfi Coast and then down and around Southern Italy and on to Greece. Would you be able to make your way home from there?'

'It sounds great, but I . . .' She couldn't abandon Roxy. They'd come out here together, though since meeting Thierry in a nightclub on their first night in Monaco, Roxy seemed to want to spend every minute she could with him.

'You don't get seasick, do you?' asked Chantelle suddenly.

Shauna laughed. 'No, I've crossed the Irish Sea dozens of times. I have very good sea legs.' She thought of Roxy again and wondered whether she might want to come back with her and see if there was any chance they'd take them both.

'Can I . . . can I let you know in the morning?'

Shauna arrived back at their hostel slightly shell-shocked from her visit to the *St Helena* and still trying to make up her mind as to what she should do. By the time she'd climbed the final flight of stairs, she'd decided to turn the job down. But when she opened the door, Roxy was stuffing her clothes into her rucksack while Thierry looked on. Her face lit up in excitement when she saw Shauna.

'Shauna, Thierry has saved our lives!'

Shauna looked at Thierry. He was middle-aged, craggily handsome with salt-and-pepper hair and tanned skin that spoke of years in the Mediterranean sun. Shauna realized she didn't know anything about this man that Roxy seemed so taken with, and she wasn't sure she shared her friend's enthusiasm.

Roxy continued, her words an excited babble: 'Thierry owns a house in the South of France, he's an artist and he's friends with all sorts of people – designers like Jean Paul Gaultier and John Galliano, I could really learn a lot from them. Thierry says we can both go, it's really near the beach and we wouldn't have to pay . . .'

Thierry and Shauna eyed each other.

'That's right, isn't it, Thierry? Me and Shauna come as a pair, we're completely inseparable.'

'*Oui*.' Thierry shrugged, but didn't smile. 'You may come along, if you wish?'

Shauna could sense that Thierry would much prefer that she didn't come.

'Look,' Shauna blurted, 'I've just been offered a job on a yacht. I was going to turn it down because I didn't want to abandon you. But now it seems . . . well, it would be for the best.' She flashed them a smile. 'Three's a crowd, and all that.'

'Shauna, you're not a gooseberry.' Roxy dropped the clothes she was stuffing into her bag and rushed to embrace her friend. 'This could work out brilliantly for both of us. Where is this yacht going?'

Shauna told her that they'd be dropping her off in Greece at the end of August. Roxy clapped her hands. 'That's perfect!' I'll come and meet you in Greece; that way we can have a couple of weeks together before we have to go home! Oh, Shauna, going on a yacht sounds so glamorous.'

'I'll be mopping the decks and cleaning bathrooms,' Shauna said, hugging Roxy back. 'But I'll miss you.' Suddenly feeling anxious, she leaned in close and whispered, 'Are you sure about Thierry? We don't know anything about this guy.'

'Don't worry, he's a pussycat,' Roxy whispered back. 'And who knows who else I might meet? It's who you know in the fashion world.'

Shauna felt a tightening in her tummy. What if something went wrong and she ended up stranded, without Roxy?

Roxy saw the look that passed across her friend's face. 'Hey, none of that. This is what we both wanted: an adventure, right?'

'It's bijou,' said Chantelle with a laugh later that afternoon when she was back at the *St Helena*, opening the door to a tiny cabin with barely room for a bunk bed. 'But you have got an en suite. You'll be sharing with Freya, she's one of the engineers, so she's on the bridge most of the time. She's nice. Earthy Scandinavian, with a good sense of humour, but don't play poker with her whatever you do; she'll take you to the cleaners.'

Shauna nodded, trying to take in the information and gazing around the cramped cabin that was to be her home for the next eight weeks.

'Tell me about the people who own the boat.'

'The family's in shipping.' Chantelle shrugged. 'They're incredibly wealthy. Demetrios Theodosis is the eldest son, and his father wants him to take over the business.'

'He seems a bit of a playboy.' Shauna felt herself blushing

again as she remembered the flirtatious way Demetrios had looked at her.

'He's a red-blooded male, that's for sure, and he's a bit torn – wants to please his family, but wants to have a good time, too. He's still only in his late twenties.'

Shauna thought about Normandie, the glamorous woman in the skimpy bikini who had been with Demetrios. 'Who is the girl he is with?'

'Normandie Chappelle? You obviously don't read the glossy gossip mags! She's a French model, already been linked to Jack Nicholson and Sting. She's got everything, and now she's got Demetrios wrapped around her little finger.'

Shauna felt her heart sink, and was surprised by the feeling. She told herself to stop being ridiculous. She might as well be invisible in this world. Demetrios was way out of her league, and she was just a glorified chambermaid. She could look, but that was all she'd ever be able to do.

Chapter 5

'Shauna, when you've finished those, can you take a couple down to the master cabin?' said Gordana, the *St Helena*'s housekeeper. According to Chantelle, she knew everything that went on aboard the yacht, from who was sleeping with who, to the guests' medical conditions – whether they wanted them known or not.

Shauna nodded and pulled the last of the warm towels from the tumble dryer, folding each of the soft, plump bath sheets into a neat stack. She couldn't wait to trade the hot stuffy confines of the laundry in the bowels of the yacht for the glamour of the upper decks.

Their trip to Corsica had been cancelled, so they'd spent the week in Port Hercules. Shauna didn't mind as it gave her a chance to get to know her way around the *St Helena*. As a member of the housekeeping crew, she was also mastering the art of being invisible so far as the well-heeled guests were concerned. Jeremy had drilled into her that staff should be discreet when slipping in and out of rooms to carry out the necessary tidying, cleaning and changing.

Some of their guests had departed, including the exquisite

Normandie. Shauna had not seen much of her and Demetrius, though she had been given the task of tidying up the master bedroom suite one morning. Try as she might to maintain a professional distance, it was impossible not to let her mind run riot when she picked up the Chanel silk camisole and knickers thrown carelessly across the bed. Shauna could imagine the fevered passion, Demetrios's hands lifting the camisole over Normandie's head as his lips travelled across her body . . .

She tutted at herself. *The sun has gone to your head, Shauna O'Brien.*

Scurrying up the stairs, she arrived on the upper deck and, without thinking, pushed open the door to the master suite.

'Oh . . . I'm sorry.' Like an idiot she stood in the open doorway gaping at Demetrios, who was just buttoning up his shirt. His hair was damp, as if he'd recently showered. Of course, it was. Hence the request for fresh towels.

'No problem.' He carried on buttoning his shirt. 'Go ahead.'

She scurried into the bathroom, her cheeks flaming. Gosh, he must think she was a complete idiot. Quickly, she unfolded one towel onto the rails, placed a couple more on the shelves and scooped up the damp one hanging on the back of the door.

She darted out of the bathroom, hoping to escape without having to speak to him. She hadn't seen him since the day she'd arrived, but it hadn't stopped her wondering if he was as good-looking and self-assured as she remembered. Her memory had served her well. He was extremely good-looking and very sure of himself.

'So, you're still here,' he said, before she had taken a pace across the room.

Something about his tone triggered a sharp response that

was out of her mouth before she could stop herself: 'Is there any reason why I shouldn't be?'

He grinned. 'Catering to every whim of a bunch of rich assholes isn't everyone's idea of a great job.'

Shauna felt he was testing her in some way. 'I haven't met anyone who's an asshole on this ship.'

Demetrios grinned. 'Yet. There's still plenty of time until we finish our voyage.'

'Anyway, they haven't sacked me yet. Unless you decide that you don't like the way I folded your towels.' Again, she'd surprised herself, but there was something about the way he challenged her with his smug self-assurance that brought out her feisty side.

'I'm sure they'll be perfect. Although that talent is probably somewhat wasted if you're going to be an accountant.'

'How do you know about that?' Shauna was puzzled.

'I make it my business to know about everyone who comes on board my yacht. We don't let just anyone work for us, you know.'

Shauna noted again his rich voice, his Greek accent tinged with something else, an American twang perhaps. She felt slightly disconcerted as he took a step closer.

'I even know your name.' He was inches away from her now and she could see his hazel eyes more closely; they almost seemed to be flecked with gold. She caught a waft of citrus and sandalwood. 'Shauna O'Brien.'

Shauna thought her name had never sounded so glamorous or sensuous as when he said it, and wished she looked the way it sounded rather than standing there clumsily in her staff uniform of white vest and navy shorts. He reached towards her, and for a moment Shauna thought he was going to touch her face, but instead, he took the last clean towel from her and rubbed his hair with it. He sauntered over to the mirror, dropped the towel and pushed his hands through his hair, regarding himself in the large mirror. Shauna caught her own reflection standing behind him; she was horrified to see she appeared to be gawping.

'How good are you with numbers, Shauna?'

'Pretty good,' she answered without hesitation. Her father had taught her there was no point in false modesty.

'Good. You can help me sometime, Shauna O'Brien. It's not all play for me, despite what you might think.' When he said this, there was a seriousness to him that Shauna hadn't noticed before. She wondered what sort of help it was he wanted. 'I will call for you tomorrow.'

The following morning was a busy one, they would be leaving Monaco soon and Jeremy wanted the yacht shipshape for the onward leg, but he was pleased with the work the crew had done and gave them all the afternoon off.

'So, have you any plans for the rest of the day?' asked Chantelle, slipping onto the bench beside her as Shauna kicked off her deck shoes and sipped at a Pepsi.

Shauna shook her head. 'I might just explore a bit more of the old town. I love the buildings up there.' And she still hoped for a glimpse of the princess. Only yesterday, two of the other crew members had come back from an outing and said they'd seen the royal couple leaving the palace in a limousine. Princess Grace had waved from the window at the tourists gathered outside.

'I'm going to nip down to the coast, visit some old friends who are staying at Port de Cap D'Ail. Make the most of my free time. Shame Demetrios is on board, otherwise I'd be spending this afternoon lapping up rays on the sun deck.'

'Are we allowed to do that?' Shauna's eyes brightened at the prospect; that would be heavenly. Despite her typically

Irish white skin and red hair, she could get a tan if she was careful.

'Only when there's no one on board. If you know he's on shore and not likely to come back for a couple of hours, it's fine.' Chantelle laid her fork down and called across the table. 'Jeremy, do you have any idea of Demetrios's movements today and tomorrow?'

'Tomorrow he's booked a driver to pick him up at ten and bring him back at three. I believe he has meetings at the casino and lunch with someone. In the evening, there's another car booked to take him to . . .' Jeremy paused, his eyes gleaming, '. . . the Grimaldi palace. Some party there.'

Shauna sat transfixed by the news. Demetrios was going to a party at the palace. Did he know the princess? Had he met her before? Was she as lovely as she looked?

'He knows how to enjoy himself,' said Eric, who was sitting further down the table, helping himself to more French bread. 'When we were in Naples last year, we had a party on board and Dudley Moore and Liza Minelli came.'

'And Kathleen Turner, Jerry Bruckheimer and Michael Mann,' chipped in his girlfriend, Rebecca.

'That was some party,' said Jeremy. 'We almost ran out of champagne.'

With widening eyes, Shauna listened to the tales of famous names, people she couldn't imagine ever meeting.

The afternoon found her creeping up to the top deck with a couple of *She* magazines left behind in one of the guest cabins and a borrowed striped towel that co-ordinated with the sunshine yellow of the cushions on the sun loungers. She also had a tumbler full of ice, a couple of candy-striped straws and a can of Coca-Cola, which seemed the height of luxury.

Even though she'd taken the precaution of checking with

Jeremy that it was OK to come up here and made sure that she had the boat to herself, with the exception of the skeleton crew of two who were doing maintenance work on the engines, she moved quickly and stealthily, unable to shake the feeling she really shouldn't be doing this. But once she'd stripped off her jersey dress, covered herself in sun cream and laid down on the wooden sun lounger in her bikini, she began to relax. Even so, she was too excited to pay much attention to the glossy pages of her magazine. Instead, she used it as cover while taking surreptitious glances at her surroundings.

Across the marina, she could see the stark white stone of the royal palace on top of the hill, and to her right the pinks, oranges and creams of the buildings that perched on the steep slopes of the town. Below her the water lapped at the hull with a somnolent rhythm that made her want to close her eyes. Two yachts down, on a boat nowhere near as big as the *St Helena* – she grinned to herself with a flicker of pride – a group of twenty-somethings were flitting about with glasses of wine, talking in loud voices that carried across the water, making sure the tourists could see and hear them. The girls were all in jewel-bright bikinis topped with sheer kaftans, displaying their bodies like a group of brilliantly coloured hummingbirds.

A smile lit her face as she thought how wonderful it all was. Moments later, her daydreams turned into dreams as she drifted off to sleep.

When she eventually floated to the surface again, luxuriating in the warmth of the sun and gentle breeze, she had no idea how long she'd been asleep. Reluctant to break the spell, with a murmured sigh she stretched her body, enjoying the sensation, smiling to herself – and then a shadow fell across her.

Her eyes shot open. Demetrios was looking down at her,

a soft teasing smile playing around his mouth. 'Hello, Sleeping Beauty.'

Suddenly feeling very vulnerable and naked, she swung her legs over the side of her chair and grabbed a towel to shield her body.

'Oh, don't do that. I was admiring the view.'

'How long have you been here?' she demanded, feeling at a disadvantage given that she was faced with a man wearing a tie, shirt and trousers with a suit jacket hooked on one finger tossed casually over his shoulder. She wrapped her towel around her like a dress and attempted to snatch up the magazines, which slipped and slithered about on the table, making them impossible to hang on to.

'Not long. My meeting finished early so I thought I'd come back. And now I'm glad I did.'

Shauna glared at him, annoyed that her heart, currently pounding at a thousand beats per second, chose to betray her. 'I need to go.' She took a step forward, expecting him to move aside, but he remained where he was, so she found herself almost nose to chest with him.

'Please carry on,' he purred in his deep voice, a boyish mischief twinkling in his eyes. 'You looked like you were enjoying sunning yourself, and I won't tell if you don't.'

'I didn't realize you were coming back . . . I have work to do.'

Demetrios grinned. 'Now I know you're telling lies, Beauty. You have the afternoon off, along with the rest of the crew, as a reward for working so hard and looking after my guests so well. If you're not careful, your nose will grow – and that would be a shame because it's quite a pretty nose.' He crossed his arms and held his position, making it difficult for her to get past him.

'And now I know you're talking rubbish, because noses

aren't pretty,' she observed acerbically, taking a step back. 'Now, if you'll excuse me, I really must—'

'It's only one o'clock. Do you really want to spend this beautiful day making beds and cleaning bathrooms?' He tapped his foot, a bit impatiently, she thought. 'Besides, if you really want to work, you can help me.'

'With what?'

'Follow me and I'll show you.'

Shauna followed him below deck to a small office, where Demetrios took a seat behind a mahogany desk and indicated that she should sit next to him.

'Have you heard of the Greek island of Ithos?' he asked her as he opened a large ledger which appeared to be full of figures.

Shauna shook her head. 'Can't say I have. I've only really heard of Corfu.'

'It's nothing like Corfu.' He sounded horrified, but his eyes gleamed with amusement. 'Your education is sadly lacking.'

'I haven't travelled much, and Greece is a long way from Enniscrea. Anyway, you must think I have something to offer in terms of education, otherwise you wouldn't have asked for my help.'

Demetrios nodded in apology. 'You are right and I forget my manners. This is your afternoon off, and I appreciate your time.'

Shauna was surprised to see he was sincere.

'We must focus, Shauna O'Brien. Here, let me show you something. These are my father's ledgers. You know we sell boats and ship goods all over the world?'

'Yes,' she answered, 'Chantelle told me.'

'I must earn my keep by attending to the family business. We have many customers, many suppliers, and some of them cannot be trusted. Given the chance, they will try to take advantage of us, so we must be vigilant. I know there is something amiss in this ledger, but no matter how many times I look, I cannot get to the bottom of it. Will you help me?'

'I don't know anything about business.'

'But you know about numbers.' He drew his hand across his face, suddenly looking younger than a man pushing thirty, though the strain he was under showed in his eyes.

'What do you see around you?'

Shauna didn't hesitate. 'A lot of money and wealth.'

'*Nai*.' He nodded. 'But this wealth, this money, all these beautiful things – we have worked for them, Shauna. People are jealous and too lazy to work for themselves. They think we do not deserve all this, but the truth is my father and his brothers have made many sacrifices for this – and I must protect my father's interests and keep this business thriving for the generations that will come after us. We put our family first.'

'It sounds almost like a family code.' Shauna laughed.

There was no humour in Demetrios's face when he replied, 'It is a code. We live by it.'

'Then I'll help you, if I can.'

'Let us concentrate.'

For the next hour or so, Shauna and Demetrius pored over the books together; Shauna found it disconcerting to be so close to him, but her interest in the problem and her tenacity soon kicked in. Eventually, her scrutiny paid off and she spotted a discrepancy.

'These two figures don't correspond.' She pointed to a line in the ledger. 'This company, Valma and Partners . . . The hours they worked for you don't correspond to what they billed. According to my calculations, you should have been billed $6,400, but this invoice is for $64,000 dollars. That's why the columns don't tally.'

'Those sneaky bastards!' Demetrios thumped his fist on the desk. 'The head of the company is one of my father's oldest friends. You'd think he could be trusted, no? But this isn't the first time we've been cheated by people we should be able to trust. That's why we try to keep everything in the family.' He was lost in thought for a moment, his brow creased in concentration. 'My father will not like this.'

Shauna could see that it was a serious matter but she wasn't sure how to respond. To her relief, Demetrios shook off his anger at the decption and said, 'I must repay you for saving my company a lot of money. When we get to Ithos, I'm going to take you out myself in one of our boats. Then you will see the Ithos that I want you to see.'

Shauna felt a thrill at this, but couldn't help thinking that, by the time they got to Ithos, she would have been forgotten. While he was genuinely grateful in the moment, he was a busy man and she was just a chambermaid, a helpful one who had just saved his family a lot of money, but a chambermaid all the same.

'There's nowhere quite like Ithos in the whole of the Greek Islands,' he went on. 'It is a jewel. It's also my home.' His eyes were distant for a moment.

Moved by his sudden quietness, she said softly, 'It sounds as if you love it very much.'

'I do. It's the one place where I can be me.'

Shauna saw something in Demetrios then, a seriousness and honesty that his playboy persona belied, and it touched her. 'I don't think I know who me is,' she said, wondering where her own candidness had come from.

'One day you will, but first you must live a little, Sleeping Beauty.' He looked at her then, holding her gaze, and Shauna felt her heart quicken. She was convinced that he was going to reach out to her, and it was all she could do not to touch him first. For a moment she thought of the underwear strewn across his bed and wondered what it would feel like if she were the one sharing that bed.

Then Demetrios dropped his gaze and reached for the satellite phone. 'Now you must excuse me, I have calls to make. Thank you again, Shauna O'Brien, I can see you are an asset to the Theodosis Shipping Company.'

Shauna hunted for an ironic smirk behind that comment but was surprised to find only sincerity. He was already punching out a number on the telephone and, as she crept out, she could hear him talking animatedly in Greek. As she made her way to her cabin, she couldn't stop thinking of Ithos and wondering what might await her there.

Chapter 6

The following day, Shauna found herself on duty in the master suite again. She half hoped that she would run into Demetrios, but he was nowhere to be seen so she tidied his suite quickly, noting with satisfaction that there was no sign of Normandie's lingerie this time.

As she went about her work, her thoughts kept returning to Demetrios. Jeremy had said that Demetrios would be attending a party at the Grimaldi palace tonight. What Shauna wouldn't give to be to be a fly on that opulent wall right this moment. She imagined Princess Grace sitting on a Louis XV chair in her enormous dressing room, flicking through a copy of *Vogue* distractedly while her maid paraded a series of glamorous and elegant gowns before her so she could select what she would wear later for the reception. Her seventeen-year-old wild-child daughter, Princess Stephanie, beautiful, tanned and tempestuous, would come running in, demanding her mother's attention, and the business of tonight's outfit would have to wait while her mother listened to Stephanie's excited chatter. Perhaps they would be catching up on the latest gossip about the rich and powerful Monaco elite . . . or maybe they'd be planning a trip to watch John McEnroe play in the French Open, or to visit Elton John backstage at his latest concert . . .

She was startled from her daydream by the rumble of tyres down below on the jetty as a bright red Ferrari screeched to a halt. She stepped forward to look over the side of the yacht at the open-topped sports car. In the driving seat was the unmistakable Normandie with Demetrios sat beside her. It was clear that all was not well. Shauna took a small step back to avoid being seen. She knew it was wrong to eavesdrop, but she was afraid to draw attention to herself by moving. So she stayed rooted to the spot as their words drifted up.

'You are a shit, Demetrios! How dare you treat me this way.' Shauna could hear the anger in the girl's voice, and she could sense that the girl was on the verge of tears.

'You are exaggerating,' Demetrios answered her, his own voice cool and unemotional.

'I saw you with that little whore, you didn't even try to hide it.'

'Sofía Constantis is the daughter of one of my father's business associates. Of course I must spend time with her – it is my duty to show her around Monaco while she is here.'

'Is it also your "duty" to take her back to her hotel for the night and then screw her?' She spat the words at him, her voice rising a couple of notches.

'Keep your voice down,' he hissed. 'You're letting your imagination run away with you. Why must you be so jealous and childish? Always demanding attention and throwing tantrums.'

'You were seen leaving there this morning at seven a.m.' Normandie's voice was ragged with emotion.

Demetrios's patience seemed to snap. 'So, you're having

me followed now? What the fuck do you think you are playing at?' Shauna was surprised by his anger. 'I don't answer to you, I'm not one of your horny little tennis players or ageing rock stars who think they need you on their arm to make them look good.'

'You're a bastard!' Normandie sobbed.

'And you're an insecure, needy brat.' His voice was like steel. 'You can't control me, and all you'll get for trying is my contempt.'

'Demetrios . . .'

Shauna couldn't resist taking a peek. She saw Normandie reach out to Demetrios and try to put her arms around his neck, sobbing uncontrollably. Demetrios calmly took her arms, pushing them firmly away and then opened the car door and stepped away.

'Tidy yourself up,' he said, 'you look a mess.'

Normandie didn't answer but hung her head on the wheel of the car. Shauna could see her shoulders heaving as she cried. She didn't know anything about Normandie, other than what she had heard, but she felt a tug of sympathy and wondered how Demetrios could treat her this way.

'I'll get one of the crew to drive you back to your villa; you aren't fit to drive in your current state.'

At this the girl threw her head up and said defiantly, 'I don't need one of your minions, fuck you to hell.' With that she reversed the car, the tyres throwing up gravel and smoke as she spun the vehicle around. But Demetrios was already making his way up the gangplank without a backward glance, heading to his quarters no doubt.

Shauna stepped out from the shadows and wondered at this new side to Demetrios. He was certainly a man of many faces.

* * *

That evening, after she had finished her day's work, Shauna made her way to the small deck at the stern. She'd found an old paperback in the staff lounge: *Chances*, by Jackie Collins. According to the back cover, it told the story of Lucky Santangelo, the daughter of a gangster, and was set in the playgrounds of the rich and famous. It sounded just the thing to take her mind off the incident she'd witnessed earlier – try as she might she couldn't stop thinking about Demetrios's cold indifference to Normandie's tears. How could the sensitive man she'd spent time with the previous day suddenly have turned into this heartless rat?

It was still preying on her mind when she sensed someone approaching along the gangway behind her. She turned to see Demetrios, clean-shaven, dressed in a sharp black Armani suit and bow tie. For a moment, she wondered if she'd conjured him up; he looked like a Greek James Bond, almost dazzling in his handsomeness. It was all Shauna could do to tear her eyes away and the realization made her want to laugh.

'What are you doing, Beauty, with that secret smile on your face? Don't you have somewhere exciting to be tonight?'

'No. Some of the crew were going drinking in the town, but I didn't want to go with them.'

'Why not? All work and no play makes Shauna a dull girl, no?'

'I'm not dull.' She was piqued by his teasing. 'It's not my scene, that's all.'

'And what is your scene?' He nodded at her book, and Shauna felt a little ashamed of her trashy paperback; no doubt the sophisticated girls he mixed with would have better ways of spending the evening. She thought then of Normandie, and wondered if she was still drying her tears after his treatment of her.

'Anyway, I'm glad you didn't go,' he said. 'I have a favour to ask of you.'

'Me?'

'Yes, tonight I must attend a reception at the Grimaldi palace. I would like you to be my guest.'

Shauna's jaw dropped, making the shape of a large O. She didn't know what to say.

'But I . . . I . . . why me?'

'Why not you?'

'I'm just an ordinary girl, I don't even have a dress.' Shauna felt completely blindsided; could he really be serious? She felt annoyed at him, why would he want to take one of the ship's crew to a party at the Grimaldi palace. 'You're teasing me, aren't you? I don't think this is very nice of you. I know I'm not important but I do have feelings, and making fun of me like this . . . well, it's just cruel,' she said, her voice shaking a little.

Demetrios shook his head and gently took her hand in his. 'Shauna, the reason I am asking you is precisely because you do have feelings. If I have to spend one more hour in the company of the attention-seeking, insincere little fakes that take up way more of my time than they should, then I think I'd . . . well . . .' He looked around him, trying to find the right words. 'Well, I'd jump into the Mediterranean and swim back to Ithos.'

Shauna thought the look on his face was so sincere that she couldn't help bursting into laughter. 'That bad, is it?' she asked.

He grinned. 'You have no idea.'

'Maybe I do,' she replied, and the two of them smiled at each other. For a moment, Shauna felt his equal, two friends sharing an intimate joke. Then she remembered. 'I really don't have anything to wear.'

'Leave that to me.'

Within half an hour, Chantelle had arrived with an armful of designer eveningwear. She suggested they go to her cabin, which was larger than Shauna's, to try them on. Some were stylish, simple and elegant, while others were glittering and glamorous, but they were all beautiful and worlds apart from the fanciest thing Shauna had worn: a velvet Laura Ashley ballgown with puffy sleeves that she'd bought second-hand for her first university ball.

Shauna couldn't contain a gasp. 'Where did all these come from?'

'Honey, this is Monaco, where fancy events happen on a daily basis. Trust me, this is a town where you can easily find a decent dress at the shortest notice.'

'I can't believe I'm going to be wearing one of these.' Shauna suddenly felt overwhelmed by the thought of the evening ahead. What if she said the wrong thing, or was left alone and somebody asked her who she was? She voiced these fears to Chantelle, who laughed.

'Chérie, you have nothing to worry about. I have been to one or two events of this kind and, let me tell you, most of the guests are so self-absorbed and up their own arses, they won't even care who you are.'

'Does Demetrios usually take crew members on nights out?'

Chantelle hesitated, but didn't meet her eyes. 'Er, no, but he must have a good reason. And he'll have had to square it with Jeremy.'

'But Demetrios is the boss.'

'And Jeremy's in charge of the crew. He doesn't like the boss fraternizing with his staff. It can make life . . . complicated.'

Had it got complicated in the past, Shauna mused. Chantelle seemed to read her mind.

'Look, Shauna, Demetrios knows the rules, but he gets these whims and we just have to roll with it. He won't want to piss Jeremy off, though, so you're safe. Now let's get you into one of these beauties.'

Shauna decided on a shimmering green satin strapless dress with a slit in the front up to her thigh. It was understated yet elegant, and daringly sexy at the same time. Chantelle helped her pile her hair up into a chignon, and shared some of her expensive Estée Lauder make-up. The blue eyeshadow and dark blue kohl seemed to give her eyes a cat-like appearance, and when Shauna put on the gold strappy sandals and looked in the mirror, she didn't recognize herself.

Chantelle whistled and grinned broadly. 'Wow, you are going to blow them away, you look a million dollars! Now grab a clutch and you'd better go – the boss is waiting.'

Shauna tottered a little on her heels as she made her way to the lounge area where he was waiting for her. He had his back turned, and Shauna suddenly felt like a shy child again. It all seemed too much: the yacht, Demetrios, an evening at the palace – this was someone else's world. She had to fight the urge run away.

Demetrios was pouring out two glasses from a bottle of Dom Perignon champagne. He must have heard her approach because he started speaking before he turned around. 'I hope you found something that you—' As he turned to hand her a glass, his eyes widened and he broke off, lost for words.

'What's wrong?' Shauna said. 'Don't you like it?' She looked down at herself, thinking that she must have picked the wrong outfit. 'Should I have gone for something more formal? I can go and change—'

'No,' he answered quickly, then took a step towards her. He came so close that Shauna once again could see the golden flecks of his eyes. 'No, I . . .' He hesitated, then seemed to recover himself. 'You will do just fine . . . More than fine.' He swallowed, then continued, 'In fact, I think you will turn quite a few heads. I doubt they will have seen anything like you in the Grimaldi palace.' He handed her one of the crystal flutes. 'Here, have a glass of champagne while we wait for the car to collect us.'

Shauna took the glass. 'We're going in a car?'

'Of course, how else would we get there?'

'I thought we would walk. It's only a few minutes away.' She looked down at herself and laughed. 'Actually, I can barely walk in these.'

'Drink,' he urged her. 'It will give you the Dutch courage.'

Shauna raised her glass. 'Sláinte,' she said, and took a hesitant sip. 'Oooh.' She laughed again, feeling a buzz of excitement enter her along with the effervescence of the champagne. 'The bubbles went up my nose. It really is fizzy. I've never had champagne before.'

He tilted his head as if intrigued by this admission, then lifted his glass and touched it to hers. 'I hope it will be your first of many.'

Impulsively, she said, 'I've always wanted to go to the sort of party where they serve nothing but champagne or have it for breakfast like Holly Golightly in *Breakfast at Tiffany's*.'

'I seem to recall she has it before breakfast.' Demetrios observed her gravely over the top of his glass.

'You know it?'

He nodded.

'It's one of my favourites, it's so glamorous. Audrey Hepburn is just sublime, although Grace Kelly is my absolute favourite actress.' She looked over towards the castle on the hilltop. 'That's why I came to Monaco. Sounds silly now.'

'Not silly at all.' He paused and then, looking away into the distance, added, 'We all need dreams. What's yours?'

For once there was no need for secrecy. It didn't matter if this stranger found it odd or funny. 'If I could be anything in the world, I'd like to be an actress one day.'

'Why?' The simple question caught her off-guard, but when she tipped her head up to look at him, he seemed genuinely interested.

'Because . . . Look, I know it sounds a bit fanciful – my mam would think I was mad if she knew. You see, I'm quite shy, but when I'm pretending to be someone, I'm not shy any more. It's as if I can leave myself behind. It's empowering and liberating. I can be anything, anyone I want.'

'I can understand that. It's difficult being the person other people want you to be.'

Her skin tingled as their eyes met in a moment of understanding.

'I know that feeling better than you think.' He pulled a self-deprecating face that tugged at something deep inside her, making her want to offer sympathy and comfort.

'And you want to do something different?'

He sighed. 'I am expected to run the family business, to be the next patriarch.'

'But you don't want to?'

'It seems ungrateful. Look' – he spread out his hand, indicating the plush surroundings – 'I have everything I could possibly wish for. But I have a dream of my own, too.'

'What's that?'

He stood up quickly as if irritated and went to the guard rail at the side of the yacht. For a while he remained there, looking out over the marina, both hands gripping the metal. Because there was a touch of loneliness about him as he stood there, she rose and went to join him, each caught in the shadows of their own thoughts as they stared out at the horizon and the crisp line where the cobalt blues and dusky pink and oranges of the twilight met the deep blue sea.

'We are a family of boat builders, but you know what? None of us build boats any more; we pay other people to do it.' He looked at her. 'I want to build my own boat one day. From scratch. Hand-crafted. A sailing boat that is built to respond to the wind and the sea. That works in harmony with nature.'

She smiled. 'Sounds wonderful.'

Demetrios looked self-conscious now. 'And now I am the one who is being . . . what did you call it? "Fanciful".'

Shauna put her hands on the guard rail, small and slender next to his dark capable hands. She could picture him working the wood himself.

'You know, I can see you doing just that, right now in my head.'

Demetrios held her gaze. 'Shauna, I find myself quite liking the idea of being inside your head.'

'Oh, it's full of stuff and nonsense.' She dropped her eyes. 'Like being an actress,' she said with a wistful sigh.

'Hey . . .' He reached up and gently touched her face. 'Always remember, those dreams keep our souls burning brighter.'

She swallowed, lost for words. It was a beautiful thing to say and all she could do was smile back at him.

He lowered his hand. 'Never lose your dreams.' Then he was businesslike once more. 'Now we are strengthened with our liquid courage, it is time for you to play a new role. Tonight, you will be one of Monaco's finest. It's your time to shine – think you can pull it off?'

Shauna didn't know if she could, but she was now filled with a fizz of anticipation as well as alcohol. 'I'll give it everything I've got,' she said.

'That's my girl,' he replied, and a thrill of pleasure shot through her.

Chapter 7

Hardly an auspicious start, she thought to herself with a slightly giddy giggle as she tiptoed awkwardly on her heels down the gangplank.

A black car glided to a halt beside them and, even though she was expecting it, she gave a start. For a moment, she stood there, staring at the tinted windows, until Demetrios opened the door for her and said, 'Jump in.'

She got in first and he slid in beside her. It was impossible to ignore his nearness.

As they drove the short distance to the palace, Shauna felt the question burning inside her that had been at the back of her mind since Demetrios had asked her to join him this evening.

'Can I ask you something?'

'Of course.'

'Why did you choose me to come with you tonight?'

Demetrios turned his head to look out of the window. Shauna followed his gaze; the twinkling lights of the harbour looked so pretty in the dusk.

'Look at it out there,' he said, 'it's beautiful.'

'Yes, it is,' she answered.

'But it's fake . . .' He paused. 'Like most of the people here.'

'I thought you would want to take Normandie.'

He turned back to face her. 'Not today. There are things you don't know about Normandie. She's not always the best-behaved guest, for starters.'

'I might know more than you think,' she said boldly, and when he looked at her sharply, she thought she had over-stepped the mark.

'Did you see or overhear something today?'

Shauna bit her lip, reluctant to admit that she had been listening when she shouldn't have, but he seemed to read the answer in her face. To her surprise, he wasn't angry.

'You know, Shauna, Normandie is an actress too. Her moods come and go so fast, I'm sure by now she will already have her attention elsewhere.'

'But she's your girlfriend?'

He laughed without humour. 'Shauna, you really are naive. Normandie has a string of lovers. What she wants is for me to worship at her feet the way the rest of them do. She wants to be famous and applauded. I assure you, she does not want me for myself, only what she thinks I can do for her.'

'And what about you – what do you want?'

The car was now ascending the hill to the palace. It passed through a set of wooden gates and several stone arches before he answered her. 'Shauna, when I give my heart to someone, it won't be an "It girl" like Normandie. Tonight, Shauna, I just want to talk to a real person for once.'

Shauna wondered what sort of girl he would give his heart to, but before she could give it much thought, the car pulled up beside a red carpet. The butterflies in her stomach seemed to soar and dive in a great fuss. She froze in her seat while the driver opened the door and Demetrios stepped out.

'Time for you to play your role, Beauty,' he said, smiling.

Giving herself a little pep talk, she waited until he reached in and extended his hand to help her out. *Imagine you're a famous actress*, she told herself. *Or a new actress fresh from your first award-winning role. You've taken Broadway by storm.* And with that she lifted her chin, pulled her shoulders back and gave him her hand, imagining being regal and queenly. The image was dispelled a little when her hand shook as she put it into his, but he gave her fingers a gentle squeeze and her spirit reasserted itself when he tucked her hand through his arm as if she were his princess.

'You're supposed to enjoy this,' he reminded her with a gentle smile. 'Any tighter and your grip will cut off my circulation – and I'm rather attached to this arm.'

She let out a small laugh. 'Nervous. Sorry.'

'Don't be. They're all human beings, just like us.'

'Hmm, but with a lot more money,' observed Shauna faintly as a woman passed by, a large diamond and sapphire necklace flashing at her neck.

'You'll be fine.' He briefly put his free hand over hers. 'You look very beautiful and every bit as elegant as the other women here. And we can have a little fun too, you know.'

She knew he was being charming and trying to set her at her ease, but for a moment Shauna could only stare at him, too bemused to speak. Then she lifted her chin and told herself, *I can do this*.

They followed the line of well-dressed people towards a horseshoe-shaped marble staircase. Ahead of them, women were ascending the staircase, lifted their long skirts an inch or two to avoid tripping. Shauna smoothed the expensive fabric of her dress. This was the most exciting thing that had ever happened to her. In response, Demetrios stroked her arm gently, sending a shower of sparks fizzing through her bloodstream.

To steady herself, she stared at the people around her. To their right was an elegant, statuesque woman who wore a black strapless dress of unrelieved simplicity that was set off by half a dozen rows of pearls around her neck. 'Christy Turlington,' murmured Demetrios.

'What?' she squeaked and moderated her voice quickly to add, 'The model?'

He nodded. 'And there's Bianca Jagger.' He nudged her arm and she turned to see the dark-haired woman in a red halter-neck sequinned dress that shimmered as she walked with undulating grace in the company of two other equally attractive women.

'Oh, my, it's Farah Fawcett-Majors.' Shauna ducked her head as the famous actress walked by in a billowing gold lamé dress on the arm of a familiar-looking man. 'And the Bionic Man.'

Demetrios laughed softly. 'I don't think you should call him that if we're introduced.'

'Do you know him?'

'No.'

A thought struck her. 'Do you know the prince and Princess Grace?'

'Monaco is actually very small. My father has business dealings with Prince Rainier. He asked me to come in his place as he's unavoidably detained in Athens.'

There was something about his tone that made her ask. 'Didn't you want to come?' She couldn't believe anyone wouldn't.

He hesitated. 'It's business. These aren't my friends. There are so many people here, it's difficult to talk to anyone. It's all an act. A game. Some of my father's friends and associates will be here and I'm expected to mingle with them. Will you think me very dreadful if I say it's a duty I must fulfil?'

'Very,' she said cheerfully, determined to make sure that tonight he enjoyed himself.

He laughed, a rich low rumble that made her tummy tingle.

Now it was their turn to climb the steps. They passed through ranks of white-uniformed guards armed with guns into a reception room. 'It's exquisite,' Shauna whispered, entranced by the huge glittering chandelier that sparkled and shimmered with golden light refracted and reflected by the mirrors lining the white plaster and gilt walls.

'I find it a bit stuffy.' Demetrios shrugged, looking around him.

'Yes, it's like being in a museum, except real people live here. Look at the chairs.' She discreetly pointed to the plump, silk-brocade-upholstered Louis XV gold-leaf chairs, 'And the walls.' Her eyes widened as she realized the walls were covered in matching silk brocade. Her attention turned to the painted walls curving up to the ceiling with frescoes depicting scenes of voluptuous cherubs and a titian-haired goddess with flowing locks.

Her head twisted this way and that as she tried to take in every detail so that she could share it in a postcard to her parents. It was magnificent, spectacular, marvellous, glorious . . . and she was never going to be able to describe it properly.

At last they came to a room so crowded with people that it took her mind off the sumptuous surroundings. The hum of chatter filled the high-ceilinged room and Demetrios took two glasses of champagne from the smart waiter standing to attention by the doorway.

'Gosh, before today, I'd never had champagne, and now I'm having my second glass.' Shauna raised her glass in a playful toast.

'I feel like I'm leading you astray. I think my mother might disapprove.'

'My mother definitely would. She doesn't approve of enjoying yourself.' With a defiant grin she took a swig of champagne.

'Ah, the rebel,' teased Demetrios.

'Not really, just determined to make the most of this moment,' she replied, beaming at him before looking around her. 'I didn't expect this many people. It's quite a crush.'

'And now you see why I'm not so keen.'

'But it's all so pretty, there's so much to look at. And that doesn't even include the people. Look at that old couple there, the lady with the iron-grey curls and the black walking stick. They're like something out of an antique painting.'

'The Von Hapsburgs – they're German former royals, and he's in pharmaceuticals.'

Shauna felt like she was wandering around with her mouth open and told herself to look less obviously like an interloper. Demetrios wanted her to play a role, so that's what she was going to do. They began to circulate around the edge of the room. 'Who's the tall blonde over there with the rather elderly gentleman?'

'Greta Mitterand, niece of the French president, and that's her tennis coach.'

'Tennis coach?'

'Oh, yes, despite his advanced years, he's still rather handy on the tennis court – she almost got to Wimbledon last year.' She could feel Demetrios shaking with laughter as he spoke. 'He's also her husband.'

'Really?' Shauna took another look at the pair. 'That's . . . Do you think she really loves him?' With a perplexed frown, she glanced up at him. 'I mean, he's, well, quite old, and she's . . . very beautiful.'

Demetrios shook his head. 'Shauna, you really do need an education in the ways of the moneyed classes.' Then he caught sight of someone and steered her in their direction.

'How about this couple?' he said, indicating a very striking pair standing under one of the glittering chandeliers beside a long window.

'They . . . oh, my.' Her mouth dropped open in a gasp. 'It's them, her. The princess.' Desperate not to be caught staring, Shauna ducked her head and tried to peep surreptitiously at the royal pair. The princess was resplendent, it was the only word for it, in a purple taffeta dress, her signature blonde hair in an elegant chignon and her favourite pearls at her neck. She was chatting with easy charm to an uncomfortable-looking woman who kept fidgeting with her skirts and nodded a lot. Shauna could imagine how she felt. It must be daunting coming to face to face with a movie legend who was also royalty and an international icon.

'Shall we?' Before she realized what he was doing, Demetrios had cupped her elbow and was guiding her towards the royal couple.

Prince Rainier looked up and smiled in recognition.

'Monsieur Theodosis, what a pleasure to see you.'

'Sir, may I present Miss Shauna O'Brien.'

'Enchanted.' The prince nodded and gave her a smile.

Overcome with shyness, Shauna gulped and smiled back. Fortunately, her mother's voice in her head, chiding *Shauna, where are your manners?*, came to her rescue. 'Pleased to meet you, Your Highness, you have a very lovely ho— palace.'

'Thank you.' His eyes twinkled. 'The family has been here rather a long time. Over nine hundred years. We've accumulated quite a lot of treasures over the years.'

'Haven't we just,' the princess joined in. 'And I can tell you, when I first came here, I was terrified I might break something very valuable.' Her face, though heavier now than in her acting days, creased into a smile that still possessed the same luminous quality that had been her hallmark.

'Oh, I can imagine,' said Shauna, her shyness and awe vanishing thanks to the princess's friendly demeanour. 'Some of the furniture looks quite fragile. I'd be scared to sit on it.'

Princess Grace let out a peal of laughter. 'Exactly. Poor Rainier. I was extremely nervous.' She patted his arm. 'All this history and protocol. But one learns with experience. I'm quite old now.' Her eyes sparkled with laughter. 'But experience and age bring wonderful insight, as you will learn one day.'

Shauna could only nod, committing the words to memory, determined she would never forget them.

'Please do give our best regards to your father, Mr Theodosis. And lovely to meet you, Miss O'Brien. Enjoy the party. You'll find the chairs are quite sturdy, but terribly uncomfortable.'

Shauna stared after the royals as they moved away, still dazed that the princess had noted her name.

'Regular people really, aren't they?' said Demetrios quietly as the royal couple were swallowed up in the crowd.

'They were much more friendly than I expected. I thought they'd be quite formal and stuffy. She was . . . she was lovely.'

'And so are you.' Demetrios smiled down at her. 'I think you charmed them because you weren't trying too hard. A rare thing in this world.' He held out his arm. 'Shall we fight our way through this melee and find some food?'

'Do you think they'll have caviar?' she joked. 'Now that I've tried champagne, I feel I ought to try caviar as well.'

'If they don't, I'll order some in.' Shauna realized when he said this that he wasn't joking.

It turned out there was caviar, along with smoked salmon and fresh anchovies and foie gras – which she really didn't like – and super-thin slices of cured ham, delicate slivers of Swiss cheese, tiny meringues, miniature roulades of sponge and raspberry, miniature lemon tarts . . .

Demetrios encouraged her to sample everything, which she did eagerly, and he laughed at her as she tried not to stuff her face, though it was hard to resist the delicious array of new delicacies to try.

'Are we starving you on the ship?' he joked.

'Not at all, Chantelle is a wonderful chef. But I've never eaten anything this good – or expensive!'

'I'm very glad I brought you with me this evening.'

'So am I,' she said, and she meant it. It was a lot more fun and less restricted by protocol than she'd thought it would be.

A band started up in the elaborate ballroom and Shauna thought she recognized the tune: 'You're Sensational' from *High Society*.

'I love this one,' she said.

'Then let's dance.'

'I'm not sure I can. Can you?'

'Of course, I have been trained for every social situation.' He grinned.

'I can dance a little.'

'Then let's take to the floor.' He grabbed her hand and pulled her towards him, holding her close as he smoothly glided across the dancefloor, one hand around her waist and the other holding her hand as they swayed to the music.

'You're quite the dancer!' Shauna told him.

'You're not too bad yourself.'

'You're doing a good job for both of us. I hardly have to do anything.'

They were so close now, and he was leaning towards her so that, although he was a few inches taller than she was, their cheeks were touching. It occurred to her that he would barely have to move an inch to kiss her, and for a crazy second Shauna wondered what he would do if she kissed him instead. But before she could act on the urge, someone tapped her on the shoulder and she almost gasped to see Princess Grace and her dancing partner, a handsome young man.

'You two look sensational together, quite the glamorous couple!' she purred. 'Demetrios, where did you find this adorable girl?'

She winked at Shauna, still swaying in time to the music. 'I always make sure the orchestra plays this, but Rainier will never dance with me as he's still sore about Frank Sinatra.'

Shauna couldn't tell if she was serious. She noticed that the princess's dance partner looked as starstruck as she felt.

'You might want to hang on to this young lady, Demetrios, she's a one-off,' Princess Grace added with a smile, and in a flash she was gone, chattering away to her young companion as they danced.

Demetrios turned to Shauna and grinned mischievously. 'She's right, you know: we do look good together.'

'Now I know you're teasing.'

Demetrios's smiled faded. 'I never tease, not when it matters.'

Shauna didn't know what to say to this, and for a moment they stood together, everything else fading away into the background. His eyes were studying her so intently it was as if he was looking deep inside her, and again she felt the urge to reach out and draw him towards her. Before the impulse could get the better of her, the band stopped playing and she realized they were back where they started. Demetrios smoothly retrieved their champagne glasses from the balustrade, handed one to her and then lifted his own in a toast. 'To a night of surprises, Beauty.'

She raised her glass in response, but somehow knew the spell had been broken and the magic dispelled. They drifted back into the main hall, where Demetrios was stopped several times, usually by older couples who knew his parents or business associates of the family firm. None of them paid much attention to Shauna; it was as if she were merely an accessory. This didn't trouble her, because the conversation invariably turned to people she'd never heard of and she had nothing to contribute. So she smiled a lot, nodded even more, and although she had little to add to the general small talk, she was quite happy soaking up the atmosphere, watching the other women and compiling a mental inventory of their dresses. There was so much to see and observe that she wasn't at all bored, but she could tell that Demetrios was wearying of the frequent enquiries about his parents' health, his company's interests and what he thought of the latest takeovers and mergers in the shipping industry.

They had just been introduced to a tall blond Englishman called Richard, and were both listening with polite interest as he told them in great detail about the recording studio he was building in his Cotswold manor house, when Shauna registered a sudden change in Demetrios's expression. She followed his gaze, which had fallen upon a strikingly beautiful woman who was wearing an incredible low-cut white gown that left little to the imagination. She locked eyes with Demetrios, and then her steely glare swept over Shauna. There was a flash of annoyance before the woman composed herself.

Demetrios touched the small of Shauna's back. 'Shauna, Richard, please excuse me for a moment.'

He walked over to the woman and as he kissed her on both cheeks, the woman's eyes flickered over to Shauna. She then leaned in, whispering in his ear, and Demetrios whispered something in reply, but the woman did not appear pleased. As Richard carried on chattering, oblivious to Shauna's lack of interest in the club he was thinking of buying in London, Demetrios and the woman pulled away from the small circle of people she was with and began talking animatedly to each other. Again the woman looked at Shauna, this time with undisguised animosity and, a moment later Demetrios returned with her by his side.

'Richard, Shauna, this is Sofía Constantis, a dear friend of my family.'

Shauna immediately recognized the name of the woman that Normandie had accused Demetrios of sleeping with. She smiled and extended her hand. 'Hello, Sofía. Nice to meet you.'

The woman's eyes narrowed; she pointedly kept her own hand by her side, and made no attempt to return the smile. Instead, she turned to Demetrios and demanded, 'Where did you find this one? She looks and sounds like an Irish peasant.'

For a second, Shauna was bewildered. Why had this woman picked her out for a fight? Richard, clearly embarrassed by the outburst, coughed politely and excused himself.

Shauna briefly considered doing the same, but then she heard father's voice urging her: *Never let anyone tell you you're not good enough, Shauna O'Brien. Always hold your head high.*

Before she knew where the words came from, they were out of her mouth: 'Oh, I think you've mistaken me for someone else. The O'Briens are descended from a long line of Irish kings – but I don't suppose you'd know that, not being royalty yourself.'

Demetrios let out a snort that he covered with a cough. There was a glint of laughter in his eyes and she could see he was working hard at suppressing a smirk.

'Yes,' he said, composing himself and turning to Sofía. 'Shauna here is doing an excellent job of representing her country.' Casting an apologetic look at Shauna, he asked her to excuse him for a moment, then he took Sofía's elbow and said, 'Come, Sofía, I believe Prince Albert wants to hear all about your recent trip to New York . . .' and they set off for the other side of the room where the son of Rainier and Grace was chatting with his guests, Sofía turning one last time to shoot her a look of pure venom.

Shauna felt like a bird that had been singled out as prey by a rather vicious cat. She wondered what she had done to warrant such treatment. Though she tried to shake it off and focus on her grand surroundings once more, her feathers were ruffled all the same. Was this what it would be like to live in Demetrios's world? An endless round of parties, batting away pampered and demanding hordes of women? No wonder he wanted a break from it all.

It seemed he was living up to his playboy reputation, in some respects at least. But she couldn't stop thinking about the hardworking and serious side he'd revealed to her: the young man trying so hard to live up to his family's expectations. Which one of these was the real Demetrios?

She sighed and drained her champagne glass. Barely a second later a waiter in a crisp white jacket and bow tie appeared, raising a bottle to fill it again. She placed her hand over the top of the glass as she had seen other guests do, to indicate that she didn't want any more.

There was no way she would ever get to know the real Demetrios. It had occurred to her in the last hour that the reason few of Demetrios's acquaintances paid any attention to her was because they were used to him having a different escort on his arm each time they saw him. The realization brought with it a welcome dose of common sense. She might be inexperienced and somewhat gauche, but she wasn't stupid. This evening Demetrios had enjoyed the novelty of playing Pygmalion, casting her as his Eliza Doolittle, but as soon as the next group of his rich friends arrived he would lose interest. She'd been no more than a brief diversion so far as he was concerned.

Tomorrow they would be leaving Monaco to begin their voyage. In a few weeks she would be flying back to England to resume her education. The memories of tonight would fade and seem like a distant dream, something to tell the grandchildren: her night with the handsome playboy and the fairy-tale princess.

They left the party soon after. Demetrios said little while they were in the car, but when they arrived back at the marina he asked the driver to drop them off so they could walk the rest of the way.

As they made their way along the harbourside, he told her, 'I would like to apologize for Sofía's rudeness, it was inexcusable.'

Shauna thought it sounded as though apologizing for Sofía's rudeness was a regular occurrence. 'Who is she?'

'A close family friend. Her father is my family's closest competitor in business, so he is both a friend and a rival of my father. Keep your friends close and your enemies closer, isn't that what they say?'

'Sounds serious.'

'Yes and no. Sofía . . . Well, let's just say she embodies the qualities of both friend and enemy. She loves me and she hates me, probably in equal measure. My father and mother would have me marry her and put an end to her indecision.'

Shauna felt a jolt pass through her. 'And will you do what your parents would have you do?'

'When I marry, it will be for love. But enough of me. Tell me, has this night lived up to your expectations?'

'Oh, yes.' She gave him a dazzling smile. 'I met Grace Kelly, what could be better than that?'

'I am glad we made one of your dreams come true.'

Shauna couldn't help the thought that there was one more thing that would make her night complete.

He looked at his watch. 'Do you know, it is midnight already.'

'Just like Cinderella – the only thing missing is a glass slipper.'

'And a kiss from a prince?'

'Now that would be a fantasy. Remember, no fraternizing,' Shauna laughed.

He laughed too, but reached out and took her hand. 'I think you played your part very well tonight, Beauty. I was impressed.'

Shauna felt a tingle as he touched her and didn't pull away. *Maybe the champagne really has gone to my head*, she told herself. 'I loved every minute of it. Apart from Sofía, everyone was utterly charming. It was wonderful to be someone else for a night.'

'She is jealous.'

'Why would she be jealous of me?'

'You really have no idea? She is angry because you are with me. And she knows I wouldn't take just anyone along to the Grimaldi palace. You are special, Shauna. I thought tonight was just . . .' He trailed off and took a step closer to her. This time she moved towards him too and looked once more into his hazel eyes flecked with gold.

'Perhaps we should put the final touch on our evening,' he whispered, waiting as if to give her the chance to say no, but she was mesmerized by the way his eyes seemed to drink her in.

'Yes, perhaps we should,' she breathed, proud of her unexpected boldness.

Slowly, he slipped an arm around her waist and drew her closer, his gaze never leaving hers.

She thought that he must be able to hear the thudding of her heart as he lowered his lips to hers. The first gentle touch surprised and delighted her as, satin soft, his mouth glided over hers, barely there but sending a delicious shock wave through her.

His hand slid up her back, pressing her to him. She felt a growing sense of urgency and kissed him back. Beneath her fingers she could feel the warm skin of his neck. The warm night air wrapped around them, bringing the scent of the sea and the faint chimes of the halyards clinking on the sailing boats in the harbour.

Eventually, he pulled away, 'Our night together now has everything. Tomorrow it is back to reality for both of us, but at least we will both have a little dream to keep in our hearts. You can be my Cinderella, and I . . .'

She touched his lips with her fingers. 'Don't say any more. It's perfect as it is. Goodnight, Demetrios.'

Shauna slipped off her gold sandals and skipped up the gangway feeling the slight rock of the boat as she stepped aboard. It had been a magical evening, a glimpse of another life, but now she was back with a very gentle landing rather than a bump, and for that she was very grateful.

The yacht was silent with no one to see her clutching the gold sandals and lifting her skirts as she padded down the stairs praying that she wouldn't meet anyone. After she'd peeled off the beautiful silk dress, she lay back on her bunk with a dreamy smile on her face, wondering if this was this how Cinderella had felt after the ball.

Chapter 8

It felt as if they were setting off on a big adventure when the yacht finally nosed out of its berth accompanied by the Port Hercules harbour pilots in their zippy little speedboats, buzzing around like small aquatic flies. Excitement thrummed through her veins in tandem with the low throb of the engines as Shauna stood on the starboard side of the boat ready to haul in her assigned fender. She was doubling as a deckhand and in her smart uniform she couldn't help feeling rather important as a crowd gathered to watch the *St Helena*'s departure.

As soon as the harbour pilots buzzed off, abandoning the *St Helena* to the open sea, the crew dispersed to their usual rostered jobs. There was no sign of Demetrios and she couldn't decide whether that was a good or a bad thing. Last night at the Grimaldi palace had been heavenly, a glimpse into another world which she knew she might never see again, but it had strengthened her resolve that one day she would be somebody.

Despite the hard work, Shauna discovered that she loved the rhythm of life at sea. The ship had a completely different feel to when they'd been in port. Somehow, the yacht seemed to come into its own as it cut its way across the Mediterranean. Over the following days, the sea proved an ever-changing chameleon. Some days it was calm and still; on others, the waves would be gently whipped by the wind. It was a far cry from ferry crossings on the turbulent Irish Sea; here the waves had a hypnotic quality, while the sky was always a cloudless azure blue.

Their route took them via Corsica, where they stayed for one night. Even in that short time, she found herself enchanted by the lively town of Bonifacio. Demetrios had left the yacht for dinner with some business associates, leaving the crew free to amuse themselves for a few hours. The marina was a hive of activity and the other crew members were eager to sample all it had to offer, but Shauna had set her heart on making the long climb up the hill to the thirteenth-century citadel. Having agreed to meet up with the others for drinks later, she set off, enjoying the solitude and marvelling at the unrivalled view out across the harbour.

When she joined up with the crew in the bar where they were drinking beer and cheap wine, it brought it home to her that she was just passing through. She liked the other crew members, but she wasn't quite one of them – even if that was how Demetrios saw her. It felt as though she must have imagined the night at the palace with Demetrios and their fairy-tale kiss, but then she remembered the way he'd looked at her and felt a jolt of pleasure. She found herself wondering what he was doing right now. Since that night, she was certain he'd been avoiding her. He no longer spent each day passing backwards and forwards, making his presence felt, exchanging cheerful banter with the crew and getting involved in day-to-day life on the *St Helena*. These days, he made his way up to the bridge first thing in the morning and stayed there, taking his dinner with the captain and the senior officers in the evening. She thought he must be regretting their night together, and she told herself that was what happened when girls like her got mixed up with men like Demetrios. Rich people didn't have feelings.

The next day, Shauna saw even less of Demetrios. Jeremy explained that there was a change to their plans and they weren't going to be stopping at either Malta or Crete on the way to Ithos as originally planned.

'Demetrios has decided he wants to get back to Ithos.' Jeremy pushed a hand through his hair. 'It's turned everything upside down. Funny, because it's not like him at all.'

'In what way?' she asked.

'Don't get me wrong, Demetrios is demanding and expects everything his way, but he's not usually capricious. Not like this. Changing the plan at the last minute is not like him at all. And on top of that he's told me that he's acting as chief mate on this journey, assisting the captain.'

Which explained why, when Demetrios did appear, it was on the bridge, directing the voyage with the captain. He looked so absorbed in what he was doing that she commented on it to Chantelle as she helped her prepare the crew's lunch.

'Well, they are a shipping family. Yes, they are concerned with commerce, but the family have their roots in sailing and his father will want Demetrios to learn about ship life from top to bottom. How can one know about the challenges of running a shipping company without the insider knowledge of how a boat is handled?'

'Do you know why he's suddenly in such a hurry to get back to Ithos?'

'Probably something to do with the business. The family divide their time between Athens and Ithos. You'll like it there – it's very beautiful and unspoiled.'

'So I've been told.' Shauna paused, wondering how to broach the next subject. In the end, she gave up and just blurted it out: 'Tell me about Sofía Constantis.'

'Oh, so you have had the pleasure of meeting the tigress?'

'She was at the Grimaldi party. I can't say she was too friendly.'

Chantelle laughed. 'She never is. Sofía's father is determined that she and Demetrios will marry, bringing two of Greece's shipping dynasties under one roof. If it is good for her father, it will be good for Sofía too – Demetrios is quite the catch!'

'Is that what Demetrios wants?'

'No one knows what he wants, not even Demetrios!' Chantelle turned the marinated chicken over the open coals – they smelled delicious and Shauna's tummy rumbled. 'He's very good at fending off over-enthusiastic lady friends, but Sofía is different – he won't have it all his own way there. Mama Theodosis will have been scheming behind the scenes too. Never cross a Greek mother!'

'I'll try not to,' Shauna responded.

'Papa Theodosis is the head honcho on paper, but Elana wears the pants. She always gets what she wants.'

Shauna was silent, thinking about the forces bearing down on Demetrios and wondering what it must be like for a young man with dreams to know that he wasn't free to pursue them.

Chantelle seemed to read her thoughts. 'Demetrios isn't always so diligent about working for the family business.' She gave Shauna a sideways glance. 'I hear you've been helping him.'

Shauna shrugged. 'Is that what everyone is saying?' She hated the idea that the rest of the crew might be gossiping about her. 'It's nothing really . . . It's nice to use my brain occasionally.'

'No one thinks anything. You're far too . . . Don't take offence, but you're the innocent, sweet type and we all know Demetrios's tastes run to sultry, tempestuous brunettes, like Normandie. Anyway, Demetrios knows his own mind and won't be pushed into anything, but he also knows that his family want what's best for the business. In an uncertain world, there is strength in numbers.'

Shauna bit her lip.

'Hey,' said Chantelle, 'why the frowning face? You're not getting romantic ideas about Demetrios, are you?'

'Of course not,' Shauna said. 'That would be ridiculous!'

Chantelle looked at her kindly. 'Listen, chérie, you wouldn't be the first to get attached to Demetrios, he has that knack of making everyone feel a bit special. But that way only heartbreak lies, I promise you.'

'You've got the wrong idea completely,' Shauna said quickly, taking her plate of Greek salad and skewered chicken to sit alone, thoughtfully eating it on the deck.

Up above, through the smoky glass of the bridge, she could see Demetrios and Captain Elias poring over their charts.

He looked up momentarily and Shauna thought he could see her. But instead of giving her a wave he turned away. Her heart sank. Chantelle was right: she'd been a fool to think there was anything in his kiss.

The following morning, Jeremy tackled her as she was tidying the linen stores.

'Shauna, are you taking those to the master suite? Can

you give this telex to Demetrios, he wanted it as soon as it came through – it's urgent. He's also asked for coffee, so make yourself useful.'

The last thing Shauna wanted was to see Demetrios, having convinced herself that he no longer wanted anything to do with her after having fun at her expense. Nevertheless, she couldn't keep the butterflies from fluttering in her stomach as she approached his suite.

She knocked but there was no answer. Thinking he was probably having his shower, she left the telex on his desk with the tray of coffee but as she was about to leave the bathroom door opened and Demetrios stepped through from his cabin, a towel wrapped around his hips, both hands towelling his hair. 'Ah, is that the message I was expecting? I need that coffee, too. Could you pour for me? I'm running a little late.' He tossed down the towel and sat down on the sofa, completely unselfconscious about his bare chest. Shauna dropped her eyes and focused on pouring him a cup before walking over to hand it to him.

'Sit down. I don't want you towering over me, it gives you an unfair advantage.'

'You aren't dressed.'

'You're being rather prudish. Surely, you've seen a man's chest before?' He sounded irritable and cross.

'Maybe I'll just leave you to it. I'm sure we both have plenty of work to do.'

'Are you always such a calm, collected beauty?' he snapped icily. He stared at her, resentful and arrogant.

Taken aback by the fierceness in his words, she froze. She might be unworldly and unsophisticated and from a humble background, but she deserved some respect. She lifted her chin. 'I'm an employee. I can't fight back, as you well know, but I can tell you that I think you're being rude. If I'm not required here, I will leave.' She turned on her heel and marched to the door, her heart beating a little faster, roused by the unexpected conflict.

'Stop! Wait.' He lurched to his feet and intercepted her, standing between her and the door handle.

She looked up at him, defiantly refusing to be intimidated.

His face softened and he smiled at her, his brown eyes full of warmth and regret. 'I owe you an apology. I'm sorry. You're quite right, perhaps I got out of the wrong side of the bed, as you would put it.'

Shauna nodded stiffly, still determined to leave the room.

'Please, Shauna, come and sit down with me.'

She felt herself relent. 'I'd rather you were dressed first.'

It was his turn to raise an eyebrow. When he saw her mouth firming into an implacable line, he laughed.

'As you wish, Miss Prim. We must have standards.'

She bristled at the description; it made her sound staid, dull and boring and everything that her mother wanted her to be, when she wanted to be anything but that. More than ever, she wanted to be one of those tempestuous and beautiful women that he was so taken up with, the ones who wore Chanel and had Bollinger and sex for breakfast.

When he returned, it was in a pale green linen shirt and navy cotton shorts. 'Better?' He enquired, his mouth twisting in barely contained amusement. 'Do you want anything to eat? There's plenty there.'

'I had breakfast with the crew. At half-past six.'

'Touché,' he said, lifting his coffee cup in salute. 'What would you say if I told you I'd not slept well?'

'I'm sorry to hear that.' She paused before adding, 'I always sleep exceptionally well.'

'Do you?' He eyed her. 'There is nothing that keeps you awake at night?'

Shauna felt as if he were pulling her into a dangerous force field.

'Surely you have everything you want?'

'You'd think so, but sometimes even those who seem to have everything don't have the one thing they truly need.'

'And what are you missing?'

He hesitated, as if about to reveal something, but then he stopped himself and reached out for the message. After reading it, he let out a sigh. 'I have been very busy these last days. I have been focusing on my father's business and not able to spend time getting to know you further. I need your help again, Shauna. Will you spare me your time?'

He seemed so sincere when he said these words, she couldn't resist. 'OK, it's a truce. What do you need my help with. More figures?'

'Not this time. My father wants me to go home to Ithos as soon as possible for family reasons.' He pointed at the telex. 'He thinks I have been wasting my time enjoying myself.' He smiled ruefully. 'Maybe he is right, though I will keep him waiting a little longer. You can help me with my excuse. I'll tell him that I have been looking at new avenues for our shipping routes, but I'll have to show him some proof. You can help me map the routes on these charts.' He pointed to a pile of papers.

'I don't know anything about shipping or maps.'

'We can do it together. All you need is a ruler and a steady hand. While we do this, I will show you what a gentleman I can be, you will tell me about yourself and I will tell you about myself; that way we can be friends again – but let's sit out on the deck to do it.'

That morning as they pored over the charts, she learned that he'd studied at Harvard, that he'd lived in London for a year, that he'd been to New York many, many times. He learned that she liked living in Manchester, that she'd grown up on the coast and that she'd played Lady Macduff, despite longing for the part of Lady Macbeth, in the recent university drama club performance.

'You need to be more pushy,' he told her. 'I think you have to show your hunger – and you don't. You want everyone to like you. Shy, demure, Shauna. The nice girl.'

He'd said it kindly, so she didn't take offence. 'I've always been taught not to push myself forward but to stand up for myself when I need to. It's difficult,' she sighed.

'You don't find it difficult with me.'

'You're different.'

'How?'

'I don't know.' Shauna gazed at him intently, trying to figure out why Demetrios didn't scare her. She pinched her lips together, honesty forcing her to go on. 'I think that first time we met . . . I saw something. Your hopes and dreams. You were open with me and I was open with you . . . I see you as that person, rather than the playboy prince that you pretend to be.'

His eyes widened. 'Shauna, how is it that you seem to see inside my soul? Perhaps you are an Irish witch?'

'We don't call them witches in Ireland. They're known as *Cailleach* and they can cause all sorts of mischief.' She grinned playfully at him.

'In Greek mythology, we have a goddess of witchcraft called Hecate, who can be both good and evil. Are your *Cailleach* like that too? Perhaps you can summon one to cast a spell that will save me from my father's commands and my mother's temper.'

'Oh dear, is it really so bad?' Shauna couldn't help laughing.

'There are days I would give anything just to be an ordinary fisherman, to tend my nets, drink beers with my friends on Ithos . . . fall in love' – he looked at her closely – 'and have a family, just like the men down on Ithos harbour.'

Shauna looked out over the dazzling sea with sunlight bouncing off the deep sapphire blue of the water. 'You'd miss this glamorous life.'

'There would be other consolations.'

When he said things like that it made Shauna's heart dance in her chest. The more she got to know him, the more she felt that she was falling under his spell, even though she knew she shouldn't be.

To her surprise, he reached out and touched her cheek with his fingers, leaning closer until she could smell the sandalwood soap that he used.

'Shauna, would it be so wrong of me to want something that other people take for granted? I've never met anyone like you. I've tried to ignore you these last few days because I can feel you exerting some power over me that I'm unable to resist. Since we kissed, I can't get you out of my mind. When I lie awake at night, I can see you in my head, your red hair and those green eyes like emeralds.' He looked at her, and Shauna thought there was a touch of annoyance in his face, as if she were an inconvenience to him.

A flash of anger reared up in her. 'How can you keep toying with my emotions this way? You know a girl like me and a man like you . . . we could never be together.'

'Why not?' He too was angry now and his eyes flashed with passion. 'It isn't so hard to imagine.'

'The prince and the pauper,' she said quietly, although her heart was pounding so hard in her chest she thought it might leap out at any moment and go frolicking in the sea with the dolphins.

'I don't give a shit about money.'

She knew then he was going to kiss her and she knew she wanted him to with every last cell in her body.

When his lips claimed hers, she felt the delicious electricity touching every nerve end. It seemed the most natural thing in the world, her body like warm wax, moulded to his. She sighed with sheer pleasure. When his kiss deepened, she rose in response, feeling an urgency in her body. And when his hand slid over her breast she was too electrified by the sensation to push it away. Instead that urgent ache between her legs made her arch towards him, wanting more.

It was only when his hands began tracing small teasing circles along her thighs that she panicked and gasped, 'Stop,' and grabbed his wrist. 'I shouldn't . . . this is . . .' Her voice shook as she realized how close she'd come to not caring about the consequences. It was horrifying to discover all the Catholic teaching that she'd been brought up with had so nearly been cast aside.

'I'm sorry, I didn't mean to frighten you.'

'I'm not frightened.' Shauna lifted her chin, 'but we shouldn't be doing this.'

'You're very beautiful, Shauna. I think I might be falling in love with you.'

'You don't mean that. I can't, Demetrios.' She stood up and smoothed down her shorts. 'I need to get back to work.' With that she ran across the deck and down the stairs without a backward glance.

Chapter 9

Shauna threw herself into her work for the rest of the day, avoiding the other crew members and Demetrios. That night, she found that, like him, that she couldn't sleep. The memory of how she'd felt when he touched her lit a fire in her mind. Luckily, she was distracted as in the morning they would finally be docking in Ithos, and she was eager to see it. Though she knew that matters with Demetrios were complicated beyond measure, she still wanted to see the place that meant so much to him, in the hope it would give her some insight into the real man.

The yacht was easily the largest in the whole port. It nosed slowly into the furthest berth, which had been specially constructed for the *St Helena*. As they approached the island, Shauna was aware of Demetrios on the sun deck high above her, but she deliberately avoided looking his way. The island was every bit as beautiful as he'd said. White-painted buildings tumbled down the steep hillside towards the harbour, their walls so brilliant in the bright sunshine that she had to squint to look at them. Rising behind them, scrubby green shrubs were scattered across the sandy soil, covering the hills which were outlined against the deep azure sky. Not a cloud marred the perfect horizon over the sea, where diamond-bright light skipped across the bobbing waves.

She studied the pretty sand-coloured stone-built harbour with its wooden-shuttered tavernas and vine-clad terraces. A few people were sitting at tables in the shade and she longed to be up there, enjoying a moment's solitude while she mulled over all that had happened. Living cheek by jowl on a busy yacht was beginning to take its toll and she was delighted that the crew were to be given a much-needed break.

Once every surface was spick and span, the perishable food divvied up, the engines shut down and the boat secured, the crew disembarked with their luggage and were immediately besieged by a group of young boys, all arms and legs and enthusiasm, chirping like baby birds: 'Cheap, cheap taverna. Come. Come.'

Smiling at them all, she was at a loss as to how she could choose one boy as a guide without upsetting the rest.

Jeremy took pity on her and intervened. 'Hold your horses,' he told the boys, then turned to Shauna. 'How much can you afford to pay?'

After a minute's haggling with a wiry, dark-eyed boy, he settled on an acceptable rate for the night. 'There you go, Shauna. You might find you want to move on after one night,' he warned her. 'It will be basic, but bigger than your cabin.'

'Anything's bigger than my cabin,' she grinned. 'Thanks for helping me out.'

'No problem. Are you sure you'll be OK? You don't want to come with us?'

'No. I fancy staying put and exploring for a while. This is my first time in Greece.'

'Well, enjoy. See you in a week's time.'

She picked up her backpack, hefted it on her shoulder and without a backward glance at the yacht set off after the boy, who watched her like a lion determined that his prey shouldn't get away. But with each step she found herself longing for the familiarity and safety of the *St Helena*. She wasn't entirely sure she was built for adventure on her own.

The room above Níko's taverna was small, and it had a tiny balcony looking out over the harbour. Dropping her bag on the bed, she pushed back the faded blue shutters and leaned on the iron balustrade. She gazed at the view, almost laughing out loud at the antics of a couple of elderly men making their battered fishing boat bob up and down as they argued about something, gesticulating wildly. Below her she could hear the low, murmured conversations of people in the taverna and the clink of cutlery. Her room was sparse but clean and she had the use of a bathroom shared with two other rooms which were currently empty. Níko, the owner, had already brought up a plate of stuffed vine leaves, a half-bottle of retsina and a bottle of water. He spoke excellent English and had fallen on Shauna with great delight as soon as she opened her mouth. He'd worked in Dublin for a few years in his twenties and as far as he was concerned Shauna might have been his long-lost daughter. His enormous moustache twitching with delight, he had called his wife and daughter to come meet the Irish colleen. Even though she'd only been to Dublin twice in her life, he assumed she knew it intimately and asked if Paddy and Maureen still ran O'Donoghue's on Merrion Row and whether the bakery on Thomas Street still sold his favourite soda bread.

Being on land for the first time in a week felt odd and

everything seemed to sway in a disconcerting way, but Shauna was ready to explore her new surroundings. Níko had told her that the best beach on the island was only a short walk away. With the day promising to be a hot one, she set out with her swimming costume, a towel and one of the bottles of water. En route she passed a few tourist shops and treated herself to an English newspaper, a large shady straw hat and a new bottle of high-factor sun cream to protect her pale skin. From under the brim of her hat, she sat quite happily on the beach people-watching for most of the afternoon, not feeling as lonely as she'd thought she might. She took after her dad like that; she'd always been quite happy with her own company.

Smiling at the children playing noisily in the water, she gazed out at the turquoise blue of the sea. At one end, the little horseshoe bay finished with a steep bank of rocks rising to a high cliff overlooking the beach. Now she was on her own, she had more time to think. Confusion dogged her. Had she overreacted the previous day? Demetrios had stopped as soon as she'd asked him to; she hadn't exactly been fighting him off.

She put the paper away in her bag and lay down for a doze in the sun, her mind already running away to a distant imaginary landscape where she was able to kiss Demetrios with languorous pleasure without having to worry.

On her return, Níko insisted that she come down to the taverna at seven o'clock for dinner.

'I will reserve the best table in the house for you.' He beamed at her and she smiled back as she climbed the stairs that curved up the side of the building up to her room and a very welcome cool shower where she washed the salt and sand away from her skin and let the water flow through her hair. Afterwards she sipped a glass of beer on the balcony while watching tourists disembark from a tour boat. It looked as if plenty of alcohol had been involved as they were all in high spirits. A couple wrapped themselves around each other, leaning against the harbour wall, kissing without inhibition, completely oblivious to everyone around them. She envied them their lack of self-consciousness, remembering the pleasure that Demetrios's kisses had brought her.

At seven o'clock, wearing the one dress she'd brought with her, feeling Níko's kindness deserved it, she slipped down the stairs to the taverna.

'My Irish *despoinída*! Come, come.' Prancing ahead of her like a delighted show pony, with a touch of pompous pride that made her smile, he skirted around the main dining area and led her up a small flight of steps to a pretty terrace under a pergola laden with clouds of pink and orange bougainvillea. With a picture-perfect view of the harbour, it held three tables discreetly separated by olive trees in large pots. The aromatic scent of scores of rosemary bushes bursting from window boxes on the balcony filled the air.

'Please.' Níko pulled out a chair at a table set for two with a candle already burning in a delicate white china votive. She lowered herself into the seat, grateful for Níko's gallant ministrations. He was very sweet and this was all very romantic, but she felt a bit silly sitting out here on her own. He fussed over her, bringing her a menu, a complimentary glass of retsina and brushing a stray leaf from the table. Then he bustled off. She opened the menu, resolving to ask him when he came back if she could move into the main dining room, where she'd have people to watch instead of sitting out here on her own.

'Would you mind if I joined you?'

Her heart leapt into her mouth at the familiar deep voice. 'Demetrios!'

'Would you mind?' The diffident question made her smile expand with sudden joy. Couldn't he see the light in her eyes, her hands shaking on the menu?

Unable to say anything, she shook her head and took in every delicious detail of him as he lowered himself into the chair opposite. He raised an eyebrow at her choice of wine.

'I think we can do better than that.' Without him uttering a word, Níko appeared. He threw his arms around the younger man and the two greeted each other like long-lost brothers, talking rapidly in Greek, none of which she could understand. Whatever Demetrios had said, Níko quickly snatched her glass away and hurried off.

'What did you say to him?'

'I said that a woman as special as you deserved a better wine.'

'What are you doing here?' she asked, lifting her chin and giving him a direct look.

'I will leave if you'd like, but I wanted to apologize in person.' His smile was rueful as he fiddled with the tines of the fork in front of him. 'I'm sorry that I wasn't as respectful as I should have been. My mama would have been ashamed. I think she would like a good girl like you.'

Honesty prevented her from letting him continue. She held her hand up to stop him.

'You stopped when I asked.'

'But still, Shauna, I should—'

'I wouldn't apologize for kissing you.' Her voice was calm and her gaze on his handsome face direct. He deserved honesty.

Those dark eyes studied her face before he picked up her hand. 'Does that mean you forgive me?'

'There's nothing to forgive.'

'I feel I've been clumsy. I'd like to . . . will you come out for the day with me tomorrow?'

A whole day with Demetrios, without having to look over her shoulder and worry what anyone might think.

'Yes,' she couldn't help a smile breaking across her face. 'I'd like that very much.'

Níko returned with a bottle of chilled white wine, the condensation running down the elegant glass bottle. He made much of opening it and pouring it to taste.

'You taste it first,' Demetrios told her firmly, pushing the glass towards her.

'I don't know anything about wine.'

'All you need to know is whether you like it or not,' said Demetrios, watching her face with that careful intensity she was now becoming familiar with.

She sipped at the cool, fresh wine, instantly knowing that this wasn't anything like the cheap plonk she'd downed in the student union bar. 'It's lovely.'

Níko filled both glasses and with beaming approval backed away as if he were their very own fairy godmother. Shauna narrowed her eyes. 'How did you know I was here?'

'News travels fast. There aren't many beautiful, red-headed Irish women on the island and . . . Níko is a cousin of my father.'

She raised an eyebrow, surprised by this.

'Don't be taken in by the humble surroundings. Níko is an extremely successful businessman. This is one of five tavernas he owns, as well as a hotel in Crete. Like me, he gravitates back here in the summer months. This island is our home. Tomorrow I hope to show you why I love it so much.

'Now, what would you like to eat? Níko's wife, Teresa, is an excellent chef; she has worked in Paris, Athens and London. Her spanakopita is the best I've ever tasted – but don't repeat that, my yaya would never forgive me.' Over the top of the menu his eyes crinkled at her with a conspiratorial smile that made her think of a small boy up to no good.

'I promise.' She grinned back at him. 'But only if you tell me what it is. And what is a yaya?'

'In Greek γιαγιά means grandmother. And spanakopita is a filo pastry pie with a filling of feta cheese and spinach flavoured with dill and parsley. It's delicious.' He leaned forward and added in a confiding whisper, 'Chantelle makes a very good version on board the yacht.'

'She spoils you. Doesn't it get . . .' Her voice began to trail off, but he tilted his head encouragingly, 'I'm not sure I'd like it if everyone always said yes to me.'

'You have it all wrong,' he replied, with a twitch of his mouth. 'My father is harder to please than most. The work we did has pleased him, though. I am in his good books for once.'

'Weren't you before?'

Demetrios tilted his head, thinking before he spoke. 'My father . . . some people think he's a hard man, but all he's ever wanted was provide for his family. He helped Níko get started. He's generous to people who are prepared to work hard, and he despises laziness. He thinks I need direction, and that's what he's been trying to provide me with for the last couple of years.'

When the food arrived, it was every bit as good as Demetrios had promised. Shauna bit into the crisp flaky pastry and sighed with pleasure at the contrast of sharp, salty feta with herby spinach. 'This is delicious.'

'I told you.'

His smug arrogance provoked an exasperated roll of her eyes. 'And you are always right.'

'No, not always. That's what I like about you. You challenge me. You don't care who I am.'

'As my mother would say, in the eyes of God we are equals.'

She studied the open vee of his shirt and the crisp glossy dark hair revealed before sliding her gaze to the strong masculine forearms and then the chiselled jawline. 'I'm not sure my mother would approve of you at all.'

She grinned at him as he burst into delighted laughter.

'You always know how to put me in my place, Shauna O'Brien.'

They finished their meal and carried on talking long after the guttering candlelight had sputtered out. It was only when Níko apologetically came and said the restaurant was now closed that they realized the other diners had long since gone and the harbour lights were starting to go out.

Demetrios escorted her to her door.

'Thank you for a lovely evening, Shauna.'

'Thank you.'

When her eyes met his with a shy smile, the tenderness of his gaze shook her.

He leaned forward and gave her a chaste kiss on the forehead. 'Goodnight. I'll see you in the morning, after breakfast. Say, nine thirty?'

She gazed up at him, longing welling up and took a step forward, but he stepped backwards, lifting his hand in a sharp salute.

'Until tomorrow.' He turned and walked away, leaving her restless and twitchy. It took ages for her to fall asleep, it seemed impossible to settle. When she finally stilled, the bed felt as if it were swaying and she was back on the boat. Her dreams, when she did fall asleep, were full of Demetrios.

Chapter 10

The white hull of the speedboat bounced over the waves as the wind tugged at her hair, tossing it around her face as she held onto her hat with both hands.

'This is wonderful,' she cried above the sound of the engine, looking back at the foaming wake spilling out behind them, cutting through the dark navy sea like a plume of feathers.

Demetrios stood at the wheel, his face turned into the headwind. He shot her a quick smile and pushed the throttle to increase their speed.

'Want to drive?' he asked.

'Absolutely not, I want to enjoy every minute of this.'

He'd arrived earlier with a heavy cool box and a large bag, refusing to tell her what was in either, although he did hand her a bottle of water after he'd helped her into the stylish, streamlined speedboat. She tried to play it cool but couldn't help examining the small boat; she'd never been in anything like it in her life. Leaving the harbour, he'd steered right so that they hugged the coast for a while, travelling parallel to sand-coloured cliffs that teemed with birds launching and landing on the sheer sides. She was fascinated by the changing shades of the sea and the magnif-icent rainbow of blues and greens from the pale turquoise, to the sun-dappled pockets near the shore, through to the rich, secretive dark navy of the deeper water.

After a while he slowed the boat and they rounded a towering cliff into a small bay with a tiny strip of white sand fringed by turquoise shallows.

'Our very own beach.'

'It's gorgeous.'

'Inaccessible except by sea. Not many people come here. Certainly not tourists.'

He brought the boat to within a few feet of the beach and then switched off the engine and dropped the anchor. When he climbed over the side, the water was only at waist height. She handed him the box.

Then she jumped in, bracing herself for icy cold.

'Oh,' she squealed in delighted surprise. 'This is lovely. It's . . .' It wasn't warm but it wasn't the freezing cold that she was used to. Looking down through the crystal-clear water she could see the shadows of tiny fish darting across the sandy surface. Sunlight dappled through the water, creating dancing streams of light and movement.

She followed Demetrios to the beach, her feet sinking into the softest sand she'd ever known.

'I think I might be in heaven,' she sighed contentedly, watching as he dropped the box and turned straight back to the boat to retrieve the big canvas bag.

From this he pulled plush velvety beach towels, a parasol, a bottle of sun cream.

'You've thought of everything.'

'I hope so.'

She sat down on one of the towels, glad that she'd put her bikini on under her light cheesecloth dress.

Demetrios stripped off his shirt and in averting her gaze from his chest she found herself looking at his tanned legs instead, which was almost as distracting.

'Did I tell you I am going to build a boat?'

Shauna laughed, 'You might have mentioned it a hundred times.'

'I am going to build a boat for you. You make me want to create something, something that is as beautiful and unique as you are.'

'I'd be happy with a bunch of flowers,' she said, 'or just a smile. My dad always says, "May your heart be happy, may your smile be wide, and may your pocket always have a coin or two inside."'

'I think I would like your father.'

'And I think he would like you . . . especially if you build me a boat to sail home in.'

'The Irish Sea is a bit choppy, no? I think I could do it.' He waved his arm dismissively at the sea.

She laughed. 'Remind me not to get a lift home in your boat.'

'I will call it *Beauty*, after you.'

Shauna giggled, not thinking for a moment that he meant it.

They whiled the day away reading on the beach, swimming in the sea and eating a picnic of freshly made pitta bread, tzatziki, a crunchy salad of sweet tomatoes, cucumber, onion and feta, and glass bottles of chilled Coca-Cola. Demetrios told her about his magical childhood growing up on Ithos, until it was cruelly snatched away from him when he was sent to a first-rate private boarding school in Athens.

After lunch Shauna lay on her stomach and picked up her book; she had finished her Jackie Collins and was now reading *The Thorn Birds*. It had been left behind in one of the cabins and found its way into the pile of lost items in the corner of the galley. Her mother would have been utterly shocked at the thought of a Catholic priest falling in love, but Shauna was enjoying the romantic element and the idea of forbidden love. Today though, with Demetrios so close to her, it was impossible to concentrate.

Beside her, Demetrios lay dozing. She couldn't stop herself gazing at his face while his eyes were closed, his hazel eyes protected by the fringe of dark lashes. If a man could be said to be beautiful, then he was. It was a strange kind of torture being so close. She realized she really wanted to touch him and for him to touch her, but he'd been the perfect gentleman all day. Even when they'd been swimming, he'd kept his distance. She sighed and went back to her book but before long found her eyelids drooping. Eventually she gave in and rolled on to her back, letting sleep envelop her.

She woke to Demetrios's lazy feline smile. 'Welcome back, Sleeping Beauty.' It reminded her of the first time she'd met him, and she lay looking up at him, willing him to close the distance between them and kiss her. She wanted his mouth on hers and there was a dull ache in her heart.

'Come on, one last swim and then we ought to go back.' Demetrios jumped up and ran down into the sea. Surprised by his sudden burst of speed, she scrambled to her feet and laughing ran after him into the water. By the time she neared the water's edge he'd already swum out into the bay, his powerful crawl eating up the distance as if he were trying to escape something. Not being a strong swimmer, she paddled in the shallows watching tiny silver streaks of fish dart this way and that.

When he finally waded out of the sea towards her, she simply stared at him as the water droplets sparkled on his skin in the sunshine. He was simply gorgeous and the yearning to touch him was stronger than ever.

He came closer to her, and in that moment she knew what she was about to say; she couldn't have resisted her body even if she wanted to. 'Demetrios,' she asked, her voice full of desire, 'have I done something wrong?'

'Oh, Shauna,' he said. 'You have no idea what you are doing to me. Being in your company and trying to be a saint is quite a burden.'

She narrowed her eyes. 'I didn't ask you to be a saint.' She stepped forward, and gently touched her lips to his, desire shooting through her. He responded with a groan, pulling away.

'Shauna,' he pleaded, 'I'm not made of stone.'

'Who says I want you to be?' She softened her mouth, whispering her lips over his and pressing her body against his. It was almost a relief after the constant longing to feel his body against hers, the heat of his skin next to hers and to finally give in to the desire that had been plaguing her for days.

He pulled away and with one tender hand cupped her cheek, his eyes boring into hers with an intensity that sent her senses into high alert. 'I've been wanting you too . . .'

The touch of his fingers stroking her skin sent tingles racing down her spine, stirring heat between her thighs and bringing an unfulfilled ache to her breasts. In that moment she realized she loved him with a depth of passion she hadn't know she was capable of.

'Shauna,' he murmured, bending to kiss her, placing a chain of tiny kisses across her cheeks, 'my heart is lost to you.'

Her whole body sighed and softened, relief and joy mingled with excitement and anticipation.

When their kiss spiralled out of control, this time she embraced the storm, her body eager and her desire desperate. He picked her up, his lips caressing her face, then her breasts, as he carried her to the shade of the parasol. When they tumbled onto the velvety towels, her hands were as keen to know his body as to feel his on hers.

Demetrios laid a hand on top of hers where curiosity had her tracing the dark hair above his waistband. 'Shauna, we have to stop.'

Both of them were breathing heavily and she rejoiced in the effect that she was having on him.

'Do we?' she asked, empowerment and desire thrumming through her veins. Leaning down, she kissed his mouth with slow reverence, revelling in the fierce burst of power that shot through her. 'What if I don't want to stop?'

'Dear Shauna.' His hands raked through her hair, holding her at a distance. 'Are you sure?'

'Very sure.' Even though her body felt shaky with need, her voice was resolute. And then they needed no more words.

Afterwards, their arms and legs entangled, Shauna lay for a moment savouring the delicious feeling of excitement and euphoria. Demetrios, with infinite care and tenderness, had made her feel the most precious woman in the world and now she felt wonderful. Turning her head, she could scarcely believe he was there lying next to her, both of them naked under the sun; it was intoxicating.

Almost shyly, they had helped each other get dressed, packed up their things and clambered back into the boat, Demetrios had kissed her longingly and passionately and she had felt his desire stir again, arousing her own. Her hand moved down to caress him.

'If you keep doing that, we'll never end up leaving here,' he said.

'What makes you think I want to?'

When they arrived back at the harbour, twilight had fallen and Shauna felt a little apprehensive. Would this be another dream that she'd have to awake from, her bubble burst again by reality? She wished the day would never end. However, instead of steering the boat into the jetty where he had picked her up, he tethered the boat to the *St Helena*.

'Why have you brought us back here?'

'I'm not ready to say goodnight.' He pulled her close. 'I want to say good morning to you instead.'

'What do you mean? We can't stay here tonight.'

'Why not? The ship is almost empty, everyone is on shore leave save a few who won't notice us – besides, this is my boat and I can do what I like.' He grinned at her like a Cheshire Cat.

'That certainly has its advantages.'

As they climbed up the ladder that hung over the side, he pulled her up and onto the deck, drawing her towards him.

'O lover, with your skin so white, the purest alabaster. Delicate as the whitest lily that only opens its petals at night,' he whispered in her ear.

'That's beautiful, what is it?'

'Sappho. I didn't put all that expensive education to waste, you know.'

'You're teasing again.'

'Not tonight, Beauty. Tonight, I want you more than ever.' He took her to his suite and Shauna thought of nothing but Demetrios until she fell asleep in his arms.

* * *

The next day, as the sun streamed in through the window, Shauna realized she had no experience of waking up with a naked man in a bed that wasn't her own. For a moment she wasn't sure what she should do. Thankfully, Demetrios snaked a hand around her waist and pulled towards him before putting one thigh between hers, claiming one naked breast with his hand and kissing the last of her breath away and rendering her incapable of thinking any more for the next half-hour.

The last of her shyness vanished when he insisted on showering with her. It seemed that he had no inhibitions as he walked around naked without a qualm. She wasn't quite that bold and wrapped herself in one of the robes as they went down to the empty galley to forage for breakfast. There were slim pickings, but Shauna made them black coffee and Demetrios lounged on the bench watching her.

'What would you like to do today?' he asked.

She looked back at the craggy hills that rose beyond the harbour. 'I'd like to see more of the island. Find out what living here is really like.'

'That can be arranged. I've got a jeep which is perfect for the local driving conditions. Some of the roads up in the hills are little more than tracks. There's a monastery that sits on a promontory on the other side of the island which has a stunning view, and there's a pretty fishing village at the head of a deep inlet which is home to the local stone-masons.'

She tidied up, making the bed, all the while smiling to herself at the memories of unmaking it last night.

When she was done, she looked around with satisfaction. There was little sign they'd ever been there, which for some strange reason suited Shauna. She wanted to keep their love a delicious secret for a while; it made her nervous to think that anyone might suspect she'd been here with Demetrios – but where did that leave her when everyone came back?

'Hi. All set?'

'Yes, I'm ready.'

'Unless you want to go back to bed for another couple of hours?' He slid his hand up the inside of her thigh and she felt a tingle of pleasure.

'Demetrios Theodosis, you are incorrigible.'

'Yes,' he swept her into his arms and swung her around, 'but you love me.'

As his hands came to rest on her waist she looked up into his face. 'Yes, I do.'

Chapter 11

Demetrios woke from another disturbed night and turned to see the empty space beside him in the bed. Yet another dream that he couldn't remember, but as always it had left him with a sense that storm clouds were gathering. Then he remembered – he was due to see his mother and father today. They had returned from Athens and there would be no avoiding them.

He stretched out a hand to brush across the empty space, wishing Shauna had woken with him in the sun-filled stateroom instead of slipping silently back to her cabin sometime in the night. A week ago the crew had come back to the boat and Shauna had insisted on returning to work and keeping their relationship to themselves. In truth, that suited him too, much as he wished that they could go back to the week when they'd had the yacht to themselves. Shauna could be very stubborn when she wanted to be, but they had spent as much time as they could together.

Now that he was back in Ithos, his time was taken up with running the business, meeting his father's financiers and looking at plans for the future. The company was struggling financially; his father's investments had not been doing well recently, with stock markets in turmoil and a glut of crude oil bringing volatility to the shipping industry. Demetrios knew that today would be a day of reckoning; his father had been vacillating about handing over the reins of the business for some time. His health had been poor of late, but it was hard for him to give up the thing that was his life-blood.

These last few weeks, Demetrios had been struggling with the knowledge that the family juggernaut was bearing down on him. The time he and Shauna had spent together exploring the island and the yacht had been a magical interlude, an interlude he wished could go on for ever. A smile curved his lips as he thought of the way they'd explored each other's bodies and how, much to his surprise and pleasure, Shauna had embraced her sensuality, learning to tease and taunt him with seductive confidence. She had reawakened something in him. Maybe her innocence had played a part in that, but there was something else too: she gave him new purpose.

With a grunt of irritation, he rolled off the bed, and then remembered with even more frustration that she wouldn't be waiting up on the sun deck for him today. It was her day off and she'd said she had errands to run. He'd wanted to meet her somewhere for lunch, but she was adamant that she had things to do. And now he had to wait until this evening to see her. Another delay, and it didn't suit him to wait. He crossed the cabin and opened a drawer in his dresser. The envelope nestled there among his T-shirts. Two return tickets from Heathrow to New York. He'd already booked a suite at the Waldorf Astoria. Anticipation danced in the pit of his stomach. He couldn't wait to get there and show his favourite city to the woman he loved – to show her around and watch those big eyes of hers go wide with surprise and delight.

He pulled on his clothes quickly, leaving the envelope on top of the dresser. The thought of having to wait any longer was unbearable, especially for a man who was used to getting what he wanted. Did that make him spoiled, he wondered, or resolute and focused? He knew his own mind, there was no crime in that. It was time for him to move on to the next stage of his life, to fulfil the promise he had made to himself, and he needed the right woman beside him to do that. He had made up his mind.

Usually, after a few days enduring the flippant chatter and indolent lifestyle of the Ivankas, Tamaras or Normandies – they were, he realized, quite interchangeable – he would be driven to seek refuge in his office, craving the mental relief of work. Now he could see how his life could, or should be.

Demetrios had always known that one day he'd have to fully commit to the family business, but he'd been delaying it as long as possible. A showdown was looming, and Shauna had helped him reconcile himself to the idea. Her sharp observations and clever insight made him realize that the work could actually be interesting. She'd opened his eyes to the world in more ways than one. He looked at his Rolex. He was due to be at the family home at twelve; perhaps he could find a moment first to talk to Shauna. It was time she knew what he wanted to do. What was expected. He hoped that she would be strong and understand.

The Theodosis family home on Ithos was a large white villa that had been in the family for generations. While each firstborn son who had inherited the Theodosis home had put their own stamp on it, some things never changed, like the breathtaking views from the hilltop groves over-looking the sea. Its grandeur dwarfed the smaller villas with their shuttered windows and colourful awnings lining the narrow winding streets down to the small harbour town.

As he approached the villa in his Porsche, Demetrios saw his mother, Elana, sitting out on the balcony overlooking the sea. Her dark hair was flecked with a few strands of grey, but she was still beautiful, and while the soft features of her girlhood had gone, her striking cheekbones, hourglass figure and mane of perfectly coiffed hair gave her the appear-ance of someone much younger.

After parking between a Ferrari and a Mercedes in the ample driveway, Demetrios bounded up the stairs and greeted his mother at the entrance with an embrace and kiss on each cheek.

'Where is Papa?'

'He is in his office, shouting at his lawyers again.'

'What is going on?'

'I will let him tell you. It is not good.'

Demetrios ascended the marble staircase that ran though the centre of the main hallway. The ground floor was where the family entertained guests: vast rooms filled with lux-urious white leather sofas and discreetly expensive antique furniture from Sotheby's and Christie's, along with tastefully modernist art on the walls.

His father, Aristotle, was upstairs in his study, sitting behind a large mahogany desk, a Cuban cigar smouldering in the enormous crystal ashtray in front of him.

'Where the hell have you been? Have you any idea what has been going on – I expected you back here ages ago!'

'Calm down, Father, you will give yourself a heart attack.'

'A heart attack, he says!' His father threw up his hands.

'You know what's going to give me a coronary? You. Fooling around with the hired help when you should be here attending to your responsibilities.'

Demetrios narrowed his eyes. 'Jeremy has been doing your spying again, I see?'

'Never mind.' Aristotle waved a hand dismissively. 'We have bigger problems. To put it bluntly: we're in the shit.'

Elana had entered the room behind her son. She went to her husband's side and placed her hand on his shoulder, then said, soothingly, 'Demetrios is right, we must be calm. Pour me a drink, Demi. And put that cigar out, Ari, it's getting in my eyes.'

As her son poured her a Campari and soda from the small bar in the corner, she perched herself on the edge of her husband's ample leather desk chair. Aristotle was as plump as his wife was slim, his thinning hair was slicked back and he wore a pair of black heavy-rimmed glasses through which shrewd eyes glared out at his only son.

Demetrios handed the drink to his mother and she sipped it calmly. 'The business is in serious trouble,' she told him.

'We invested heavily in oil production and now there's a glut,' his father explained, crushing out his cigar. 'The markets are volatile and the banks are foreclosing. Over the years we have run up considerable debts, and now they want their money back. Either we do something to pump some major equity in, or we lose everything.'

Demetrios was shocked. 'Those lousy lawyers who've been advising you have been trying to embezzle—'

His father threw his hands up. 'We're losing millions of dollars right, left and centre. Every bastard is out to get us.'

'We have to take immediate action and consolidate the business before it is too late,' Elana put in.

'Lukas Constantis wants our companies to merge. He's prepared to bail us out, provided he gets a controlling share of the company in return.'

'Never!' Demetrios said. 'Over my dead body, I'd rather lose everything.'

'Demetrios, you foolish, foolish boy,' Elana snapped, her voice dripping disdain. 'This is not about you, it is about the family. We have considered all the options open to us, and this is the only way.'

'I will never give control of the business to him. He is a snake and will take the whole business from under your nose if you give him an inch.'

'There will be nothing left of the business if we do not agree to this.'

Demetrios paced the room. 'He has always wanted our business. He'd like nothing better than to be sitting in your chair now, Papa.'

'You think I don't know this? But there is no other way to save the business.'

His mother stood and walked to the enormous window that looked over the Bay of Ithos. Aside from the bay, there were few places for safe harbour on the island, which was why the community had sprung up here. She looked out, her eyes focused not on the spectacular view but on her family's future. 'There is one thing we have to offer.'

'What is that?' Aristotle asked.

'He loves that daughter Sofía of his more than anything, and has always wanted to build a dynasty through her.'

'Oh, yes, that crazy daughter who always gets what she wants,' Aristotle sneered.

'Mother, you are playing a dangerous game here,' Demetrios warned her.

'How so? It is our duty – the duty of every one of us – to

put the family first. Sofía will make the perfect wife for you and give you sons.'

'No, Mother, you ask too much.'

'We must all make sacrifices. You want to save the business, do you not?'

'It is for the good of the family, my boy,' his father chimed in.

'Yes, for the good of the family. That matters to you, surely?' his mother purred.

Demetrius gave nothing away, looking at his mother coolly.

'Come, my son, it is time for you to take your place at the head of the business. It is time for your father to retire.' She looked at her husband with steel in her eyes, daring him to disagree with her.

'Oh, yes, you're right,' Aristotle said weakly, 'I'm getting too damn old for this.'

'So, Demetrios, are we agreed then?'

'Mother . . .'

She walked to the bar and pulled out a bottle of chilled champagne from the cooler. 'Let us celebrate.'

She popped the cork and poured out three tall flutes, handing the first one to her son. 'Let's drink to the future: your future and the future of the business. To a grand dynasty.' She handed Demetrios a glass and tipped her own to him. 'What do you say? To the future? Stay for dinner this evening and we can talk some more.'

He looked at her coldly, and as she clinked her glass to his, it felt like a door was slamming shut.

Chapter 12

Shauna was excited as she left the post office in Ithos. On arriving to the island, she'd sent a postcard to Roxy, telling her to write to her at the poste restante on Ithos as soon as she knew when she would be arriving. It seemed like a lifetime since her friend had left Monaco for a French adventure with Thierry, and Shauna knew they would both have so much to tell each other. She couldn't wait for Roxy to meet Demetrios; she knew they would like each other.

She ripped open the airmail letter and scanned the page quickly but was surprised when there were only a few scribbled lines:

I'm leaving France and Thierry and heading your way.
Will be there sooner than we said. Don't leave without me.
Roxy XXX

Shauna wondered what on earth this could mean. Maybe there'd been a falling out between them? Roxy could be quite intense and full of enthusiasm; she'd thought all along that Thierry was too old for her. Whatever the reason,

Shauna couldn't wait to be reunited with her friend. Life on the boat had been amazing and Demetrios was . . . She smiled, remembering how his touch made her feel. She'd longed to be able to talk about how much he meant to her, how special he was, to let someone else in on their secret romance, someone who would be happy for her.

They had spent every day of that first week on Ithos together, and even after the crew came back from leave they had continued to sneak away whenever they could, taking the small boat out to their private island. She felt as if there had never been a moment when she hadn't known him – he seemed to fill up every part of her, her heart and her mind as well as . . . She felt that familiar flutter in her stomach at the thought of their lovemaking, the way he explored every inch of her body and encouraged her to be adventurous.

The town clock in the village square chimed and Shauna was astonished to see that it was four o'clock already. She had completely lost track of the time. She'd taken the steep walk to the foot of the mountain that dominated the village to drink in the view. Since arriving, the place had stolen her heart almost as much as Demetrios had. Time seemed to stand still here, as if nothing had changed in centuries. The local farmers still loaded up their donkeys with fresh produce for the weekly market. Old ladies dressed in black sat on their doorsteps, shelling white broad beans; younger women sat chatting to one another as they fixed their husbands nets. The younger locals would gather in the village square of an evening, their flirtatious laughter ringing out through the cobbled streets. The scent of wild jasmine filled the air, while bright red geraniums struggled to gain a toehold through cracks in the paving stones, and the pink bougainvillea that was so typically and unmistakably Greek flourished everywhere you looked. Ithos really was a magical place.

Shauna took a seat outside one of the small tavernas and wrote a postcard to her parents. She didn't tell them about Demetrios; she wasn't ready to admit to them that she was rethinking her entire future. She'd been wondering whether she should apply to defer her studies in Manchester for a year, so she could stay on with Demetrios. She'd even fantasized about how it would be if he came to Manchester to be with her. She smiled to herself, struggling to see Demetrios slumming it in student halls. Would he do that? She frowned, realizing that she was running away with herself. He had told her he loved her, and she believed him. No doubt they would talk about it over the coming weeks.

Of one thing she was certain, though: there was no way she was ready to go home yet.

Shauna took the gangway in giant leaps. Demetrios might be a little cross with her as she was back later than she'd said, but she'd placate him with the new bikini she had bought with the wages she had saved. It was silver, with little strings at the side of the bottoms – they could have fun untying them . . .

There was no sign of him on any of the decks, so she hurried to his suite. He wasn't there either, and the place had a strange, empty feel about it. She looked into the wardrobe and his clothes and belongings were gone. She pulled open his T-shirt drawer, which was empty too, apart from a white envelope. Shauna lifted it out to look inside. There were two First Class tickets to New York. What could that mean? She knew he loved the city, but he hadn't mentioned anything about a trip.

She looked around, puzzled now, and then she saw a

postcard on the bedside table. A sick feeling washed over
her. She didn't want to pick it up or to read what was
written on it, but she found herself drawn to it all the same.
The picture on the front was of the harbour at Ithos; just
an ordinary postcard that any tourist might buy to send
home. She turned it over and recognized his handwriting
and read the words Demetrios had written:

My dear Beauty
Always have hope. We have our dreams. Remember our
souls will always burn brighter.
Don't wait for me . . .

Shauna gasped, a wave of anguish gripped her. Was he
saying goodbye? Before she could even process that thought,
she heard a footstep outside. Relief flooded her, her imagination was running wild, of course, that would be him
now. He'd take her in his arms and tell her off for being
silly.

But instead of the face that made her heart sing, it was
Jeremy who appeared at the door. His face was set hard,
no smile for her, and none of his cheery banter.

'Shauna, I've been looking for you. Please collect your
things. There is no easy way of saying this, so I won't try
and cushion it for you – you're fired.'

Shauna's heart beat furiously in her chest. 'I . . . what
do you mean . . . I haven't done anything wrong.'

'I'm afraid that's not true, is it? We have rules about the
crew abusing their position and you've been seen skiving
off when you should have been working to conduct an illicit
liaison with a member of the Theodosis family. It's strictly
off limits, and I've been instructed to dismiss you.'

She could barely get the words out. 'By whom?'

'By me.' A beautiful woman in her late forties or early fifties entered the cabin. There was no mistaking the family resemblance, this was Elena Theodosis, Demetrios's mother.

'Pack your things and get out,' she said, her voice cold and harsh.

Shauna stood her ground. 'I won't go until I see Demetrios. He won't let this happen.'

The woman took a step towards her, her eyes flashing. 'Demetrios does as he is told.' She eyed Shauna as if sizing her up. 'You are different from his usual type. A pretty thing, but just one of many, I am afraid. You think you are something special to him, but you are wrong.'

'You're the one who's wrong. Demetrios loves me.' Shauna felt her voice crack, she felt so vulnerable, so alone in that moment. Where was he, how could he abandon her to this cruelty?

The woman turned to Jeremy. 'Get her out, will you? Give her money if necessary, but I want her off the island tonight.'

Shauna's tears were flowing now but she could feel her anger rising. 'I don't want your money. I don't want anything from you.'

'Suit yourself . . .' She took a step closer, and Shauna could smell the woman's expensive perfume – Chanel or Givenchy. Something classic. 'Your tears are very sad, and I would feel sorry for you if only I hadn't seen this happen so many times before. But Demetrios has his priorities, and this little holiday romance isn't one of them.'

With that she turned away and left Shauna with Jeremy, who jerked his head and told her, 'Time to pack up.' If he felt any remorse, he didn't show it as he marched her to her cabin, the postcard still gripped tightly in her fingers.

He stood in the doorway, arms folded, as Shauna began

to fill the small rucksack with her belongings. After a minute or two he stepped in to gather her belongings for her, helping more from expediency than kindness, because she found herself unable to stop crying.

They were interrupted by Chantelle. 'What the hell is going on here?'

'Stay out of this, Chantelle. Elana wants Shauna off the boat and that's all there is to it. You know the rules.'

'Sure, I know the rules – but where is your fucking decency, Jeremy?'

'That doesn't come into it.'

'Get out, Jeremy. Mama Theodosis will get what she wants, but we're going to do things my way. So off you go, and leave this to me.'

Jeremy looked as if he was going to erupt with anger, but he kept his lips tight and turned on his heel. Chantelle took Shauna in her arms and held her tightly.

Shauna was so grateful for this woman's kindness that fresh tears fell down her cheeks.

'Oh, chérie, I told you this could happen, but you didn't want to listen.'

'He said he loved me.'

'And maybe he does a little, but he is not free to do as he wants – as you are now finding out.' She lifted Shauna's chin to look at her. 'This is the first time your heart has been broken, it probably won't be the last, but you'll never forget it. One day the pain will be gone, and you will have these precious memories.' She took an embroidered handkerchief from her pocket and dried Shauna's tears with it. 'When you are older and wiser, like me, you will learn that the love that is cut short is the more precious because it never truly dies.'

Shauna hung her head, certain that there would never

come a time when she would want to remember this feeling. 'Please, let's just go.'

'Yes, darling . . .' Chantelle looked around her to check they had packed everything, 'One day you will want to look at this, too.' She tucked the postcard into Shauna's rucksack.

Shauna took one last look around, knowing that whatever dreams she'd had of love and the future were now just ashes.

She stood on the jetty, waiting for the tourist boat that ferried visitors to and from the island to arrive. This would be the last boat of the day and Shauna did not want to miss it. Chantelle had walked with her to the jetty and spoken to the harbour master, who told her that it was only minutes away.

Still struggling to hold it together, she heard a voice in her head. This time it was her mother rather than her da, telling her, *Dry your tears and hold your head up, Shauna O'Brien. Never give them the satisfaction.*

When the boat came into view, Chantelle enveloped her in a hug. She'd tried to force some money on her, but Shauna had refused. 'I still have some of my wages left,' she insisted.

'I am so sorry, Shauna. The crew of the *St Helena* will miss you, and you deserve better. Jeremy will find it hard to get anyone to work for him for a while now, but unfortunately it won't change anything. It's Mama and Papa who pay his wages, not Demetrios.'

They hugged once more, Chantelle waving sadly as she headed back to the yacht. More than anything, Shauna wanted to get as far as possible from this place. The last couple of hours had been the worst of her life. In spite of everything, she'd kept hoping Demetrios would show up and tell her there had been some mistake, that none of it was true, he loved her and they were going to spend the rest of their lives together.

She scanned the harbour, and even looked up into the hills where she could just make out the high turrets of the Theodosis villa poking through the trees. Maybe she should go up there now and confront him? How could he be so cowardly and let his mother do his dirty work for him?

She turned back towards the jetty as she heard the horn blast of the little ferry. At this time of day, there were few tourists; unlike the morning boats that came in loaded with day-trippers, this one carried islanders home from work on other islands, or backpackers who were hoping to find a beach where they could sleep under the stars. As the boat approached, she spotted someone waving on the deck. Shauna blinked, unable to believe her eyes – it was Roxy, and she was jumping up and down, waving madly. It was as if the universe had heard her pain and sent her a friend.

The boat pulled into the jetty and Shauna saw Roxy push her way through, drawing protests from the other disgruntled passengers, some of whom gesticulated at her and shouted in Greek.

Oblivious, Roxy leapt off the boat and grabbed Shauna in a fierce hug. It seemed like ages before they let go of each other. And when they did, Roxy said, 'How did you know I was on this boat?'

'I didn't.'

Roxy shook her head and the two of them looked at each other for a moment. It was then that Shauna realized there was something different about her friend. Roxy's eyes were dark from lack of sleep and she'd lost weight.

Her own troubles forgotten, Shauna asked, 'What's happened Roxy? What's wrong.'

'I can't—' Roxy's eyes darted around the jetty and the

boat. 'Not here, I'll tell you later, when we get to . . .' Her eyes alighted on Shauna's rucksack and she frowned.

'I've been given my marching orders,' Shauna told her.

'Says who?'

'It doesn't matter. But I'm afraid it means I won't be giving you the grand tour of Ithos. This is the last boat of the day and we need to be on it when it leaves.'

Roxy shrugged. 'Doesn't bother me, I only came because you're here. Go on, lead the way, I'm right behind you.' They hoicked their bags onto their shoulders and boarded the ferry.

As the boat pulled away and the island retreated into the distance, Shauna thought of everything that had happened. In a matter of a few weeks her life had changed – *she* had changed. She had fallen in love and allowed herself to dream of a future. Now she could see that Demetrios was right – the rich weren't like other people; they didn't have hearts. At least she knew that now and wouldn't fall into the same trap again.

She turned away from Ithos and vowed that she would never return.

Shauna and Roxy sat side by side on the deck, drinking from cold bottles of beer that they'd purchased on board. The sun was low on the horizon and seemed huge to Shauna, a giant orange ball that looked as if it was melting into the sea as it slowly dipped below the horizon.

Roxy sipped at her beer and listened in silence as Shauna described the emotional rollercoaster her life had turned into since they'd last seen each other. 'I can't believe that Demetrios would do that to you. You sure big Greek mama didn't strong-arm him into it?'

'Even if she did, what sort of man would let his mammy rule his life in that way? No, I was just stupid, I should have realized the sort of man he was when I saw how badly he treated Normandie. He's a selfish spoiled bastard.' Inside, Shauna knew she still loved him and part of her always would, but right now she needed to hate him, to convince herself she was better off without him. Otherwise the pain would eat away at her until there was nothing left. No more tears for Demetrios after today, she resolved to herself.

'Enough about me,' she said. 'What happened with Thierry? Something bad, right?'

Roxy looked away. Shauna remained silent, waiting. She could see her friend was struggling to find the right words.

'Thierry . . .' Roxy laughed bitterly. 'Well, turns out he was also a liar, but much worse too.' She gulped down another mouthful of beer.

'He took me to this big villa in a place called Cap d'Agde. Soon as I got there, I realized he'd fed me a pack of lies. Instead of an artist's colony, it was more like a hippy commune, lots of people bumming around, stoned or high on something or other. There were a few painters and artists there, but mostly it was a bunch of old guys screwing young chicks. I stuck it out for a couple of weeks, then told him I was ready to move on. Thierry tried to talk me out of it, said that the people I wanted to meet were on their way and I should just be patient. He kept telling me, "Cheeel out, Roxy . . ."' She impersonated his accent, but without humour.

She seemed to be steeling herself. 'One night, a bunch of musicians turned up and there was this real party vibe. Everyone was dancing – it was fun . . . for a bit.'

'Go on,' Shauna gently encouraged her.

'You know me – I don't take drugs, ever. But I think

someone spiked my drink. I started to feel woozy, like I couldn't speak properly, and my legs didn't seem to work. I'd been chatting to Thierry and some of these other old guys he was with. They seemed OK, but I couldn't understand half of what they were saying. The next thing I remember, Thierry was saying, "Let's get you to bed, chérie, you are tired, no?"'

'I had to lean on him to stand up, it didn't feel right – it wasn't that feeling you get when you're drunk, it was like I was . . . helpless. He took me into one of the bedrooms. It wasn't the one we were sharing, and I remember there was already someone in there. But it's so fuzzy.' Her voice cracked. Shauna could see she was finding it hard to go on, so she put one arm around her, then reached over with the other and squeezed her hand.

'I lay on the bed and I could feel this other guy move onto the bed and start to touch me. I wanted to shout out or scream but I couldn't, it was like my voice wouldn't work. Then he was on top of me and I think I passed out. The next thing I remember is waking up, and I wasn't wearing any clothes. I could see this other guy asleep; he was older than Thierry, with thinning grey hair.' She choked back a sob.

'Oh, Roxy.' Shauna could feel tears streaming down her own cheeks.

'Shauna, he raped me, and Thierry let him do it.' She took a deep breath. 'I didn't hang around, just grabbed my things and got the hell out of there. It was still early and there was no one about. I didn't see either of them again.'

'Roxy, I'm so sorry. I wish I could kill them both.'

'Me too – but that's not the worst of it. I've missed my period. I think I'm pregnant.'

The two friends were silent. How had their dream trip

turned into this nightmare? How had so much happiness been snatched away from them? Shauna knew her heart was broken, but she also knew it would mend. Now, she had to help Roxy.

'What can I do?' she asked.

'Shauna, just get me home.'

'I will . . . and I'll be here for you, whatever happens.'

'I know, Shauna, I know . . .'

PART TWO

Hello! Magazine

Eight months after their engagement, Sofía Constantis and Demetrios Theodosis have tied the knot at a private ceremony in Athens. Sofía is one of the world's richest heiresses who stands to inherit millions from her shipping tycoon father. Until his engagement, Demetrios was one of Europe's most eligible bachelors. His name had been linked to a string of beauties, including model Normandie Chapelle and actress Brooke Shields.

Hello! has learned from a source close to the couple that the wedding took place behind closed doors, and guests included Jerry Hall, Mick Jagger and Niki Lauder.

The couple honeymooned in New York, a favourite city of the happy groom. Construction has begun on a new wing at the family villa on the Greek island of Ithos, and they plan to move in as soon as work is complete. 'They can't wait to start a family,' our source tells us.

Chapter 13

Manchester, March 1983

Shauna looked at the piece of paper in her hand and checked the address at the top of the page against the plate on the wall at the entrance of the building. As the rain lashed down on them, she squinted at the lettering, trying to make out if it was a match, then nodded. 'This is it: the Next Step Agency.'

'Are you sure it's the right place?' Roxy asked anxiously, her shoulders huddled up to her neck, trying to stop the rainwater from trickling down the inside of her raincoat, but without much success.

'Yes, it says so on the letter.'

'Do we really want to do this?'

'Let's go inside. No sense hanging around in this miserable weather. It will only make things worse.'

They climbed the two flights of stairs to a shabby landing covered with threadbare grey carpet. There was only one door, and the two of them hovered in front of it, peering through the glass panel at a woman seated at a small desk.

Her mousy hair was tied up in a bun and she was chatting animatedly on the phone. When she caught sight of them through the glass, she ended her call and beckoned them in.

'Here goes,' Roxy said and went in first, followed by Shauna.

'Hello, ladies, isn't the weather shocking!' she said in a heavy Northern accent. 'Been raining cats and dogs for days – it's a wonder we haven't all floated away down the canal!' She laughed and her eyes crinkled up at the sides behind her glasses. 'Now what can I do for you two?'

The girls looked at each other and Shauna handed the woman the letter. 'It's all in here.'

The woman took the letter and read over its contents. 'Ah, I see. Which one of you is the addressee?' she asked, lowering her voice confidentially and looking them up and down.

Roxy hesitated, 'Um . . . it's—'

'Both of us,' Shauna leapt in.

The woman glanced from one to the other in confusion. 'I'm not sure I understand.'

'Look, we just want to go in together, you know . . .'

The woman seemed to consider this for a moment and then nodded. 'Of course, it's good to have a friend, isn't it. Why don't you both take a seat in the waiting area and someone will be out to see you shortly.'

They did as they were told and sat next to each other on low armchairs that had seen better days. The woman got up and made her way to an office door, knocked once, then disappeared inside for a few minutes. When she returned, she announced, 'Sandra will just be a few minutes, she's with another client.'

Shauna took off her flared trench coat. Outside, the

Manchester rain made it feel as if it was still winter, but now they were sitting in the airless waiting room she was finding it unbearably hot and stuffy.

Roxy looked around at the blank walls. 'You'd think they'd put a few pictures up the wall, wouldn't you – brighten it up a bit.'

'Most people who come here probably aren't worried about the décor,' Shauna replied.

They sat there for a few more moments, Roxy tapping her foot impatiently. Shauna touched her knee. 'Hey, just try to relax.'

'I can't help it. I keep hoping this is all a bad dream and in a minute, I'll wake up.'

'Me too. But we're here now, we might as well see this woman. It's not like we have to sign anything right away, is it?'

'I hope not.' Roxy reached out for Shauna's hand and squeezed it tightly. 'Honestly, Shauna, I think we should go. I meant what I told you: I can do this.'

Shauna gave her friend's hand a squeeze in return. 'Roxy, we've talked about this so many times. It would mean you'd have to give everything up. Your studies, all the work you've put in, all that would go to waste.'

'I don't care. You know I don't.'

'But I do.' There were tears in Shauna's eyes. 'Please . . . You'd be putting your whole future at risk. I know you'd be willing to give it all up – you've got a big heart and that's what makes you such a wonderful person – but it's too much of a sacrifice.'

Roxy was crying now, hot tears splashing down her cheeks. 'Shauna, I know what you're saying makes sense, but it all seems so unfair.'

Shauna took a tissue out of her pocket and handed it to

Roxy. 'Dry those tears. We've got to be brave. Otherwise we'll never get through this.'

Roxy nodded, and blew her nose just as the door to the office opened and a couple in their late thirties came out. The man was beaming with happiness as he took his partner's hand and said, 'After all this time, we're finally going to be a family. I can hardly believe it!'

She was almost crying with joy as she kissed his cheek, then she turned to the woman in a tidy navy-blue suit who'd escorted them to the door and said, 'Sandra, we just can't thank you enough. This means everything to us.'

As the couple left the office chattering happily, Sandra smiled and said, 'Hello, thank you for coming, would you like to come through?'

Shauna and Roxy looked at each other and after a moment Shauna stood up and held her hand out. 'Come on, it's time, let's go.'

Roxy stood and followed her through the door, which the woman closed quietly behind them.

The receptionist, who'd been watching them out of the corner of her eye, resumed sorting through the contents of her in-tray. Then the phone rang, breaking the silence; she picked up the receiver and announced, 'Good morning, Next Step Adoption Agency, how can I help you?'

Chapter 14

Los Angeles, 1986

Roxy screamed and jumped up and down in excitement. *'Oh my God oh my God oh my God, I can't believe we're here!'*

Shauna screamed, too. *'It's huge!* I never thought it would be so big, and it looks just like it does on Oscar night!'

Grauman's Chinese Theatre on Hollywood Boulevard dominated the stretch of sidewalk, and the whole world seemed to be thronging outside the theatre as tourists gawped, ooohed and ahhed at the handprints of Hollywood royalty in concrete. Japanese tourists took pictures of each other, the shutters of their cameras clicking rapidly; a fat American boy in a baseball cap and a *Top Gun* T-shirt slurped a giant cup of Coca-Cola through a straw as his mother, her coal-black hair coiffed to within an inch of its life, cooed over the handprints of Frank Sinatra. 'Hey, Joey,' she shouted in a New Jersey accent, 'c'mon over here and put your hands in Frank's!'

'Shauna, look here,' Roxy squealed. 'It's Elizabeth Taylor

and Rock Hudson. And here's John Travolta – ooh, he's dreamy, I loved him in *Grease*.'

Shauna picked her way through the throngs of people, her eyes cast down as she looked for the handprints of the one person that would truly make this day extra special. But even though she methodically walked up and down, scanning the ground, she didn't find what she was looking for.

Roxy appeared by her side. 'Those hawkers are asking ten dollars for a "homes of the rich and famous" tour in Beverly Hills. Fancy it?'

'Hmmm?'

'What're you looking for?'

'Oh, nothing . . .'

'Ah, I get it, you're looking for Grace Kelly, aren't you?'

Shauna grinned sheepishly. 'How did you guess?'

'It's only like your one obsession!'

'I don't think she's here, though.' Shauna's shoulders slumped briefly before Roxy reached out and gave her shake, doing another little squeal.

'Oh, this is the best day ever! I can't believe we're here, in LA.'

Shauna laughed her momentary frustration away. 'I know, who would have thought we'd make it here?'

'We did, remember?'

'How could I forget! What shall we do now? I'm hungry.'

'Me too, let's go find a diner.'

Ten minutes later, they were sitting in an all-American diner around the corner, drooling over the menus. A row of chrome stools lined the gleaming counter, but they chose one of the booths with leather seats and a Formica top instead.

'I'm going to have blueberry pancakes with maple syrup.' Roxy said.

Shauna licked her lips; it all looked delicious. When a waitress in a frilly apron came to take their order, she told her, 'Eggs and bacon on French toast, hold the sugar.'

'You sound like a local,' Roxy said as the waitress bustled over to the kitchen hatch and shouted the order at the harassed chef, pinning the ticket next to the others.

'I guess. You get used to things pretty quickly here. I love this place, the portions are huge and it's cheap, but everything comes covered in icing sugar. It's weird for an Irish spud like me.'

'And a Liverpudlian like me,' said Roxy. 'What I wouldn't give for a plate of scouse! I haven't been home for ages.'

'How are your folks?'

'Me mam and dad are still fighting like cats and dogs, our Sheila is getting married to that lazy fella of hers – she wants me to make her dress. What about yours?'

'You'd think this was Sodom and Gomorrah the way Mammy goes on about it. She keeps telling me not to talk to any strange men – all the men are strange in LA,' she laughed. 'So, tell me about Milan.'

'Oh my God, it's wild, Italians are just crazy, the men all have mistresses and the women all look a million dollars until they reach fifty, and then they all turn into widows wearing nothing but black.'

'Seriously?'

'I'm kidding – just. I love it there, Shauna.'

Roxy had beaten four other interns to the much-coveted role of fashion apprentice at the house of Missoni in Milan. So far, her job seemed to involve inventorying the fabric and making copious amounts of strong coffee for the design team.

'I'm learning so much. Everyone there is super-creative.'

'I'm happy for you, Roxy. It's just what you wanted.'

Their food arrived, giant portions steaming as the waitress placed the plates in front of them. 'Enjoy. Have a nice day.'

'This would feed my entire family.'

'I've given up trying to finish the portions here, I'd end up as fat as a house if I did.'

'I hate you, Shauna O'Brien, you can eat what you like and never put on an ounce.'

'So can you. You're as tall as a basketball player.'

They tucked in and after a few mouthfuls. Roxy returned to the subject of Milan. 'It's really hard work, we have to work long hours for a pittance, but the clothes are mind-blowing, and the men . . . well, let's say I'm taking an accelerated course in Italian!'

They both giggled.

'So, how about you?'

'I feel so lucky, Roxy. It's taken me a while to make friends, but we never have any time for socializing anyway.'

'It's funny how things turned out, both of us landing up in our dream destinations.'

'Yes, if that accountancy firm I worked for after uni hadn't opened an office in LA, I would still be slogging away in a dreary office in Tottenham Court Road, rather than in Hollywood.'

After her finals at university, Shauna had applied to work for large firm of accountants in London. It was as dull as she had thought it would be, but when the company opened an office in LA, Shauna had badgered her boss to let her relocate there for a year. He liked her and agreed. Her first few months had been an eye-opener. It felt like she'd stepped into a movie: Hollywood seemed to be full of roller-skaters sailing along the sidewalks with huge earphones clamped over their ears, cute dogs trotting along beside their Lycra-clad owners, agitated taxi drivers arguing noisily with other drivers at the lights . . . Best of all, you could get pizza and Chinese food delivered to your home, something unheard of in Ireland. Shauna had also discovered that Americans tended to be hardworking, ambitious and upbeat. Everyone and everything seemed larger than life.

She had got herself noticed and after a year in the LA office followed one of her colleagues when they moved to a large production company based in the city's financial district. Shauna had worked hard; she was always the first to arrive and the last to leave. She put herself forward for extra duties, networked like crazy between departments and had managed to move sideways into location work, assisting the location manager on shoots, helping keep a tight rein on budgets. She shared a tiny apartment with another girl who worked at the same company, though they never seemed to see each other much as they were always working.

'What about this movie you're making?' Roxy said with a mouthful of pancake.

'Don't talk with your mouth full, Roxy. I'm not involved with making the movie as such; my job is just to try to stop us going over budget. But, Roxy, it's incredible. Tom Cruise is the star, and he's amazing. Works harder and longer than anyone else. It's being directed by Dan Jackson – it's his first really big-budget movie and he's so intense and meticulous when he's working, but when he isn't, he's the nicest fella.'

'Shauna O'Brien, your eyes are shining! This Dan Jackson must really be something!'

'Oh, don't be silly, it's nothing like that. He's so inspiring, that's all. I've learned so much about movie-making even in the small amount of time I've been allowed on set.'

'How are the acting classes going?'

Shauna blushed. 'How did you know?'

'You can't hide anything from me.'

'I feel silly, to be honest. I'm going to have to give them up. The hours are too long at work and I keep missing lessons – the teacher has completely lost faith in me.'

Roxy shook her finger at Shauna and tut-tutted. 'Never give up on your dreams, honey.'

For a moment, Shauna was taken back in time, to a moment when someone else had told her that. Her face clouded but she shook away the memory, then looked at her watch.

'Oh, Lord, is that the time? I have to be back at the office. We've got another crisis budget meeting. The film is about to move locations and the producer, Jerry Bruckheimer, is worried about overspending. I think we're going to get hauled over the coals.'

'Shit, that bad?'

'We'll put up a good fight – I've learned not to get walked all over here, they'll eat you for breakfast.'

'Fighting talk.'

'You bet, though what Jerry says goes. What are you doing this afternoon?'

Roxy leaned in conspiratorially. 'I can't believe I'm telling you this – it's my Cinderella moment! I'm going with one of the head designers to a fitting. You'll never guess who.'

'Tell me immediately!'

'It's only Kathleen Turner – she wants a dress for the Oscars.'

Shauna's mouth dropped open. 'She's gorgeous!

'Doesn't seem real, huh? I'll just be making notes and measurements, but I hope they'll let me make the dress! Well, maybe cut some of the fabric and do some stitching at any rate.'

'There'll be no dress and no job for either of us if we don't get going, eat up!'

Roxy shovelled in another couple of mouthfuls.

'It was so much fun today, Roxy,' Shauna said. 'I'm glad we found the time before you go back to Milan.'

'I'm sorry you didn't find Grace's handprints though.'

'Me too.' Shauna paused. 'I still can't believe she's gone.'

In September 1982, Grace Kelly had been killed in a car accident; her daughter Stephanie had been lucky to escape with her life. It felt as if the whole world was in shock, unable to absorb the tragedy that had cut short such a glittering and extraordinary life. Shauna had nursed her own private grief, one more terrible blow in that awful year of sadness and heartache.

'Did I ever tell you I met her once?'

'Sure, you did, and only about a million times . . .'

It had been wonderful to see Roxy, and Shauna had felt the familiar pang of separation as they hugged goodbye a few days later. Roxy was going back to Milan and who knew when they would see each other again. But Roxy had left her something beautiful to remember her by. It was a trouser suit, wide-legged pants matched with a double-breasted jacket made of oatmeal wool that felt as light as a feather. She felt so grown-up and sophisticated in it and the tailoring was beautiful.

'Sometimes I get to use off-cuts for my own designs. I made this for you – I wanted you to have something fabulous to wear in your new job.'

She'd thanked Roxy with over-zealous hugs, but Roxy had waved away her thanks. 'You're my muse – this is only the start. Keep taking those acting classes and soon I'll be making *your* Oscar dress!'

Shauna headed to the studio, knowing that she'd be in for another fourteen-hour day. The crew had recently returned from a location shoot in the Rocky Mountains, where everyone's skills and patience had been put to the test filming a lengthy scene in which the star and his nemesis engaged in a life-and-death struggle while descending from a mountain pass into a spectacular ravine. It had been fraught with difficulties and tempers had frayed, but Shauna's admiration for Dan Jackson had grown with each stressful and exhausting day. She and her boss, an Englishman called Terry Sullivan, had been charged with keeping a tight rein on costs while making sure everyone was safe. It often meant having to say no to people who were used to getting their own way, and this didn't endear them to directors as a rule, but Dan had been a complete pro, handling the situation with patience and good humour while always remaining true to his vision.

As usual, she spent the day assisting Terry while the cast and crew filmed a couple of interior scenes. Terry was coming down with flu after weeks of working too hard, and by evening he was feeling too ill to continue. He called her over and asked her to take over the reins.

'Jerry wants a detailed breakdown of location costs for the New York shoot. The whole thing is a fucking nightmare and the mayor's office are breaking my balls about closing off Times Square for the final scene. Can you type me up a state of play so I can get my head around it before I talk to him tomorrow?'

'Sure, chief, I'll get started now. Go home and make sure you have a hot toddy – Irish whiskey and lemon with a shot of honey.'

'Thanks, love. I can do the whiskey, not sure about the rest.'

Shauna sat typing it up for a couple of hours, but despite the fact everyone else had gone home by the time she finished, she didn't feel tired, just restless.

She decided to take a walk down to the lot where they'd been filming, just to clear her head after staring at spreadsheets all day. It felt as though her brain was beginning to turn to mush.

If only I could do something else instead, something I really love, she thought.

It wasn't that she hated what she was doing – she was lucky and she knew it. The world of Hollywood movie-making was frightening, exciting, intoxicating, exhausting and fun all at the same time, but she knew deep down that what would make her truly happy was acting.

The lot was in semi-darkness and appeared to be empty. It had been set up for an office scene; a showdown between a corrupt chief of police and the hero.

Shauna sat down in one of the chairs. It was strange to be on the other side of the camera for once. She tried to imagine what it must feel like to be an actor on set, with the director and camera crew on one side, make-up artists running in to apply finishing touches while you went over your lines, the hustle and bustle of runners dashing here and there, then a hush falling as the director called for quiet on set, the clapperboard sounding as they rolled.

Suddenly, Grace Kelly's lines came into her head. Grace had won an Academy Award for her performance in *A Country Girl*, in which she played the long-suffering wife of an alcoholic actor. Grace had delivered a memorable mono-logue which had probably clinched her the famous statuette.

Shauna had first seen the film in her teens and remem-bered crying as Grace Kelly's character, at the end of her tether after years of supporting her drunken husband, stands before William Holden and describes the pain she has endured, the sacrifices she's made, and the terrible cost to her soul. Without thinking, Shauna stood and delivered the monologue, the words rasping in her throat as slipped into the role of Georgie Elgin.

'Can you stand him up on his feet again? Because that's where all my prayers have gone . . . and I might forgive even you, Mr Dodd, if you can keep him up long enough for me to get out from under—'

Shauna was suddenly shocked out of her rapture by the set lights being slammed on. She heard the sound of someone clapping.

'Bravo, Shauna! Bravo!'

Shauna blinked against the lights, squinting at the voice coming out of the darkness. It was a moment before Dan Jackson came into view, still clapping and smiling broadly at her.

'Isn't it at this point that William Holden kisses Grace Kelly?'

Shauna was speechless. 'Dan, I'm so sorry, I didn't know that anyone was here.'

'Never mind about that, finish the scene.' He stepped forward and held her arms tightly, just as William Holden had done to Grace Kelly. 'He kisses her and then she says . . .?'

Momentarily Shauna felt like a rabbit in the headlights, but she could see that Dan was serious and there was something so direct and reassuring about him that the words came to her without thinking:

'How could you be so angry at someone that you didn't even really know . . .?'

'Maybe I really wasn't . . .'

Together they finished the scene and Shauna was astonished that Dan knew all the words too. When the scene was done and Georgie agreed to stay with her husband so that the show could go on, they regarded each other in silence for a moment before Shauna started to laugh, and Dan joined her. Soon they were giggling like teenagers, 'That was so . . . exhilarating.'

'George Seaton was a brilliant director and *A Country Girl* was one of his best. I've watched it a hundred times.' His eyes twinkled with interest. 'It seems maybe I wasn't aware enough of you, Shauna – that's quite the emotional punch you packed there. Why don't I know you're an actress?'

'I'm not.

'Not at all?'

'Well, maybe an aspiring one.'

'We aren't short of those in Tinseltown.'

She looked at the ground ruefully. 'I'm aware of that.'

Dan smiled kindly. 'There are very few actors who could do what you just did, Shauna.'

Shauna didn't know what to say, but once again she heard her father's voice in her head: *When opportunity comes knocking, Shauna, open the door . . .*

'I've been taking acting classes.'

'What you've got can't be learned in an acting class.'

He looked at her, studying her face. 'It's late, and we both need to get some sleep before tomorrow, but I don't feel tired. Do you fancy a drink?'

Chapter 15

Shauna couldn't pinpoint exactly when she fell for Dan Jackson. It might have been the very first day she saw him at work on set, or it could have been while they sat drinking in Molly Malone's Irish bar near Melrose Avenue that night after he'd caught her off guard on set.

They'd laughed at each other's stories. Dan told her that, though he had Irish grandparents, he'd been brought up in a typically middle-class English fashion: a private-school education followed by Cambridge, where he'd been part of the Footlights drama club. He told her of the terrible reviews he received after his first performance with his friend Julian Fellowes, which made him realize he was much better off the stage than on it.

What Shauna liked best about Dan was the way he listened to her and seemed genuinely interested in what she had to say. He was over a decade older but didn't look it. He had a full head of thick brown hair that stuck up boyishly and never seemed to do what he wanted. He had warm brown eyes that always seemed to have a smile in them for her. Dan had been married before. He and his wife, Helen, had separated amicably; she hadn't been part of the acting world. 'It's tough for sweethearts and wives, Shauna,' he told her. 'Directors are never at home and it can be a lonely old business. Only the strongest relationships survive, but you're too young to know about that yet.'

'I've had my fair share of an education on that front, I can assure you.'

He'd looked at her quizzically but didn't pry. He asked her about her acting ambitions and told her to keep practising, that acting was a constant process of learning and something that you could get better and better at.

'Why don't you change your name?' he suggested.

'Why would I do that?'

'It might help you make that mental leap into believing you're an actress. Sometimes, taking on a new persona can be freeing, it can give you the confidence you need to move on to the next stage in your life.'

Shauna thought about what he'd said. 'Then I'll take your name, as a thank you for your inspiration.'

'Jackson is as good as any, and I'm flattered. Welcome to the world, Shauna Jackson.'

Dan was usually too busy on set for chit-chat, but occasionally their eyes would meet, and he would always give her that boyish smile and a wink. Shauna found herself looking forward to those special moments.

When the film, *A Hard Line*, wrapped there was the usual raucous party. The star and all the crew mingled together, and Shauna was starting to feel like she belonged. Tom Cruise and Dan both made speeches in which they thanked the crew for their contribution; Tom's was emotional and heartfelt, while Dan was his usual self-deprecating and modest self.

'I've been privileged to have worked with some dear old friends, and with new ones, and every single one of you feels like family.' The crew whooped and whistled in appreciation. 'Mind you, some of you are like the sort of family I only want to hear from in the yearly Christmas card – Tom, you know I mean you!' Everyone laughed and Tom Cruise good-naturedly told him to fuck off. 'But there are others I hope that I'll be seeing a lot more of.' When he said this, Dan caught Shauna's eye in the crowd, and she felt herself blush.

While the crew were enjoying the lavish spread that the studio had put on, and drinking copious amounts of the free booze, Shauna noticed Dan wend his way through the crowd in her direction. Many of the crew clapped his back and shook his hand as he went past. Despite his approach-ability, there was a natural deference to the director in Hollywood Shauna had noticed, each cast and crew member knowing that, even if the director was as seemingly normal as Dan, they were still extremely powerful people and had the influence to make or break careers.

Dan had brought over a bottle of red wine and he joined the small cluster of Shauna's team, chatting to everyone and topping them up. When he came to her, he offered her the bottle and she said, 'I'll just have a drop. Red wine goes to my head.'

'It's a good one,' he said. 'I told Jerry I didn't want any of his Californian vinegar – this a good French claret, I'll have you know.'

'That'll be even worse for a hangover!'

Dan hardly left her side for the next couple of hours and Shauna was well aware he'd sought her out. She found herself not wanting to chat to anyone else, and when he asked if she wanted to slip away and have dinner, she nodded.

'It's like you've left your own birthday party,' she told him as they crept out.

'Rubbish,' he replied. 'No one will even notice I've gone. They're all drunk and getting off with each other.'

He took her to Spago, his favourite restaurant and one the most iconic in Beverly Hills. As they sat eating clam linguine, Robert De Niro and Martin Scorsese were having dinner at an adjacent table, and Meryl Streep was dining with her agent. Shauna was almost becoming used to rubbing shoulders with the stars, but tonight she only had eyes and ears for Dan.

'What's next for you?' she asked.

'My next picture is about a family torn apart by the Irish Civil War. It's got a great script and a smaller budget than this one, it's more of an ensemble piece. The big blockbusters are great and they pay the bills, but this is something much closer to my heart.'

'It sounds wonderful. Every Irish person has a story about their own family during that time.'

'I'm casting right now. I want Richard Harris as the patriarch, and we're in talks with a couple of actresses for the lead.'

'How exciting.'

He paused before adding, 'There's a small part as the daughter. She's only in a couple of scenes, but it's a key role. She leaves Ireland with her new husband to get away from the Troubles, and it breaks her father's heart.'

'Who have you got in mind?'

'I want someone fresh, someone who isn't jaded – a new voice.' He looked at her intently. 'I've been watching you and I think you might have what I need.'

Shauna's jaw dropped. 'Dan, I—'

'Don't say yes or no yet, you'd have to do a screen test. I need the rest of the production team to buy into the idea of a non-professional, but you have a . . . certain poise and a calm centredness that is just what this part needs . . .'

Shauna felt she was dreaming when her new agent, recommended by Dan, negotiated a fee that was more than she'd earn in ten years as a location assistant. Her screen test had gone well, after a shaky start. With Dan teasing an understated and naturalistic performance out of her, she had felt herself slip into the persona of her character, Maraid O'Gallagher.

She still found it hard to get her head around this new Shauna Jackson person that she didn't really know yet. She couldn't even bring herself to tell Roxy of the incredible opportunity that Dan had singled her out for, it felt too good to be true. She left it until she was on location in Galway before dashing off a quick letter to break the news.

Though Dan maintained a consummate professionalism throughout the shoot, Shauna knew her feelings for him were moving beyond the deep admiration she'd always had for him as a director. She could feel the tug of a deeper emotion drawing her to into his orbit, and she wasn't sure she wanted to resist.

Dan had dealt with Harris's wild behaviour with a patience and sensitivity that meant the actor gave one of his best performances. The cast and crew all felt that they had been part of something truly special and there were whispers of Oscar nominations for Dan and Richard.

After the shoot finished, there was time for her to take a short break before heading off to start on post-production back in LA. Shauna decided to spend the time visiting her family. She was surprised when Dan offered to drive her there. 'It's God's own country,' he told her. 'I'd be a fool not to enjoy it.'

Shauna could tell that her mother was slightly flummoxed by the appearance of this handsome and debonaire Englishman, and that she was desperate to work out his part in her daughter's life. It didn't take long for Dan to win her over, and Da was soon regaling Dan with tales of his uncle who had been sent to prison for his part in the Irish Uprising of 1916 and who had been lucky not be hanged for it.

Nevertheless, as they said goodbye to her parents at the end of the visit, her mother couldn't resist a dig. 'It will all come to nothing, Shauna, this acting lark. It's bad luck to give up your own name.'

'Hush, Kathleen,' her father had said, but Dan had put his arm around Shauna.

'You should be very proud of your daughter, Mrs O'Brien,' he told her. 'She's a wonderful actress, and everyone in Enniscrea will know Shauna Jackson's name one day.'

Maybe that was the moment when she knew she had fallen in love with Dan. He made love to her that night for the first time, in a small hotel that looked out over Galway Bay. He told her that she was beautiful, and that he would take her dreams and keep them safe with his own. His lovemaking was slow and unhurried, and brought her passion to life again, Shauna knew then it didn't matter *when* she had fallen in love with him, only that she was in love.

Dan had become her soulmate, his career was part of the fabric of his existence, and Shauna was like a thread that had been woven into it. She knew that he loved her with every part of his being and she felt the same way.

That first film with him, *One Day in April*, won him his first Oscar and he told her she was his good luck charm. Her role, though small, got her noticed. Although there were no awards nominations for her, she received glowing reviews in both the Irish and the American press.

Refusing Dan's entreaties to attend the Oscar ceremony, Shauna opted to stay at home and watch it on TV with only a Chinese delivery for company, not quite ready to put herself under the scrutiny of the flashing bulbs of the red carpet, although Roxy had badgered her to.

'I'm terrified – they'll ask me questions and I'll give stupid answers and I'll look silly.'

'You should have let me make you a dress,' Roxy told her on the phone from Milan.

'I'm sorry, maybe next time.'

'You'd better promise!'

She had cried when Dan had won, knowing how much it meant to him, but also knowing that it would take him into the stratosphere. Would this mean that he would drift away from her, that their lives would now be too far apart and he would find someone else more suited to his Hollywood royalty status?

Instead, Dan had shown up at her apartment at 3 a.m. looking the worse for wear and reeking of booze. She'd laughed and tried to help him out of his tuxedo, which was harder than it should have been as he wouldn't stop talking about how long and boring the ceremony had been, and how he was glad he'd smuggled in a hip flask of brandy because they weren't allowed to leave their seats for long periods.

'You'll have to come with me next year, Shauna – it's too tedious to bear alone. You will say, yes won't you?'

'Put me down as a maybe,' she'd said, as she struggled to get him out of his trousers.

'But you'll be my wife then, so of course so you'll have to.'

'Now I know you're drunk,' she laughed.

'No, I'm not. Look . . .' He'd fumbled drunkenly in his pocket and pulled out a small box which had the unmistakable stamp of HW – Harry Winston, jeweller to the stars. He proffered it to her. 'Go on, open it.'

Shauna took the box from his fingers and gingerly opened it. She gasped. Inside was the hugest solitaire she had ever seen, the many facets of its cushion cut throwing a rainbow kaleidoscope across her bedroom ceiling as it caught the light from the vintage Art Deco lamp by her bedside.

'Dan . . .?'

You will say yes, won't you?' He swayed in front of her, his face a mixture of drunken love and a touch of anxiety.

'Oh, Dan – yes, yes, yes!!'

She threw her arms around him, which caused him to collapse on to the bed. They lay there hugging each other in a messy jumble of laughter and tears.

Dan kissed her with the lazy passion of a drunk. 'I love you, Shauna Jackson.'

'And I love you, Dan Jackson.'

At this, Dan promptly fell asleep with a huge grin on his face.

They married a few months later on the island of Mustique, with only a handful of guests. Dan's mother came, along with his brother and his wife. Roxy was Shauna's maid-of-honour and she was accompanied by her current beau, Jacob, a pizza-delivery man from Brooklyn, where she was now living. 'He brought pepperoni pizza and never left!' Shauna had also invited her new friend, Mel Rosaria, a make-up artist she had formed a bond with on set and who she now requested whenever she signed on to a movie – as Dan had instructed her to do. 'Make sure you have good people around you, people that you trust.'

Her parents had declined to make the long journey, but her father had given Shauna her grandmother's wedding ring to wear. Even her mother had shed a tear as she told them her news on a visit home.

Shauna had worn a dress made by Roxy: sleeveless, strapless and figure-hugging, it was a world away from the eighties trend for shoulder pads and princess puffs. They had written their own vows and Shauna had cried when Dan made his vow that, every moment of every day, he would carry her in his heart. She in turn vowed to be forever by his side, no matter what life would throw at them. She tossed the bouquet, which was shunned by Roxy and caught instead by Mel. Then they adjourned to Basil's Bar where everyone danced under the stars to the sound of a calypso band.

When they said goodnight to their guests, Shauna reserved an extra-long embrace for Roxy.

'You look so beautiful and happy,' Roxy said, looking stunning herself in a floor-length black sequined number which was the perfect negative image of Shauna's dress.

'That's because I am – are you?'

'Yes, Jacob gives me everything I need right now – he's a great lay and doesn't pretend he loves me.'

'We've come so far, hard to believe that just a few years ago . . .'

'Hush! Today is not the day for those sorts of memories.'

'You're right, but I'll never forget, not even today.'

'I know, but you're happy now and that's what matters.' She mimed raising a glass to toast the bride: 'Here's to the start of a new chapter. Here's to the rest of our lives.'

Chapter 16

Shauna had taken her first steps on the path to stardom before she married Dan, but once his ring was on her finger, doors seemed to magically open for her. She hated to think that it was because of Dan, and he took pains to reassure her that it wasn't, but she was determined to make it on her own merits.

She chose only projects that would enhance her reputation and where she could learn from people she admired. She shied away from blockbusters, though the offers poured in, and the agent Dan had recommended, Isaac Orvitz, supported her in her choices. Isaac was old school; expensive but fiercely protective of his clients, he drove a hard bargain and treated Shauna like his daughter.

He was the one who told her about *Only the Brave*, a film that was in the early stages of development. The leading role had already been given to Jessica Lange, but there was an interesting supporting role as the wife of a paraplegic Vietnam veteran who faces a long road to recovery on his return home.

'She's not a likeable character,' Isaac explained. 'Turns

out, she can't cope with what's happened to him and she winds up dumping the guy – but you can give her a heart.'

After reading the script, Dan was of the same opinion as Isaac. He urged her to go for it.

The director was an auteur with a clear idea about who he wanted for the role – and it wasn't Shauna. He wanted Mary Elizabeth Mastrantonio, and Shauna knew she would have to do something extraordinary to get him to take a risk on her. Thanks to her old boss, Terry Sullivan, pulling some strings – thanks to Mel for transforming her appearance so that she was unrecognizable as Shauna Jackson – she passed herself off as a new waitress in the director's favourite bar, serving drinks incognito for a few nights to get to know him. She invented a sob story that her violent ex-husband was out of jail and threatening to kill her and she needed a thousand dollars to skip town. He was so convinced by Shauna's performance that he gave her the money in cash and offered to drive her to safety himself.

Shauna returned the money via a courier, along with signed picture of herself accompanied by a note that read, 'Do you think I can do it now?'

The part was hers. And when word of the subterfuge spread, it cemented her reputation as an actress who was prepared to take risks for her craft.

It was a gruelling shoot, months of doing scenes repeatedly, tempers boiling over in the process. She rediscovered emotions she hadn't felt in a long time and when she finally walked out on her on-screen husband while he screamed at her not to abandon him, it nearly tore her in two. The director had to give her a day off set to recover.

When they finally wrapped filming, Shauna felt drained but at the same time exhilarated. She tapped into her emotions and brought that character to life in a way she wouldn't have believed herself capable of – and she had never felt more alive.

The following year, the film received nominations in virtually every major category in both the Golden Globes and the Oscars. It was Shauna and Dan's first year of attending awards-season events together, and Dan encouraged her to revel in it.

'This is what Tinseltown is all about, baby,' he told her out of the corner of his mouth in a fake American accent as they stood on the red carpet at the Golden Globes. Shauna, having kept her promise, was wearing a gown made by Roxy. It was ice blue, fitted her like a dream, understated enough not to overshadow the other actresses who'd been nominated in her category, with a subtle nod to Grace Kelly in the elegant styling. Shauna kept having to pinch herself that she had been nominated. The film had garnered worldwide acclaim and her turn as the brittle, resentful but damaged wife had fully pushed her into the spotlight.

The evening passed in a blur of flashing bulbs and sound-bite interviews, and then suddenly the names of the nominees were being read out by Shirley MacLaine. Shauna, certain that she wouldn't win, concentrated on keeping a smile on her face so the camera wouldn't catch her looking disappointed. Even so, she couldn't keep a pang of longing from flaring up inside her when she heard her name among the nominees, wanting the coveted award so much, yet not daring to hope.

Shirley MacLaine slowly opened the envelope and time seemed to stand still for a second until she squealed and said, 'The best supporting actress goes to another redhead: Shauna Jackson!'

Dan's eyes shone with love and approval as she got to

her feet. She accepted her award with humility, thanking the director and the cast, and dedicating the award to the many damaged veterans and their families who had suffered so much in the aftermath of war. Dan had insisted that she rehearse an acceptance speech even though she'd been convinced there was no chance of her winning; she was thankful that he had.

As she posed for pictures and fielded reporters' questions while clutching her Golden Globe to her chest, she realized that the one person she had forgotten to thank was Dan.

Chapter 17

Cannes, 2000

Ordinarily, Dan Jackson loved the Cannes Film Festival. It lacked the mania of Hollywood, and its European focus meant that Dan was able to meet like-minded directors and talk to thoughtful interviewers about his passion for film. The junket was gruelling nonetheless, today alone he'd been interviewed by Jonathan Ross, *Entertainment Tonight*, the BBC and by a Dutch film crew. He'd had lunch with Sam Mendes to discuss financing on a new project he wanted Dan on board for, and tonight he and Shauna were having dinner with Tim Robbins and Susan Sarandon after the screening of *Cradle Will Rock*, which was in the running for the coveted Palme D'or. His busy schedule was the least of his problems.

His schedule allowed him only one short break. While Shauna was off being interviewed by a French TV show, he had their hotel room to himself. He was planning to make use of the time by taking a quick shower and freshening up.

He stood in the bathroom and regarded himself in the

large well-lit mirror, which hid nothing. He was now in his late forties, and no amount of hours on the treadmill in his home gym, or pounding the boardwalk outside their Malibu beachfront mansion could shift the tyre that had accumulated around his middle. His brown hair was peppered with more than a little salt, and his face was lined – or craggy, as he preferred to think of it – with bags sagging under his bloodshot eyes. God, he needed some sleep.

He splashed some of his usual 4711 eau de cologne, the one that Shauna ensured he had a ready supply of. *I like to smell you coming*, she would joke. He opened his wash bag and took out a vial of tablets. *You need to slow down*, his doctor had told him. *Cut out the fags and the booze, and the nose candy, for Chrissakes – your blood pressure is through the roof*. He threw his head back, swallowed the daily dose of tablets to keep his blood pressure down. He wasn't sure they were working.

He padded from the bathroom to the bedroom and sat on the edge of the bed. They were staying in the Hôtel Barrière Le Majestic, and their suite looked out across the Croisette to the Mediterranean Sea. Not for the first time, Dan contemplated taking a walk down to the shore, taking a swim and never coming back.

That familiar pang of conscience was back again, the knot in his stomach. He pushed down the fear, the sense that life was out of control, and tried to focus instead on getting ready, of finding his socks, his tie . . . He felt useless without Shauna here and knew that he would be useless without her in his life. Why the hell had he let himself get involved in this dreadful mess?

The phone jangled, and he picked it up, hoping it would be Shauna – knowing that her voice would reassure him, even if only momentarily.

'Dan Jackson,' he said.

'Dan . . . it's me.' It was a woman's voice, American, with a touch of Latino.

His stomach lurched. 'I told you not to call me – how did you get them to put you through?'

'I'm not just a pretty face,' she snapped. 'And what else was I supposed to do? You don't answer your mobile, or take my calls from your office.' There was no mistaking the anger in the voice. 'You can't just erase me from your life, Dan. I won't let you.'

Dan grimaced and drew his hand across his forehead, wiping away the sweat that was beading on his brow.

'I'm not trying to dismiss you, but you must understand, I can't do what you're asking—'

'You didn't say that when you were screwing me. You wanted me then.'

'Yes . . . please . . . I know, but I wasn't thinking straight.'

'You bastard, you took what you wanted and now you think you can leave me – and our son – with nothing.'

'I've given you money, more than enough, but I can't . . . I won't be held to ransom by you.'

'That's where you're wrong. You're going to pay, Dan. Believe me, you'll pay.'

She hung up, leaving Dan drenched in his own sweat, his heart pounding. At that moment, Shauna entered the room, accompanied by a waft of No.5 and clad in a classic pink-and-black Chanel two-piece. She threw her Hermès Birkin handbag onto the bed and kissed his head. 'Thank God that's over! If one more interviewer asks why I turned down *Shakespeare in Love*, I'll scream. Gwynnie was the right actress for the role. Pour me a drink, darling.'

It took her a moment to notice that Dan was ashen-faced. 'Dan – oh, God, what's wrong?' She quickly dropped down beside him. 'Should I call a doctor?'

'No fucking doctor!' he snapped. Then he took a deep breath and held his hand up in a gesture of restraint and said more calmly. 'Really, Shauna, I'm fine. Probably overtired, that's all.'

'Are you sure? You look awful.'

'Charming,' he laughed mirthlessly.

'Dan, you know what I mean. Something isn't right.'

It took a supreme effort, but Dan did his best to smile and reassure her. 'Darling, I'm perfectly well. Cannes always does this to me – too much cordon bleu and fine brandy. Please don't fuss.' He made a show of looking at his Patek Phillippe watch, a present from Shauna for their tenth wedding anniversary. 'You'd better take a soak; we've got another long night ahead of us.'

'Look, we can cancel. It's more important that you rest – you know what the doctor said about your blood pressure.'

His patience snapped. 'The doctor isn't a fucking film director forced into this year of hell by the film studio that pays his wages.'

Stung, Shauna retreated. 'You chose this life, Dan – we both did, but that doesn't mean it has to ruin your health – or our marriage.'

'You didn't say that when you swanned off for a six-month shoot with Richard Gere, did you?'

Shauna's eyes flashed at the accusation. 'You told me to take that movie. "It will be good for you to do a comedy," you said.'

Dan rubbed his eyes, sick and tired of the endless arguments, but knowing he was the cause. 'Oh, Shauna, can we please stop talking about your fucking career for five minutes.'

'Fine. I'm going to take a bath.' She went into the enormous bathroom with its marble and gold sunken bath and slammed the door.

Annoyed with himself because he recognized that Shauna didn't deserve his barbs, Dan raked his hand over his chin and reached for the nightstand. He removed his medication organizer from the top drawer and took out a small paper wrap of white powder that had not been prescribed by his doctor. Using a tiny spoon, he measured out a small amount, used his credit card to chop two lines and snorted them with the aid of a rolled-up twenty-euro note.

Feeling better now, he lifted the phone and put in a call to his accountant in New York. His foot tapped impatiently as he waited to be connected.

'Abe, it's Dan Jackson. You remember that hundred-thousand-dollar transfer I had you make to Frankie Martinez? Well, I need you to make another one.' He pulled the phone away from his ear as Abe squawked down the line at him.

'Yes, I know she's just some bit-part actress, I know it's madness – but do what I'm asking you and send her another hundred grand. And keep your mouth shut, OK? I can't have Shauna finding out.'

Shauna felt detached as she and Dan posed for pictures outside the cinema that was the venue for tonight's feature. Although the festival was tiring and repetitive, with way too many late nights, the effort involved in looking glamorous and delighted to be there wasn't exactly coal mining. Red-carpet events like this kept the wheels of the industry turning. The publicity generated was good for business, and vital to smaller movies that might otherwise struggle to get noticed. Tonight, however, she was operating on autopilot, her mind preoccupied with the nagging concern that had dogged her for months: Dan was keeping secrets from her and something was terribly wrong with their marriage.

It wasn't just the increase in the amount of cocaine he

was taking. Their Malibu home was enormous and they both had their own suites, but they still slept together and, despite his attempts to hide the evidence, she had spotted the tell-tale signs. The clues had been easier to spot this past year, as he'd grown sloppy about sweeping away the residue on the glass table in his office. His unpredictable mood swings were now a constant. When she tried to broach the subject, his male pride wouldn't allow him to open up to her. Dan was a wonderful person in so many ways, but he was old-fashioned and kept his troubles to himself.

Their marital problems had gotten worse over the last couple of years. A shoot in Scotland that ran into problems when the director quit halfway through had meant an extended and enforced absence from each other's lives. It had been a mistake; she could see that now. Dan had begged her to come back to LA when the shit hit the fan, but her loyalty to the cast and crew wouldn't let her. By the time she returned, Dan was in South America, fulfilling a contractual obligation to shoot a drama set in the rainforest, even though he was in no condition, physically or mentally.

By the time they saw each other again, six months had gone by. The physical toll on Dan was obvious; he'd lost weight and looked as if he'd aged ten years. But the worst thing was, he seemed to have grown emotionally distant from her. When he was tired or under stress, he would rail against her, accusing her of being self-absorbed and only caring about her career. Afraid there might be some truth in his criticism, she did everything she could to restore his trust in her, turning down projects that would take her away from home. But whatever she did, it never seemed to be enough.

The photographers hailed them both, some throwing questions at her in Spanish, Italian and French as well as

English; it was dizzying, she didn't even try to answer, acknowledging with smiles and waves instead.

Maybe it was time for her to take a break from acting. She knew Dan's doctor had put him on medication for his heart, and tonight had really worried her. Yes . . . taking a year or two out would be good for both of them, if she could persuade Dan to do the same. They could go back to Ireland. Maybe not to Enniscrea, but to somewhere not too far away so she could look in on her father. Dan loved the west coast of Ireland, they both did, and they could easily find some beautiful remote spot where there'd be no distractions. Maybe Dan could write that book about French Cinema and she could have a go at writing a novel . . .

As they headed through the doors into the reception, Dan dropped her hand and took off without a word. She watched as he greeted David Lynch and struck up a conversation with him. These days, it was quite a novelty to find herself alone at a party, even for a few moments. She accepted a glass of champagne from a waiter and cast her eye around the crowded room to see who she could spot. Susan Sarandon, who was chatting with Bill Murray and Emily Watson, caught sight of her and mouthed, 'See you at dinner.' Shauna responded with a smile and a thumbs-up.

Suddenly, Shauna's heart skipped a beat as she caught sight of a face she'd hoped never to see again, one that dredged up unwelcome feelings and took her back to a time and a place she'd tried hard to forget. She was older than the last time Shauna had set eyes on her, but there was no question it was Sofía Constantis; she still had that imperious feline air that had led Chantelle to call her 'the tigress'. Shauna took a sidestep and dropped discreetly behind a pillar to watch as Sofía airily surveyed the room, ignoring the short fat bald man who seemed intent on talking to her.

And before the thought was even in her head – that Demetrios might also be in the room – a man appeared at Sofía's side. Though she only glimpsed his face for a moment before he turned away again, Shauna recognized Demetrios. He still had the same confident bearing, his tanned face was as handsome as ever, his hair now sporting a few annoyingly attractive grey hairs.

Much as she would have liked to stay in her hiding place to drink in the sight of him, she was afraid if she did she would be unable to resist the magnetic pull he apparently still had over her. *Don't be ridiculous* she told herself, *it's just the element of surprise that's thrown you*. When Roxy had glee-fully reported that the European tabloids were all claiming the marriage was on the rocks, Shauna had told her she wasn't the least bit interested. At the time, she'd meant it, yet here she was, unable to take her eyes off him. What was it about Demetrios that always brought out the idiot in her?

Before she could examine the thought further, Dan appeared at her side.

'Why are you hiding? I thought the whole point of coming here was to be seen.' He glanced over his shoulder. 'Here we go, they're ushering everyone in now.'

She took Dan's arm, put on her best smile, and together they crossed the room. If Shauna had allowed herself to glance in their direction – which she didn't – she would have seen Sofía regard her with stony features and Demetrius knit his brow as they swept past, a questioning and confused look flitting across his face before she disappeared up the red-carpeted staircase.

Chapter 18

Demetrios Theodosis looked out over the Hudson River from his office at the top of Manhattan's Rockefeller Centre. He'd taken the decision to move the company headquarters from Athens to New York four years ago, when his daughter left Greece to attend a boarding school in England. With her gone, he had no reason to stay and every reason to escape. Had Lukas Constantis still been president of the company, he would have vetoed the move, if only for the reason that Demetrios had suggested it. But after Lukas's death in 1996, Demitrios had finally taken control of Hellenic Ventures – the company formed by the merger of the Theodosis and Constantis family holdings.

'United for posterity!' Lukas had announced triumphantly, toasting the bride and groom at the wedding which sealed the merger. But there had never been any unity between them, Demetrios thought ruefully as he looked down at the papers in front of him: the Decree Absolute that would put an end to the charade.

So far, they had manged to keep the divorce out of the tabloids, but Demetrius had long stopped caring what anyone thought about his marriage. He and Sofía had never been suited; they'd argued constantly from the start. She had never understood the nature of the business or the demands on his time, and he . . . well, he had never loved her. He had hoped that it would come in time, but on that he was mistaken. Their differences only became more exaggerated as the years ticked by. For the sake of the family, they had kept up the pretence and stayed married, though both of them had conducted a series of affairs, discreetly and other-wise – a fortune had been spent on bribes and court injunctions to keep the ensuing scandals out of the news-papers and the long lenses of the paparazzi at bay. Demetrios wouldn't have bothered suppressing the stories if it weren't for the fact Ariana's heart would have been broken if she'd found out how much her parents despised each other.

He picked up the gold-framed photograph of his daughter that sat on his desk. Ariana was sixteen now. Already she was starting to think about which university she wanted to go to. Demetrios would have liked her to follow in his footsteps and study at Harvard, while her mother wanted her to go to Oxford or Cambridge. He knew that Sofía would be doing everything in her power to make sure Ariana stayed in England, but he wasn't about to intervene. His greatest wish was that his only child should have the freedom to make her own choices in life.

He took out his Waterman pen, hesitating only briefly before signing with a flourish. Their lawyers had spent months negotiating the settlement. Sofía had never been interested in the business and, while they couldn't bear the sight of each other, they both had Ariana's best interests at heart. That meant safeguarding the legacy that would be handed down to her: the family business, Hellenic Ventures. They'd therefore agreed that the divorce should be as quick and painless as possible. Sofía could now move on to the next stage of her life, probably marry a hedge-fund manager and relocate permanently to London, where she spent most of her time shopping in Bond Street or Harrods.

As for him . . . Demetrios stood and took his coffee cup to the window. He had loved New York when he was a young man, but now he longed for the uncomplicated life he'd known on Ithos. New York, well, it was the perfect place for a hungry young man, but what was he hungry for now that he was older . . . and lonelier?

He chided himself, *When did you start falling victim to pity, old man?*

Returning to his desk, he placed the papers in his out-tray. He would ask his secretary to courier them over to his lawyer that afternoon. His eyes shifted to the copy of *Empire* magazine he'd purchased from a newsstand the day before.

On the cover was a picture of the actress Shauna Jackson, her green eyes looking out coolly at him, her blonde high-lighted hair hinting at a redness underneath.

He stared at the picture for a few moments, scrutinizing every detail of the beautiful face underneath the headline:

Shauna Jackson, Ireland's Greatest Export – we join her on the set of her new movie

Demetrios folded his hands and rested his chin on them. How could he have been oblivious all these years? While it was true the only time he had for watching movies was on transatlantic flights, and even then he was liable to be distracted by paperwork or catching up on his sleep, he must have been walking around with blinkers on to have missed her.

Or could it be that he was mistaken? He looked again at the picture. No, it was definitely her. He'd been certain of it from the moment he almost caught her eye in Cannes last month. That had been the last time he and Sofía had gone anywhere together, and he'd only agreed to it because Ariana had seen the invitation sent to him by a new production company looking for investors and had pleaded to be allowed to attend. After the actress had passed them by, presumably with her husband, he had asked Ariana who she was. With a roll of her eyes, she'd told him, 'Papa, have you been living under a rock? That's Shauna Jackson, she's an A-lister.'

Since then, he'd bought copies of every film and gossip magazine going, trying to find out more. All he'd learned so far was that both she and her director husband, Dan Jackson, zealously guarded their privacy; she was rarely photographed in LA and her background seemed to be a bit of a mystery. He'd tried to recall some of the detail of what his Shauna had told him about her background. He remembered it was somewhere in the west of Ireland, but where? What had it been called? He cursed himself, realizing how little he had known about the woman he had fallen in love with.

Those cool green eyes continued to regard him impassively from the cover of the magazine. Was it really his Shauna? His face twisted in a grimace as he reminded himself that she had ceased to be *his* Shauna . . . he had let her go and it was too late to make amends or rectify the situation.

He placed the magazine in the bin beside his desk. There was no point raking over the past after all these years.

Frankie Martinez tucked her son Alexander into his bed. Their small bedsit in Lincoln Heights was all she could afford. It was only six o'clock in the evening, but the nightly symphony of wailing sirens was already seeping through the open window as the cops rounded up teenage gang members after yet another drive-by shooting. The thought of her little boy growing up in this neighbourhood filled her with dread; she'd seen what it had done to her two brothers.

'Mommy has to go out now, honey.'

'Please don't go, Mama,' he pleaded, his eyes wide and anxious as he always was when he was left alone.

'I won't be long, I promise.'

'You promised before and you didn't come back for a long time.' His brown eyes looked at her reproachfully.

'I'm sorry, I won't do it again.'

Frankie hoped it was true this time. She hated having to leave her young son on his own, but there was no alternative. Since last year he'd been enrolled in a state preschool that took kids from the age of three, which had allowed her to work a seven-hour shift in the local dime store, but her minimum-wage salary wouldn't stretch to paying for additional childcare. Sometimes the old lady down the hall would help out by having Alex for a couple of hours, but she wasn't home right now. If Frankie didn't get to the hospital soon, visiting hours would be over and she wouldn't be able to see her sister.

'Remember what I told you to do to get to sleep?'

'I have to think of all the llamas up on the mountains and count them jumping over the wall to get to the alfalfa plants.'

'That's right, sweetie. So hold on to Alfie the Alpaca, start counting, and you'll fall asleep in no time.'

A large tear trickled down the boy's face as he hugged his cuddly alpaca to him.

'That's right, sweetie, now be brave and settle down and I'll be back soon, OK?'

He nodded and Frankie kissed him before slipping her bomber jacket over her black T-shirt and jeans. Then she slipped out of the apartment door, making sure that it was firmly locked. She ran down the dingy hallway, passing other shabby apartments on her way. She could hear the wailing of a baby and a couple arguing in one, and the theme tune of *Who Wants to Be a Millionaire?* blaring from another.

The 251 bus that would take her to the general hospital was due any minute, so she raced down the street, arriving in the nick of time. She had barely a second to catch her breath before the familiar orange bus pulled up. After paying, she headed for the back, passing a homeless man fast asleep in layers of tatty clothing, and an old woman who sat muttering to herself. Once seated, Frankie tuned everything else out and stared out at the freeway, the cars whizzing past the bus as it trundled along the slow lane for the 25-minute journey to the hospital, her mind a jumble of thoughts and terrors as she thought about what lay ahead.

Frankie's parents had been illegal immigrants from Mexico. She had never known her father; he'd walked out soon after she was born, leaving her mother to raise four children alone in a poor district of South Los Angeles. She had struggled to make ends meet with an endless succession of cleaning jobs that took her out of the house for much of the time. Though she'd done her best to instil good values in her children, she was no match for the twin evils of street gangs and the grinding poverty that the gangs exploited to expand their membership.

Disaster struck when her mother contracted an aggressive form of breast cancer. With no medical insurance or savings, her treatment options had been limited. She died, barely into her forties, leaving Frankie's big sister, Isabelle, as head of the household. Though Isabelle had done her best to be sister and mother to them all, the boys were beyond saving. The younger boy was killed in a knife fight and the older was currently serving two consecutive life sentences in San Quentin jail.

Frankie had always been the dreamer of the family. As long as she could remember, she'd wanted to be an actress, but even though the Land of the Free promised riches to those who worked hard enough, success had eluded her. Before she'd had Alex, she'd worked the casting couch as hard as she could, but it had only resulted in bit parts in bad movies. All that seemed set to change when she landed a small speaking part in a film directed by Dan Jackson. As usual she'd played the part of a prostitute – she was invariably cast as a hooker or a waitress – but though she only appeared in a few scenes, in her short leather skirt and low-cut black lace top, she'd made an impact. Or so she thought, until the acting jobs dried up and Frankie had to take a job in a bar to help her sister pay the bills. Then one night, who should walk into the bar but Dan Jackson.

'You're a long way from home, Mr Jackson,' she'd said to him as she handed him his neat Scotch.

'Do I know you?' His English accent sounded incongruous in those surroundings, drawing attention from the lowlifes who frequented the bar.

'You'd better watch out; you might not get out of here with your wallet if you're not careful,' she'd warned him, but he'd paid no heed, steadily getting drunker as the night wore on, while she warded off any sharks who singled him out as easy prey by giving them the evil eye.

Frankie knew she turned heads with her black hair and black eyes, strawberry red lips and hourglass figure, but she was only interested in men who could give her a way out of poverty. She knew her only chance of a better life depended on putting those God-given gifts to good use.

'Do I know you?' Dan slurred, his eyes narrowing as he tried to place her through the fog of alcohol that was clouding his vision as well as his memory.

She introduced herself and reminded him of the picture they'd worked on. 'Oh, yes – Hooker Number One. As I recall, you made quite an impression.'

Though wounded that he only remembered her part and not her name, she smiled.

'What are you doing in a dump like this?'

'I have bills to pay, and there are always a hundred more actresses with blonde hair and blue eyes and rich daddies to pay for their apartments in Bel Air. Me, I'm not so lucky. Anyway, I should be asking you the same question. What are you doing here – shouldn't you be at home with your wife – what's her name, Shauna Jackson?'

'Ah, yes!' Dan raised his glass. 'Here's to the marvellous, radiant and venerated Shauna Jackson, everybody's darling.'

Frankie caught the whiff of a discontented husband. She'd seen enough of them in her time.

'My wife is in Ireland . . . and I . . .' he sank his Scotch and held up his glass for a refill, 'I am doing whatever the hell I like while she's perfecting her craft with Richard Gere!' He sank the next one too, his shoulders shuddering slightly as the golden liquid hit his insides. 'Anyway, pleased to meet you – you must call me Dan.'

'Hey, Dan, maybe you should slow down a little,' she told him, but she poured him another refill anyway.

Where there was misery there was opportunity. Frankie made it her business to please Dan Jackson; she asked him about his life, sounded knowledgeable about his work, and gently drew his attention away from his wife and on to her instead. She'd bundled him into a taxi that night, but to her satisfaction he'd returned the following night and the one after that, seeking her out. Frankie knew she was flattering his ego – the guy was two decades older than her, for God's sake – but she liked him. He was kind, and despite his obvious unhappiness with his marriage, he didn't bad-mouth his wife. He seemed interested in Frankie too, so why not encourage him?

One night, he'd been drinking even more than usual, and when he returned from a trip to the bathroom Frankie saw telltale traces of white powder around his nose.

'Something getting to you, Dan?' she asked.

He told her that his wife had been held up on a movie shoot in Europe and would be away longer than expected. Months longer. Frankie could tell that Dan was lonely, and she was lonely too. All the guys she'd dated were only interested in screwing her, while Dan had a gentle side to him. So she asked one of the other girls to cover her shift, promising to make it up to her, then came around to Dan's side of the bar.

'Let's get out of here, Dan. Tonight you need more than booze and cocaine.'

She took him to a decent motel in a better part of town and made love to him. And as he spent himself inside her, she smiled, certain that Dan Jackson was her ticket to the big time.

The bus pulled to a halt outside the hospital and Frankie thanked the driver and headed quickly through the lobby and up to the tenth floor.

After years of doing her best to be a sister and mother to her siblings, hardship had worn Isabelle down until, by a cruel twist of fate, she'd fallen prey to the same cancer that had killed their mother. Thanks to Frankie, she was receiving the best treatment possible.

A nurse was at her bedside, checking the various monitors and making notes.

'Hi, Ruby,' Frankie greeted her.

'Oh, Francesca, can I just have a word with you?' she said kindly. Once they'd stepped out into the hallway, she explained: 'Isabelle hasn't had such a great day today – the chemo has been taking its toll. She's been vomiting a lot, and now she's exhausted. So don't stay too long, OK?'

Frankie nodded, went back in and slipped into the chair by her sister's bed. Isabelle wore a beanie hat that covered her head, now devoid of hair. Her skin was pallid and looked paper thin, while her lips had an almost blueish tinge. Her eyelids were closed.

'*Hola, cariño mío*.' She reached for Isabelle's hand and her sister's eyelids fluttered.

'*Hola, hermanita*,' Isabelle whispered in return, a small smile playing across her lips.

'Don't speak, OK,' Frankie said.

'Crap day today.'

'I know, just rest now.'

Isabelle opened one eye. 'Where's Alex?' she asked, alert now.

'He's OK, a friend is watching him,' Frankie lied, knowing that Isabelle would give her hell if she knew that Frankie had left him alone, but it was the only way she could see the sister that she adored.

'You give that nephew of mine a big hug, you hear?'

'The biggest. You want me to go?'

Isabelle looked at Frankie, her eyes fluttering with the struggle to stay open. 'Don't leave me yet, Frankie, stay a little longer.'

Frankie sat quietly, holding her sister's hand, singing their mother's favourite lullaby, 'Luna Lunera', about a lover who asks the moon to tell his sweetheart he loves her.

As her sister dosed, Frankie's thoughts returned to Dan. She'd hoped that he would open doors for her, help her land a part that would pay big bucks and set her on the road to stardom. After all, he'd done it for his wife. Frankie didn't believe her expectations were unreasonable; she knew it would always be her body and not her acting that would get her parts, but why shouldn't she have a shot at *Baywatch* or *Diagnosis: Murder*? But things hadn't worked out the way she'd planned. Dan wouldn't play the game. Told her that their brief affair was a mistake and that he was ending it. Frankie didn't think of herself as a cruel person, but she'd taken a certain amount of pleasure in breaking the news to him that she was pregnant with their child.

At first, he had refused to give her anything, told her that she was a crook and a liar, but Frankie bided her time and, once Alex was born, she was thrilled that he looked just like his daddy. She had sent a package to Dan's office in Burbank Studios containing Alex's plastic identity bracelet from the hospital, with his name, Alexander Rodrigo Jackson, and an enlarged photograph of their son, with his shock of brown hair and his eyes just like Dan's.

Dan had agreed to meet her alone, without the boy. 'What do you want from me?' he'd demanded, his mouth set hard. Frankie saw that, despite the 'decent man' façade, this was a man like all the rest: happy to use her and then discard her afterwards, taking no responsibility for the predictable consequences.

'I want a hundred thousand dollars and a lead role in your next movie.'

'You've got to be kidding.'

'I'm serious. I've got a journalist from the *National Enquirer* on speed dial and I'm ready tell them everything.'

Dan had refused to give her a part in one of his movies, but he had paid up.

Frankie had intended to leave it at that. If she was careful with the money, it would last them for years, or at least long enough to give her son a decent start in life. Isabelle adored her nephew and had insisted on helping to look after him, so the three of them moved in together, a happy little family. Until Isabelle started to feel unwell and they found out it was cancer. That had changed everything. When Isabelle's doctor told Frankie that her sister would die within months without chemotherapy, she used every penny they had to pay the medical bills. And when the money ran out, she called Dan to demand another hundred thousand.

Isabelle's breathing deepened and the rise and fall of her chest became more rhythmic. Frankie rose, put her jacket back on and kissed her sister's forehead with the words, '*Te amo, pequeña madre*.' Little mother, the name she had always used for Isabelle.

It was now eight o'clock and the bus was due in ten minutes, but as she headed for the lift, she saw a doctor approach, He was quite young, in his thirties, and Frankie had always thought he looked a little like George Clooney in *ER*.

'Hello, Francesca, do you have a moment?'

'Umm, hi, Dr Scott, I kinda gotta run . . .'

'This won't take long, I just wanted to let you know that your sister's treatment is working well. We did some scans and we're confident that the cancer is shrinking.'

Frankie felt her heart lift. 'That's great! Does that mean she'll be able to come home soon?'

'Well, as we discussed before, this is a very aggressive

cancer. Isabelle will need many more months of treatment before we can say she's in remission.'

Frankie's face fell a little. 'But it's good news, right?'

The doctor nodded. 'Yes, it is . . . As long as you can afford the treatment. It's cutting edge, but very expensive.'

Frankie frowned. 'I told you, you don't need to worry about the money. I found it for you, didn't I?'

'Yes, Francesca, but we will need more—'

Frankie jutted out her chin. 'Whatever it takes, I'll get it for her. That's a guarantee. Listen, Doc, I have to run.'

'Of course. Goodbye, Francesca.'

Dr Scott watched Frankie as she skipped the lift and headed for the stairwell, running. He shook his head. Cancer treatment could run to hundreds of thousands of dollars. He had no idea where Frankie had got the money for her sister's care – it wasn't his job to ask those sorts of questions. The medical system was unfair enough in the USA; sticking his nose in where it wasn't wanted wouldn't help matters. He only hoped that, however Isabelle's sister had found the money before, she'd be able to do the same again.

Chapter 19

Shauna didn't think she was nosey, but it was in her nature to be inquisitive, she couldn't help herself, so she tried not to feel guilty as she listened at the door of Dan's home office.

That something was wrong with Dan was all too clear. He'd been drinking too much again, and she'd found more telltale signs around their Malibu home that hinted at his increased drug use. Whenever she attempted to talk to him about it, he bit her head off and told her to mind her own business, so she'd resorted to subterfuge to find out what was going on.

At first it was difficult to hear anything through the thick wooden door, but then he began shouting about being bled dry, accusing someone of extortion.

Shauna knew that Dan was having problems financing his latest project, perhaps it was something to do with that. In the movie business, drama wasn't confined to the big screen. Actors, directors and producers tended to get emotional, sometimes to the point of hysteria, when they couldn't get what they wanted. That must be what was

185

going on with Dan; after all, he couldn't be serious about blackmail, could he? She shook her head and padded up to her own office which looked out over the Pacific Ocean. Their home had cost $3,000,000 and boasted ocean views from virtually every room. While Dan had a library office, Shauna's was filled with her beloved art deco collection which she had been building up ever since she had moved to LA.

She was more convinced than ever that what they both needed was to get away from LA altogether and take a long break. They'd both been working too hard and had been promising themselves a trip to Europe for years – Shauna would love for them both to go to Rome and Paris and be like tourists again. Maybe then, in a more relaxed environment, she could talk to him again about having a baby. They'd been married almost thirteen years now but it felt as though work had come first for both of them during that time. She hadn't been ready . . . but now she longed to feel the grip of a baby's fingers on one of her own. That sweet smell of a son – or a daughter – lying across her breast, sleeping soundly. Shauna knew Dan would make a wonderful father.

And what sort of mother would she be? She rarely allowed herself to indulge in these thoughts, but today she couldn't help it. Yes, away from all the pressures of Hollywood, they could just be themselves, and they could find each other again.

Shauna threw herself onto her large leather sofa and eyed the pile of manuscripts that Isaac had sent her way this week. He only sent her the most interesting ones, but before she had a chance to look at the first one, a script from Julian Fellowes, one of Dan's old friends, the phone rang.

It was Isaac. 'Hey doll, how you doing?' He was calling her from his office in New York and Shauna could picture him in her mind's eye, looking out over Central Park while chomping on a Cuban cigar.

'Hey, Isaac, tell me about this *Gosford Park* script—'

'Hold everything, I've just heard about a project you won't want to miss.'

'I don't know, Isaac. I've been thinking of taking a break for a while, so Dan and I could get away from LA. He's been working too hard and badly needs some time out. A shoot in England would be a great compromise: Dan could relax and spend time with his family while I'm working, and—'

'Hear me out before you do anything.'

'OK, Isaac, I can see there'll be no peace until you tell me.'

'Wait for it . . . There's a Grace Kelly biopic in the making.'

Shauna laughed; Isaac knew her so well. 'OK, you got me, who's making it?'

'Columbia Pictures – they want Steven Spielberg, and he'll only do it if he can get you on board.'

Shauna felt that familiar rush of adrenaline, that special tingle an actress only feels very rarely. Spielberg directing her as Grace. She must be dreaming. 'Isaac, are you sure about this?'

'Never been surer of anything in my life. He wants to meet you – to talk about the part.'

'When?'

'Soon. How badly do you want it?'

Shauna took a breath, trying to steady her racing heart. 'I want it more than I've ever wanted a role in my life.'

'That's what I thought . . . leave it with me.' And with that, he rang off.

Shauna was still for a moment, his words ringing in her ears, then she leapt off her sofa and did a dance of joy around the room. *Easy, Shauna,* she told herself, *nothing is certain in this town until you've signed on the dotted line.* Rome and Paris would have to wait.

She raced out of the room and down the stairs and knocked on the door to Dan's office. When he didn't reply, she started to go in to tell him the good news, but he was gone. As she set off in search of him, she saw movement through the windows in the lobby. Dan was leaping into his vintage Jaguar, which was parked next to her more everyday BMW in the drive. With a screech of tyres, he was gone.

Shauna wondered what could have caused him to leave in such a hurry. Neither of them had been planning to go out until this evening, when they were having dinner with friends. Then she remembered his phone call earlier and felt anxious. Determined to get to the bottom of whatever was going on with Dan, she resolved that tonight, when they got home from dinner, she would insist that he tell her the truth.

Gary Fisher was one of Dan's closest friends. Old enough to be Dan's father, he'd been blacklisted during the McCarthy era and forced to spend years in exile in Europe. The wilderness years came to an end when his work with David Lean earned him an Oscar; after that he'd enjoyed a renaissance in Hollywood and he was now respected as one of the finest cinematographers of his generation. His partner, Eric, younger than him by some decades, was a Hollywood stylist who knew all the latest gossip – who was sleeping with who, and who'd been thrown off the set of their latest picture. Dan loved spending time with the two of them. He knew how difficult it had been for Gary when he was ostracized by Hollywood's elite, and it made him happy to know that in his golden years his friend was getting the recognition he truly deserved, and that he'd found a partner who truly loved him and looked after him.

Usually, Dan loved nothing better than to relax in their company, but tonight he felt trapped. This afternoon had been one of the worst of his life. Frankie had called him at home, demanding to see him right away and refusing to take no for an answer.

'I need more money,' she'd told him when he picked her up downtown. Her eyes blazed darkly as she sat in the passenger seat of the Jaguar.

'You've had two hundred thousand dollars out of me already. I can't keep giving you money, Frankie, this has to stop.'

'It stops when I say it does,' she'd spat. 'You have everything you need, a home worth millions of dollars, your fancy cars, your beautiful wife.'

There had been a time when Dan felt some sympathy for her, but now he saw that she was out to destroy him. He should never have let it go this far.

'No, Frankie. I'm not giving you another penny.'

'Then your beautiful life will be in ruins, because I'll tell the whole world about your dirty little secret.'

Dan had felt his anger snap, and he'd grabbed Frankie by her shoulders. 'I don't care any more, Frankie. You'll not get a penny more from me, do you hear? Take your filthy story, your lies and your dirty secret and sell them to whoever will pay you the most money.'

'I'll destroy every shred of your life, I'll tell them everything – about Alex, about your drug habits . . .'

It was all Dan could do to stop himself from physically throwing her out of his car. Instead, he'd leaned across and opened the passenger door, then commanded her: 'Get. Out.'

Frankie took one last look at him, her face full of hatred and anger, then stepped out of the car.

Dan had driven straight home, and when he opened the front door, Shauna was standing in their enormous hallway, her face full of concern.

'Dan, where have you been? I've been so worried.'

He took her in his arms, gave her a brief hug and said, 'I'm OK, I just had to take care of something. I'm back now.'

'Dan, please, I know something is wrong. You have to let me in.'

His shoulders sagged. 'I know . . . these last few years have been tough on both of us.' He kissed her on the forehead and held her tight. 'I love you, Shauna, and after we've had dinner with Gary and Eric tonight, I promise I'll tell you everything.'

'Everything?'

'Yes, no secrets, not any more.'

Dan had ordered a steak and a crème brûlée at dinner and Eric had ribbed him about it. 'You English guys are all the same, everything is full of calories and cholesterol.'

'These public schoolboys are still obsessed with school dinners,' Shauna joked. She'd squeezed Dan's hand and he'd squeezed hers in return. She looked dazzling tonight, he thought, casual yet elegant in a tailored grey trouser suit which showed off her curves. She'd sparkled all evening, bouncing off Eric and making him and Gary laugh with stories of her Irish childhood, stealing a penny from the collection plate in church and then being made by her mother to apologize to the priest in person, who told her to pray the five joyful mysteries a thousand times on her rosary until she was truly sorry.

His heart ached with the knowledge that things would

never be the same after tonight, when he finally told her the truth about Frankie and the son he had denied. Dan knew his marriage might not survive. He felt shame not only at that, but also at the terrible unkindness he had inflicted on a child who was completely blameless. He couldn't even blame Frankie; this was his fuck-up and he'd have to pay for it. He felt his chest tighten and a pain shot up his left arm.

'Excuse me,' he said, standing up and pushing his chair back.

'Are you OK, darling?' Shauna asked him.

'Yes, of course, I'll be back in a moment.'

He walked to the Men's washroom and locked himself in a cubicle, taking one of the small paper wraps from his pocket; these days he was never without a supply. On his knee, he rested the mirror, the chopped up the lines and snorted them quickly, his hands shaking as he did so. But instead of the usual high, he felt his tight chest worsen, along with the pain in his left arm. This time the tightness was worse, and it was a struggle to breathe. It took a great deal of effort to make his way out of the washroom and back to the table. As he approached, he could hear Eric saying, 'Apparently they're heading for divorce, it's the worst-kept secret in Tinseltown. She is sick of his controlling ways and that weird cult he's in thrall to. Trust me, she's gonna walk.'

Shauna looked towards Dan and stood up immediately, 'Darling, you're ill . . .'

Eric stood up quickly too, shouting for the waiter to call an ambulance, but by now the pain was radiating from Dan's chest across his entire body. He tried to reach out for Shauna but suddenly if felt as if she were a million miles away. Try as he might, he couldn't get to her.

The voices around him faded away. All Dan wanted was to speak to Shauna, to tell her he loved her and that he was sorry, but the only sound that came out of his mouth was a strangled gasp. He fell to the floor with Shauna beside him, tears streaming down her face, as her lips seemed to be saying, 'Don't leave me, Dan . . . don't go . . .'

Then everything around Dan went black and there were no more words, only silence.

Chapter 20

Beverly Hills, July 2000

Shauna O'Brien adjusted the neat pillbox hat on her head and pulled the net down over her face, praying it would blur her swollen, red-rimmed eyes. Even a make-up artist as gifted as Mel couldn't disguise the storm that had ravaged her face, leaving it dry and cracked, as if all her tears had sucked the very moisture from her skin. Was it really only a week since this nightmare had begun? With a shaking hand, she smoothed down the skirt of the Chanel suit, a little looser around the waist than when she'd worn it last.

Stiffening, she straightened and tugged at the neat, nipped-in-at-the-waist jacket. Her fingers shook as they closed over the heavy silk-satin fabric.

'You set to go?' Isaac's voice was gentle but businesslike. Today, she was grateful for his steadiness, his guidance and his admin assistant's near-perfect organizational skills. Lifting her chin, she nodded. Like him, she knew that the moment she stepped through that door the television crews and paparazzi clamouring at the gates of the funeral home would be straining to capture a glimpse of the grieving Shauna Jackson.

Without a word, she reached out and gently squeezed Issacs's arm as he pulled open the door, letting the Californian sunshine spill inside. She was aware of the sudden flurry as everyone moved forward, first the funeral director and his team, then Mel and Roxy flanking her on one side with Isaac on the other.

At the sight of the big black hearse waiting in front of the limousine and the formally attired undertaker holding the door open, all her hard-won composure almost crumbled. Nothing had prepared her for this. She slid into the car and stared straight ahead as the others climbed in on either side of her. Roxy laid a hand on her gloved hand and squeezed but didn't say anything as the car smoothly drew away.

As the gates opened, the paparazzi began snapping away, despite the heavily tinted windows. No one said a word in the car as it followed the stately hearse, the car sweeping down the hill and through the streets to join the four-lane highway of Santa Monica Boulevard, a sedate convoy among the flashy Bentley convertibles, behemoth Range Rovers, open-top Ferraris and Lamborghinis that cruised the street at this time of the day. Isaac had told her to expect the service to be packed to the rafters. People instinctively liked Dan. What wasn't to like? Good-looking, personable and always the first to support the underdog. He had a streak of kindness in him as wide as the Shannon River back home.

After a smooth left turn and then another, the car slowed and came to a halt outside the historic Church of the Good Shepherd. As she stepped out into to the mid-morning heat, Shauna stared at the cream stuccoed building with its twin four-tiered bell towers topped with golden domes that shimmered in the brilliant sunshine. A cloudless blue sky framed the pretty church, seeming merciless in its endless expanse. Shauna searched the sky, wishing there was just one cloud she could focus on so that she wouldn't have to acknowledge the oak coffin with its brass fittings glinting gaudily in the sunshine. One cloud to which she could anchor her imagination to take her away from this. She'd deliberately asked for the service to be held without mass. Her mother would have been horrified, but Shauna couldn't bear to prolong the agony of saying goodbye.

The cool interior of the church was already full as the solemn procession made its way inside. The priest greeted them and sprinkled holy water on the coffin. Just another day for him in a holy place that had seen many funerals, including those of Rudolf Valentino, Alfred Hitchcock, Frank Sinatra and Rita Hayworth, to name but a few. Heads began to turn as Shauna made her way to the pew at the front of the church. So many familiar faces. Brad and Jen, looking as chic and beautiful as ever in near-matching tailored suits. A few rows in front were Harrison Ford and his wife Melissa, who both gave her sober, emotionless nods. Dan's family were waiting for her at the front, except his mother, too heartbroken and elderly to make the trip. Shauna tightened her lips as a burst of resentment bloomed in her chest. Her mother had said it was too short notice for her parents to fly to LA.

Horribly aware of all the gazes settling on her, she focused on the ornate marble altarpiece, her eyes occasionally straying to the coffin. Shauna wished for a moment that she had just an ounce of the faith that had shaped her mother. She would not think of Dan's body lying in there. Not think that he'd never give her that slow, easy smile again. That those warm brown eyes wouldn't twinkle at her over the tops of his Raybans when they shared a private joke. An involuntary sob shook her. She lifted her chin higher. She'd get through this and make Dan proud of her. Even though she had no idea what she was going to do without him. Her mouth crumpled and her lower lip shook as she desperately tried to reign back the emotion. Her tears for Dan were private, not for public consumption. She was an actress, for God's sake. Act, you fool, she told herself. But it was no good, the sobs hiccoughed their way into her throat no matter how hard she fought them, and tears brimmed and fell. Roxy's hand found its way into hers as she stared straight ahead.

The service seemed interminable and her knees, despite the homely handstitched hassock beneath them, ached. She managed to calm herself when Gary rose to give the eulogy. The tribute from the renowned cinematographer was everything that Dan deserved; Gary hailed him as 'one of the finest directors of our generation, who never forgot that every single person counts'.

At last, the coffin left the building and Shauna blotted her tears with Roxy's never-ending supply of tissues.

'You're doing brilliantly. Not too much longer,' Roxy told her.

'Shauna, darling. I'm so sorry for your loss. Dan was . . . was a wonderful man.'

Shauna blinked and gave Barbara Draven, anchorwoman on the local news show, a perfunctory nod.

'I hope you caught the obit we did,' Barbara simpered.

'I'm afraid I didn't.' Shauna was polite but she certainly wasn't going to apologize. Seeing Dan's coffin lowered into the ground had almost broken her, and she still had the wake to get through.

'Is she for real?' murmured Roxy into her ear as they drifted on into the Beverly Hills Hotel reception room where the mourners were gathered.

'Well, she's LA news real, anyway – only interested in the next story. Why are there so many media people here? Hollywood's not usually that interested in directors, even if he was brilliant and talented and wonderful.' She felt her control start to slip again.

'Because he was brilliant, talented and wonderful and married to you, one of Hollywood's hottest properties.'

Shauna had never forgotten that her lucky break had been meeting Dan and she'd never shied away from admitting that he had been her springboard into the industry. She was also aware that the story of how she got started certainly added to the romance of her and Dan's marriage and their reputation as a Hollywood power couple. But everything after that had come from hard work, determination and dedication. She couldn't believe it was over: their life, everything they had built up. Now she would never know what it was that had been eating away at Dan; all she knew was that the stress and anxiety it had caused him was part of the reason he was dead.

The autopsy had shown that Dan had cocaine in his system when he died. Shauna had been aware that he was a user – the late nights, the long shoots, the protracted editing process, the Hollywood lifestyle that demanded it. She'd rarely touched the stuff herself, preferring a stiff drink, but she should have done more to get Dan to stop. Something else to beat herself up about.

The hubbub of the room softened to a low murmur; mourners seemed to have spread out in a circle around her, an invisible barrier between Shauna and the mourners that no one wanted to cross. She had never felt so alone in her life and thought she overheard someone say, 'Poor woman, always the last to know . . .'

To know about what?

'Shauna?' She jumped at the tap on her arm. It was Isaac. 'You OK?'

'Bearing up,' she said, looking with longing towards the open doors. 'People are saying lovely things about Dan. I knew he was wonderful. I forget that other people did too.'

'Yeah . . . he was a regular saint.' Isaac stared off into the distance, his grey eyes stony before he turned to face her and patted her on the arm. 'You eaten today?'

Shauna raised an eyebrow, her mouth turning downwards. 'What do you think?'

'I think, although don't quote me on it, there's such a thing, even in Tinsel Town, as too skinny.' He waggled a grey bushy eyebrow. 'Don't forget I've got to protect my asset. You need to eat.'

'Thanks, Isaac.' She knew his gruff tone hid how much he genuinely cared. 'I don't think I can.' But she knew she ought to; she didn't want anyone realizing that grief was making her a little crazy.

'You can, kid. Dan wouldn't want you wasting away.'

'Low blow, Isaac,' she muttered, linking an arm through his.

'Hey, I'm a businessman. Remember?' He winked and steered her away from the doors.

She did her best, nibbling at a couple of hors d'oeuvres, but the smell of the caviar dotting the dainty vol au vents turned her stomach and the delicate crustless triangle sandwiches tasted of sand in her mouth. Shauna would happily see every crumb on her plate go into the trash. As soon as Isaac's attention was diverted elsewhere, she abandoned the plate and slipped to the next, much quieter room where she was able to step out into the courtyard.

Outside, she inhaled a lungful of the warm air and drifted unnoticed into the shade of a fragrant honeysuckle climbing its way up one of the slender columns of the small cloister area. Screened from view by the column, she watched a young boy darting about the garden, playing with a small car. She envied his absorption in his game, oblivious to the heavy emotion weighing down the adults around him.

Out of the corner of her eye she saw Isaac emerging from the building. Wanting a little more time on her own, she drew back further into the shadows. Isaac was with a young woman, or rather she was with him, because he had a strong grip on her arm and was almost dragging her through the doors.

Shauna was startled by this; she'd never seen Isaac so angry. She was about to step out from her hiding place to intervene, but then she saw the woman's face. Though she didn't recognize her, from the feline, calculating look in the woman's eye, she wasn't sure she wanted to.

'What the hell are you playing at?' Isaac hissed, and Shauna winced at the tone of his voice. Isaac rarely lost his temper. That was one of the things she liked about him: he was even-tempered and impervious to the histrionics of the industry. 'You shouldn't be here.'

'Shouldn't be here? You're kidding me, right?' The dark-haired woman's voice rose. Her accent matched her Latin-American appearance.

'Keep your damn voice down. And show some respect.' Isaac shook the woman's arm.

Shauna peered through the foliage and saw that the woman's face was screwed up in anger as she and Isaac exchanged agitated whispers. What was all this about? Who was this woman and what was she doing here?

The little boy cannoned into one of the wrought-iron tables in the garden, sending a chair spinning into Shauna's corner. She caught it easily before it rammed into her legs, then looked to make sure he was unhurt. Big brown eyes, shimmering with alarm, looked up into hers as his face began to crumple at the sound of the crash. She smiled down at him. 'It's O—' For a moment, her legs threatened to buckle beneath her, and she had to grab the nearby pillar. 'Dan,' she breathed, confused and suddenly breathless, her heart racing with a charge of adrenaline. The floor shifted and she felt lightheaded and dizzy.

The boy's bottom lip quivered as he stared up at her, hovering between tears and curiosity. She stared at him, shaking her head. Grief made ghosts of real people, she realized. Her mind was playing tricks on her. She'd barely slept in the last seventy-two hours.

'No harm done,' she reassured him, reaching out a hand to his shoulder to reinforce her words.

With a fierce shove her hand was pushed away.

'Don't you touch him.'

'I wasn't . . .' Shauna reared back in surprise, her legs still shaky, her pulse racing. She felt as if she'd lost touch with reality.

'Alex.' The woman grabbed the child possessively and held him in front of her like a shield, her eyes narrowing as she stared at Shauna.

Shauna stared back, taking in the attractive features of the woman. There were dark shadows under her eyes which were almost black in colour, she was extremely beautiful.

Isaac came over. 'Frankie, you need to . . . I can—'

'Need to leave. Oh, you'd love that, wouldn't you? Duck

outta here with my tail between my legs. It ain't gonna happen, old man. I need the bucks to raise my son. What's due to him.' Her voice rose, and Shauna could see a fierce pride behind her hostile demeanour.

Shauna frowned, her eyes drawn back to the boy and those oh-so-familiar eyes. He was the spitting image of Dan. A relative? The boy was only about three or four years old.

Shauna looked at the woman again and felt her heart sink to her feet as the penny dropped.

Over Isaac's shoulder, people were gathering at the French windows, peering into the courtyard and whispering to one another. Shauna realized then that there was more than one way to break a heart as she felt hers crack in two. Betrayed by a husband on the same day as she buried him.

There was a look of triumph on the woman's face, her face calm as a storm raged inside Shauna's mind. There was no denying it, Shauna understood exactly who the boy was now.

PART THREE

Chapter 21

Ithos, June 2002

From his vantage point sitting at a table under the blue-and-white awning of Níko's taverna, Demetrios watched the girl on the harbour wall as she packed and unpacked her backpack repeatedly. It was obvious that she had lost something important, and there was something about her predicament and the fact that she looked to be about the same age as his daughter made him want to come to her assistance. He resisted the impulse, telling himself it was no business of his and she might not welcome an offer of help from a middle-aged man. Though he was sure he didn't look like a Lothario in his navy chinos, espadrilles and an open-neck linen shirt, he was conscious that his thick dark hair was streaked with little strands of grey. No, Ithos was known for its hospitality, he reasoned, and if this young woman was in need of help then the locals would come to her aid. Besides, he didn't need any more complications today.

He returned to his newspaper and sipped at the strong, sweet Greek coffee. Despite the early hour, around him, Ithos harbour was a bustling scene. In the main square, traders were setting up their market stalls, arranging baskets piled high with fat tomatoes and olives, rows of purple aubergines and courgettes, ripe plums and nectarines.

Though he made every effort to focus on the news of the day, Demetrios's eyes kept returning to the girl. Perhaps it was that she reminded him of his daughter, Ariana. She could almost be Greek, with her light tan and her dark hair tumbling around her shoulders, but something told him she wasn't. Most likely she was one of the European backpackers who came in on the tourist ferry; she had that unmistakable air of the curious stranger that set her apart from Greek visitors.

Ariana . . . He frowned. His quick-tempered, temperamental, excitable and exhausting daughter had arrived back home on the island like a hurricane, and now they were all swept up in her turbulence. She was like her mother in many ways . . .

He was shaken from this thought as he noticed the girl had moved from her spot and was now sitting down at the table next to his.

Blue-and-white checked tablecloths covered each table and the taverna was shaded by a vine-covered pergola. Teresa, the owner's wife, approached the girl's table and asked her in English, 'What would you like?'

'How much is a Coca-Cola?' the girl replied, pulling out a meagre handful of coins from her pocket, counting them carefully.

'Two euros.'

'Oh . . .' The girl looked crestfallen.

Out of the corner of his eye, Demetrios saw Teresa cock her head sympathetically.

'That's OK, there is enough.' Teresa was in her early sixties, long grey hair braided in a thick plait hanging to her waist.

Demetrios knew she was a hard-headed businesswoman who kept her extroverted and not always wise husband, Níko, in check, but she had a heart of gold. She gave the girl a kind smile, nodded her head and bustled off inside.

It seemed that this unexpected kindness shook the young woman's composure. Tears began to splash down her cheeks and she swiped at them ineffectually, unable to stop a sob escaping her. Enough was enough, he decided, and moved across to sit next to her. When the girl looked up, he offered her a napkin, which she took and blew her nose with.

His hazel and gold-flecked eyes regarded her silently while she blew her nose loudly and tried to compose herself. She pulled a scrunchy out of her pocket, shook her mane of thick black hair and pulled it back into the hair band.

'I'm sorry,' she said, 'I hate crying.'

'There is nothing wrong with tears,' he said, giving her time to recover. He was in no hurry.

Teresa brought over a long, cool glass of Coke for the young woman, and a short tumbler of ouzo for Demetrios.

'*Yiamas.*' He lifted his glass in toast.

'Thank you.' She gulped quickly at the Coca-Cola.

He nodded but didn't press her to speak, feeling sure she would do so in her own time. Instead he watched the busy waterfront, where the day-trippers who'd disembarked from the first ferry of the day along with the girl were happily taking photos of everything in sight.

'Feeling better?'

'A little. I'm sorry, you must think I'm a right wet blanket.'

It was a long time since he had heard someone use that term and it made him want to smile, but he suppressed it. 'Ready to tell me what happened?'

'The usual stupid mistake: I fell asleep on the boat and someone stole my money and my passport. Now I'm stuck.'

'And here I was thinking that you were about to tell me your story of betrayal and a broken heart.'

She gave him a weak smile. 'Nothing that exciting, I'm afraid.'

'How disappointing. I'm sure it would have been a very romantic and dramatic account, and we could have shed tears together.'

The girl laughed despite herself and Demetrios saw the way her face lit up, lending her a beauty he was sure she was not aware of.

'It is quite dramatic, being robbed,' she told him.

'Yes, I agree. But it is good news, in a sense, because we can help you. A broken heart? Maybe we would not have been so helpful, no?'

'True. But I'm not sure there's a consulate here, so I'd have to go all the way back to Crete.' He saw the girl's lip wobble, and she bit down quickly on it to make it stop, 'They took all my money, I'll have to go home . . .'

'I have a few connections here,' he told her, hoping he didn't sound as if he were boasting. 'If you trust me to make a few phone calls, then I may be able to help. What is your name?'

'Grace Taylor.'

He called Teresa over and told her what had happened. She gave a shocked cry then immediately began to make a fuss of Grace.

'Please, I'd like to call my parents, if possible.'

Teresa nodded and took her inside to use the payphone, giving the girl a handful of coins from the till.

Meanwhile, Demetrios took his Nokia out of his pocket and made a few calls. Moments later, the police arrived. Demetrios sat by and listened while she told her story. The taverna began to fill up with locals, intrigued by the police

208

presence and wanting to know what all the fuss was about. Unfazed, the girl patiently repeated her story. Observing her poise and cool-headedness, Demetrios couldn't help but be impressed.

Eventually, the police went away and the crowd dispersed, and Demetrios came to sit with her again. 'Did you speak with your father?' he asked.

'Yes, he's offered to wire me some money.'

Demetrios nodded. 'A good man.'

'He's definitely that. I think he wants me to come home, though.'

'And do you want to go home?' he asked her.

'No, not at all. I've been looking forward to this trip forever, it would be awful to have to turn around and go home when I've only just got here.'

He clapped his hands in a gesture of finality. 'Then Ithos will take you to its heart and keep you until everything is well. But first you must eat.'

Without asking, he called for Teresa, who hurried over from the other table she was serving. Demetrios spoke to her in Greek, then she hurried off and returned a few moments later with a Greek breakfast: olives, cheese, eggs, cold cuts, yogurt with a fruit compote, and a basket of fresh bread rolls.

'Please, eat,' he insisted, and after a polite, but brief hesitation, the girl fell on the food like a starving person, tucking into the delicious fare and trying not to speak with her mouth full as he gently questioned her.

'Where are you from, Grace Taylor?'

'England. A town just outside Manchester – it's so small, you'll never have heard of it. Who are you?'

Demetrios laughed.

'Sorry, I didn't mean to be rude.' She shovelled another mouthful of the delicious bread and cheese into her mouth, her troubles briefly forgotten. 'You look less serious when you laugh, and your eyes crinkle up nicely.'

'My name is Demetrios Theodosis, and my family have lived on this island for many generations. Perhaps always.' Demetrios grinned. 'I'm in shipping, hence those many lines you describe kindly as crinkles, and Teresa here is the wife of Níko, owner of this taverna. Níko is a cousin of my father and one of my oldest friends; the two of us are like brothers.'

Teresa had been following their conversation as she waited on the other tables. Her eyes sparkled as Demetrios beckoned her over, and the two started speaking rapidly in Greek.

She peered over Demetrios's shoulder and studied Grace, as if assessing her. 'Are you looking for work?'

Grace hesitated for a moment, then nodded. 'Yes.'

'Have you waitressed before?'

'Yes.'

'Can you start this evening?'

'Er . . .' Grace looked at Demetrios.

'Let me explain,' he said. 'You need money and somewhere to stay?'

Grace nodded.

'Teresa and her husband Níko need a waitress – their last one has run off to get married, so they are a pair of hands short.'

'But I don't have anywhere to stay, and no money—'

Demetrios held his finger up to stop her talking. 'They have a room above the taverna that you can stay in. They will pay you a week in advance, which I will act as guarantor for, in case you do a moonlight flit, which I don't think you will.'

Grace shook her head fervently. 'Of course not, but I couldn't possibly let you—'

'I insist. The sea has delivered you to Ithos, and Ithos must provide. You have a job and a room, Teresa has the help she needs. Everyone is happy, no?'

'What about my passport?' the girl asked.

'You gave the police your details, yes?' She nodded. 'Then leave it with me,' he said, standing to leave. He leaned down and kissed her lightly on both cheeks in the Greek fashion, leaving a hint of citrus and sandalwood in his wake.

The girl blinked, not quite believing what had just happened, but Teresa didn't give her time to think. 'Come, let me show you to your room.' Grace grabbed her backpack and Demetrios smiled as he looked over his shoulder and saw her running to keep up with the departing Teresa.

Ariana ran a brush through her long thick hair, her amber eyes looking back at her angrily from the mirror. Her father was so infuriating – why would he never listen to her or care about what she wanted in life? She was furious with him.

We have provided you with the best education in the world and this is how you repay your parents? he had berated her.

Ariana slammed the brush down. What would he know about what was best? Neither of her parents could wait to be rid of her, bundling her off to an English public school when she was thirteen. Best education, indeed! They had done what suited them, not her.

'You only sent me to Marlborough because you wanted to get on with your own lives without me in the way,' she had shouted at him.

'You asked us to send you there. I wanted you to stay in Athens!' he had yelled back at her.

Ariana huffed, picking up the brush once more, dragging it through her hair vigorously. One hundred brushes a day, that was what Yaya – her grandmother – had told her to do to keep her hair beautiful and silky. So what if she had asked to go to an English public school, she huffed to herself, suppressing the memory of the way she'd badgered and nagged at them for months about it.

For the first few terms, it had been fun. She'd found it a relief to be away from her parents, who could never be together without arguing, so they spent most of their time in different parts of the world. Her mother had immediately moved to London to be nearer to her, but whenever she went to visit her at her Chelsea townhouse, Sofia was usually preoccupied with one of her lovers or lunching with friends at Harvey Nichols or Cipriani's.

It hadn't taken long for Ariana to become bored with the school. Most of the English girls were alike, they all had long blonde hair and fathers who were investment bankers or peers who spent their days in the House of Lords. There were a few exceptions, girls like her who didn't want to marry a prince. Her best friend Maddy, or the Honourable Lady Madeleine Dorchester, was one of them. They'd discovered they were kindred spirits – Ariana doubted there was anyone else at the school who knew how to catch tuna with a line, or could free-dive up to fifty feet. As the second daughter of a English Lord, Maddy had been raised in a ramshackle stately home in Derbyshire by a succession of nannies until she was bundled off to public school when she was nine. By the time she arrived at Marlborough, she was already a wild child. Ariana quickly became her willing disciple. Eventually, they were both caught smoking weed, and while Ariana had taken the punishment of a suspension and the loss of all her privileges with a shrug, Maddy had gone completely off the rails. Still only sixteen years old, she ran off with a musician. Rumour had it her parents eventually tracked her down to a squat in Camden Town, where she was living in squalor and hooked on hard drugs. Ariana had never heard from her again.

For Ariana, her father's disappointment at her suspension had been the worst part. She'd tried to be a dutiful daughter after that and to focus on her studies, but it was so boring. Now he wanted her to go to a good university, but all she wanted to do was stay on Ithos. She had everything she needed here. Her old friends down in the harbour town, her grandmother who let her do exactly as she pleased, and her father – who she loved, but who didn't understand her . . . OK, so she missed the shops of London and Paris and New York, but how many clothes did a girl need?

Of course, the one thing that Ithos really had in its favour was Christian, Níko and Teresa's son. Ariana smiled dreamily at the thought of his blue eyes and hair the colour of golden sand. His sister was already married with two children, but Christian was still a bachelor. All he needed was a push in the right direction, she figured. Her father treated Christian like the son he'd never had, so he was bound to want him as a son-in-law, wasn't he? She imagined herself on her wedding day – the hundreds of guests, the tradition of wearing stefana crowns, the dancing afterwards . . . For a moment her anger at her father was forgotten as she imagined him walking in the bridal procession alongside her, his face full of pride as she shone with radiance in her beautiful dress.

The thought cheered her up and Ariana smiled to herself. She'd get her grandmother to plait her hair for her and then she would go down and see Christian. It was well into the afternoon and, if she was lucky, Christian would be back at the harbour after working with her father at the boathouse on the other side of the island.

Ariana padded over to her walk-in wardrobe. When her mother and father were first married, her mother had insisted on a complete remodelling of the Theodosis villa if she were to live there. A new wing had duly been added. It was modern compared to the rest of the villa, which was still occupied by her grandmother. Ariana's bedroom was more like an apartment, with a large en-suite bathroom, and a balcony that looked out over Ithos Bay and the harbour.

She eyed the long row of clothes, the Guccis, Alexander McQueens and Balenciagas all catalogued and arranged by colour. She tilted her head to the side; today she would be casual yet eye-catching, an outfit that showed a little of her taut and toned body, but not too much – just enough. Her eyes settled on a pink and cream boho-style beach dress, that criss-crossed over her bust and had a slit up the side to show off her legs. She might be nearly ten years younger than Christian, but this would grab his attention.

She slipped out of her strappy vest and shorts and caught sight of her naked body in the large full-length mirror, feeling pleased with what she saw. Her olive skin was now tanned and golden again after being hidden away in England all winter.

Yes, there was no way Christian would be able to ignore her today. He might have thought of her as a child before, but she was eighteen now and he was about to see just how much she had grown up.

Chapter 22

'Come on, a touch more mascara.'

Shauna groaned and laughed. 'It's a good job I like you, Mel.'

'You have to,' said Mel, in her nasal New York accent with her usual sassy belligerence. She was as much a friend as co-worker. 'I'm here to make you look good and if you piss me off . . .' She raised her dark, finely plucked eyebrows in mock threat.

'I'll be on my best behaviour,' Shauna promised.

It felt strange to look in the mirror and see Grace Kelly again, though she'd grown used to it during the months of filming at Pinewood Studios near London and on location in Europe. She had loved seeing herself transformed into her idol each day, mastering her voice and her mannerisms. There had been only one occasion when she faltered: the day they arrived at the Grimaldi palace. The place had barely changed since her first visit, and memories of that night in the summer of 1982, when a young Shauna O'Brien was presented to Princess Grace of Monaco, came flooding back. Chantelle's parting words had echoed in her mind: *One day,*

the pain will be gone, and you will have these precious memories.
The memories were as vivid as ever, but she wasn't sure the pain had gone. Shauna had pushed the memories away and focused only her work.

It had been her first time working with Spielberg and she was impressed by his technique, his ability to get what he wanted – all the actors got on well and Spielberg had taken such good care of her. Although it was draining being in every scene, Shauna rose above it to give the performance of a lifetime. Spielberg had put his heart and soul into the film, and she had done the same.

For the Love of Grace was still in post-production, with the release date still to be fixed, yet already there were whispers of Oscar nominations. The publicity machine wanted to exploit the rumours to full advantage, so today she was recreating the moment in 1955 when Grace had won her Best Actress Oscar.

Mel stood back and admired her work. 'There, that'll do, Grace. I'd better win an Oscar for this too.'

Shauna studied herself in the mirror and the soft gold of her hair swept up into a sophisticated chignon that emphasized her features. Mel had brought an elegance to her today which fitted the occasion. 'I'm more than ten years older than Grace was when she retired from acting.'

'The camera never lies,' Mel told her.

There was a sharp rap at the door. 'Ten minutes.'

'That's my cue.' Shauna rose and pulled off the light silk dressing gown protecting her costume. It was as breathtaking as the original and for a moment she wondered what Princess Grace might have said to her if she were here. She took another look in the mirror at the faithful replica of the dress Grace Kelly had worn to the Oscars: a figure-hugging mint-green satin sheath with elegant spaghetti straps.

Outside, the photographer, Kevin, and his lighting assistant were waiting.

'Hey, Shauna,' Kevin threw down his clipboard and began to clap, 'you look amazing.'

She inclined her head, still in her Grace persona, and smiled. 'That mine?' she asked, and picked up the replica gold Oscar being watched over by the young assistant. She turned around to face the camera and held it in the same pose as her idol had done forty-seven years previously. Then she let out a girlish laugh, herself once more.

'I hear on the grapevine that you nailed it,' Kevin said.

'It went well,' said Shauna, with a quiet smile of real satisfaction.

'Ever the understatement. Rumour is, that production is *hot*.'

Shauna had heard it all before and although quietly confident in her performance, she knew anything could happen. Politics in Hollywood played a huge part in who won and who didn't, which films the Academy took to their hearts and which they hated. It didn't pay to make bets.

'I can't think that far ahead.'

He laughed. 'Isaac can. By the way, he called a couple of times. Says he really needs to speak to you.'

'He always says that.' Shauna shook her head and leaned back in her chair 'Right, let's get to work.'

After Dan's death, Shauna had sold the big house in Malibu and downsized to something a little less ostentatious. It was a much smaller, classic Art Deco home in West Hollywood. Shauna loved its classic design and the vintage features; it was the perfect setting for her antique collection. Somehow the place had immediately felt like home, the intimate size more suited to her than the house in Malibu, especially now that she was living alone. As she closed the heavy oak door behind her, she paused for a moment to savour the calm ambience of the house. This was her sanctuary now; though she'd hung on to the apartment, she hadn't used it in months, perhaps because she no longer needed a bolthole to escape to. Maybe it was time to let it go.

So much had changed since Dan died. She was still feeling her way, trying to come to terms with it all. Overnight she had gone from being a wife to a widow, and though almost two years had passed, she found it a struggle to recognize herself in that role. She was no longer sure who Shauna Jackson was. As for Shauna O'Brien, she was so far removed from her old self, all that remained were a collection of faded memories.

She'd had little contact with her mother since her father died. While he was alive, Shauna had made the effort to play happy families, keep up the pretence. Now they only called one another on birthdays and Christmas, and even then the conversation was stilted. Shauna was convinced her mother felt the same way she did: they were too tired of each other to keep trying.

Shauna kicked off her shoes, poured herself a drink and took it outside, debating whether to take a dip in the heart-shaped pool to unwind. In the end she decided to postpone her swim until later. There was admin to catch up on, and she needed to return Isaac's calls – judging by the last message he'd left, he was on the brink of apoplexy. He wanted a decision on the two scripts that were currently sitting on the desk in her office, and would no doubt have another try at getting her to write her memoirs – a couple of international publishers had expressed an interest.

'About damn time, too,' he barked when his secretary put her through. His crotchety tone amused her; he liked to forget that he actually worked for her and not the other way around.

'I haven't decided on either of the scripts – I'll be honest, they aren't giving me that tingle. When do you need to know?'

'Yeah, yeah, maybe you're right.' There was an uncharacteristic pause at the other end.

'What's up, Isaac?'

'Look, you're not going to like this . . .'

'Isaac, not that again. I told you, the lawyers took care of it all. I have no intention of speaking to her.'

'Just hear me out—'

'No, I don't want to talk about that woman again.' Shauna felt her voice rising in anger; why did he have to keep raking this up? It was done.

'Shauna, listen . . . Frankie Ferreira is sick. Real sick.'

'I'm still not going to see her. Please, Isaac, this is my final word. I don't want anything to do with her.'

'The woman's dying, Shauna. She's called, collect, five times in two days. She's desperate to speak to you.'

'How do you know she's telling the truth?'

'I called the clinic, spoke to her physician, Dr Scott, he didn't pull any punches. It's cancer – terminal.'

Despite herself, Shauna felt a jolt of shock. Frankie was a young woman, with a child. Whatever the woman had done, there was no denying how cruel a prognosis that was.

'Did she say what she wanted to speak to me about?'

'She said it wasn't money.' Isaac cleared his throat. 'She . . . she said she wants to talk to you about the child.'

Shauna closed her eyes. She'd done her duty in that regard. The child was provided for. Generously so. What more could the woman want? 'I'll have to think about it, Isaac. I can't promise anything . . .'

* * *

Shauna sat in the hospital corridor sipping the dark liquid masquerading as coffee and feeling incongruously out of place with her immaculate make-up. A couple of the nursing staff shot her curious glances as they squeaked past in their sensible shoes on the glossy rubberised floor. She had spent a few sleepless nights since Isaac's phone call, her slumber troubled by dreams of Dan trying to reach out to her, jumbled with the cries of a child just out of reach that stayed with her when she awoke, drenched in sweat, and left with a profound sense of loneliness that she couldn't shake. Torn by indecision and an unwanted feeling of responsibility, she called Isaac in the middle of the night and demanded the name of the hospital where Frankie was a patient.

And now here she was. She'd been waiting over an hour, buried in melancholic thoughts, when a doctor came to speak to her.

'I'm afraid it is not good news. Miss Ferreira is very unwell.'

'Can you tell me what's wrong with her?'

'She has a very aggressive type of breast cancer. It was very advanced before she sought treatment; we tried chemotherapy, but there is little more we can do for her.' His staff ID said his name was Dr David Scott. His kind, grey eyes bored into her and she understood the unspoken message. 'Are you a friend?'

Shauna couldn't bring herself to say yes. 'Um, we have a friend in common. What about her family?' she asked.

'Her sister was here earlier with Frankie's son, they come every day. Would you like to go in? She is tired but awake.'

The doctor was already moving towards the door, taking her silence as acquiescence. She swallowed in trepidation, but her feet seemed to be doing the thinking for her and she followed him into the room.

Frankie lay propped on pillows, a small, almost childlike, figure. Beside the bed was a drip stand, the line leading into a cannula in her thin arm. Her bedside was decorated with a child's drawings. Propped up by the bed was a toy llama, which lent the scene a little joy and normality.

Frankie's eyes were closed and in one of her hands she loosely held a rosary.

'She's on morphine for the pain most of the time, but she asked us to hold back on it when we told her you were here.' He spoke in a low voice. 'If you need a nurse, there's a call button above the bed. We're trying to make her as comfortable as possible.'

'I can hear you, David.' Frankie's voice, though rasping, had power, and Shauna saw the woman open her eyes. Despite her frailty, she was alert.

'I don't doubt that for a minute, Frankie.' He turned to Shauna. 'Don't stay too long.'

A small smile flitted across Frankie's face, and the doctor touched Frankie's hand before he left the room. Shauna could see that the doctor liked Frankie a great deal. Had Dan cared about this woman, too? She knew very little about their affair, hadn't wanted to know, but now she was filled with curiosity. Had Dan loved her? Had he seen his son? She'd asked her lawyers to make a fair monthly settlement to be paid until the boy was eighteen, but once that was done, she'd tried to put him out of her mind.

The woman's eyes darted towards her with a suddenness that made Shauna start. As they stared at each other, the woman twisted and tried to sit up.

'No, stay there,' said Shauna, realizing that she needed to conserve what little energy she had left.

'I'm glad you came.'

'Isaac told me about . . .' Shauna didn't know how to continue the sentence.

'I'll save you the trouble, I'm dying.'

I know,' Shauna said softly.

'I don't care for me. It's Alex.' Frankie turned her dark expressive eyes on Shauna; fierce and intelligent, they seemed to burn from her face, gaunt, but still beautiful. 'He's with my sister—' Frankie shut her eyes, gripped by a spasm of pain.

'Do you want me to call a nurse?' asked Shauna, her finger reaching for the call button.

'No, don't. They'll just give me more morphine and then I can't talk . . . and I need to talk to you about Alex's future.' Shauna opened her mouth to speak, but Frankie cut her off: 'It's not about money. It's about what will happen to him when I'm gone.'

For the first time, Shauna saw fear in Frankie's eyes; fear for herself, but also for her boy. 'I'm sure your sister will—'

'Isabelle is in remission. The same cancer as I have, but hers was caught earlier. The only reason she's alive is because I blackmailed your old man to pay for the treatment.'

Shauna was stunned at this revelation but tried not to show it. 'Dan would have given you the money if he'd known what it was for.'

'I know that now . . .' Beads of sweat formed on her forehead and her jaw clenched as another wave of pain hit her. Once it had passed, she was seized by a new urgency, as if she had to get the words out while she still could: 'Look, Shauna, my sister loves Alex, but this cancer, it's a bitch. It killed my mother, it's gonna kill me. If anything happens to Isabelle, Alex has no one. He doesn't deserve that. He's a good boy, despite having me for a mother, and you saw how cute he is – just like his father, no?'

Shauna recalled the day of the funeral, how unnerved she'd been by the child's resemblance to Dan.

'I want you to take him. You can give him a better life, opportunities, connections.'

Shauna shook her head, panic rising in her. 'I can't.'

'Please . . . you have to.' Frankie reached out and clutched Shauna's hand with surprising strength. 'I want Alex to be safe. I don't want him to wind up in a street gang like my brothers.' Frankie grimaced again. 'Dan . . . he said you were kind. Good.'

Shauna knew that if Dan were here, he would have said yes in a heartbeat. Dan hadn't left a will, dying before his time, but she knew that he would want her to take the boy and love him as her own. Yet still she hesitated. Her heart went out to the child; losing his mother at such a young age would be a terrible blow and, however conflicted her feelings about Frankie, she couldn't stand the thought of him suffering. But would it really ease that suffering if he came to live with her rather than staying with his aunt? Yes, Shauna could give him all the material things, the opportunities and connections Frankie wanted him to have, but she was a stranger to him. If his aunt loved him and he loved her, surely it would be in the boy's best interest to stay where he was?

Frankie sucked in a laboured breath, her eyes losing focus. 'I know what you think of me, but I can tell you that Dan loved you. And I really wanted some of that. It was why I tried to ruin him. I'm sorry for that now. I can see a lot of Dan in Alex – he's got his dad's genes, thank God.'

Shauna could see that, despite the pain and exhaustion, Frankie would go on pleading with her until she agreed, but she didn't want to make empty promises just to placate her. Choosing her words carefully, she took Frankie's hand and said, 'OK, I will look after him. But first he needs to get to know me, to learn to trust me. I'll leave my phone number with you so you can get Isabelle to call me and we can talk about things.'

'Promise me.' Frankie didn't let go of Shauna.

'I'll work with Isabelle and together we will do what's best for him. Alex is going to need her in his life. Does he have any other family?'

Frankie shook her head. 'Just Isabelle. If anything happens to her, he will have no one.'

'He will have me.' Shauna held Frankie's gaze. 'I promise you.'

Her sincerity seemed to satisfy the woman, because she let go of her hand and closed her eyes.

Chapter 23

It had been well over a year since Roxy and Shauna had seen each other. Shauna had hoped to spend time with Roxy while she was in Europe filming *For the Love of Grace*, but her friend's new clothing line had taken off in a big way and she'd seized the chance to consolidate her success in Milan and Paris by opening a flagship store on Melrose Avenue in Los Angeles, so once again they'd found themselves on different continents. Even when filming wrapped and Shauna returned to the States, their busy schedules kept them apart. With ROX clothing now being worn by A-listers in all the fashionable places, Roxy needed to put in an appearance at every fashion week on the planet: at London Fashion Week, she was seated next to Anna Wintour, who was wearing a ROX drop-waisted silhouette dress. In Paris she was photographed with Kate Moss. At the launch of the New York store, Sarah Jessica Parker made an appearance in a jaw-dropping black ruffled swan dress that made the pages of hundreds of women's magazines around the globe.

Shauna was excited to be back in LA once more; they were breakfasting in the Fountain Room at the Beverly Hills Hotel, Roxy's favourite hangout. Shauna had ordered an egg-white omelette with spinach, while Roxy had ordered the buttermilk pancakes.

'I can't believe you can still eat those! I can't even look at one of them now! I might as well smear them on my hips, that's where they are going.'

'Nonsense! Women should enjoy their food. I'm sick of all these size zero LA women. I'd rather dress a good old size-fourteen Liverpudlian lass any day of the week.'

'I daren't put another pound on, we still have publicity to do for the Grace movie. The camera never lies.'

'Rubbish! You're going to look incredible, and that is what Spanx are for, isn't it?'

'I've never mastered the art of wearing Spanx, I usually end up with them stuck around my knees, unable to move!'

'Anyway, what's happening with the publishing house, how much are they offering for your "tell all" memoirs?'

'A million dollars for global rights.'

Roxy whistled. 'That's a lot of money. You going to take it?'

'I don't know. I'd like to tell my story, my way. That's assuming I'm going to do it.'

'What's holding you back?'

Shauna paused. 'The truth.'

Roxy nodded. They were silent for a moment, then Roxy said, 'If you really want to tell the truth, then you have to face up to the past.'

'What do you mean?'

'You know exactly what I mean. I know all about that box you keep hidden away, the one with all the letters and cards that you write but never send.'

'Roxy . . . I don't want to talk about this.'

Roxy put down her fork. 'Shauna, you never want to talk about this. Look, I haven't mentioned it before now, but I've been seeing a therapist.'

'Oh . . .' Shauna's eyes widened in surprise. 'Why didn't you tell me this before?'

'I'm telling you now.' Roxy frowned. 'For years, I've needed to get some things off my chest, stuff that's been buried for too long. About Thierry.'

Shauna suddenly felt stupid and self-centred. 'I'm sorry, Roxy, I should have asked about it more over the years, but I thought, well, I wanted to forget about everything, and I thought you did too.'

'I can't forget, *we* can't forget. Shauna, I've spent years waking up with night terrors. I've avoided forming relationships with men who are equals because I want to stay in charge all the time. That guy tried to steal my peace of mind. I want to claim it back.'

'Oh, Roxy.'

'Peace of mind doesn't come for the asking; we need to work hard for it. I want you to come away with me – we can look at it as a life cleanse. We've been talking about a trip for ages and I think you should go back to Ithos. This is the first time for years that I feel able to get away. The team will do a great job looking after the store here while I'm gone. I know I can leave ROX in good hands. The retail team say I only get in the way anyhow, and with Marco on the design side, I don't have anything to worry about.'

'Funny that he never made it back to Italy.' Shauna smiled. Marco, the young model that Roxy had introduced her to a couple of years previously was now one of her key employees.

Shauna looked at her watch. 'That reminds me, Isabelle

will be dropping Alex over at the house and then we're going to Universal Studios.'

'Alex will love that – how is he?'

'He's sensitive and intelligent. It's hard to know how much he understands, but he misses his mom, and he's frightened. Understandably, he's wary of me, and I don't know how to overcome that.'

When Shauna had arrived at Isabelle's apartment to collect him for his first sleepover, she was so nervous. She and Isabelle had agreed that they would do a few trial runs, and that sometimes Isabelle would stay over too. Isabelle was calm and kind, but wary of Shauna and she knew she would also have to win her trust. So many times she'd told herself she was doing the wrong thing – as had Isaac, who'd tried to talk her out of it, but a promise was a promise.

He stood in Isabelle's apartment, clutching his toy llama, the same one that Frankie had kept by the side of her hospital bed. 'Hello, Shauna.' He smiled and, to her surprise, he pointed to a newspaper cutting of a photo of her propped up on a rickety shelf clinging to the wall. Perhaps it was the way Dan's blue eyes stared up at her, guileless and innocent before frowning with sudden concentration, he was so quiet and so brave. 'Do you have a garden?' he asked her.

'Yes, I do,' Shauna said.

'Can we grow alfalfa sprouts? Alfie likes alfalfa.' He held his cuddly toy out to her and Shauna took it. 'Hello, Alfie.' She gave the toy a hug and then handed him back to Alex. 'We also have a pool. Can you swim?'

Alex looked up at Isabelle, who nodded at him encouragingly. 'I'm learning. I can swim with arm bands!'

'Have you packed them?'

Isabelle nodded. 'Then we can have a swim this afternoon. We're going to have so much fun, Alex,' Shauna had said.

She reached out her hand and he took it, then he turned and waved goodbye to Isabelle.

'See you in a couple of days, *pequeño*,' she said, and Alex gave her a little wave as they left the house.

'It's still tough, but we're taking it slow. He still has nightmares and calls out for Frankie in the night. I'm so glad he and Isabelle are so close. Alex is spending longer periods with me, and Isabelle's presence keeps him close to his mom.'

'How is Isabelle?'

'She's still in remission, thank God, but she's heartbroken about Frankie.'

The last month had been a roller coaster ride, but Shauna had devoted the time to building a relationship with him.

She'd taken a court injunction out to stop any reporting by the gutter press, and the whole experience had been an eye-opener for her. Alex was endlessly curious, and asked questions about every aspect of life – How did crickets make such a loud noise? Why were grasshoppers green? What made the sun rise every morning? He loved maple syrup on pancakes, *Barney and Friends* and she was growing to love him. Alex kept her excited about life and each day she loved him a little more. She had cleared her diary for the foreseeable future so a holiday was something she could contemplate. But wasn't it better to leave the past where it belonged?

Later that afternoon, Shauna had put Alex down for a nap in his new room. It was decorated with llama wallpaper and was already filling up with Transformer toys and merchandise from all of their daytrips. Alex loved amusements and rides and Shauna hadn't been to a fun fair since she was a child; they had both loved every minute and Shauna felt like a kid herself again. Despite her worries it had really thrilled her to see Alex so joyful and she tried not to spoil him, as she knew that Isabelle didn't approve, but Alex had never been spoiled before and it gave them both pleasure.

'We went on the *Back to the Future* ride, Tía!' Alex told Isabelle on the phone when they'd got home. Alex called Isabelle *Tía*, which was Spanish for auntie; that was fine with Shauna who had no interest in trying to erase Frankie's place in his heart, she only wanted to carve out her own.

As he napped, Shauna took a call from Isaac, putting her feet up on her large couch in her lounge which looked out over the lush garden and pool.

He was calling from his New York Office on Fifth Avenue. 'How's the boy enjoying himself?' he asked.

'He's happy and exhausted!' She laughed. 'I can't believe it's only been a few months since I've known him. I don't know how I'd live without him now.'

'Shauna, I'm scratching my head here. We've got a package delivered for you and I'm not sure what to do with it, so I've couriered it over, you'll get it this evening.'

That wasn't strange in itself – as a top agent, Isaac got plenty of mail for his clients, usually fan letters or scripts from aspiring writers hoping to be discovered; sometimes it was weird and unwanted post, like love letters written in blood, sometimes it was a request that Shauna was happy to grant, like a signed photo.

'What is it?'

'It's a book of poetry and a letter. The covering note says that we should give it to you personally and that it is from an old friend.'

They finished the call and Shauna was intrigued: who

would be sending her poetry? Maybe it was related to a film part, but Isaac would have known that . . . She wracked her brains to think: could it be an old friend from university, or an old school chum from Ireland?

A short while later, there was knock at the door and Shauna took the parcel handed to her by a UPS delivery man, tipping him ten dollars.

She sat with the parcel on the comfortable leather chesterfield by the window and turned the package around in her hands. It was an ordinary Jiffy bag but when she looked at the postmark her heartbeat fluttered as she saw it was from Greece. Part of her wanted to stop right there and throw it into the trashcan and never find out what was inside, but there was another part of her, the Shauna O'Brien part, who had left something of herself in that beautiful country two decades previously and was itching to see what was inside.

Slowly, she opened the package and took out a book. There was a covering note which read:

Many years ago, I had the privilege of making the acquaintance of Shauna Jackson when she was known as Shauna O'Brien, I would be grateful if you could pass this to her with my kind remembrance.
  Regards,
  Demetrios Theodosis

Shauna felt the heat rise to her face. Even after all this time, he could still blindside her. She read the title, *The Lyric Poetry of Sappho*; it was a very old edition, bound in red leather. Inside the book, a page was marked with a sealed letter. She looked at the page and the sonnet, 'Lilies'.

O lover, with your skin so white
The purest alabaster
Delicate as the whitest lily that
Only opens its petals at night

The recall was instant, and Shauna was taken back to that day when Demetrios had made love to her and they'd spent their first night together on the *St Helena*.

She tore open the letter.

Dear Shauna,

For many years I have thought of you and that summer we spent together. Fortune has thrown many arrows in our direction. In one letter it is not possible for me to express all the things that are in my heart, but I would like the chance to try. You will not find me the same man as you knew then, but one thing has never changed, and that is the high regard in which I hold you.

I have never forgotten those precious weeks we spent together and every day I deeply regret not trying harder to find you. Should you ever wish to visit our magical island again, it would give me great joy to see you once more. I have so much I want to say to you.

As ever, I am at your disposal.

Yours

Shauna traced the lines of his signature, recognizing it still after two decades: the lowercase D rather than an upper-case one, the characteristic curve of the d looped around.

There was something about the letter that seemed inevitable to her now. She had worked so hard to forget, to erase all the traces of the love she had felt. Dan's love had done much to gently smooth away her anger and sadness, but it was still there, like Roxy had said, locked in that secret place, hidden from everyone, even Dan. Why had she never told him?

Taking Alex into her life had shown her that secrets will always find their way out. Roxy was right, it was time for her to face up to her past. Demetrios wasn't the only one who needed to explain himself. She owed him an explanation too . . .

Chapter 24

Ariana watched as her grandmother chopped up the pistachios and walnuts, preparing them for her traditional baklava, which everyone in the household loved. Tonight was Níko's birthday and it was always a cause for celebration at the taverna. Níko loved to entertain and no one threw a party like he did.

Her grandmother was still a striking woman, but with the death of her husband, Ariana's beloved Pappous, some of the fire had gone out of her. She suffered with arthritis and Ariana watched her gnarled fingers work the mixture with a spoon.

'How did you and Grandfather meet?'

'Oh, he made a play for me, but I didn't say yes immediately.' Elana smiled at the memory, 'He was very passionate in his courting, but my father didn't want me to marry him.'

'Why ever not? Wasn't he already a rich businessman?'

'He was still a young man with lots to learn . . . my father wanted me to be happy. He said, "Elana, this man will make his business yours, and you will have to be his boss too."'

'What did he mean?'

'He could see that your grandfather needed someone by his side to be a success. My father just wanted me to have babies and be a good wife, he thought that is what would make a young woman happy.'

'You were happy, weren't you?'

'Of course, and being part of the business suited my talents every bit as much as it suited your grandfather!' Her eyes twinkled. 'The only sadness I have, is that we were not blessed with any more children, so your father did not have a brother to share the load.' Her face grew sad at the memory.

'Well, Father loves the business, so it worked out all right.'

Elana sighed. 'I am not sure that is true. He spends more time building boats with Christian down at that boathouse of his than he does managing the business.'

Ariana rested her hand on her chin and said dreamily, 'Christian.'

Her grandmother tutted at her. 'Your head is full of romantic dreams. Why must you worry your father so, Ari?'

'I don't worry him. He just doesn't want me hanging around and getting in the way of his precious boats.'

'That isn't true. He loves you more than anything else in the world, but you are like your mother: too headstrong.' Elana spooned out the mixture onto the phyllo pastry and then drizzled sweetened honey syrup over it.

'It isn't my fault Papa has always been so dutiful. Not everyone wants to work, work, work.' She reached over to pick at the gooey mixture.

Her grandmother slapped Ariana's fingers away.

'Ouch!'

'It serves you right. No picking!' Elana said sharply. 'Anyway, your father knew what duty meant. He made sacrifices for the good of the family.'

'Didn't he ever want to do anything else?'

Her grandmother hesitated before answering. 'Maybe . . . once.'

At that moment, Demetrios came into the kitchen and kissed his mother on the cheek. Ariana was still cross with her father and turned her face away as he leaned towards her.

'Suit yourself.' He shrugged.

She scowled at him. 'When these are ready, I am going to take them down and give them to Teresa for the party tonight.'

Demetrios eyed his daughter suspiciously. 'She will think that you are after something.'

Ariana fluttered her eyes innocently. 'Who, me?'

Demetrios rolled his eyes. 'More time-wasting. You should be preparing to take up your place at Oxford in the autumn.'

'Papa, we have had this conversation a million times: I don't want to go back to England.'

'Fine, then go somewhere else – Harvard, the Sorbonne. You must have an education if you are to make your way in life. You have a good brain and you should use it.'

'What is wrong with life on Ithos? You spend all of your time here now.'

'There is nothing wrong with life on Ithos, but . . . I need you by my side running the business when you are old enough.'

'I don't want to work in shipping, it's so boring.'

'Look at Rupert Murdoch and his daughter – she is as sharp as he is. You will feel differently in a few years.'

'No, I won't! You can't force me!' she shouted.

'You should want to do it.' He had raised his voice now.

'Well, I'm not going to.'

Elana intervened. 'Stop this childish argument, both of you. Ari, pack up these pastries and take them to the taverna. Tell Teresa I will see her later.'

Ariana's eyes flashed defiantly, but she did as she was told. She was sick of being treated like one of her father's possessions, and she was going to do exactly what she wanted to, whether he liked it or not.

Demetrios sat brooding in his office, sipping at a cognac as he worked out his next step. He knew getting angry with his daughter was a mistake, but her wilfulness enraged him. He checked his post again. Still no reply. Contacting Shauna had been a mistake. He should never have allowed hope to rear its head in his life. Now he felt like a fool. An imma-ture, lovesick teenage boy.

He had received a letter from the office of Isaac Orvitz some weeks ago, acknowledging receipt and confirming that his gift had been passed on, so he knew Shauna had received the book of sonnets. He had hoped that she would remember the poems from their time together, that she would reach out to him as he had reached out to her in sending the letter. He chided himself; of course she wouldn't want to have anything to do with him. He should have tried harder all those years ago – she had probably forgotten who he was.

His mother entered his office. 'I have been looking for you.' She seated herself in one of his armchairs. 'It is early for brandy, no?'

Demetrios ignored her comment and took another sip of the vintage Courvoisier. 'Ariana has gone down to the harbour,' she continued. 'You can't keep pushing her in this way. You will lose her forever if you don't stop.'

Demetrios was in no mood for his mother's lectures. 'You

are hardly in a position to take the moral high ground, Mama.'

Her tone was conciliatory. 'Maybe not. I realize that I may have pushed you too far in the past.'

'May have?'

His mother's eyes flashed with some of her old fire. 'Family has always come first, we both know that. But I can see that, if Ariana is pushed any more, she will break or do something stupid.'

'What do you suggest then? Let her waste a good brain on clothes and baubles?'

'No, but there is another way.'

Her son narrowed his eyes. 'What are you planning, Mother?'

She waved her hand at him. 'Don't give me that look. What you really want is someone to help you with the business?'

Demetrios made a non-committal noise.

'Listen, Ariana will never want to join you.' She paused, weighing up her words. 'You know she has a strong attraction to Christian, don't you?'

'Níko's son? What are you suggesting?'

'You are preparing him, are you not, to join you? He already works for you and wants to do well in the company?'

'He is a good boat builder . . . and he is keen to learn the shipping side of things.'

'That's why you have been teaching him the way your father taught you: sending him out on the yacht, making sure he knows how to handle a boat. And he has a good business brain, you have said so a thousand times.'

He nodded. 'Yes, he is serious-minded and hard-working. He will be an asset to the company. What are you getting at, Mother?'

'If Ariana and Christian were to make an "alliance", then she would have what she wanted, and you would be able to keep the business in the family.'

Demetrios regarded his mother in silence; after a moment, he spoke. 'An old leopard is a leopard nonetheless and this one has not changed its spots.'

She gave him a cool smile. 'I will take that as a compliment, my son.'

His face remained stony. 'It wasn't meant as one.'

'Demi, you can't have it both ways. If you want her to go along with your wishes, she needs a little . . . motivation, shall we say?'

'I think when it comes to matters of the heart, a father should leave well alone. Ariana is too young, and—'

'Nonsense, I was only eighteen when I married your father.'

'I seem to remember you knew what was best for me once, and look where that ended.'

'Sofía did not know her duty, she was not a good wife.'

'And I was not a good husband, Mama.'

'Demi, you are over-dramatizing this. All we will be doing is helping your daughter with her dreams. You must trust a woman's intuition . . .'

Grace had found herself slotting into the rhythm of life on Ithos without even realizing it. She had picked up some Greek and while she wasn't quite speaking like a local, she could chit-chat with the regular customers who came to the taverna.

Tonight, even though it was a Saturday and the busiest day of the week, the taverna would be closed for business. It was Níko's birthday, and the staff had all been given the day off and invited to the party. Grace, however, liked helping and didn't mind spending the morning with Teresa in the kitchen getting the food ready.

Níko's son, Christian, had come by to wish his father a happy birthday. Teresa had immediately put him to work too, checking out a discrepancy in the taverna accounts. Which was why he was sitting at the family table inside the restaurant, munching on one of his mother's homemade kalitsounia pastries while tapping numbers into a calculator.

Christian had returned to Ithos only a week ago – he was a crew member on one of Demetrios's yachts. Already, Grace had come to look forward to his occasional visits to the taverna. He was the eldest of Níko's three children, in his late twenties. Grace didn't think she had ever seen him let his hair down, but there was a quiet self-possession to him that she admired. Something that she wished she had.

She found herself at the coffee machine studying his features as he knitted his brow in concentration. Unlike most Greeks she had met, he had sandy blond hair. Níko would joke that he had been left at the door of the taverna by the stork, but Teresa told her that her own grandmother had German blood and that was why he didn't have dark hair like her other children.

Grace was just wishing she could get a little closer to see what colour eyes he had when, almost as if he had heard her thinking, he looked up and caught her eyes with his own. She quickly looked away, blushing. *Definitely blue.*

When she glanced back again, he was still calmly looking at her, smiling, so she smiled in return. He beckoned her to come over and chat.

'I'm a bit busy, I don't want to make Teresa cross.' Grace tilted her head in apology.

He smiled. 'I am a valued customer and my mother will not mind if it's me you're chatting with.' He gestured to his mother, pointing at Grace and indicating he wanted to talk to her. Teresa shook her finger at him and made the universal sign-language motion for 'five minutes only'.

Grace wiped her hands down on her apron and smoothed the stray strands of dark hair from her face; the rest of it was pulled back in a scrunchie.

'Sit down, Grace. I have a present for you.' Grace liked the way his tongue rolled around the r in her name. He reached behind him into his back pocket and pulled something out of it with a flourish.

'My passport – finally!' She clapped her hands in delight and had to strongly resist the urge to kiss him.

Demetrios had placed some calls shortly after she had arrived, and his contact in the police had phoned him a week later to say that the thieves who'd robbed her had been apprehended on Kythira. She'd thought that her passport would have been sold on the black market, but it turned out one of them had given it to his sister. Demetrios had arranged for Christian to pick it up on her behalf.

'Oh, thank you, Christian, I can't believe it has taken so long to get here.'

He blushed. 'Sorry about that. Demetrios had arranged for me to collect it from police headquarters in Crete, but it turned out someone had sent it to Athens – so local bureaucracy was partly to blame for the delay. But then we took a longer route back to Ithos than we'd originally planned, and by the time I got here I'd completely forgotten I had it.'

'It doesn't matter, I'm just so glad to have it back. I must find some way to thank you.'

'The smile on your face is enough for me.' Grace found her grin spreading even wider at his words. 'Now you are free to leave,' he told her.

'Oh, I don't think I can; Teresa says this is the busiest part of summer with all the day-trippers from the other islands. I don't start university until late September, so I can stay on for another month or so.'

A grin broke across Christian's face that matched her own. 'That's wonderful!' He checked himself, 'I mean, it's wonderful that my parents won't have to find another waitress at short notice. They are always saying what a help you are,' he added.

At that moment, there was a commotion at the front of the taverna. The sound of wolf whistles and a honking of horns drifted in from the square. Grace looked out to see a young woman wearing the tiniest pair of denim shorts and a crocheted bikini top with a wide-brimmed sun hat. She was attracting the attention of the local boys as she headed into the restaurant carrying a box filled with baklava; she turned around and blew them a kiss, which was returned with more blaring of horns and good-natured catcalls.

'Ariana,' Christian said with a shake of his head, 'must you always make such an entrance?'

'Those boys, they are so juvenile . . . Christian!' Ariana leaned in and gave him a kiss, lingering a little.

'Hi, Ariana,' Grace said. 'I love your Roman sandals.'

Ariana gave a her a brief glance and looked down at the golden strappy sandals. 'Oh, these old things.' She then turned to Christian and proceeded to completely ignore Grace.

Grace had become used to Ariana's high-handed manner. She was a frequent visitor, especially since Christian had showed up, but Grace thought he seemed to know when Ariana was on the lookout for him and deliberately made himself scarce.

'I can't wait for the party tonight, Christian. I've brought baklava from Yaya. She and Papa are both coming later.' She took off her hat, and her straight dark hair spilled out fetchingly across her shoulders.

'Grace is coming too, aren't you?' Christian said, politely bringing Grace into the conversation.

Ariana gave her a dismissive look. 'Yes, it's nice that the staff are allowed to come as well as the real guests.'

'Grace is also a guest, Ari, and a very welcome one.' He looked at Grace warmly and she couldn't help but smile back.

'I'm really looking forward to it.'

Ariana was trying to hide a scowl and failing. She turned her back on Grace and leaned into Christian. 'You must dance with me, Christian. I'm wearing a special dress for the occasion.'

Christian pulled back from her slightly. 'I'm not much of dancer, Ariana.'

'Spoilsport.' Ariana changed tack. 'When are you going to take me out in the boat? You always say you will and never do. You must take me out tomorrow, you have a day off, it's Sunday and Papa never works on a Sunday.'

'I can't,' he answered quickly.

'Why not?' Ariana stuck her lip out petulantly.

Grace noticed a split second of hesitation cross his face before he said, 'I promised to take Grace.'

'What?' Grace and Ariana both spoke in unison.

'Don't you remember, Grace? I promised to take you out tomorrow, to show you Fengari Bay.'

Grace caught up quickly. 'Uh, oh yes, that's right. You did promise me that.'

Ariana couldn't hide her annoyance. 'Oh, I see.'

'We must look after our visitors to the island, Ariana. We are known for our hospitality, are we not?'

A flash of frustration blazed a trail across Ariana's face. She tossed her hair back and said airily, 'I'm going to see Teresa and give her Yaya's gift.' She stood and headed for the kitchen, reminding Christian she would be looking for him later for their dance. She blew him a kiss over her shoulder, managing the feat of glaring at Grace at the same time.

Grace looked at Christian expectantly, and he stuttered a little. 'I . . . I've been meaning to ask you if you'd like to come to Fengari Bay. I can show you the boat Demetrios is building.'

'Well, the good news is that tomorrow is my day off, too.'

Christian was hesitant. 'You'll come then?'

'I'd love to!'

He smiled. 'Bring a swimming costume.'

Chapter 25

Grace put the final touches to her outfit. She hadn't expected to stay as long as she had on Ithos, but since her arrival, she had manged to supplement her meagre wardrobe with a few extra items: a pair of brown leather sandals, a new bikini and a couple of cheap but pretty summer dresses, all picked up from the weekly market in the square, where the traders had enjoyed her haggling and given her a good price for the items.

Tonight, she had a choice, either a yellow knee-length gypsy-style dress, or a pale blue halterneck with a slight flare that gave it a vintage feel. Blue, she decided, and slipped it on, pulling the dress up over head, and enjoying the feel of it as it slipped over her hips.

She brushed a little grey shadow over her lids, some dark grey eyeliner – she found black too harsh – and a slick of pink lip gloss.

'You'll do,' she told herself, pleased with how she looked.

She could already hear the hubbub of the guests from her window, which gave her a delicious sense of anticipation. As she made her way down to the taverna, she saw that all the individual tables on the terrace had been re-arranged to form two long tables that filled the space, and the whole square was crammed with people dancing to the music of a traditional dimotika band. She drank in the lively scene; everywhere she looked, guests were laughing, drinking, eating and having fun.

Grace held back for a moment, a sudden shyness giving her pause. Maybe she should go and read a book in her room; no one would miss her, she reasoned, she was just the English waitress.

Before she could turn tail, she was spotted by Níko, who was entertaining a table of guests with an anecdote that was making them roar with laughter. As soon as he saw her, he dashed over and embraced her. 'Grace! My favourite young agapitós! Come meet my friends and join my party!'

He grabbed her hand and, laughing, led her over to the table, seating her next to Demetrios.

'This is Elana, Demetrios's mitéra,' he told her, introducing her to an older woman seated next to Demetrios.

Then Níko indicated the lady seated opposite, who looked old enough to be a great-grandmother. 'And this is my mitéra, Katerina,' he teased. 'She is ninety years old, but she makes the rest of us look old, don't you?'

'*Stamáta na me peirázo gios.*' The old lady shook her finger at him.

'Nonsense, I would never tease you, Mama! You are a spring chicken!' He gave the old lady a noisy kiss then rushed off to greet more new arrivals.

'Welcome, Grace, you must eat, drink and be merry. It is demanded tonight.' Demetrios poured her a glass of red wine and served her up a plate of the lamb stew called kleftiko that was a speciality of Teresa's.

She lifted a forkful of it into her mouth, savouring the flavours of lamb, oregano, lemon and garlic that danced over her tongue. 'This food is delicious.'

At that moment, Christian joined them at the table. He was wearing a pair of white linen trousers and a navy-blue shirt. A few of the shirt buttons were undone and Grace tried hard not to stare at his toned chest.

'Hi, Grace,' he said. 'You look . . . very nice. I'm glad you came.'

'So am I. This is the best food I've ever eaten.'

'Now, Grace,' Demetrios said, 'you must tell us about yourself. It must be three months that you have been here, and yet still you are woman of mystery with your reserved English ways.'

'Do you have a boyfriend?' Christian asked her.

Grace almost choked on a bite of stew. 'That's very direct!'

Christian coughed awkwardly, 'I'm just wondering what sort of fellow would let his pretty girlfriend go off to spend the summer without him.'

Grace felt herself getting sucked in by his blue eyes again and tried to concentrate on the plate in front of her.

'No boyfriend. I'm due to start university in September, but I'm taking a working holiday first so I can earn some money to help finance my studies, and then spend a few months travelling.'

'Why did you come to Ithos?' Demetrios enquired, looking at her quizzically. 'Ithos is not on most young people's list of must-see destinations. We are a little "square" here. I feel it is no accident that you were brought here though. You already feel like one of the family.'

Grace noticed that, although Elana made no comment, her eyes narrowed as Demetrios said this. Grace had seen Demetrios's mother a handful of times in the town, occasionally wandering through the market examining the fresh fruit. Despite her age, she cut an imposing figure.

'I've always wanted to come to Greece, but Ithos I only learned about recently.'

'We are a little off the beaten track.' Christian said. 'How did you hear about it?'

'Well, I—'

Before she could speak, Elana cut in: 'Demetrios, where is your daughter, she must join us now Christian is here.' She turned to the young man. 'I hear you have promised her a dance?' Her eyes twinkled mischievously.

'Elana, you know I cannot dance.'

'That is not true, I taught you myself. Ariana, come over here!' Elana waved to her granddaughter, who was laughing and joking with a group of friends. At that moment, the band struck up the famous traditional dance, the Sirtaki, famous all over Greece.

Grace thought Ariana looked beautiful, dressed in a white floor-length off-the-shoulder silk dress that emphasized her ample breasts and her curvaceous hips. The eyes of every young man in the square turned to watch as she glided over to their table, making a beeline for Christian, and Grace noticed girlfriends and wives nudge their men in jealous annoyance. Ariana certainly turned heads.

'Come, Christian!' Ariana grabbed his hands, pulling him onto the floor, and Grace could see he was powerless to resist. Ariana swirled around him, her dress lifting up to reveal perfectly tanned legs and a glimpse of her thighs.

'They make a handsome couple, do they not?' Elana said, watching smugly as her granddaughter and Christian dominated the dancefloor, drawing claps and encouragement from the birthday crowd.

'They do,' Grace agreed, once again feeling like an outsider.

'Some things are meant to be.' Elana nodded her head in satisfaction.

Demetrios said nothing, looking on impassively, and Grace found it hard to work out what he might be thinking.

'Elana, you are turning into a wallflower.' Níko descended on their table and pulled Elana to her feet. 'We can't have that. We all know you are the best dancer in Ithos.' The older woman laughed, clearly enjoying the attention, and they both joined the throng of dancers now joined together arm in arm, circling around the room in the traditional Greek style.

Níko's mother had been quiet until now, just watching and enjoying the festivities, but she reached out to Grace and touched her hand, making a motion Grace didn't understand. She shook her head, not comprehending what the woman meant.

Demetrios helped her out. 'Katerina is asking you to show her your palm; she wants to tell your fortune.'

'Oh.' Grace wasn't sure she wanted her palm read but she didn't want to be rude, so held it out tentatively.

'The story goes that Katerina is of Romany blood. Níko says that she has the gift of second sight.'

Grace couldn't tell from Demetrios's tone whether he thought there was any truth in it or not. But the woman examined her hand, muttering in Greek as she did so.

Then Katerina looked intently at Grace, making her squirm a little under the scrutiny. When she spoke, again it was in Greek but Demetrios was able to translate.

'Katerina says Ithos has called you and you have come.'

Katerina nodded, smiling at Grace, then she began to speak again.

'Do not be afraid to seek the truth. The light is nothing to be afraid of,' Demetrios translated.

The woman said something else. 'Katerina says that tomorrow, under a full moon, you will find your heart's desire.'

Grace laughed a little nervously, but Katerina looked at her with eyes full of wisdom and said, in broken English, 'You are looking for your own truth, but you must look for it in the right place.' She gave Grace a beatific smile, patted her hand, and went back to tapping her feet to the music.

Grace blinked, a shiver creeping up her spine. Katerina's words seem to hang in the air.

'Katerina is a wise old bird,' Demetrios said. 'We are all looking for something, no?' He took her hand. 'Come, too much introspection is not good for the soul, but dancing is.'

With that her swung her onto the dance floor and Grace was soon swept up by the music, his kindness and the thought that tomorrow would bring something new.

Chapter 26

It was well after midnight when the yacht moored in Ithos harbour. The captain had radioed ahead, and a car was waiting to greet the visitors as they stepped off the gang-plank.

Shauna held a fast-asleep Alex in her arms. He had been so excited about arriving at Ithos, but hadn't been able to stay awake long enough to enjoy the moment the ship docked. The last couple of weeks had been exhilarating for him; the Acropolis and the Parthenon in Greece, the tourist sites of Crete and Rhodes. Being with Roxy again had felt like old times; they had loved feeling like tourists again and this time, Roxy pointed out, they weren't reduced to picking up old fruit from the gutters but had dined in the best restaurants and stayed in the best hotels. Shauna was trav-elling incognito, under the name O'Brien, and she had asked her stylist to get rid of the highlights, so she was a redhead once more. So far, they had managed to dodge the paparazzi. They had chartered a yacht in Athens and their island adventure had given her a sense of freedom and lifted her spirits. She didn't miss the film world at all, and she'd been able to forget about being Shauna Jackson movie star, and focus on being there for Alex.

She looked around her at the harbour. There were still revellers in the square spilling out of the taverna, laughter and music drifted on the air and she picked up the smell of the pink bougainvillea that she remembered so well. Could she really be here again after all this time?

With their luggage following separately, they bundled into the car, Alex only briefly rousing as she settled him on her lap. As the car climbed up the narrow road to the brow of the hill, Shauna caught a glimpse of the Theodosis villa. Their own villa was a little further on, and soon they were being greeted by Delphine, the chatty and capable house-keeper, who bustled them into the cool interior. She guided Shauna up to the bedrooms, taking Alex out of her arms and tucking him up in bed. He briefly awoke, rubbing his eyes and asking where they were.

'We're on Ithos now, darling,' she told him.

He yawned. 'Sing me "Luna Lunera", Auntie Shauna.'

Shauna had learned that Alex could only fall asleep with this lullaby in his ears, but she spoke no Spanish so had leaned the words in English, which seemed to keep him happy. She quietly sang the lines, 'Moon bright moon, you have seen me crying . . .' He was asleep in moments. Shauna kissed him and turned out the light.

Roxy was eager to explore the villa now rather than wait until morning, so they went around peering into the beau-tiful minimalist rooms, oohing and aahing with delight when they came to the large lounge area that opened on to a wide terrace, beyond which there was a gate to a swimming pool which made them both gasp. It balanced on the edge of the overhanging rock, overlooking Fengari Bay to the east and Ithos harbour to the west.

'Alex is going to love it here. He'll never want to leave,' Roxy said.

'He might not be alone in that. It's magical,' Shauna said. 'How are you feeling?'

Shauna smiled. 'It's funny, but being here feels good – it feels right somehow. I forgot how much I loved this place.'

It was late and they were both tired. Shauna climbed the stairs to her room, which had a large balcony that looked out over the pool. The moon was high in the sky; not quite full, but almost so, and there was a pinkish tinge to it which seemed to bathe the bay in a warm glow.

Before they left, Isaac had made a few phone calls and found out that Demetrios Theodosis always holidayed at his home in Greece for the summer months. As the breeze rippled through her light silk shirt and her red hair billowed out behind her, Shauna found it strange to think that Demetrios was here, somewhere close, perhaps looking up at the moon at this same moment.

You're being fanciful again, Shauna, she told herself, but as she climbed into bed and drifted off to sleep, her dreams were filled with the moon whispering to her of lost love.

'Auntie Shauna, I think I can see China!'

'Hmmm, is that so?' Shauna peered over the edge of the pool across the bay, screwing up her eyes in concentration. 'You must have wonderful eyesight, Alex. Or maybe I should get new glasses?'

He giggled, bobbed on the surface like a duck for a moment, then swam underwater to the end of the pool, where he immediately climbed out, ran back to where he had started and dived in again, popping up next to Shauna. She squealed in mock surprise, and then the two of them shrieked as they splashed each other with water. Shauna broke first and begged him to stop.

The first thing Alex had done upon waking that morning was to throw his swimming trunks on and shake Shauna awake, demanding that they go for a swim. He'd been having intense lessons since he had come to live with her and was now swimming like a fish. Shauna had barely been able to drag him away from the pool, but it was mid-morning and Ithos beckoned. She was about to insist that they get some clothes on and go exploring, when Roxy appeared, coming through a vine-covered gate that she hadn't noticed until now. Shauna had assumed that Roxy was enjoying a lie-in.

'Good morning!' she hailed them both. She looked tanned and relaxed in a wide-brimmed sun hat and a full-length wraparound sarong in a tropical palm print.

'Have you been exploring?' Shauna asked.

'I couldn't resist. You'll never believe this, but on the other side of that gate there's a stairway cut into the rocks that leads down to the beach. It's like our own private path.'

Delphine appeared carting a tray of drinks and a delicious-looking Greek meze of dolmades, olives, houmous and Greek salad.

All three of them realized they were hungry at the same time. Alex scrambled out of the pool, Shauna following suit, pausing to pull on a light silk kimono over her white swimming costume. Her skin was a golden colour, but she smoothed on some suncream to protect it from the heat of the sun.

'Yes,' Delphine said, having caught the end of their conversation, 'the path is private and will take you to the beach, but it also connects with other paths, so you must be careful otherwise you will be taken off course along the line of the sea rather than down to it.'

'Why don't you let me take Alex to the beach for a few hours so you can get some rest?' Roxy offered.

'I'm not tired at all,' Shauna replied, 'but I should do a little work today, I'm supposed to be writing my memoirs.'

'You haven't taken the publisher's advance yet.'

'But I haven't said no either. Maybe I should try . . .'

Roxy bit into a big fat juicy green olive. 'You're on holiday. I think that means you should spend your days eating meze and ice cream – and drinking wine, of course.'

'That sounds like a great idea.'

'Seriously,' Roxy said, 'you could do with a few hours' head space.' She looked at Shauna meaningfully.

'Don't look at me like that,' Shauna frowned, knowing that Roxy was expecting her to have come up with a plan as to how she was going to deal with Demetrios. 'Why don't you and Alex go down and have an explore, and I'll join you in a little while?'

'It's a deal. Make sure you use your time wisely.'

Shauna put her nose in the air imperiously. 'As you have rightly pointed out, we are on holiday and I shall use my time as I please.'

'Is this you talking, or is it Grace Kelly?'

Shauna laughed. 'I'm not sure I know any more!'

Grace loved working at the taverna, but she also loved the one day she had off each week. She didn't think it was mean for Teresa to only give her one day off; the season was short and everyone had to make the most of it before all the tourists and holidaymakers went back to where they had come from. Everyone at Níko's worked hard, the owners most of all – they never seemed to have a day off.

Ever since she'd learned to snorkel on a family holiday as a child, Grace had been hooked. She and her father would always insist on going to destinations where they could get in a little underwater sightseeing. She particularly remembered diving from a boat in Malta, and being dazzled by the colourful reefs teeming with life.

Visitors left many things behind by accident at Níko's taverna, and in the lost property cupboard there were any number of flippers, goggles, sun hats and flip-flops. Níko didn't mind her 'borrowing' some of the items, and today she had spent an hour swimming up and down, not too far from the shoreline, hoping to see one of the elusive sea turtles, or maybe a shy parrotfish or two. She hadn't been lucky today and was now sitting on her beach towel watching the world go by.

The beach was busy by Ithos standards, but there were never throngs of tourists on the island. The day-trippers came to experience the picturesque Greek harbour and its narrow streets lined with shops selling traditional Greek craft: goods made from leather that was tanned locally and baskets that the local women sat weaving on their doorsteps.

She watched as a woman and a little boy played with a giant beach ball. The boy was a bundle of energy and she could see the woman was working hard to keep up. The multicoloured rubber ball was suddenly caught by a gentle gust of wind and came sailing over in her direction. Instinctively she jumped up and caught it. She'd been a netball champion at school and loved nothing better than a ball game. She threw it back to the boy and he came running towards her, tripped over his feet and went crashing down to the sand.

'Oh, no!' Grace gasped and ran forward. She was too late to catch him, but he didn't seem to be hurt. Despite the fact he had a mouth full of sand, he was laughing his little head off.

The woman came running over. 'Alex! Are you OK?'

'I'm so sorry,' said Grace. 'I think that was my fault.' She picked the boy up, saying, 'I'm very sorry, Alex. My name is Grace, nice to meet you.'

'Oh, he's fine, aren't you, Alex?' the woman said, dusting the boy down. She was taller than Grace, with short spiky hair. There was something familiar about her, but Grace couldn't put her finger on it.

'This one is steel-plated,' the woman said.

'He's certainly got lots of get-up-and-go.'

'Tell me about it.' The woman rolled her eyes. 'But I volunteered for this, so no complaining allowed. I'm his almost-auntie.'

'Almost-aunties are the best sort. Anyway, I love playing with a beach ball,' Grace said. 'If you like, I could take over for a while so you can read your book ' – she nodded over at the woman's towel, on which lay a copy of *The Life of Pi* – 'and I can enjoy making a fool of myself. It will make up for Alex falling over.'

'Really?'

'Absolutely, I could do with the exercise.'

'I want to play with Grace!' Alex jumped up and down.

'Come on, you can try and catch me.' With that, Grace grabbed Alex's ball and ran off to the shoreline, Alex laughing and chasing after her.

For the next half-hour Alex had the perfect companion in Grace. While Roxy looked on, they splashed at the water's edge, Grace pointing out the tiny fish that would nibble at his feet, making him jump, and they played endless rounds of catch. Eventually Grace realized she had lost track of time and delivered Alex back to Roxy.

'I'm sorry, Alex, I have to go now. A friend is taking me out on his boat and I don't want to be late,' she apologized.

'I'm sure we will see each other again,' she reassured him when she saw his face fall. 'Are you staying on Ithos long?' she asked the woman.

'I'm not sure yet. It depends. I'm here with a friend and, well, let's say she has some life stuff to do. It might take a while, it might not.'

'Excuse me for asking,' Grace said, 'but do I recognize you? I feel like I know you from somewhere?'

'My name is Roxy, I design clothes.'

Grace tilted her head to one side, thinking, then her eyes widened, and she said, 'Roxy Lennon? I love ROX! That dress that Kate Moss wore to the British Fashion Awards last year was incredible.'

Roxy inclined her head in a modest thank-you. 'I try to make clothes that I like. Kate Moss could make a paper bag look glamorous.'

'I love fashion, you're an icon!'

'You'd better stop now, my head was big enough already!'

'Sorry – fan girl. Not cool,' Grace said.

'I'll take the compliment. Hadn't you better run? You don't want to miss your boat?'

'Lord!' Grace grabbed her things. 'I'd better dash, lovely to meet you – bye Alex!'

She ran off and Roxy shouted after her, 'I hope he's a dish!'

Shauna felt like she'd been staring at her MacBook for hours, but in reality it hadn't been very long at all. She'd been trying to conjure up memories of her childhood in Ireland, but as she gazed out at the horizon, the azure blue of the Mediterranean called to her and all she could remember was her father telling her, *No one should be working when the sun is high and the sea is calm.*

Abandoning hope of getting anything written today, she decided to head down to the beach to meet Alex and Roxy. The long white boho sun dress and brown leather Birkenstocks she was wearing were perfect for the beach, so she stuffed a towel into her satchel, popped her favourite fedora on her head and set off for the old rusty gate that she'd seen Roxy come through earlier. The path led downhill to a junction where the path split in two. The beach appeared to be directly below her, but it wasn't clear whether she should turn right or left. She shrugged and took the right-hand path, figuring that the worst that could happen was that she would end up in the town.

There were a few twists and turns and, after a while, the path became very overgrown and nettles kept catching at her feet. Shauna thought she must have come the wrong way and decided to retrace her steps, but the path didn't look the same heading in the opposite direction and soon she had lost her bearings.

The sun beat down and Shauna regretted not bringing a bottle of water with her. The path was so overgrown now, with large bushes and branches obscuring the way ahead, that Shauna was starting to panic. What if she had come completely off the path? She had lost all track of time, the only sound she could hear was the cry of buzzards as they spied prey below and swooped down to seize it.

She pushed on through the undergrowth and was starting to feel faint when she came to a clearing. She was higher up than when she had started; down to the left was the sea, ahead of her were olive groves, and above the tops of the trees she could see the upper tower of the Theodosis villa.

Before she could process this, the heat seemed to close in on her. Feeling faint, she lowered herself onto a boulder underneath the canopy of an olive tree, took her hat off and fanned herself furiously.

She sat there for a few moments, wondering how she could get back up to the path without fainting, when she saw a figure coming towards her through the trees from the direction of the villa.

As the figure approached, Shauna could see it was a woman wearing a long kaftan. She looked to be in her seventies and her grey hair was tied up in a bun. Even after twenty years, there was no mistaking that face: it was Elana Theodosis, and the last time they had met, she had been ordering Shauna off the island and out of her son's life.

Chapter 27

The only sensible shoes Grace possessed were a pair of Nike trainers, but that didn't worry her. An uncle of hers had owned a sailboat and she and her parents had spent a few holidays sailing off Cowes, which she'd loved. Grace prided herself on having excellent sea legs and knew a bit more about boats than Christian gave her credit for.

His boat was a cat-rigged yacht with a single mast. When she had clambered aboard late that afternoon, he told her to take a seat while he unfurled the sail and readied it for casting off. Grace surprised him by securing the bowline.

'You steer and I'll cast off,' she told him.

He scratched his head. 'You didn't tell me you could sail.'

'You didn't ask me!' The dumbfounded expression on his face made her laugh. 'You look so comical! Come on, let's get going.'

It was a perfect day for sailing. There was enough of a breeze to lift the sail and for the boat to move at a lick through the water, but the sea was calm. Grace relished the taste of brine on her lips as the wind whipped around her.

'Is this your boat?'

'I built it myself with help from Demetrios. He is a patient teacher.'

The two of them made a good pair, Grace knowing what was needed and when, reading the wind as Christian used the tiller to manoeuvre the boat through the water, reading the waves and the wind as if he and the boat were one.

'Where are we going?' she asked him, as she rested on the side on the boat.

'To Fengari Bay. You can't reach it by land, only by boat. Hardly anyone knows it's there, only islanders.'

It didn't take them long to reach their destination, and Grace was pleased that the midday heat had passed, making the late afternoon more bearable. There was a small mooring, and Grace jumped off the side, catching the rope that Christian threw her, pulling the boat in and knotting the line around the dock ring to secure it.

While she waited for Christian to join her, she took in the horseshoe line of the bay. The cobalt sea meeting the chalk white sand was so inviting, she longed to take a dip but still felt a bit shy around Christian, so instead she pointed at the solitary boathouse tucked away in a secluded spot near the mooring. Unlike the boathouses and sheds in the harbour, the timbers weren't weathered and ancient but bleached and new-looking. Clearly, a recent construction.

'Who owns the boathouse?'

'It belongs to Demetrios; he comes here when he wants to get away from it all. He says he can't relax at home because the phone never stops ringing. This is where he taught me how to build a boat – we made the one I brought you here on.'

Grace turned and looked at the boat again. She hadn't noticed before, but on the side was its name: *The Selene*.

'Did you choose the name? Who is Selene?'

'Selene is the goddess of the moon, she is revered in Ithos. Let me show you inside the boathouse. Demetrios won't mind us being here, seeing as it is you.'

It was cool and dark inside. A canoe hung from the rafters, held in place by ropes, and there were fishing nets and lobster pots dangling from the walls. In one corner was a hammock and an old battered leather sofa; bookshelves filled with classic novels lined one of the walls. Grace picked one up: *Dr Zhivago*. She leafed through the scuffed pages, thinking that the book had been read many times already, then scanned the rest of the shelf: Alexander Dumas, a number of crime novels by Elmore Leonard. There was also a book of love poetry by Sappho. Christian appeared by her side.

'Demetrios likes his classic poetry,' she said, and opened a page that had been bookmarked, reading aloud from it:

> Tonight I've watched the moon and then
>   the Pleiades go down
> The night is now half gone; youth goes
> I am in bed alone.

'How sad,' Grace said. 'Demetrios must be so lonely.'

Christian shrugged. 'He is very private and doesn't talk about himself much. My mother says he had his heart broken when he was a young man.'

'And now he's divorced and alone again.' Grace placed the poetry book back on the shelf. In the middle of the boathouse a tarpaulin covered a large object held up on blocks.

'What's underneath?'

'That is Demetrios's magnus opus, his masterpiece!'

'Is it a boat?'

'Of course.'

'Can I see it?'

Christian loosened the rope around the tarpaulin and together they pulled it back to reveal the boat beneath. It was about the size of a small speedboat. Made of wood, it featured a U-shaped cockpit with a wooden steering wheel and a hand-buffed mahogany consol. But it was devoid of a motor, or any controls; it still had the feeling of a work in progress.

Grace ran her hand along the outside, enjoying the feel of the smooth wood under her fingertips, eventually resting on the curved letters of the name of the boat, which had been hand-painted.

Beauty.

'Demetrios has yet to finish it. He is often here alone working on it, but never seems to get any further along. I don't think he wants to finish it.'

'Who do you think Beauty is?'

'Maybe she is the girl who broke his heart?'

The rest of the afternoon was spent lounging around in the cool of the boathouse, eating the picnic Christian had packed. Grace found that, far from being reserved, Christian was easygoing and fun; he laughed a lot and was interested in her. He told her that Demetrios had taken him under his wing as a fourteen-year-old.

'I think he would have liked a son, someone to pass on his knowledge to.'

'He could share it with Ariana, women can build boats too.'

'Of course, but Ariana is no craftswoman, she does not have the patience. She likes dancing, music, fun, boys . . .'

'She likes you.' Grace elbowed him in the ribs.

'Ariana doesn't know what she wants. She will not like me so much when I have a middle-aged paunch and grey hair like my father. She is young – she needs to live a little before she thinks about settling down.'

'I can't imagine you with a middle-aged paunch,' Grace laughed.

He got to his feet and pulled his T-shirt over his head to reveal a deeply tanned torso, a washboard stomach and rippling abs. 'So, Grace, we have the beach to ourselves. We would be crazy not to swim – I hope you remembered to bring a bathing suit.'

'You're so old-fashioned.' She laughed, trying not to stare as he stood before her in only his swimming shorts. 'No one says "bathing suit" in England.'

'What should I call it then?'

'A cossie . . . or a bikini.'

'OK, I hope you have brought your bikini then. Not a "cossie" – I like the sound of a bikini better.'

His eyes teased her as she stood up. Grace was glad she had worn her bikini underneath her clothes, but she was hesitant about taking her vest and shorts off in front of him.

'Are you a good swimmer?'

'Pretty good.'

'I'll race you – over to that large rock and back again.' He headed towards the water. 'I'm fast, you won't beat me.' Diving in, he started to swim quickly, his arms cutting through the water in a front crawl.

'Big talk! I won a bronze medal in the county championships, I'll have you know!' she called after him, tearing off her clothes to reveal her red bikini with a bandeau top. Once in the water, her shyness was forgotten as she sped through the cool clear sea, determined not to be beaten.

* * *

Shauna looked out at Elana Theodosis from under the brim of her fedora hat, her hair pulled up underneath it.

'*Chairiete? Boró na se voithíso?*' Elana asked.

'Sygnómi . . . I'm sorry, my Greek is a little rusty.'

'Can I help you?' Elana said. 'Are you lost?' Despite twenty years passing, Demetrios's mother hadn't lost her striking looks. Intelligent eyes regarded Shauna with curiosity but there was no indication that she recognized her.

'Yes, I'm afraid I am lost. I'm staying up at the villa over the hill, and was looking for the beach, but I must have taken a wrong turn.'

'It is easy to get lost on that path, there are many twists and turns to confuse the unwary traveller.'

'That sounds like me.'

Elana smiled. 'I can show you a quick and easy way down to the beach, but you look a little sun-weary. Perhaps you would like something cool to drink first?'

Much as Shauna wanted to get away as quickly as possible, she did feel rather faint. 'I really must be going, my friends will be wondering what has happened to me, but a cool drink . . . well, that would be very kind of you.'

'Kindness and hospitality is our duty on Ithos. Please follow me.'

Shauna resisted the urge to point out that, last time they had met, Elana had been the very opposite of kind and hospitable. She followed in silence as the woman led the way through the olives grove to a small timber gazebo, under which there was a wooden table and chairs, set out with iced orange juice in a jug next to a couple of glasses.

'My housekeeper brings this down from the house for me when I come to look at the olive trees.' She indicated a chair. 'Please, sit down and rest.'

She poured Shauna a glass of the juice and handed it to

her. Shauna was desperately thirsty, but tried not to gulp it down greedily.

'Do you grow olives yourself?' Shauna asked.

'Sadly, yes. I have some gardeners who come and help me, but this was my husband's passion. And now he is no longer with us . . .' Elana said this with a tilt of her head, lowering her eyes. Despite herself, Shauna felt a touch of sympathy, knowing what it was like to feel grief.

'I'm so sorry, I also lost my husband not long ago.'

Elana looked up. 'You are young to be a widow, and for that I am sorry.' She topped up Shauna's glass. 'You are young and beautiful; you will find love again.'

Shauna suppressed a smile; this woman who had done so much to break her heart all those years ago had the nerve to talk about love!

'It would make me truly happy if my son could help me out here, there is much to do, but he never has the time.'

'What does your son do?' Shauna couldn't help this streak of deviousness, telling herself it was only her Irish nosiness at work.

'He is head of our family business, but these days he seems to prefer hiding in his boathouse to running the company.'

Shauna tried to imagine Demetrios working in a boathouse, but her mind's eye could only conjure up the young man he had been. She found it hard to remember the glimpse she'd caught of the man he had become.

'Perhaps it's time for him to do something different?'

'He may think that,' Elana sniffed disapprovingly, 'but the business needs him, and the family needs him at the helm.'

Nothing had changed, Shauna thought; still the same demands, the same pressures on him. Was that why he was divorced? she wondered.

'I am being rude. Tell me about yourself,' Elana said.

Shauna trotted out the line she always used when she met people who didn't know who she was. She hated bragging and, when she wasn't promoting a movie, she disliked all the attention her life in the spotlight brought. 'Oh, I work in the media. I'm here because . . . well, let's just say I'm looking for some peace.'

'Well, this is a wonderful place for a holiday. We have a saying in Ithos: *"Óla káto apó to fengári eínai edó"*, which means "everything under the moon is here".'

'That's a lovely saying.'

'I hope you find what yoú are looking for. Now, can I get you something to eat?'

'No thank you, I really must be going.'

'Well, it is very nice to have met you. To get to the beach path, walk in a straight line through the grove,' she said, pointing the way. 'At the end is a wooden gate; walk though it and the path will take you straight down.'

'Goodbye, thank you again for the drink. It was very kind of you.'

As she headed off following Elana's directions, the woman called out after her, 'Goodbye, I didn't catch your name . . .'

But Shauna carried on her way and pretended not to hear as she walked through the gate and headed down the path towards the beach.

Chapter 28

After hours of snorkelling and swimming, the afternoon had passed into evening and they both realized how hungry they were. There was still plenty of food left over in the cool box Christian had brought: slices of soft, fresh pitta, creamy taramasalata and tzatziki as well as slices of spanakopita, which combined the delicious crunch of filo pastry with salty feta and fresh spinach. They spread it all out on Grace's sarong, which stood in for a picnic blanket. Christian had even remembered to bring a chilled bottle of retsina, which he poured into the two mismatched glasses he'd found in the boathouse. The finishing touch was a large candle in a storm lamp he'd lit. It danced and flickered with hypnotic golden light in the balmy night air.

Now that they'd eaten, the candles were starting to gutter and Grace felt sleepily relaxed as they sat side by side.

'Look at the colour of the full moon.' He pointed into the sky. The moon was rising from the east and was already quite high in the sky. The moon was bigger and brighter than she'd ever seen it; there was a pink tinge to it that

271

she had never seen before, and a million tiny points of light seemed to sparkle in the sky like a jewelled canopy.

'I've never seen the moon look so beautiful,' she said, transfixed by its hypnotic luminescence.

'We have our own moon on Ithos,' he told her.

'Don't tease, it's the same moon for everyone.'

'Ah, but ours is special. In fact, this bay is named after it – Fengari means moon.'

'What is so special about your moon, then?'

'Can't you see, just by looking at it?'

Grace had to agree, it did seem to her to be unlike any other moonlit night.

'Selene is the goddess of the moon,' he told her. 'Her spirit is strong here in Ithos, and here on Fengari Bay I think she is stronger still.'

Grace nudged him with her shoulder. 'The moon can send you mad if you stare at it too long.'

'Here on Ithos, the moon stands for love and the passing of time. As it gets bigger and smaller, so time passes, the cycle starts again over and over.'

Grace noticed that their shoulders were still touching; neither of them had moved away from the other.

'I know very little about you, Grace,' he said. 'You are very good at listening but not so much at talking?'

'Perhaps it's all those dark secrets I've been keeping.' She hooded her eyes and attempted to look mysterious.

He moved and threw himself on the ground in front of her so he could look directly into her face. 'OK, three questions. I ask and you have to answer.'

She rolled her eyes. 'OK, unless it's something rude.'

He looked at her in mock outrage. 'As a gentleman, I am insulted. First question: Have you ever been in love?'

Grace gave a sigh. 'That's not fair.'

'You must answer.'

'All right . . . I thought I was, but it wasn't the real thing.'

'Who was it?'

'A boy at school. He dumped me for my best friend, but my heart wasn't broken.'

'Good. Next question – what is your middle name?'

'I don't have one.'

'Really?' He looked surprised. 'In Greece everyone has a least two names. I have four.'

Grace shrugged. 'Don't blame me.'

'OK, I won't. Last question . . . what is your heart's desire?'

Grace rolled her eyes again, 'What does that even mean.'

'You don't have dreams?'

'Of course I do . . .' She looked down. 'Everyone does. What's your heart's desire?'

'Me . . . I want to run a business one day, be successful.'

'For Demetrios?'

'He is the boss now, but I want to be my own boss. Don't misunderstand me, he has been like a second father to me, but it's not the same as when you do it for yourself.'

'OK. My turn. What's your star sign?'

'Capricorn.'

'Interesting! I'm a Gemini.'

'Split personality. I'll never know where I am with you.'

'Enough!' She kicked a little sand at him, and he grabbed her toe playfully. For a moment they held each other's gaze and electricity fizzed between them.

'We should be getting back,' she said.

'Why? We have only ourselves to please. Besides,' he added, 'it is lucky to swim under a full moon.'

Grace wasn't ready to go back yet either. She was enjoying getting to know Christian – he was honest and open, he knew his own mind and what he wanted from life. She would have loved to confide in him about what had brought her to Ithos, but she had kept it to herself for so long now that she didn't know where to start.

'Let's have another swim,' he whispered. 'It would be a shame to waste this night.' With that he leapt up and executed a smooth dive into the water, the sleek lines of his body lit by the moonlight.

'What are you waiting for?' he called as he popped up out of the water, his hair slicked back, reminding Grace of a seal or a merman.

She followed him in and the cool water lapped around her, heightening the sensations in her body. She pushed her long hair over her shoulder, enjoying the feel of the wet sand underneath her feet. The moon threw a stream of light through the water. They could have been castaways on a deserted island.

Christian swam towards her. 'You look like a moonlit nymph.'

'I feel like one.' And it was true. He was right, there was something magical about this place; with the moon above them they could almost have been characters from Greek mythology themselves.

He moved towards her through the water and until he was a hair's breadth away. 'Grace, you're so . . .' His hands slid into her hair on either side of her head, cradling her face and staring into her eyes before he dropped a kiss on her lips. His fingers stroked her face and down to her cleavage. He kissed her again and she responded, her body suddenly aching with a desire that had risen inside her, but after a moment she pulled away.

He smiled at her and they stood like that until she spoke.

'I . . . I'm not ready for anything else. Not yet.'

He nodded, seemingly unruffled by her restraint. 'You will know when you are, and I will still be here.'

He took her hand and together they walked back to the shoreline. He wrapped her in a towel and put his arm around her as they strolled to the boathouse to collect their things.

Grace helped him to cast off, jumping into the boat as he turned *The Selene* towards the harbour. She was sad to say goodbye to Fengari Bay, but glad that Christian hadn't noticed she had not answered his question. Her heart's desire would have to wait a bit longer.

'Come on, Ari, you know you want to . . .'

Ariana pushed the young man away as he fumbled at her breasts with one hand, his other moving up her thigh as he tried to pull her underwear aside with his fingers.

'Stop it, Georgiou.' She pulled her body away. 'Just keep your hands to yourself, will you!'

'What are you playing at?' The boy pulled back, annoyed with her now. 'You didn't seem to mind last week. As I remember, you were pretty hot for it.' He leaned in again, biting her ear and making another lunge for her breast through her low-cut top.

'That was different.' She pulled her head away, scowling at him.

'My cousin's holiday flat is still empty, we can go there and . . .' He stroked his hand up her thigh under her dress.

'No, not tonight.'

'You're driving me crazy here, you know that, don't you?'

'That's too bad. Look, I'm not in the mood tonight.' She opened the passenger door of his BMW convertible and stepped out. They had parked up in the darkness behind the warehouse on the harbour. The previous week she had gone to a party at a friend's place and Georgiou had made a play for her. She had drunk a few vodkas, he was good looking and horny for her, so why not? Ariana had lost her virginity at sixteen, during a summer festival. She and Maddy had bought tickets with fake IDs and her first sexual experience had been with a guy whose name she couldn't remember but who had plenty of drugs to share with them. The sex had been something of an afterthought to the rest of the excess. There had been plenty more lovers since, but she hadn't been in love with any of them. Not like Christian. None of them made her feel like he did.

'Ariana!' he called out after her as she walked away. 'I'll call you sometime.'

She'd felt upset and angry all day. Last night at Níko's party she had worn the sexiest dress she could find, she'd massaged oil all over her body and dusted a light shimmer of glitter over herself, she'd shown enough cleavage to drive most men crazy and thrown her skirts up at every opportunity to give Christian a glimpse of what he could have.

And when she had danced with him, she had whispered in his ear, 'Let's go somewhere private, just the two of us.' Then she had brushed her lips over his.

None of it had worked. Christian had just laughed and taken her back to her table, with a chaste kiss on her forehead.

Her Jimmy Choos clacked on the cobbles as she headed towards Níko's taverna. It wasn't so late that everyone had gone home and there were still a few customers, finishing their meal and enjoying some of the island's retsina which was made from grapes grown on Ithos.

She sat down at one of the tables, called the waitress over and ordered a Bacardi and Coke. The waitress looked at her uncertainly, but headed off inside with the order.

From her Louis Vuitton clutch, she took out a packet of

Marlboro Lights and a vintage Cartier lighter that had been her grandfather's. She lit the cigarette, drawing on it deeply, the buzz going to her head.

Looking out across the harbour, she brooded. What could she do to make Christian notice her? Maybe it was because he was embarrassed to show his feelings in front of his family; he was a reserved type of guy, so that must be it. It couldn't be how she looked; she'd never had any problems getting guys before.

She took another draw on her cigarette. That new girl Grace was getting in the way too. Ariana was sure he couldn't be interested in her. She was quite pretty, Ariana supposed, but she was a quiet squeak of a mouse and would be going back to her boring life in England soon.

She flicked her ash into the ashtray. Even with Elana on her side, she needed to be more strategic. She needed to get Christian on his own; he wouldn't be able to resist her then.

Where the hell was her drink? She turned her head to see where the waitress had got to and when she looked back at the harbour her heart jumped. Christian's boat, *The Selene*, was coming in to dock. Determined to look relaxed and cool when he came over, she stubbed out her cigarette, took out her lipstick and mirror, and began reapplying the Chanel Rouge Allure in a thick but precise layer. She pouted. A bit more eyeliner? She rummaged around, finding the black stick of kohl and deftly applied a touch around each eye, smudging it for the smoky effect. She pouted again: perfect.

She crossed her legs and threw back her hair. When Christian came in, she'd wave and invite him over for a drink; he was bound to be thirsty.

Her pout was replaced by a thin line of fury when she

saw Christian had finished securing the mooring lines and was now reaching down to help the English girl clamber off the boat. He kept hold of her hand as the two of them made their way towards the taverna, taking their time, talking to each other in low voices. What the hell could they have to talk about?

Then she saw that Christian was carrying a cool box and Grace was carrying her towel, and it dawned on her that they must have been together all afternoon and all evening.

Her eyes narrowed in a cold, angry stare. Her heart froze as she watched him reach down to kiss Grace on the cheek, lingering too long for it to be just a kiss between friends. What else had they been doing during their happy little day trip? Grace let go of his hand and walked away down the side of the building, heading for the stairs that led to her room. Christian watched her go, and then made his way towards the main entrance of the taverna. He saw her and gave her a cheerful wave. It was all she could do to plaster a tight smile on her face and wave back.

Ariana sat there, dazed, feeling like a bucket of cold water had been thrown over her.

A moment later, the waitress returned, but there was no drink in her hand. 'Where is my Bacardi?' Ariana snapped.

The young waitress wrung her hands and looked awkward. 'Teresa said your father would be angry if she served you alcohol.'

'I'm eighteen years old,' Ariana said through gritted teeth.

The waitress shrugged. 'Don't blame me. Take it up with Teresa. Would you like a Coke?'

'No, I don't want a fucking Coke!' Ariana swept the ashtray onto the floor, grabbed her bag and marched off in the direction of the harbour wall. She felt like screaming.

When were people going to stop treating her like a child? She was a woman and she knew exactly what she wanted.

'Hey, Ariana!' She turned to see Georgiou in his open-top convertible, still with the same arrogant look on his face. He eyed her lustfully.

'There's a pool party up the bay, want to come?' He put his hand into his pocket and pulled out a little packet of white powder.

A small smile crept across her lips. Cocaine.

Georgiou opened the passenger door. 'Jump in.'

Ariana climbed in beside him. She was no longer a child, and it was about time everyone knew it.

Chapter 29

Roxy and Alex were preparing to head down to the beach, as they did every morning. Shauna had promised Roxy that, if she looked after Alex for a couple of hours a day while she worked on her memoirs, she would do all the cooking and sign over 10 per cent of her royalties for the book.

'Ha!' I'll never see a dime,' Roxy had laughed. And after days of struggling to write about her childhood, Shauna was beginning to think she was right; at her current rate of progress, this book would never get written.

Alex couldn't wait to set off. He kept tugging at Roxy's hand, excited that he was going to see his friend Grace.

Shauna gazed longingly at the sea; today it was the colour of lapis lazuli and as calm as a millpond. She would have liked nothing better than to join them on the beach and meet the young waitress Alex had taken such a shine to. Apparently the girl was there most mornings for a swim before she started work, and always made time for a play-date with Alex.

'So, today's the day, huh?' said Roxy, smiling. 'No more procrastinating?'

'I've put it off long enough,' Shauna agreed. They had come to Ithos for a reason, after all.

After Roxy and Alex had gone, she set about choosing what to wear. How did you dress for a reunion with your first love after two decades? She tried on every outfit she'd brought with her, not to mention four hats and six pairs of sandals.

In frustration, she sat on the side of the bed and caught sight of herself in the mirror. Looking back at her was a thirty-nine-year-old woman. She had no grey hairs and only a few expression lines around her eyes. She was tanned and her body was in good shape. Hell, she looked good. She heard her father's voice telling her, *You look grand as you are, my darling girl.*

She grabbed a red gypsy skirt with a split up the side, threw on a see-through cheesecloth shirt over her white vest top. Applying only a touch of lipstick and bronzer, she put on her beloved fedora, grabbed her Birkin bag and headed down the path to the town.

Níko's taverna didn't seem to have changed at all. It still had the same blue-and-white awning, the same white tablecloths, the same menus with their list of traditional Greek dishes.

She sat down at a table outside and took off her fedora. There was always a chance she would be recognized, but she was glad she had dressed down although today most people were absorbed in their own affairs, either chatting or eating. Some were just admiring the view.

'Excuse, me . . .' She beckoned to the man who was waiting tables and he came over quickly. He was older, greyer and had more lines, but Shauna recognized Níko.

'Top of the morning to you,' she said, accentuating her Irish accent. Níko looked up, a puzzled expression on his face as he studied her, then he cried out, 'My Irish *despoinída*!'

He pulled her into a big bear hug, showering her with affectionate kisses. 'You have returned!'

He shouted for his wife, who came out and greeted her like an old friend too. 'There is no friend in Ithos like an old friend,' he said. 'You are more beautiful than I remember! Please, you must have a delicious meal here at our expense. Grace!' He motioned to one of the waitresses, but Shauna held her hand up and shook her head. Níko waved the waitress away.

'It's so wonderful to see you, Níko, and I'd love nothing better than to stay here all afternoon, but I have come to see someone else, too.'

'Ah yes, I see. And this other friend is more important than Níko,' he said kindly. 'I understand. He will be surprised, no?'

'Where is he, Níko?' Shauna asked. Suddenly, after so many nights, so many years, of wondering, of questions going unanswered, she couldn't bear to wait one minute longer. Níko must have seen this in her eyes. 'I will call Christian, my son – he will take you to him.'

Níko's son was a handsome light-haired man who looked like he'd been chiselled out of marble.

'I work with Demetrios in the boathouse,' he told her as they pulled away from the jetty in his speedboat.

'He works in a boathouse? I thought his company had offices in Athens and New York.'

The man shrugged. 'These last few years he has been spending less and less time there. You will have to ask him.' He looked at her curiously as he steered the boat through the waves. 'How do you know Demetrios?'

'We were friends . . . a long time ago,' she said.

'There is a rumour in Ithos that Demetrios had his heart broken. I don't suppose you'd know anything about that?' he asked her.

'I'm afraid I don't,' said Shauna, genuinely puzzled. She

was the one who had been banished, whose heart had been broken, not Demetrios.

She realized that the boat was headed towards Fengari Bay, where she and Demetrios had made love for the first time. So this must be where he had his boathouse. Why would he choose Fengari, of all places?

As they rounded the bay, the boathouse came into view. Shauna could see a small boat moored outside and only a handful of bathers further along the beach. The place still felt as secluded at it had always done.

Christian guided the boat alongside the jetty and helped her out. She looked towards the boathouse.

'He'll be inside,' Christian said, regarding her with interest.

Suddenly full of trepidation, Shauna wasn't sure she wanted to go in there alone. She turned to Christian, who'd made no move to get out of the speedboat. 'Aren't you coming in?'

He shook his head. 'Maybe you old friends don't need an audience. In fact, I think I'll just coast along the bay for a little while, then come back for you later.'

He revved the motor and pulled away. Shauna stood there and didn't move, fiddling anxiously with her thumbs. If Demetrios was inside, why hadn't he heard the boat and come out to see who it was? The noise from the motor was hard to ignore.

Figuring it was time to grab the bull by the horns, she walked along the timber planks of the jetty, her sandals making little noise. The two bleached wooden doors were wide open and inside she could hear the sound of a tinny radio tuned to the lunchtime news.

As she entered the boathouse, she took in the sailing paraphernalia on the wall, a bookcase full of Penguin classics, tools on every surface. There were a number of boats in various stages of construction. A tarpaulin partially covered a small wooden boat and she could see a man working at one end, his head down as he focused on the task in hand.

She stood there for a moment, not sure of her next step, her heart thumping in her chest. Whether it was the wind ruffling her skirt or some other movement that caught his attention, the man looked up. 'Can I help you?'

Shauna's mouth dried up and no words would come. After all these years, all the times she'd thought about what she would say if she ever met Demetrios again, now that she was standing in front of him, her mind was blank.

Demetrios stood up and walked towards her. He was wearing an old T-shirt dotted with paint splatter, and a pair of loose khaki shorts. He could easily have been mistaken for some artisan craftsman, she thought, rather than the head of an international conglomerate. 'I do not get many visitors to my boathouse, *despoinída*, you have taken a wrong turn perhaps?' He came closer, smiling in welcome, but as he neared her, his smile faltered. Shauna took off her fedora, her red hair falling loosely about her shoulders.

'Hello, Demetrios.'

They stood staring at each other in silence for a moment. Those achingly familiar gold-flecked hazel eyes were full of disbelief at what he was seeing. Now, rather than the fervour and passion of the young man that she remembered, there was caution and a touch of sorrow in them.

Demetrios cleared his throat and said, 'Shauna, you came . . .'

He reached out to her and before she could stop him, he enveloped her in his arms, holding her tightly without speaking. Shauna found herself surrendering – a surge of emotion threatening to overthrow her composure. Instinctively she knew he felt the same as she did. She didn't want to let go, to end this brief interlude and begin the painful conversation that she knew was coming. She drank in his familiar smell of citrus and sandalwood, now combined with an earthiness that spoke of days spent toiling with his hands. She pulled away.

'It is good to see you,' he told her.

She smiled and nodded, making no attempt to hide the fact that she felt the same way. 'So this is your new office?'

He ran his hands through his hair and them wiped them on his shorts, the nervous movement showing his anxiety. 'Call it the indulgence of a middle-aged man. Here I can pretend I am something else.'

'Still trying to escape?'

He laughed ruefully. 'Still trying, and still failing. But I forget my manners. I have little to entertain guests here, but I can offer a small hospitality.' He pulled out two wooden folding beach chairs that were leaning against a wall and placed them just inside the doors of the boathouse so that they looked out over the sea. 'Sit, please.' Then he hurried off to a cool box in the corner and returned with two glasses and a bottle of retsina.

He filled a glass and handed it to her, then filled the second and raised it in a toast. 'Here's to . . .' It took him a second or two to find the right words: 'Here's to you and your success. I always thought you had a very special quality and I am pleased that the rest of the world has appreciated it too.'

'Thank you.' She clinked glasses with him and took a sip of the cool, pungent wine. A little Dutch courage wouldn't go amiss, she told herself.

'I am so glad you chose to come here. I must apologize that I did not find out until recently that the Shauna O'Brien I knew all those years ago had become a famous actress. It was only a couple of years ago, when I caught a glimpse of you at Cannes—'

'It's a shame we didn't see each other,' she lied. 'And there's no reason you should have known. Our paths went in opposite directions.'

'If I had known, I would have written to you sooner, to explain myself.'

'There really is nothing to explain. We were young and from two different worlds. It could never have worked.'

Demetrios frowned. 'I see. You think it was youthful infatuation?'

'No one could expect a young man like you to have made a commitment to a girl like me. It was too much to ask – and so it proved.'

Demetrios took a slow sip of his drink and appeared to be weighing up his words. 'I have always regretted that I didn't try harder to find you. When Jeremy fired you, you left so quickly that I didn't get a chance to—'

'Honestly, Demetrios, there's no need to drag up old feelings that don't have any place now.' Shauna knew she was being harsh, but she needed to be strong.

'Then why did you come here?'

'There is something that you need to know . . .' She stood up and walked a few paces, steeling herself. 'Something about us.'

He looked at her, unsure what was coming. Seeing how nervous she was, he nodded encouragingly but didn't try to pressure her.

'Well . . . my husband, Dan . . .'

'I am so sorry for your loss. I saw the news and—'

'He had an affair.' She turned to him now.

'Then he must have been crazy.' Demetrios got up and took a step towards her.

'He had an affair and there was child. Dan's mistress called me, earlier this year . . . she had cancer and knew she didn't have long to live. She was worried about her son – Dan's son. Four years old, and he was about to be an orphan. She wanted me to take him in and give him the chances in life that she never could.'

'And did you take him in?'

'Yes . . .' She breathed in deeply. 'And I'm glad I did. I love him so much.'

'You always had a big heart, Shauna.'

Shauna felt herself start to shake and Demetrios, seeing her distress, reached out to her, but she backed away.

'There's something I have to tell you. And if I don't do it now, I never will.' She took a deep breath. 'After I left Ithos, I went back to England, back to university . . . A few weeks later, I realized I was pregnant.'

A cloud passed over Demetrios's face and his voice faltered. 'I was careful . . . I don't understand . . .'

'Not careful enough.'

His face was anguished. 'The child . . . did you . . .?'

'I didn't know what to do!' she snapped. 'I was nineteen years old. For as long as I could, I hid the truth. I wore big jumpers and baggy trousers so no one would know. Then I started skipping lectures. My tutor noticed, and came to see me at the flat I shared with Roxy.'

Demetrios worked his jaw. 'And then what?' he asked, his voice full of urgency.

'I explained the situation. Joanna – the tutor – was wonderful. I was ready to drop out, but she told me not to rush into anything, to take my time working out my options.' She swallowed. 'I was only in my second year, you see.'

'What did your parents say?'

Dredging up the long-buried memories was making her revisit the emotions too. Shauna's eyes stung with tears, undermining her efforts to keep this as matter-of-fact as possible. She shook her head. 'I could never have told my parents. They were Catholics . . . and it would have broken my father's heart. I wasn't brave enough, and I should have been.' She choked on the words.

'Shauna . . .' Again Demetrios reached out to her, but she held her hands up.

'You must let me speak.' She took a deep breath to steady herself and went on: 'Joanna put me in touch with an adoption agency. Roxy didn't want me to do it, told me that she'd give up her studies too and we'd raise the baby together.' Shauna swiped her tears away. 'She meant it, too, every word. Roxy would have given up her dreams for me.'

Demetrios face twisted, trying to hold back his own tears. 'Our child . . .'

Shauna couldn't help a smiling at the memory of her. 'She was the most beautiful little thing, Demetrios. She had a mass of dark hair like yours, and blue eyes – but the midwife told me that all babies have blue eyes when they are born.'

'What happened to her?'

Shauna needed a moment to compose herself before continuing. She sat down and took a gulp of the wine. This was the hardest part of all. 'I had signed the papers before she was born, but I knew it was the right thing – the best thing for her. We had an idyllic two days together. I couldn't stop looking at her, she was such a perfect little thing, a miracle. When they came to take her away, they told me not to cry, that it would upset the child, so, I tried hard to be brave. I gave them a letter I had written, and asked them to give it to her when she was old enough.'

Demetrios kneeled down next to Shauna and held her hand as she continued. 'She was asleep, her little rosebud lips slightly apart. I could hear her breathing. When I handed her over, she shuddered, her tiny hand reaching out for me before settling again. It was almost like she had reached out for me in her dreams . . . but I wasn't there any more.'

For a moment they held hands in silence, united in their thoughts of the child they had created and then lost.

Then Demetrios wiped at his eyes, then shook his head. 'What I will never understand is why you did not try to contact me,' he said despairingly. 'I could have helped . . . We could have found a way.'

His reaction lit a touchpaper. Shauna's anger flared: 'How dare you! I was banished from Ithos, and you never lifted a finger to help me.'

'That isn't true!'

'Isn't it? You didn't even come to say goodbye. Instead, you let your mother do your dirty work for you, just like you let your family decide your future. You could have fought for me, but you didn't.'

Demetrios looked back at her, speechless at first. Then he asked, 'My mother? What does she have to do with this?'

'Don't tell me you don't know!'

'The day you left, I had gone to my parents' villa. The business was in trouble and Sofía's father was prepared to bail us out, provided I made an "alliance" with his daughter. When I came back to the boat, you were gone.'

'Your mother had me thrown off the island. She came to the boat, told me that I was a fool to think that you loved me.'

Shauna saw a look of realization cross his face, then it hardened and he balled up his fists, his voice seething with rage and frustration. 'I found out afterwards that Jeremy had fired you, but I had no idea that my mother . . .' He reached out and held her by her shoulders, entreating her. 'When they told me I must agree to marry Sofía in order to save the business, I refused. I said no, Shauna. I was in love with you, so I told my mother that I would choose my own wife.'

'I don't understand. Why didn't you come back to the boat to get me?'

'My mother was angry, she stormed out. I stayed on to talk some more with my father, to see if there was some other way we could save the business. She must have gone straight to the boat. She couldn't get her way through me, so she punished you.' The truth sat between them. After all this time, they finally knew what had really happened that day. But what use was it now, Shauna thought? The truth had come too late to change anything. 'By the time I got to the harbour, you were gone. I looked for you . . . tried to track you down . . . but I knew so little about you.'

'I saw your wedding announcement – your mother got what she wanted.'

'Not right away. I looked for you, but I couldn't even find out where you had got off the ferry. I would have asked Chantelle, but the morning after you left she handed in her notice and took the first ferry out of Ithos.'

'At least someone showed a bit of loyalty. You still married Sofía.'

'I had no way to trace you . . .'

'Out of sight, out of mind. You forgot about me.'

'*No!*'

'Yes. Look, this is all so pointless. I came here because I needed to tell you about our daughter. For years, I tried to bury the memories because it was too painful, not knowing whether she was happy, whether I'd made the right decision. I tried to trace her through the adoption agency but they refused to help, and my lawyers say there's nothing I can do. I would give anything to be able to see her, to explain why I had to give her up, and to let her know that even though we were only together for such a short time, I loved her more than I've ever loved anyone before or since.'

Demetrios nodded sadly. 'You know, Shauna, when I wrote to you, I hoped that we could pick up where we left off, that our love would be the same, but I see now that we are not the same people. It was foolish of me to dream.'

He looked so desolate that she almost reached out to him, but she stopped herself. He was right, the spell was broken. She had done what she had come here to do, and now it was time to go.

'I must head back, Alex will be wondering where I am.'

'Is that your husband's son?'

'Yes. He's the brightest, sweetest, most loving little boy you could wish to meet.'

'He is lucky to have you.'

'It's the other way round, Demetrios. He's filled a little bit of that hole in my heart.'

The rumble of an approaching speedboat signalled Christian's return. He waved to them. Shauna turned to Demetrios. 'I want to go back to Ithos now.'

'Of course, as you wish. I will take you myself, in my own boat. I will signal Christian.'

Shauna picked up her fedora and underneath there was a volume of Sappho's poetry. She smiled. 'Your favourite.'

'Always. As she says: "Farewell, go and remember me . . ."'

'As if I could ever forget you.' Their eyes met for a moment, so much emotion suspended in the air between them. She looked away. 'What's underneath the tarpaulin?'

Demetrios paused. 'Oh, just another "flight of fancy", as you would say. Come, let us go.'

Shauna put her hat on and collected her bag, casting a last glance at Fengari Bay as Demetrios turned his boat towards Ithos harbour.

Chapter 30

Ariana looked at the brightly coloured scarves hanging from one of the stalls in Ithos market. She took a midnight-blue tasselled scarf from its hanger and tried it on, admiring herself in the mirror. The stallholder gave her an encouraging smile, but Ariana shook her head and gave it to the woman to put back. She drifted around some of the other stalls while keeping an eye out for Christian, her heart quickening at the sound of a speedboat coming in. She was surprised to see it was her father at the helm, and there was an attractive redhead with him.

Ariana watched through curious eyes as her father helped the woman disembark on to the jetty. They exchanged a few words, embraced briefly, and then her father was alone. He stood for a few moments, watching as the woman disappeared out of sight up the winding path that let past their own villa and up to the hills beyond.

Ariana felt sure that the woman was Shauna Jackson, the famous actress. Their family had always had celebrity friends, but they were mostly from mainland Europe. Her father took a tennis holiday every year with Viggo Mortensen, and

Ralph Fiennes occasionally came to the island and hung out at the villa, but this was a surprise. As far as Ariana knew, Shauna Jackson had never visited Ithos before. She resolved to ask Teresa – if anyone would know who the woman was, she would – but right now she had other plans.

Her father headed towards the taverna and Ariana saw Níko come out to meet him. They spoke for a few minutes, Níko clapped him on the shoulder and the two men went inside. It looked as if it was going to be one of those days when they would open a bottle of retsina and throw the cork away.

Ariana looked at her Gucci watch; it was only mid-afternoon, but her father had clearly finished work for the day. Christian must still be at the boathouse. There wouldn't be a better chance to catch him; she'd have him to herself there. She paused at a stall that sold dresses and checked herself out in their mirror; her bikini was clearly visible under the floor-length see-through white dress she wore. Perfect.

Satisfied, she strode over to her father's boat. Fortunately, he'd opted for a table inside the taverna rather than on the terrace; she could see him through the window, a bottle of retsina and a glass in front of him. Hopefully he would be too engrossed in his conversation with Níko to see what she was up to. As always, the speedboat's keys were in the ignition. No one would dare steal her father's boat from here, they all knew who he was. A fisherman on one of the adjoining boats eyed her curiously; he would know who she was too, so she waved and blew the old man a kiss, which elicited a gummy smile from his toothless mouth.

She sped away from the harbour, revving the engine, watching the speed gauge rise as she bounced through the water. Why go slow when you can go fast, she thought. It wasn't long before Fengari Bay came into view. A smile of satisfaction played around her lips when she spotted Christian's boat moored outside the boathouse.

As she neared the jetty, she cut the engine, letting the incoming tide guide her gently to its mooring. Instead of going inside as soon as she'd finished securing the boat to the docking post, she paused to take off her dress. They were on a beach, weren't they, why shouldn't she stroll into the boathouse in a bikini and invite him to come for a swim? Her gold Lycra bikini consisted of a plunge top paired with high-cut bottoms – Ariana loved the way it made her look and feel; whenever she was on the beach men just couldn't take their eyes off her. Christian wouldn't know what hit him. He would lose all interest in that stupid English girl after this.

She sashayed slowly through the boathouse doors and leaned one arm against the doorframe, striking a pose that showed off her figure to best advantage, then waited for Christian to notice her. His head was sticking out from the bottom of one of the boats under construction. He looked up, and when he saw it was her, he slid out from underneath the boat.

She looked down at him, giving him her most alluring smile. 'Hello, Christian,' she purred. 'I've come to tempt you away for a swim.'

Christian deftly flipped himself up off the floor trolley and narrowed his eyes. 'Does your father know you are here?'

'What does it matter if he does or not? I'm eighteen years old and I can do what I like.'

He spotted Demetrios's boat moored up outside. Ariana didn't have the necessary licence to drive the boat, so there was no way her father would have given her permission to borrow it. 'Where is he?'

'I saw him go into Níko's. He won't be coming back here, if that's what you're worried about.'

'Was that redhead still with him?'

'Who cares? Let's go for a swim Christian. I'm ready to dive in.' She pushed her shoulders back, emphasizing her breasts.

He turned away, throwing his tools down and reaching for a towel to wipe his oily hands. 'Not now, Ari, I'm too busy. Go and find one of your friends in Ithos.'

'I'm not interested in any of them. That's why I've come to see you.' She pouted. 'Come on, Christian, the day is nearly over. You need to have some fun.' She closed the distance between them, swinging her hips as if she were on the catwalk.

'Ari . . .'

'What?' she asked innocently as she wrapped her arms around his chest, running her fingers though his blond hair, her body meeting his, the warmth rising up in her as her breasts brushed against him.

'Ariana, stop this.' He pulled his head away from her hands and took a few steps back. 'You mustn't do this.'

Ariana giggled. 'Don't be shy, Christian, I'm all grown-up now . . . and I've learned a thing or two.' She reached behind her and flipped the catch on the back of her bikini top.

The straps came loose and she slowly dropped the top, revealing the perfectly tanned rise of her breasts.

'Enough, Ari!' Christian pushed the towel he was holding at her. 'Cover yourself up – you're making a fool of yourself. I'm not interested, why can't you just accept that?'

The laughter died on her lips and she held the towel to herself, covering her naked breasts. 'What do you mean?'

'Exactly what I said.' His voice was gentler now. 'Look,

Ari, you are a beautiful girl and one day someone will love you and make you happy, but it isn't going to be me.'

'Why not? What's wrong with me?' she demanded.

'There is nothing wrong with you,' he said kindly. 'But I've known you since you were a baby. You're like a little sister to me.'

'I'm not a child! Let's make love, then you'll see.' She pressed herself against him urgently.

'Ariana, I don't want to make love to you and I never will. I don't want to hurt your feelings but it's true.'

'It's that fucking English whore, isn't it?'

'Grace?'

'She's behind all this. I saw you with the little bitch the other day.'

'Ari, calm down.'

'Don't tell me to calm down!' Ariana dropped the towel and fumblingly put her bikini top back on. 'You wanted me before she was here.'

'No,' Christian said. 'That's not true. I've never led you on.'

There were tears mingling with her fury now, his words drawing out an anger that was born of humiliation.

'How could you do this to me?' Her voice was ragged, almost pleading now. 'All I've ever wanted is you . . .' Her mascara mingled with her tears and ran down her face, leaving black streaks on her cheeks. She turned and ran out of the boathouse.

Christian ran after her, shouting, 'Ariana, don't be stupid, let me take you back to Ithos!'

But Ariana had flicked the rope off the docking post and jumped into the speedboat. She thew the throttle, desperate to get away from Christian and the words that had broken her heart.

Chapter 31

It had been an exhausting day at the taverna, a large party of English day-trippers had come for lunch and stayed long into the evening, eating and drinking. By the time they left, the locals had started to arrive for dinner, Greeks preferring to eat later in the evening. It was now past midnight and, apart from a few stragglers outside on the terrace lingering over their nightcaps, the place was empty.

Even at this hour, the work was never done. Grace was busy wiping tables down and tidying away the condiments when Níko tapped her on the shoulder.

'Grace, why don't you knock off? It has been a long day and you are on an early shift tomorrow.'

'Are you sure?' She wiped her hand across her weary eyes. 'I'm happy to finish up here.'

'I want you to get your beauty sleep, otherwise you will be yawning over the breakfast orders,' he tutted. 'Run along now, goodnight.'

She popped a kiss on his cheek. 'You're so sweet, Níko. Thank you.'

Grace didn't bother bringing a handbag with her to the

taverna, since her room was upstairs and her belongings were quite safe in there. All she carried with her was the key in her pocket. Calling *kalinikta* to Níko, she left through the front entrance that looked out onto the square.

It was almost empty tonight, though she could hear the cries of the fishermen as they set off on their nocturnal fishing expedition. She turned into the side street, and walked into the small courtyard behind the taverna, going up the stone steps to the door that led to the landing. There was a noise behind her, and she jumped. 'Who's there?' she called, seeing someone following her up the stairs.

There was only a dim light coming from a bulb above the entrance and at first she didn't recognize the dishevelled figure. Grace was shocked when she realized it was Ariana. Her make-up was smeared and her eyes were glazed over, as if she'd been drinking.

'Ariana? Are you OK? What are you doing here?'

'You bitch!' Ariana lunged at her, but before she could reach Grace, she tripped on one of the stairs, fell forward and landing at her feet with a groan.

Grace bent down. 'Have you hurt yourself?'

Ariana moaned again. 'I don't know . . . I feel sick.'

'You'd better come inside.' Grace helped Ariana up. She had to keep hold of her because the girl was wobbling on her heels and struggling to stay upright. When she put the key in the door and flicked on the light, Ariana lurched forward and threw herself on to the bed. Putting her hand across her face, she groaned again and Grace quickly poured her a glass of water from the bottle by the side of the bed.

'Ugh, it's warm, haven't you got anything cold?' she mumbled.

'This is a lovely room, but it doesn't stretch to a fridge. I think what you need is a cup of tea.'

On the chest of drawers, there was a tray with a kettle and some sachets of tea and coffee in a small basket. 'Where have you been to get in this state?' Grace asked the prone figure.

'Mind your own business,' Ariana slurred belligerently.

'My mum always says that the best cure for drunkenness is lots of sweet tea,' Grace said. 'Ideally it should be Yorkshire Tea, but the mini-market doesn't sell that, so Lipton's will have to do.' She emptied a sachet of sugar and a splash of long-life milk into the mug. 'There's no proper milk, I'm afraid.'

She came and sat next to Ariana on the bed. 'Sit up and drink the tea. Honestly, you'll feel much better in a few minutes, I promise.'

Ariana glowered at her. 'How do you know what will make me feel better?'

'Maybe I don't,' Grace conceded the point. 'But this can't make you feel any worse.'

Ariana sipped at the sweet liquid and grimaced. 'It's horrible.'

'Keep drinking. So where have you been?'

Ariana sipped miserably at the tea. 'With Georgiou and some of his friends. We had a beach party on the other side of the island.'

'What were you drinking?'

Ariana looked at Grace like she was stupid. 'It wasn't just alcohol, you idiot.'

'Oh, I see. That wasn't very sensible.'

'You don't see anything at all, Miss Goody-two-shoes,' she sniffed. 'This is all your fault.'

'What has this got to do with me?'

'Christian . . .' Ariana started to cry. Big hot tears splashed down into her tea. 'He . . . he . . .' she hiccupped, 'he doesn't want me.'

301

Grace took the tea off her and put it on the side. She reached for a packet of tissues and handed Ariana one.

'He wants you, not me,' Ariana sobbed, dabbed at her eyes and blowing her nose noisily.'

'Did he say that?'

'No . . . but I saw you get off the boat, you'd been together.' Ariana pouted, sticking her bottom lip out.

'We had a day at the beach, that's all. We're friends, nothing else.'

'You're lying.'

'I'm not . . . well, not really.'

Ariana's tears started again.

'Look, we kissed, that's all. It was hardly anything. Just a nice day out.' She shrugged, but Ariana didn't look convinced. 'Besides, even if I did like him and he liked me, it couldn't go anywhere, I'll be going back to England soon.'

'Really?'

'Yes. I love Ithos, but I can't stay here forever . . . You see, I came here looking for something, but I didn't find it and, well, there isn't anything here for me now.'

'What were you looking for?' Ariana asked. 'Not that I care.'

'I'm adopted. Which has never bothered me in the slightest – I love my parents, they've given me the best life anyone could have been given. And I've always known I was adopted, so it didn't come as a big shock or anything. For a long time, I wasn't interested in knowing who my birth parents were, but then I found out that once an adopted person turns eighteen they have the right to apply for information.' She paused. 'When I look at myself, I know I'm not a typical English Rose and it has always intrigued me, like a piece of the puzzle that's missing. So, last year, when I turned eighteen, I contacted the adoption agency.'

'What happened?' Ariana looked as though the effects of whatever she had taken earlier were wearing off, and there was a flicker of interest that she couldn't hide.

'They forwarded an envelope . . .' Grace recalled her parents handing over the envelope from the agency and then leaving the room so she could open it in private. 'We'll be downstairs if you need us. And if you don't want to open it, that's OK too.' They had hugged each other tightly and Grace remembered feeling so lucky that these people had taken her as their own.

Her emotions had been in turmoil as she sat with the letter on her lap. The envelope could have contained the information that her mother didn't want to be contacted, or that she was dead. It took a while for Grace to find the courage to open it. Inside was a letter from her birth mother:

Dear Grace,

Happy eighteenth birthday to you. On the dawn of your adulthood, I wanted you to know that you were born in love. I have never forgotten those precious few days we spent together, and not a single day passes when I don't think of you and say a prayer for you. The mother and father you were placed with would never have made you feel like you were a guilty secret.

I hope that your life is full of kindness, laughter and opportunity, and that the years to come bring you joy and love. Live a happy and fulfilling life, Grace – you deserve it. I will never, ever forget you, and if one day you want to find me, I'll be waiting.

Xxx

Grace remembered sitting there, barely able to catch her breath, her mind fizzing with the thought that her birth mother had loved her and not wanted to give her away. She shook the envelope and was surprised when something else fell out. It was a postcard. It had been ripped in two and put back together, a bit of yellowed Sellotape holding the two pieces together. On the front was a picture of a place called Ithos, somewhere that Grace had never heard of. There was a picture of the harbour with all the little fishing boats, and you could just make out Níko's taverna and the central square. She read the words on the back:

My dear Beauty
   Always have hope. We have our dreams. Remember our souls will always burn brighter.
   Don't wait for me.

Who was the postcard from? It wasn't in the same handwriting as her birth mother's. In fact, it was very distinctively different. Once she had found out that Ithos was in Greece, she'd started to wonder if that was why she had olive skin and hair that was almost black. The letter and the postcard had thrown up more questions than answers and she'd found it too much to take in. She felt glad that her birth mother had loved her, but she couldn't find any real feelings to connect her to the woman who hadn't felt able to keep her. She wasn't sure she felt brave or curious enough to start the process of finding her.

The postcard, however, had exerted a mysterious influence over her. She couldn't seem to stop herself taking it out of its hiding place and reading it again and again.

'I still wasn't sure I was ready to meet my birth mother, but every time I looked at the picture on the postcard, I felt somehow drawn to the place. The more I thought about it, the more convinced I became that I was connected to Ithos in some way. But since I arrived . . .'

Ariana peered at the postcard, squinting. 'Why didn't they sign it?'

'I don't know, it's almost like a goodbye.'

'Maybe the person who wrote it was interrupted?' Ariana looked at the postcard again. 'There's something about the writing . . . and the name . . .' She winced and clutched at her head. 'If I didn't have such a bad headache, my brain might work properly. I can't think straight.' She handed the postcard back to Grace. 'Thanks for the life story.' She feigned a yawn.

Grace laughed. 'I don't know what I expected to find here. I mean, that postcard must have been written almost twenty years ago, because that's when my birth mother wrote the letter. Maybe she came here and had a holiday romance.'

Ariana let out a huff. 'Look, this is all very interesting, but I need to go.'

'Why don't you wait here a little longer, until your head feels better.'

'I don't want to, that's why.' Ariana swung her legs off the bed and stood up. She seemed much steadier on her feet now.

'Why don't we pop down to the tavern? Níko is still there, he can drop you home.'

'Níko?' Ariana pulled a face and stuck out her tongue. 'He's my father's spy. No, I can get home myself.'

'How?'

'I'll take one of the taxis that waits on the square.'

Grace stood and made to follow her, but Ariana put her hand out to stop her. 'Look, English girl, maybe you aren't trying to move in on Christian.' Her face, despite her smudged make-up and bloodshot eyes, retained some pride. 'But tonight, don't try to be my friend, OK?'

Grace sighed. She didn't like the idea of Ariana trying to make her way home on her own, but she couldn't force the girl to accept her help. Ithos was a safe place, and the taxi drivers would surely know who she was.

She watched Ariana teeter down the stairs on her high heels and walk slowly but deliberately out of the courtyard. 'Be careful, OK?' she called after her.

Ariana raised a hand, whether it was intended as a goodbye or a dismissive gesture, Grace couldn't tell. She closed the door and lay on the bed, picking up the card where Ariana had left it. She looked at it again, weathered and worn, now yellow with age.

Don't wait for me . . .

I'm still waiting, Grace thought, still no nearer to knowing how Ithos was tied up with her birth. There was only one way she was going to find out, but was she ready to take that step?

Chapter 32

Demetrios had risen earlier than usual and taken a run up into the hills above Ithos. The air up there felt clearer, more invigorating, and he usually had the place to himself running just after dawn, apart from the odd hill farmer tending to his goats. He found running alone helped him to think things over, and there had been so much to think about these last few days.

Shauna was more beautiful than even his rose-tinted spectacles remembered her to be. Her skin, golden and shimmering, a smattering of freckles over that perfect nose and eyes as green as the shamrocks in her home country. And her body . . . she had matured, her curves had filled out deliciously. He ran harder, reaching for the summit – just another half a kilometre but it was all at a gradient that made his calves ache. He reached the top and stopped dead, breathing raggedly, his chest rising and falling as he waited for his breathing to even out.

From up here in the hills, the vista of Ithos was laid out before him like a painting; this island that he called home was beautiful, and usually the sight of it eased his soul.

Today, however, he was too troubled to enjoy it. The thought that he and Shauna had created a baby girl together, a baby he had never held, whose first tentative steps he had missed, and who he might never meet. Conceived in the summer of 1982, she would be nineteen by now. A year older than Ariana. It felt like a punch in the guts. He was a family man, it was everything to him. Whatever Shauna might think, he would have made things right, if he'd known.

He didn't blame Shauna. This was all Elana's doing.

His mother had always meddled in his life. In all of their lives. Pulling strings and manipulating them as if they were puppets. Well, it was time she heard a few home truths. It might be too late for him, but he could at least put a stop to her plans for Ariana.

He turned and headed back along the path, all downhill now. His long strides powered through the kilometres.

It was time his mother was put in her place once and for all.

Shauna dipped her toe in the Mediterranean, enjoying the coolness on her painted red toenails as she entered the water up to her waist. The colour of the sea on Ithos was like an ever-changing jewel; today it was turquoise, and so clear she could see tiny fish darting around in the water. She kicked her legs out and swam to the rocks and back again, the coolness of the water and the breeze contrasting with the heat of the sun which was rising high in the sky. Ithos had burrowed its way into her soul again; it would be hard to leave, but she knew they must.

Swimming back to the shore, she waved at Roxy, who was reading a copy of *Vogue*, and Alex, who was trying to blow up his inflatable dolphin.

She threw herself on the sand next to Roxy and applied

another layer of suncream, then slipped her silk parrot-print sarong over her shoulders.

Roxy put down her magazine. 'Better?'

Shauna nodded. 'Much . . . Well, a little.'

'No regrets?'

'About telling Demetrios?' She put her head on one side, thinking. 'No. It was time that secret came out into the light. He's as much a part of that child's story as I am.'

'Do you believe him, that he tried to find you?'

Shauna considered this. 'I think that's what he wants to believe himself. He was under so much pressure from his parents to save the company, to build a dynasty.' She ran her hand through the sand, enjoying the heat of it through her fingers. 'I think he could be strong when we were together, but once I was gone . . .'

'Maybe it was for the best. You might never have made it to where you are now if you'd stayed together.'

'We were too young. We'd probably have ended up divorced a few years later.' She lowered her voice to a whisper. 'Could giving up a child you love ever be for the best?'

Roxy reached out for her hand. 'I'm sorry.'

'I know. But he made his choice, and so did I.'

'So, when are we leaving?' Roxy asked her gently. 'It's going to be hard saying goodbye to this place, I can tell you.'

'You're right, but every holiday must come to an end.'

'How about we go to Níko's for an early dinner? We can head over late afternoon. I'd like to say goodbye to Grace. I know Alex is going to miss her.'

'I still haven't met her.'

'Now's your chance.'

* * *

Elana poured herself a cup of Earl Grey tea from the silver teapot. She never thought of herself as an anglophile, but there was something so civilized about afternoon tea. She had heard that the English claimed tea cooled you down on a hot day, which sounded like nonsense to her, but she found a serenity in the ritual of brewing, pouring and drinking that was uniquely pleasurable. She looked out from the terrace, past the pool to the olive grove and beyond that to the sea. How many thousands of times had she looked out at this scene? People liked to assume that the Theodosis villa belonged to her husband, but the opposite was true. This had been her childhood home and her parents had gifted it to them as part of her dowry. She had been born in this place. She would die here, and that thought gave her comfort. Elana took consolation in the simple cycle of life, but today she felt troubled, a nagging unease was sending anxious ripples through her mind, chipping away her composure until even a cup of Earl Grey couldn't make things better. Something was bothering her, something she couldn't quite identify.

She tapped her foot fretfully. Where was everyone today? Ariana had not yet shown her face, probably still sleeping off another late night with her friends. She would normally have come looking for something to eat by now. Elana decided to cook her grandaughter's favourite dish: youvetsi, the perfect comfort food.

As she got to her feet and smoothed out the creases in her printed floor-length dress, she heard footsteps coming through the house in her direction. Seconds later, Demetrios came out onto the terrace, dressed not for leisure but in a pair of smart linen trousers and a crisp white shirt. He did not greet her with his usual kiss.

'You are going somewhere,' she observed.

'Yes, Mother. I have decided that I have lingered here

long enough. I am going to my office in Athens to make arrangements. I have decided to move to London and take Ariana with me. She needs someone to provide a positive influence in her life, and who better than her parents. Maybe we should have tried harder to work together when she was younger, instead of fighting each other. But I'm sure we can coexist in the same city for the good of our daughter.'

'What has got into you, Demi? Where has this come from all of a sudden? Why have you said nothing of these plans before now?'

'I have always known that you are a scheming, devious woman, Mother, but I had no idea how much your interference had cost me. I cannot stand by and let you wreck my daughter's life too.'

Elana felt a tremble in her legs. 'What are you talking about?'

Demetrios walked across the terrace, but his mind was not on the view. 'We get many visitors to this island, Mother, some of them returning ones. This week, an old acquaintance of yours arrived – or should I say an old triumph.'

'Triumph? Demi, I have no idea what you mean.'

'Don't you? Well then, let me help you understand. Twenty years ago, you took it upon yourself to decide my future. When I refused to go along with your plans, you took matters into your own hands.' His voice was full of vitriol and white-hot anger. 'You banished the woman I loved as if you were a god on Olympus.'

'Twenty years . . . I can't remember, it's so long ago . . .' Her voice was shaking but, despite her protestations, her mind was as sharp as it had always been and she remembered well the events of that day . . .

Carol Kirkwood

Summer, 1982

'Let's drink to the future, yours and the business, to a grand dynasty.' She had handed Demetrios a glass and tipped her own to him. 'What do you say? To the future? Stay for dinner this evening and we can talk some more.'

Her son looked at her coldly, 'Mother, this is not a game of chess and I am not one of your pawns.'

'Don't be silly, this is not about games, this is about the future. Surely you want the same as we do?'

'Do I?' Demetrios put his glass of champagne down on the table. 'You know, Mother, a few years ago you might have fooled me with all this talk, but now I can see a different life.'

'Don't be ridiculous, this is the only life we have known, it is in our blood.'

Demetrios's voice was louder now, the passion in his face evident as his eyes flashed and his voice filled with pent-up emotions. 'Constantis is a conniving bastard, but what the hell does it matter if he takes the company – you'll still be rich, you can buy another company, try something different.'

'Now you're being irrational,' his father had interjected, lighting another cigar.

'Are you seriously asking me to marry someone I don't love, to give up my dreams, just for the good of the business?'

'What dreams are these?' Elana had sneered dismissively. 'What can a young man know about love.'

'Oh, I know plenty. I know that love isn't selfish or greedy, it doesn't care about money or status. I know this because there is a woman who loves me for myself, who doesn't care about any of those things.'

Elana let a cruel laugh escape her. 'Ah, the little chambermaid you've been screwing?'

312

'Mother . . . you go too far.'

But Elana didn't stop. 'Oh yes, I have heard all about her. But you are a fool if you think that she isn't a gold-digger just like the rest of them.'

'You're wrong.'

'I am never wrong. You are an immature, lovesick puppy to think that your money is of no interest to her. This grand love affair of yours will last a few more weeks and then the moment she leaves the island, she'll be selling your story to the tabloids. You'll look even more like an idiot than you do now.'

Demetrios took a step towards her, and another, until their noses were almost touching. 'And how do you think you look now, Mother?' His eyes were cold. 'You think you are still beautiful. Maybe on the outside, but inside you are ugly and twisted.'

Elana's heart lurched; she had never before seen her son look at her with such hate in his eyes. Perhaps she had gone too far, but it was that stupid money-grabber who had turned his head.

'Demi!' his father had chided, 'don't talk to your mother like that. Whoever this girl is, she has gone to your head.'

Elana had composed herself. 'Relax. Aristotle, tempers are hot, no?' She patted her son's arm. 'We must step back a little and calm down.' She smiled serenely, determined to exert control over the situation. Things were worse than she had thought if this was how he was feeling.

'Demetrios, sit and talk with your father for a while, perhaps he can help you to come to the right decision. I will leave the two of you to discuss it in private.'

Elana had jumped into her Jaguar and driven down to the harbour, seeking Jeremy out.

'What the hell has been going on?'

Jeremy told her everything, about the young woman her son had been so taken with. The pair of them had been spending nearly every waking hour together since the *St Helena* had docked in Ithos.

'You stupid man! Why didn't you tell me about this before? She could ruin everything. We have to get rid of her. I want you to sack her.'

Jeremy had been shocked but when she'd reminded him that she was his employer not Demetrios, he soon did her bidding.

Elana couldn't resist a look at the girl who had caused her son to take leave of her senses. She was not what she had expected, and Elana couldn't help admiring the girl's dignity as she refused to take her money. The girl with the green eyes and the flame-red hair . . .

Elana gasped: the woman in the olive grove – that was her! She was older, certainly, but she could see now that she had not changed so much, still beautiful, with that inner poise.

'The woman . . . she was here . . .'

'So you have seen her, too. Well, Mother, she came here to tell me that we had a child, and she gave her up for adoption. A baby girl, a *Theododis* baby girl.' He emphasized their family name.

Elana's legs almost gave way. She sank down in her wicker chair, putting her face in her hands.

'Oh, Demetrios, how could I have known?'

'Your dirty secret is now discovered, Mother.' His voice was icy. 'You sent her away, and with her the child I never knew, the daughter I will never have a chance to know. Have you any idea how that makes me feel?'

'Son . . .' Elana sobbed. 'Demi, please, I only did what I thought was right for us.'

'Yes, for *us*, not for me. I don't think I can ever forgive you.'

'Please, Demi, don't say that.' She reached out for him, but he remained impassive.

They were interrupted by Magda, the housekeeper. 'You have a visitor,' she told them. 'Christian, Níko's boy.'

'Send him through,' Demetrios told her.

Elana was still dabbing at her eyes, composing herself, when Christian came out on to the terrace, but he seemed too preoccupied to notice anything amiss.

'Is Ari here?'

Demetrios flicked an irritated glance at his mother. 'Why?'

'I'm worried about her.' Christian pushed his hand through his hair. 'Your boat is missing from the harbour. I saw Ari driving it yesterday afternoon – she came by the boathouse, but she hasn't returned it to the harbour.'

'But she is here, no?' Demetrios turned to Elana.

Elana shook her head, a look of panic in her eyes. 'I haven't seen her today. I assumed she was sleeping in after a late night.'

Demetrios called Magda and asked her if Ariana was in her room.

She shook her head. 'I have not seen her today, and her bed had not been slept in when I cleaned her room.'

'Shit . . .' Christian said, looking more worried. 'It's late afternoon.'

'There is no need to panic, surely,' Demetrios said. 'She could have spent the night at a friend's house. She knows she will be in trouble with me for borrowing the boat, so she is staying out of my way.'

Elana was shaking her head, she felt a blast of cold dread run through her veins.

'The thing is,' said Christian, 'we had a quarrel. She was

upset and before I could stop her she took off in the boat. This morning, when I saw the boat was missing, I asked around. A couple of the fishermen said that Ariana had brought it back last night, but then someone else said they'd seen her return after midnight and take it out again.'

The colour drained from Demetrios's face. 'This quarrel, what happened?' he demanded, his eyes blazing. 'Tell me.'

'She came to the boathouse and . . . this is embarrassing . . .' He blushed. 'She tried to seduce me.'

Demetrios leapt forward and grabbed Christian by his T-shirt, 'If you have harmed her—'

Christian held his hands up, 'No, boss, of course not. I told her I wasn't interested, that I thought of her like a little sister. That was when she stormed off.'

Elana moaned. 'That is worse – don't you see, Demi, she feels shamed and humiliated.'

Demetrios rounded on his mother. 'This is your fault, you stupid old woman, filling her head with ideas, always trying to manipulate, to make "alliances"—'

Elana wrung her hands, sobbing. 'Demi, please, hate me later. Just find Ariana . . .'

Chapter 33

'Cheers!' Shauna clinked her cold glass of retsina against Roxy's. When they had arrived at the restaurant, Níko had embraced them both like long-lost daughters and insisted on giving them a bottle of his finest wine on the house and serving them himself. He had drawn attention to the table and, for the first time in weeks, Shauna had been asked for her autograph. The fans, a German couple who'd been sitting at a nearby table, chatted politely to her while she signed her name, and then left with big grins on their faces. Luckily, she didn't think anyone else had noticed.

Alex had been exhausted when they had got back from the beach and had fallen into a deep snooze by the time Shauna had come to get him ready for dinner.

'You two go, I will look after him for you,' Delphine, the housekeeper, had told them.

'He'll be sad to have missed seeing Grace,' Roxy said.

'We'll make time before we leave tomorrow,' Shauna promised.

They were now enjoying their first course, a delicious

meze of dolmades, pitta bread, olives, tomatoes and peppers stuffed with feta cheese. It was all delicious.

Roxy licked her lips. 'I think I'm going to miss this the most of all. But everything about Ithos is wonderful.'

'It is a magical place, but—'

'Hey, no regrets, remember?'

'I don't believe people who say they have no regrets. I will always hold this place in my heart, and Demetrios too.'

Roxy was shaking her head. 'This was supposed to be a life cleanse.'

'Oh, don't get me wrong, I know coming here and facing Demetrios was the right thing to do. I'm ready to focus on the next stage of my life.'

'Oscars!'

'Shh, don't tempt fate,' she warned, putting on a mock-stern face. 'My only regret is that Demetrios and I left things on such a sad note.'

Roxy tilted her head, waiting to see if she'd go on. When she'd arrived back at the villa yesterday she'd been reluctant to go into details about her meeting with Demetrios, and Roxy hadn't wanted to push her.

'I told him that I'd keep in touch, but . . . There were so many things jumbled up in my head, and he was so shaken by the news that we have a daughter out there somewhere . . . Maybe we didn't say what was really in our hearts. It was good to see him, though.' Shauna's eyes were misting with tears as she spoke.

'Oh, honey.' Roxy reached out and squeezed Shauna's hand.

Almost as if her words had conjured him up, Shauna saw a red Ferrari pull up outside the taverna and Demetrios got out. He strode across the terrace, followed by Christian, and passed by without even noticing her.

'It seems like fate,' Roxy observed. 'Why don't you ask him if he wants to have a drink with us – or rather, you. I know when three is a crowd.'

Shauna laughed. 'Don't be silly, I'd love you to meet him at long last, so I can prove he really is as handsome as I said he was.'

Maybe it was the retsina going to her head, but Shauna had a sudden feeling that she wasn't ready to say goodbye to him just yet.

'Wait here,' she told Roxy, 'I'll be back in a sec.'

She was wearing a sage-green, Roman-style cotton dress by Anya Hindmarch that trailed almost to the floor, and it swished against the terracotta tiles as she walked into the restaurant. She'd expected to find Demetrios sitting at a table, chatting and laughing, but she was shocked to see him shouting at one of the waitresses. Without thinking, she drew closer. The waitress was a young girl, and she seemed somehow familiar, though Shauna couldn't think why.

The girl was standing next to Níko's wife, who had her arm around her protectively.

'You're telling me you watched her walk off into the night, and you did nothing?' Demetrios raged, but there was a note of desperation in his voice.

The girl was on the verge of tears, but Shauna could tell she was trying hard to stay composed. 'She said she was going to get a taxi. I didn't think she was in any danger.'

'But you just said she was drunk.'

The girl twiddled the tea towel she was holding nervously. 'Well, yes, but—'

'And still you let her go alone?' He shook his head in disbelief. 'This is how you repay our hospitality? Maybe it is time for you to leave.'

Teresa said something in Greek, perhaps in the girl's

defence, judging by the expression on her face. Christian joined in the argument, waving his arms animatedly. The girl, who clearly didn't understand what they were saying, stood biting her lip, tears spilling down her cheeks.

Shauna's heart went out to the poor thing. Whatever she might have done or not done, this was bullying. Compelled to go to the girl's defence, she took a step forward.

'Like mother like son,' she said fiercely, interrupting Demetrios's tirade.

He stopped in his tracks and looked at her, confused. 'Shauna?' But then he recovered himself and snapped, 'This has nothing to do with you. Keep out of it.'

'No. I know exactly what it feels like to be treated the way you're treating this poor girl.' She placed herself between Demetrios and the girl, looking him in the eye as she reminded him: 'Two decades ago I was given my marching orders by a member of the Theodosis family who showed me no compassion. I will not stand by and let you treat someone like this.'

'You have no idea,' he said, and there was desperation rather than anger in his eyes now. 'My daughter is missing, and these two' – he pointed at Christian and Grace – 'are responsible.'

'That's no reason to bully a young girl.' Shauna stood her ground.

'Stay out of this, Shauna,' he said through gritted teeth. 'I still have a daughter . . . if anything has happened to her, I'll . . .' At this he looked past Shauna and addressed Grace: 'Get out of my sight.'

The girl burst into tears and Demetrios turned and stormed out of the taverna.

Shauna was enraged. How dare he? She ran after him as he headed towards the Ferrari, and as he put his key in the ignition she shouted. 'It's a shame you didn't put as much energy into looking for me when *I* disappeared.'

'Shauna, please, this isn't the time or the place.' Seeing the despair in his eyes, she felt a stab of pity.

'You need to think rationally,' she told him, her voice calm now. 'Tell me what happened.'

Demetrios explained to her about Ariana being seen getting into the boat after midnight. It seemed that, instead of climbing into a taxi, she had taken the boat out – and no one had seen her since.

'Could she have gone to a friend's house? Have you tried ringing around to see—'

'Christian has done that already. They told him she'd spent most of the evening at a beach party, and not only had she been drinking, she'd also taken drugs.'

'Oh no.'

'When I get my hands on that Georgiou, I'm going to kill him.' He clenched his jaw.

'Now isn't the time for anger. Have you alerted the police?'

'Yes. The coastguard is on the lookout—'

At that moment, there was a commotion in the harbour. A fishing boat was coming into dock, and its captain was gesticulating and shouting, pointing at something he was towing behind his boat.

As if they were possessed by some second sense, the two of them ran along the jetty to see what it was. Shauna didn't need to be told that this was Demetrios's speedboat, she recognized it from when he had brought her back in it the other day. She felt sick when she saw that the fisherman was holding up a pair of high heels. Though she didn't understand what he saying, she could tell from his gestures that the shoes had been found in the hollow of the deck. The boat itself was empty.

321

The captain, having told Demetrios everything he knew, handed him the shoes.

Demetrios turned to Shauna. 'They found the boat floating near Fengari Bay, but there was no sign of Ariana.'

'Demetrios . . .' Shauna could see the fear on his face.

'Shauna, my little girl . . . she is gone.'

'There is no sense trying to use logic – we need to think like a teenager who is a little drunk and a lot unhappy,' said Roxy.

Shauna had brought Demetrios back to the taverna with her. He'd wanted to go out to join the police and fishing boats searching for his daughter, but Shauna had persuaded him that it would be easier for the authorities to contact him here. The truth was, she was afraid they were looking for a body.

'But the boat . . . her shoes,' Demetrios said.

'It doesn't necessarily mean the worst,' said Roxy. Her unassailable optimism, combined with her down-to-earth Liverpudlian practicality, was the one thing keeping their hopes alive. 'Look, Demetrios, no one knows her better than you do. If she's hurting, her instinct would be to go somewhere she feels safe. Where would that be?'

'Christian said he had checked the boathouse but there was no one there.'

'Where else?' said Shauna.

'She has friends from primary school, I could ask them.'

Sensing that it would help him to be doing something rather than passively waiting, Shauna told him, 'Let's go see them. I'll come with you.'

'Thank you, Shauna . . .' His voice faltered, unable to find words to express how much he valued her steadying presence.

'You two go and do what you need to,' said Roxy, practical as ever, 'while it's still light.'

'I'll call you when we have some news,' Shauna told her, and they hugged.

Roxy watched them go. It was strange to meet Demetrios under such circumstances after having heard Shauna talk about him all these years. The two of them seemed so right together. It wasn't just that they were both so striking, that they made such a handsome couple. It was the way they slotted together, as if Shauna was the light to his shade, or maybe she was the calm and he was the storm.

Despite her encouraging words, she was worried about the missing girl. She hoped Ariana would turn up soon, unharmed and wondering what all the fuss was about; she dreaded to think what it would do to Demetrios if anything had happened to her.

She was about to finish her glass of retsina and head back to the villa when she spotted Grace heading towards the harbour.

'Grace!' she called, waving frantically. 'Over here!'

Grace had her head down and her backpack on her shoulder. She turned to see where the voice had come from. Spotting Roxy, she waved back and came over to see her.

'Where are you off to?' Roxy asked, pointing at her backpack.

Grace shrugged in reply, and Roxy noticed that she was dressed for travelling in sturdy shorts and a polo shirt, rather than her usual vest and shorts.

'I've decided to move on,' the girl told her. 'There's a night ferry to Athens. I really should be getting back to England, and now is as good a time as any.'

'Listen, Demetrios didn't mean what he said earlier. He's just out of his mind with worry.'

'How do you know about that?'

'I was out here on the terrace, I couldn't help but over-hear. You shouldn't leave because of that. Seriously, once he has calmed down, he won't want you to go.'

Grace looked rueful. 'You may well be right. But I think my time here was coming to an end anyway. Now is as good a time as any to leave.'

Roxy stood and gave the young woman a hug. 'Grace, honey, you look so sad. Why don't you stay and have a drink with me? You'll feel better.'

Grace hugged Roxy back and then pulled away. 'Honestly, I'm not sad. I've had a wonderful time here and met some amazing people, I'll never forget this place. It was lovely to meet you, and Alex, too . . . Oh, I almost forgot . . .'

She took her backpack off and dug around in it for a moment before pulling out a small stuffed toy goat. 'I bought this for Alex.'

'Oh, Grace, that's adorable!'

'It's a little friend for Alfie the Alpaca,' Grace said. 'Tell Alex he can call her Grace the Goat if he likes.' She laughed.

'Nothing wrong with a goat; they're independent, intel-ligent and tenacious.' Roxy laughed, too. 'Well, goodbye, Grace. If you ever get to London or New York, give me a call, OK? I'd love to see you again. I'm sorry you didn't get to meet Shauna.'

'I can't wait to see her Grace Kelly movie. Tell her I said hello.'

They hugged again and then Grace headed towards the ferry. Roxy looked down at the little toy; Alex would be sad he had missed her, but he'd have this as a consolation. And, who knows, maybe Grace would look them up one day.

* * *

'Calm down, he won't tell you anything if you threaten to kill him,' Shauna said.

Demetrios's face was a picture of fury. They had already driven to see several of Ariana's friends, all of whom had heard about Ari's disappearance and had spent the afternoon calling other friends and other acquaintances, trying without success to locate her. But one name that kept cropping up was that of a young man: Georgiou Andino.

They had learned that, over the past few weeks, Ariana had been seen frequently with the boy, that they had been to various parties and gatherings. More ominously, they learned that Georgiou had a drug habit. Though Shauna had suggested that they inform the police and let them question the boy, Demetrios had insisted on driving to the Andino family home. They found him lounging by the pool in a pair of tight swimming trunks, casually smoking a joint.

The boy shrugged nonchalantly. 'I don't know anything, old man. Your daughter does what she likes, and so do I.'

'And one of the things you like is taking drugs,' Demetrios observed coldly.

'Ari doesn't need any help from me in that department. She's crazy for cocaine – in fact, she showed up at the party last night and offered me a wrap.'

'You liar!' Demetrios snarled. Shauna stilled him with her hand.

'Look, we're just trying to find her, that's all. Did she say anything about where she was going when she left the party?'

Georgiou shrugged again. 'She kept going on about that English chick – how she was going to confront her about something. I don't know what.'

'What had she taken?' Demetrios asked.

'Just a few lines of coke, not much. Kept saying she was tired and wanted to go to sleep.'

As they sat in the car afterwards, Demetrios looked bleak.

'I pushed her too hard, trying to make her do what I wanted. Shauna, if anything has happened to her, I'll never forgive myself.' He put his head in his hands. 'I should have been a better father to her. If her mother and I had been less selfish, she wouldn't be so wild.'

'You don't know that. I seem to remember that you had that wild side too. She's young, and she's got to work out what to do with her life.'

'When she was little, I used to take her with me out on the boats. She can sail as well as I can, you know.'

Shauna smiled. 'I bet you're a good teacher.'

'Sometimes . . . She helped me to build my boathouse. She was only eight when I started to work on it, but she wanted to get involved in everything I was doing. I would bring her with me and she would help until she tired herself out, then I would find her curled up inside one of the boats, asleep under a blanket.' His eyes were shining at the memory.

'Oh, my God, Demetrios! Christian said he'd searched the boathouse, but would he have thought to look . . .?' They looked at each other, eyes wide.

'The boathouse . . .'

He turned the key in the ignition and slammed his foot on the accelerator, and didn't stop until they reached the harbour.

Chapter 34

Roxy looked at her Bulgari watch; the sun was setting and it was time to head back to the villa. Delphine and Alex would be wondering where she and Shauna had got to.

After leaving an enormous tip – Níko had refused to take any money, no matter how much she had argued with him – she packed her purse, her glasses and her phone into her handbag, a ROX black snakeskin satchel accented with her signature shield and R charm dangling from the handles. Then she stood up and pushed her chair back. She didn't fancy the long trek up the hill with darkness falling, so she was planning to take a taxi; there were always a few idling by the harbour. As was her habit, instilled by her mother, she paused to make a final check that she hadn't left anything behind. Nothing on the table, or the seats . . . but what was that under the table?

She bent to pick it up and saw that it was a passport. Like hers, it was an EU passport, but she could have sworn hers was back at the villa. She flipped it open at the photo-graph page and saw the unsmiling face of Grace looking back at her with that slightly wide-eyed statue look that characterized passport photos.

A postcard marked the page where she'd had her passport stamped on arrival in Greece. It was an old faded postcard of Ithos that had been torn in two and then stuck together again with Sellotape, which was now yellowing with age and peeling away.

Roxy felt as if the world had stopped turning for a moment. She hadn't seen this postcard for a very, very long time, but she recognized it immediately. As she turned it over and read the words on the back, she was transported back in time to the moment it had been ripped apart . . .

Manchester, 1983
Shauna was sitting on the side of her bed in their shared flat in Manchester. Her face was desolate, and Roxy knew that it could only hint at the inner turmoil she was going through.

'I've made you a cup of tea, chuck,' she said, taking Shauna's hand and wrapping it around the handle of the mug.

Shauna looked at her blankly. 'Thanks.'

For once in her life, Roxy was utterly at a loss. What could you say to someone who had just given away the child that they loved? With no words of comfort to offer, she made do with sitting down next to Shauna and wrapping her arms around her. They sat like that, with Roxy holding her tightly, for what seemed like ages. Finally Shauna spoke.

'If I'd known how I'd feel today, Roxy, I'd never have taken that job on *St Helena*. I'd have walked away as fast as I could in the opposite direction.'

'I know, honey.' She looked down and realized that Shauna was holding a postcard. 'What's that.'

Shauna handed it to her. 'It's his goodbye to me.'

Roxy read it. '"Don't wait for me"? Funny way to say goodbye.'

'When I look at it now, it makes me feel sick.'

'Then why don't you throw it away?'

'Something keeps stopping me.'

'Want me to do it for you?'

Shauna nodded, a lone tear carving a path down her face. Roxy's anger flared at the reminder of what that bastard had done, dumping her friend like this. He was the one who should have been suffering the consequences, but instead it was poor Shauna. When they had left Ithos, Roxy had thought that it was herself who was pregnant, but that, thankfully, had turned out to be a false alarm, only for Shauna to discover instead that she was. It was a horrible, cruel twist of fate.

She took the postcard and tore it right down the middle, then tossed it into the bin. 'There. Done.'

'Thank you,' Shauna said in a small voice.

'Come on, let's tuck you into bed,' Roxy told her, pulling back the duvet. Shauna slipped under, folding herself into a ball. Roxy tucked her in and kissed her on the forehead, as if she were a child . . .

Roxy turned again to the picture of Grace at the front of her passport. She looked at her date of birth: 8 April 1983.

Her heart pounding, she studied Grace's picture: the long dark curls, her hazel eyes . . . *just like her father*. Her rosebud lips . . . *just like her mother*.

'Shit!' She looked up, her eyes frantically scanning the harbour. Where did Grace say she was going?

The tyres screeched loudly as Shauna and Demetrios pulled up at the harbour wall.

'Where the hell is Christian? I need his boat.' He jumped out of the Ferrari, not even bothering to open the door, simply leaping over the side of it. He exchanged some words in Greek with one of the boat owners and gestured to Shauna.

'He said we can use his – quick, jump in.' He held his hand out to her and she stepped over the side of the speed-boat, but then turned at the sound of her name being called.

Roxy came running along the quay, waving and shouting at her. 'Stop! Shauna, wait!' She caught up with them, breathing heavily, trying to catch her breath.

'Shauna, we do not have time for this,' Demetrios said impatiently, keeping the engine running.

'Shauna,' Roxy panted, 'you need to see this.' She got into the boat and thrust the postcard into Shauna's hand.

For a moment, Shauna didn't recognize it. Then she flipped it over and saw the writing on the back.

'How . . . why . . . I don't understand, where did this come from?'

'It was in Grace's passport.'

Demetrios looked over Shauna's shoulder and reached out for the postcard. He read it and frowned. 'I wrote this.'

'Your goodbye note,' Shauna said.

'No, not goodbye.' He shook his head, confused. 'Look, we don't have time for this. Roxy, you will have to tell us later – right now I need to find my daughter.'

The waves were choppy as they set out into the bay, and the sun was slowly sinking below the horizon. When they got there, the beach was deserted, but there was a dull light filtering out from the boathouse.

Shauna risked a look at Demetrios: his lips were set in a hard line. *Please let Ariana be safe*, she thought, but her mind was still in turmoil after discovering that the postcard had been in Grace's possession. It had been too noisy on the boat to question Roxy about it, and now that they were here their first priority was to find Ariana.

The boat bumped to a halt against the jetty and Demetrios leapt out, followed by the two women. As they entered the boathouse, Demetrios cried out, all of his pent-up fears and anxiety spilling out as he saw his daughter, sitting hunched with her knees underneath her chin, looking tired but safe. He scooped her up in his arms and she buried her head in his neck.

'Papa, I'm so sorry,' she sobbed.

His own voice was strangled with emotion. 'My darling girl . . . I thought the worst . . . Thank God.'

At that moment, Shauna realized that they were not alone in the boathouse. Quietly standing to one side was Grace, looking as if she wanted to disappear.

'Demetrios . . .' Shauna said quietly, and his eyes followed her gaze to settle on the quiet English girl who seemed to be trying to shrink into the background.

'Grace?' he said. 'You are here?'

'Grace was the one who found me,' Ariana said.

Demetrios searched his daughter's face. 'Why don't you tell us what happened, Ari.'

Shauna took in the striking resemblance to Sofía. Right now, though, Ariana looked much younger than her eighteen years, vulnerable and scared.

'Last night, after I went to see Grace, I'd been planning on going straight home in a taxi, but I knew that you'd be angry if I came home drunk.' She looked sheepish.

'Ari . . . I'd rather you came home drunk than not at all,' he said.

'You say that now, but you would have been furious!' Her eyes flashed and her father said, 'OK, OK, let's not argue already.'

'I saw the boat in the harbour, and that was when I came up with the idea of going to the boathouse. You remember how I used to curl up and sleep in the boats when I was little, when you used to bring me out here while you were building your boat? I wanted to feel the way I did then . . . safe, loved.'

As she spoke, she pointed to the boat Demetrios had built, and Shauna saw the name on the bow: *Beauty*. She remembered his promise to build a boat and name it for her. Her heart soared.

Demetrios held his daughter tightly as she continued: 'When I woke up, it was ages later, the speedboat was gone. I can't have tied it up properly. I took a path up the hill, trying to find somewhere I could get a view of the coast and see if it had washed up somewhere, but it was nowhere in sight. Then it took me forever to find my way back down again. Grace heard me calling for help and came to find me.'

'But, Grace, how did you get here?'

'I saw Christian at the harbour just after I said goodbye to Roxy. He was going out to join the search for Ariana and I asked if I could help.' She fiddled nervously with her hands. 'I felt guilty about not doing more to help her last night, and I realized I couldn't leave Ithos without making sure she was OK. When we got to Fengari, there didn't seem to be anyone searching the beach, so I suggested that I take a look around while he went back out and made the most of what light was left to search the bay.'

'Where is he now?'

'Still out there searching. He was going to come in when it was too dark to see any more. We were planning to stay the night—' She stopped, suddenly embarrassed.

'It's OK,' said Ariana. 'I know he doesn't want me, not in that way. He likes you.' She shrugged. 'I'm over it.'

'No, it wasn't like that at all. If we hadn't found you, we were planning to start searching again at first light. I was going to sleep in the hammock and he was planning to sleep on the floor,' she added primly.

'Grace,' said Demetrios, letting go of his daughter and taking a step towards her, 'I owe you an apology. I lashed out in anger, which was inexcusable. I am sorry. Will you forgive me?'

Grace nodded, and Roxy moved across the boathouse, pulling the passport out of her handbag. 'Grace, honey, you left this behind at the taverna.'

'Oh, my passport,' she laughed. 'I wouldn't have got very far without that.'

Roxy opened the passport and removed the postcard. 'I know this is going to sound odd, but where did you get the postcard?'

Grace frowned. 'My postcard? Why would you be interested in that?'

Shauna took a step forward, her hands visibly shaking, her voice unsteady. 'Please, Grace, tell us how you came to have it.'

Grace blinked. 'I'm not sure why you want to know, but when I was eighteen I wrote to the agency that arranged my adoption, asking for information about my birth parents. They sent me a letter from my mother. And with it was this postcard.'

Demetrios let out a gasp.

Trembling, Shauna asked, 'What did the letter from your mother say?'

Looking more perplexed than ever, she told them. 'She wished me a happy birthday, and said she wanted me to know that I was born in love and that she hadn't wanted me to feel like I was a guilty secret.' The words were so familiar she could recite them by heart: '"*I hope that your life is full of kindness, laughter and opportunity, and that the years to come bring you joy and love. Live a happy and fulfilling life, Grace – you deserve it . . .*"'

Shauna took a step forward, and finished for her: '". . . *I will never, ever forget you, and if one day you want to find me, I'll be waiting.*"' Her voice was filled with emotion. 'It's true, Grace, I never did forget you. Every day I have kept you in my heart, but I never dreamed that I would see you again.'

Grace backed away, shaking her head. 'You're my mother? It can't be.'

Demetrios moved to stand alongside Shauna. 'Grace, I know this is hard for you to understand – and for you, too, Ariana,' he added, looking at his daughter. 'But twenty years ago, Shauna and I . . . we fell in love.' He looked into Shauna's eyes as he continued: 'I was a young man who was weak. I should have tried harder – if I had, things would have been different.'

Ariana stepped across to look at the postcard in Grace's hand. 'When you showed it to me last night, I knew there was something about it that bothered me, but I couldn't work it out. Now I know.' She pointed to the swirl of the d in darling. 'That's how my papa writes his ds.' The two girls stood together, and looked to Demetrios. Shauna was struck by the similarities between them, their soft hazel eyes with just a hint of gold, like their father's; their long dark hair, almost the same height.

Grace shook her head again, clearly distressed. 'No, you can't be my father . . . this is too much, I don't believe you.' Then her voice broke and a sob escaped her.

Roxy stepped in and put her arm around Grace. 'Give her some space, it's a lot for her to take in.'

Shauna's heart contracted, knowing that Roxy was right,

but all she wanted to do was take Grace in her arms, the way she had dreamed of doing so many times. Now she felt as though she had come so close to realizing her dream only to feel it all slipping away from her.

They heard the noise of a speedboat outside and a moment later Christian came into the boathouse. 'Ari! We've been looking for you everywhere.'

'She's been found,' said Demetrios. 'As you can see.'

Christian took in the scene with an elated grin, then he saw Grace sobbing in Roxy's arms and his face fell. 'What happened?'

Grace tore free of Roxy's embrace and ran to him. 'Christian, take me back to Ithos, please.'

'What's going on?'

She shook her head. 'Please, just take me, I want to go now.'

Shauna couldn't stop her own tears from falling. 'Grace, darling, I'm sorry . . .'

Demetrios stepped in. 'Christian, please ask your mother and father to take care of Grace tonight,' he said.

They watched as Christian collected up Grace's things and gently led her to the boat. Roxy laid a gentle hand on Shauna's arm. 'Let her go,' she whispered, 'just for now. It will be OK.'

As Christian started the engine, Ariana ran to the boat. 'Wait, you forgot this.' She handed Grace the postcard, then reached her arms around her and the two girls embraced.

As the boat pulled away, Grace turned her back on the four people who watched her go. In that moment, Shauna thought her heart was breaking all over again.

'Demetrios, that's our daughter. How can we let her go?'

'She knows we are here. All we can do now is pray that she will come back to us . . .'

Chapter 35

Demetrios fidgeted impatiently next to Shauna as they sat on the terrace of Níko's taverna. 'What if she has changed her mind?'

Shauna was feeling a huge sense of trepidation herself, but working herself up into a lather wouldn't help anyone. As it often did when she was worried, her father's voice found its way into her head: *There is no better cure for old wounds than a bit of patience.*

Initially, Grace had been hell-bent on taking the first ferry out of Ithos. It had taken days of patient mediation by Roxy, Christian and Ariana, before Grace had agreed to talk to Shauna and Demetrios, and even now they were on tenterhooks, wondering whether she would show, wondering if she would want to listen to what they had to say.

Shauna found it hard to believe she and Demetrios were sitting side by side, waiting for the daughter they'd lost. She could never have imagined the events of the past few days would lead them to this moment, but at the same time she felt as if it was meant to be.

'Just try to stay calm, we don't want to scare her off,'

she urged, with a composure that surprised her. Inside, she was anything but calm herself.

'I know, I know, but what if she is angry with us?'

'She has every right to be angry, and confused, and upset. We'll just have to soak it up, however much it hurts. If we get defensive or argue, we'll only drive her away.'

'You are right.' He looked at his watch and bit his lip, and Shauna couldn't help laughing.

'You haven't changed at all; still as impatient and irascible as ever. Still wanting life to fit around you.'

He frowned. 'That is unfair. Who wouldn't be impatient in this situation? Besides, you too are the same . . . still getting under my skin, even now.' His face softened. 'I can't pretend I mind, though.' He touched her hand.

'Demetrios . . .' But before she could finish, she saw Roxy approaching from the beach path. 'Delphine and Alex are having a playdate in the sea. Is Grace here yet?'

It was then they saw her, walking along the harbourfront with Christian, the two of them holding hands and talking quietly. She saw them, said something to Christian, and the two of them shared a brief kiss before she came running over. Shauna felt her pulse quickening as the girl approached. Grace was a total stranger to her, yet she seemed so familiar. It was almost like looking at another version of herself in a mirror. She had dreamed about this face thousands of times and now here she was, reunited with her daughter. Smiling, laughing.

'Hello,' Grace said, a mixture of shy politeness and inner confidence. 'I'm sorry I'm a bit late.'

Shauna and Demetrios told her not to apologize, awkwardly stumbling over their words and speaking at the same time.

Demetrios spoke first, Shauna noticing that he had taken

it upon himself to speak for both of them and decided to let him. 'Thank you for seeing us, Grace, and for giving us the chance to explain.'

'Yes,' Shauna added, 'I imagine you've got lot of questions.'

'I do have some. But I wanted to ask first if you had any questions for me.'

Shauna was speechless for a moment, her mind a blank under the pressure of wanting to say the right thing, as if this was a test. Then, unbidden, the question that had haunted her over the years, that had tormented her and kept her awake on countless nights came into her head. She felt Demetrios squeeze her hand under the table and she was glad of it.

'Grace, you have to tell me, are you . . . did you . . .' Her voice faltered. 'Were you happy? Have you had a good life?'

For the first time, Shauna and her daughter locked eyes, and Shauna could see a touch of O'Brien looking back out at her. She knew then that she had asked the right question.

'I've had the best life. My mum and dad are amazing. I always knew I was adopted, but they love me to bits and have given me the best start in life.'

Shauna felt a wave of relief wash over her. As Grace told them about her parents and her childhood, she lapped up the details. Her mother was teacher and her father ran an electronics firm. She had gone to a grammar school and had excelled at sport, especially swimming and racket sports.

Then came the moment Shauna had been dreading:

'So . . . why did you have me adopted?'

For years she had done everything in her power to suppress the memory. Even now, she was breaking out in a cold sweat at the thought. But her daughter was entitled to an answer.

'When I found out I pregnant, I was scared, but I knew

I wanted to keep you.' She turned to Demetrios. 'This is the one thing I couldn't tell you. It still hurts too much. You see, I went home to Ireland . . .'

Shauna knew she was starting to show, but she'd hid her bump under an oversized knitted cardigan and baggy T-shirt. Her mother looked at her over her glasses, her shrewd eyes never leaving her daughter.

'Come on then, spit it out.'

'What do you mean?'

'You've come back here for a reason. We weren't expecting you home until the summer.'

'Would you rather I wasn't here?' Why did her mother always make her feel like this, like an unwanted intruder in her parents' lives?

'Don't be so dramatic.' Her mother's face hardened. 'Anyway, I'm not stupid. Did you think I wouldn't notice that belly on you?'

'Mammy, I—'

'Be quiet, Shauna O'Brien. You are a filthy slut and I'm shocked at the gall of you, bringing yourself back here in that state.'

'How can you say that, Mammy? I'm your daughter.'

Her mother got up from the table came to stand over Shauna.

'No daughter of mine would get herself into that state and expect sympathy.'

'I should have known I wouldn't get much of that from you.'

'What do you want then? Money? You've got a cheek!'

'I don't want any money from you.' Shauna tried hard to keep her tears of shame and anger bottled up, it would only goad her mother to more spiteful remarks. 'Let me talk to Daddy.'

Her mother grabbed her by the arm, gripping her tightly. 'Don't you even think of mentioning this to your father. It would break his heart to see you like this. Sure, the shame of it would kill him. How could you have been so thoughtless and selfish?'

'Me, selfish? Anyway, you're wrong about Daddy – he'd help if you would let him. It's your own embarrassment you're concerned with.'

Her mother's face set in a hard line. 'If you cared about anyone but yourself, you'd do the decent thing and have the child, then put them up for adoption. No one need ever know.'

Shauna knew her stupid dream had died that moment, her foolish idea that her mother would be angry but not for long, that she would tell her they would find a way, that they'd love their grandchild no matter what anyone else thought. Her mother continued her diatribe, the words cold and hard.

'If you insist on keeping it, it's life will be blighted. People will point their fingers at Shauna O'Brien's bastard. Is that what you want? Well, I'll have no part in it, so you can get out of this house right now and take the fruit of your sin with you.'

'How could you be so cruel, Mammy?'

'There's nothing cruel about it, I'm just being realistic. If you ever want to step foot in this house again, or to see you father again, you'll do what needs to be done . . .'

'I left the house that same day, and if it hadn't been for my father I would never have returned. When I did, later that year, after the baby—' She corrected herself: 'After *you* had been adopted, my mother never asked me what had happened to you, and I never told her. It was like it had never happened.' She looked down at her hands sadly. 'Now I know she denied herself and my father the chance to be grandparents. It wasn't only my loss, it was theirs too.'

Demetrios took her hand. 'Oh, Shauna, you were let down by the people who should have cared the most.'

'Everyone except Roxy.'

She smiled at her dearest friend, who turned to Grace and said, 'I offered to raise you myself.'

'That could have been fun.' Grace smiled. 'You can be an almost-auntie to me now.'

'I'd be honoured.'

'But I still don't understand how the postcard fits in.'

'I wrote the postcard,' Demetrios said. 'But not for the reasons you think,' he added, turning to Shauna.

'What do you mean?'

'I had written it to cheer you up. I knew you were sad that the summer would soon be coming to an end; about what would happen to us. I intended it to encourage you: *Always have hope. We have our dreams.* I meant every word.' Shauna felt a little bit of her melt inside; *how did he still do that to her?*

'Then why didn't you finish it?'

'Jeremy interrupted me. He told me my father was trying to hunt me down. I figured I'd finish it later. I wrote "Don't wait for me" because I expected to be late returning; I knew my parents would give me hell.'

'I see.' Shauna's brow was creased in thought. 'So all of that was a misunderstanding?'

'When my mother ordered Jeremy to pack up my things, he must have found the note and left it for you to find, knowing how it would look.'

'Or by mistake. I guess we will never know.'

'But how did I end up with it?' Grace asked.

'Ah, that. *Mea culpa* on my part,' said Roxy. She explained how she came to rip it up, then went on: 'Once Shauna was asleep, I fished it out of the wastepaper bin. I knew it wasn't my place to destroy it, so I mended it with Sellotape and popped it in the envelope by the side of the bed.'

'That must have been the envelope containing my letter; I posted it the following day. The agency had told me I could write something for them to keep on file to give to you when you turned eighteen. They'd explained that I wouldn't be allowed to have contact, and you wouldn't be able to apply for information about your birth mother until you were an adult. I wanted so much for you to have something from me, so that you would know the truth one day.'

'The postcard and the birthday card were in the same envelope,' Grace confirmed.

'So that's how you ended up with them,' Demetrios said. 'But Grace, how did you end up in Ithos if that was all you had to go on?'

'I wasn't actually trying to trace my birth mother.' She looked at Shauna. 'Don't be offended, but I love my parents, and I'd never want them to think I'd rather things had been different – because I don't.'

'I admire your honesty, Grace, and it does both you and them a great deal of credit. They must be wonderful people.'

'They are. But I couldn't stop thinking about the postcard – it was so intriguing. I've always wondered about my origins; it's pretty obvious I'm not typically English.'

'No, you are a Greek beauty,' Demetrios said with pride.

Grace laughed. 'I was hoping I might find a few hints as to my background, but after I'd been here a while, I realized that my dream of finding answers was disappearing. I was on the verge of giving up, but then I met Roxy.'

'So maybe I was right before: Ithos brought you here, and now you know everything,' Demetrios said. He hesitated slightly before asking, 'So, what are your plans now? There will always be a home for you on Ithos, if you want it.'

'That's very kind of you. Christian has asked me to stay on too, but I miss my parents. I really need to tell them what's happened, and I want to do that in person.'

'Of course,' Shauna said.

Carol Kirkwood

Grace hesitated then looked at them both, but her voice was full of self-assurance and honesty. 'I'm sorry I made you wait. I wasn't intending to be rude or mysterious. It's just, well, I know who I am you see; I wanted to be sure getting to know you both won't change that.'

Shauna felt a flush of emotion, at her daughter, wise beyond her years. *Please let me be good enough.* 'And how do you feel now?' she asked.

Grace tilted her head to one side. 'Now I think – I *hope* – that everything is going to be OK.'

Their eyes met and for a small moment Shauna felt a little connection pass between them. 'OK' sounded like music to her ears right now. 'When will you leave?'

'Today. Christian has stowed my things on his boat, and he's going to take me to Rhodes to catch a flight back to England.'

'No, I will take you to Rhodes on the *St Helena*,' Demetrios said. 'I insist. It is the least I can do.'

Shauna, Roxy and Alex stood on the quay as Christian took Grace's rucksack on board the *St Helena*.

'Are you sure you won't come with us?' Demetrios asked Shauna, as he prepared to follow.

'No, I think one biological parent on the journey is probably enough. You can show her the ropes.'

'Christian tells me she is quite a good sailor already.'

'Why doesn't that surprise me?'

'You and I created a very beautiful and creative daughter.'

'Her mum and dad must be wonderful people.'

'Shauna, there is something I want to say to you before you leave Ithos. When I wrote to you before, I was serious about telling you how I feel.'

'Demetrios, we've said so much already.'

'Maybe, but let me speak – this may be my last chance and I don't know when we will see each other again.'

He was standing so close to her now, Shauna could smell the familiar aroma of citrus and sandalwood. 'I'm listening.'

Demetrios took her hands and held them in his own. 'I fell in love with you when I hardly knew what the word meant. But after you were gone, I had time to learn. Now, looking back, I can see that you were the one truth in my life. With every woman who has come since, I was only trying to recapture what we had, always destined to fail.'

'I loved Dan, Demetrios. He meant the world to me and put me back together again.'

'I am glad to hear it. But please, Shauna, give me one more chance to love you again? To love you as a man, not as a boy.'

Shauna lifted his hand and brought his palm to her cheek, holding it there, feeling his rough skin, the hands that could mould and shape the wood that built his boats. Could she put her heart in these hands again?

'Give me some time, Demetrios. I don't know my own mind yet. It's not just about being sure of you, I need to be sure of myself too.'

He nodded and brushed her lips lightly with his own. 'I have plenty of time. When and if you are ready, I will be waiting for you.'

They turned at the sound of footsteps. Grace was approaching, accompanied by Níko and Teresa and Elana and Ariana. They came to a halt beside the gangplank and Grace turned to hug Níko and Teresa and thank them for their kindness.

Then it was Ariana's turn. 'Perhaps I'll see you in England,' she said, breaking off from their embrace to cast a glance at her father. 'I've decided I might take up my place at university in the autumn after all. I miss England a bit – sun, sand and scenery can get a little boring,' she said.

'You can come and stay with me and my parents – you might enjoy slumming it with us.'

'I'll bring my own butler,' Ariana answered, and the two girls laughed.

Elana stepped forward. 'Having another granddaughter has made this old woman very happy.' She held out her hand and passed something to Grace. It was a blue amulet in the shape of an eye, known as a *mati*. Grace had seen charms like it all over Greece; it was made from blown glass hanging from a silver chain. 'This will protect you and keep you safe,' she said, embracing her.

'Thank you, it's beautiful.' Grace put the amulet around her neck.

'Are you ready?' Demetrios asked.

Grace nodded and turned to Roxy and Shauna.

'Remember, if you ever decide you want to work in fashion, you known where I am,' Roxy said.

Grace rolled her eyes. 'I don't know one end of a needle from another. Give me a reef knot to tie or a tiller to turn.'

'Sailing must be in your blood,' Demetrios said proudly.

Grace turned to Shauna, and said, a little shyly, 'You know, I saw you once.'

Shauna was surprised. 'Really? When was that?'

'In Cannes. My father took me, he had some business in Nice and took me with him. It was only a few years ago. I remember seeing you on the red carpet and thinking how beautiful you were. I never could have imagined that I'd meet you one day or that . . .' She broke off, shaking her head in bewilderment.

'It's going to take a bit of getting used to, Grace, and I don't expect you to accept me overnight. I know you need to get used to the idea. You have two brilliant parents already. I'll be happy just to . . .' For a moment Shauna felt overwhelmed by the enormity of what was happening, but was determined to hold it together, for Grace's sake. '. . . Even if you only ever see me as a friend, I'll be grateful for that.'

Grace's face broke into a huge smile and for Shauna it was like a million lightbulbs all turning on at the same time. 'I'm sure I can do a bit better than that,' Grace told her and with those words she threw her arms around Shauna and held her tight. Shauna stroked her daughter's hair, drinking in her vanilla scent. For a brief moment it was as if she was holding her tiny baby in her arms again.

Inside her heart, the empty space that had remained since she and Grace were parted was finally filled and Shauna knew that this time it wasn't a goodbye, but a beginning.

Chapter 36

Ithos, March 2003

Demetrios scratched at his eyes; he was struggling to stay awake, but he hadn't sat up half the night like a lovesick teenager to watch the woman he loved on TV, just to fall asleep when it mattered.

He had sat through the endless parade of dresses on the red carpet outside Grauman's Chinese Theatre, had laughed as Joan Rivers poked fun at the great and the good, all the time desperate to catch a glimpse of Shauna.

He knew that Roxy had designed her dress for her, but when he first caught sight of her posing on the red carpet for photographers, waving to the crowds and good-naturedly answering the hundreds of questions fired at her by the world's press, it took his breath away. Her dress was floor-length black ruffled chiffon, with a sheer torso embellished with tiny crystal skulls. With her dramatic eye make-up, it was bold departure from her usual timeless elegance. It spoke of a new confidence and acceptance of herself, able to step out of the shadow of her late husband

and the tabloid stories of the last few years and stand proud.

And now here it was – the moment that the world was waiting for, the Best Actress category, arguably the toughest category this year. Shauna was up against the best actors in the business, including Nicole Kidman, the front-runner. The camera panned across the nominees' faces as Denzel Washington read out their names and the screen showed excerpts from their respective films.

When Shauna's name was read out, the camera lingered on her face, serene and calm, her green eyes composed and cool, but Demetrios knew that her legs would be shaking beneath her ruffled dress.

'And the winner is . . .' There was a horrible pause which seemed to go on forever. '. . . Shauna Jackson in *For the Love of Grace*.'

The auditorium erupted and Demetrios was surprised to find himself jumping up and down shouting in jubilation.

Shauna took to the stage. Her hands were trembling as she grasped the Oscar, her fingers moulding around the statuette's legs.

She reached for the microphone and adjusted it, her voice trembling as she spoke. 'Thank you so much for this . . . to the Academy . . . When this script came in, I knew I wanted to do it more than any other part I've ever been offered. Grace Kelly was my heroine. My role model. It was when I was watching *High Society* with my mother that I decided I wanted to act. Playing Grace Kelly, it never felt like work . . .'

After thanking the rest of the cast and crew, she went on:

'I want to say thank you to Grace herself. I once had the pleasure of meeting her, a few months before she died. I was only nineteen, I'm not sure I should have been at the party, but she was as gracious and kind as you'd expect. She also had a touch of mischief.

'She once said, "experience and age bring wonderful insight". I don't think I could have played Grace if I hadn't known both the joys and sorrows of life. This Oscar is for her.'

Demetrios picked up the remote and switched off the TV. After the euphoria of seeing her win, he felt deflated, knowing that she was in Hollywood and he was here on Ithos. Thousands of miles separated them, but it was the emotional distance he was desperate to close.

He only realized that he was sitting in darkness when the light was switched on, making him blink as his mother padded quietly into the room.

'Goodness, Demetrios, what is all the racket about?'

'I didn't mean to wake you, Mother. Shauna has won the Oscar.'

His mother made a prayer gesture, raising her eyes to heaven. 'Thank God, now you can stop pacing up and down the house day and night. But I am delighted, she is very talented.'

'I know.'

His mother eyed him shrewdly. 'You will have to accept that her working life might come first sometimes.'

Demetrios raised his eyebrows. 'That doesn't sound like you, Mother – rather modern thinking, wouldn't you say?'

She shrugged and said airily, 'Young women now don't have to choose the way my generation did. We were stuck in the old traditions when I was her age, but I still found ways to do what I wanted.'

Demetrios grinned. 'And didn't we all know it!'

She sighed. 'You look tired, and it isn't just staying up

all night.' She came and sat next to him. 'I hear you in your office, calling her and sending flowers and gifts.'

It was true, Demetrios and Shauna spoke often. But despite his efforts to woo her, so far she had been holding back.

'What can I do, Mother? I don't want to put pressure on her, but I worry I am losing her all over again.'

Elana patted his hand. 'Son, you told her that you would give her time. But it isn't her own time she needs, you must give her some of yours.'

He scratched his chin. 'And how do I do that?'

'To win her heart you must go to Shauna and make a place for yourself in her world. Trust me, I may be an old bird, but I have learned a few things over the years. And as a woman myself, I know that Shauna needs to know you are willing to change your life to accommodate her, instead of expecting her to fit in with your world.'

'But I don't know anything about Hollywood.'

'Then you must learn. You have been promising Christian a chance to hold the reins and he has proved himself more than capable. We can all live without you for a while.'

'I have been thinking about diversifying my portfolio . . .' he said thoughtfully.

'Family is everything, Demi, it always had been. Ours has now expanded and I want to enjoy it before I'm too old.' Elana reached for the cordless phone and handed it to him. 'British Airways are open twenty-four hours a day. Call them now.'

He took the phone and moments later found himself saying, 'I need a one-way ticket to Los Angeles, please. First Class.'

Epilogue

Ithos, Summer 2003

The early morning sun streamed in through the windows as Shauna brushed out her long red hair, the rhythm of the strokes giving her an almost hypnotic feeling of calm.

She was dressed and ready to go, in a pair of light shorts and a loose cotton blouse, perfect for a boat trip. Alex was going to love this fishing trip, he'd been badgering her about going out for days and she'd finally agreed, as long as she was allowed to go too.

She looked at herself in the mirror, examining her face for new lines, but didn't find any. She didn't mind them anyway, she liked the way she looked now and was determined not to fall prey to Hollywood's obsession with plastic surgery. Grace Kelly never had plastic surgery, and if it was good enough for Grace, it was good enough for her.

She'd definitely put on a bit of weight; taking some time out from movies had allowed her to indulge in her love of good food and cooking. Well, so what if her bust was a bit more buxom and her clothes a bit tighter around the middle?

She found herself smiling, Demetrios certainly didn't seem to mind her extra curves.

Shauna stood and walked out on to the balcony. Beyond the olive groves, she could see the sparkling cerulean blue of the Mediterranean in the distance.

On the terrace below her, Demetrios and Alex were playing football.

'Are you two ready? I'm coming down!' she shouted.

By the time she got downstairs, they had picked up their fishing rods, and Demetrios was also juggling the cooler box loaded with drinks and food. Shauna followed behind, enjoying the sound of their excited chatter.

They arrived at the quay and *Beauty* was there waiting for them with Christian at the helm. The schooner really lived up to her name; fitted out in wood, she gleamed and glistened in the sun and Shauna never tired of looking at it.

'Your carriage awaits, my lady,' Demetrios told her.

'I'll be back in a minute,' she told him as they clambered aboard. He turned to wave at her and blow her a kiss, and a flood of love washed over Shauna as she glanced over her shoulder at the two most important men in her life. There was just one more thing that would make this day completely perfect.

Grace heard the steps outside as she picked up her rucksack and looked once more at the postcard on the dresser in her room above Níko's taverna. Such a small, simple thing, but one that had opened up her whole past to her and perhaps her future too.

Coming back to Ithos felt so right, more than she had ever dared to believe it could. Christian had been patient and understanding, knowing that she hadn't felt able to commit herself to him before now, but this time it was different. Demetrios had invited her to stay up at the Theodosis villa, but Grace liked the independence of staying at Níko's. Or maybe she still wasn't quite ready to be taken fully into the family fold.

At least she knew where that piece of the puzzle fitted now. She was a little bit Irish, a little bit Greek and plenty of the sensible English girl with modest parents who adored her.

Now she had her new family, too. Grace knew that there was a world of opportunity waiting for her and it could be here on Ithos if she wanted it to be. Her mum and dad just wanted her to be happy; after their initial shock, they'd been pleased that Grace knew where she had come from and who her birth parents were. They hoped it would help her to work out where she was going.

There was time for all of that, though. Today was a day for fishing and for fun. She heard the knock on the door and the voice of the person she was getting to know a little better every day.

Grace opened the door and Shauna stood there, her face full of anticipation and an excitement that was infectious.

'Good morning, darling, the boys are getting the boat ready. Have you got everything? Need a hand?'

Grace patted her backpack, put on her sun hat and closed the door, not giving the postcard a second look.

'It's OK, Mum, I've got everything I need right here.'

Acknowledgements

My thanks to the plethora of family and friends who have believed in me and my ability to do this, and also for their encouragement and patience, especially to Steve and Donald, who lived this experience with me. Heartbreakingly, my wee pussycat Donald isn't physically here any more but will live on for ever in my heart. He would open an eye from his slumber, briefly, as I read a chapter to him, before closing it again (no reflection on the book, I hasten to add!). To Steve, who has been so incredibly supportive, encouraging and enthusiastic, questioning me along the way when I felt something wasn't quite working, there are not enough words . . .

Phil and Chris, you are like family to me, always there and always 100% supportive of everything I do.

My family who are unfaltering in their support and pride in what I do.

Kerr MacRae, my publishing agent. Without you, none of this would have happened. Thank you for your belief in my abilities, and your wisdom throughout this whole process.

Kate, my editor at HarperCollins . . . one incredibly talented, wonderful lady. You totally understood my vision. I have never written a book before and you made this experience so enjoyable and so much fun. You have taught me a lot and given me a new appreciation for the publishing industry.

Finally, my grateful thanks to HarperCollins for publishing this book and to the wider team who made it all possible, including publisher Kimberley Young for her support, Elizabeth Dawson and Emma Pickard for their marketing and publicity wisdom, and to Claire Ward and Caroline Young who designed the wonderful cover.

If you loved *Under a Greek Moon*,
don't miss Carol Kirkwood's sensational next book!
Turn the page to find out more.

Escape with *Carol Kirkwood* to

The Hotel on the Riviera

Heiress Ariana Theodosis wanted everything that Hollywood had to offer, took it all, and is now paying the price. When she inherits a hotel on the beautiful French Riviera, she hopes it's a chance to start again.

Elizabeth and Robert Chappell were Hollywood's fiery English golden couple. Their legendary breakups and passionate make-ups were tabloid gold, but now they are headed for divorce. Will they say their last goodbyes by the sparkling waters of the Mediterranean?

Madame du Lac has watched the rich and famous pass through the faded doors of the Hotel du Soleil for over four decades, and has kept its secrets too. As the past catches up with her, is it time to break her silence, or are some things best left buried…?

Available now for pre-order
Coming July 2022